VIZ GRAPHIC NOVEL

INU-YASHA
A FEUDAL FAIRY TALE™

VOL. 2

This volume contains INU-YASHA #6 (second half)
through #11 (first half) in their entirety.

STORY AND ART BY
RUMIKO TAKAHASHI

ENGLISH ADAPTATION BY
GERARD JONES

Translation/Mari Morimoto
Touch-Up Art & Lettering/Wayne Truman
Editor/Julie Davis
Assistant Editors/Annette Roman & Bill Flanagan
Cover Design/Hidemi Sahara

Editor-in-Chief/Hyoe Narita
V.P. of Sales & Marketing/Rick Bauer
Publisher/Seiji Horibuchi

Printed in Canada

Published by Viz Communications, Inc.
P.O. Box 77010 • San Francisco, CA 94107

10 9 8 7 6 5
Fifth printing, February 2002

- get your own vizmail.net email account
- register for the weekly email newsletter
- sign up for your free catalog
- voice 1-800-394-3042 fax 415-384-8936

www.viz.com

Get your free Viz Shop-By-Mail catalog! (800) 394-3042 or fax (415) 546-7086

"This is a fantastic comic; well-drawn, tightly-plotted and scalp-crawlingly creepy. The bickering interplay between the characters is spot on, making the reader feel at home with them after only a few pages, and the sinister nature of the tale is lightened just enough by Rumiko Takahashi's trademark humor. People tend to forget that the author of **Urusei Yatsura** can tackle horror with the same skill as she writes comedy, but **Inu-Yasha** is the perfect way to be reminded."

Manga Max

"Rumiko Takahashi seems to deliver nothing but hits. Though very different in style from **Lum** or **Ranma 1/2**, this series shows the same excellent storytelling ability... Takahashi's excellent sense of humor is sprinkled liberally throughout, lending balance to the darker parts of the tale."

TheComicStore.com

"This is a great series, if only for the loads of Japanese myths and legendary creatures Inu-Yasha and Kagome meet. (Everything from ghosts to talking fleas...) And with this large array of characters comes the potential for an almost unlimited variety of stories...and for longtime Takahashi fans, **Inu-Yasha** delivers."

EX: The Online World of Anime and Manga

"This is the magic of Rumiko Takahashi--she has woven an intriguing historical fantasy that is filled with horror, humor, and romance in a way that most people would not think possible."

Amazon.com

VIZ GRAPHIC NOVEL

INU-YASHA
A FEUDAL FAIRY TALE™
VOL. 2

STORY AND ART BY
RUMIKO TAKAHASHI

CONTENTS

SCROLL ONE
YURA'S WEB

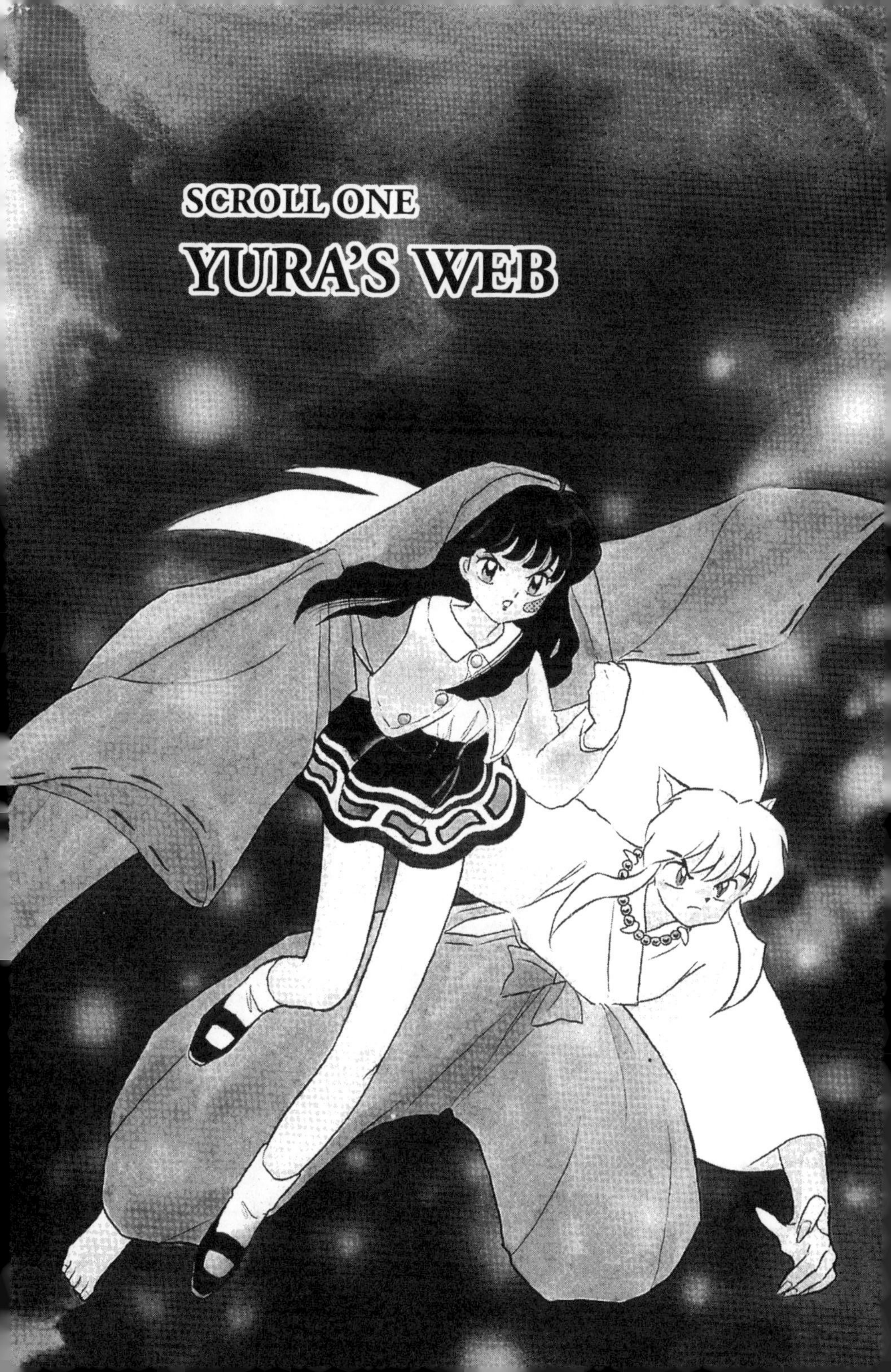

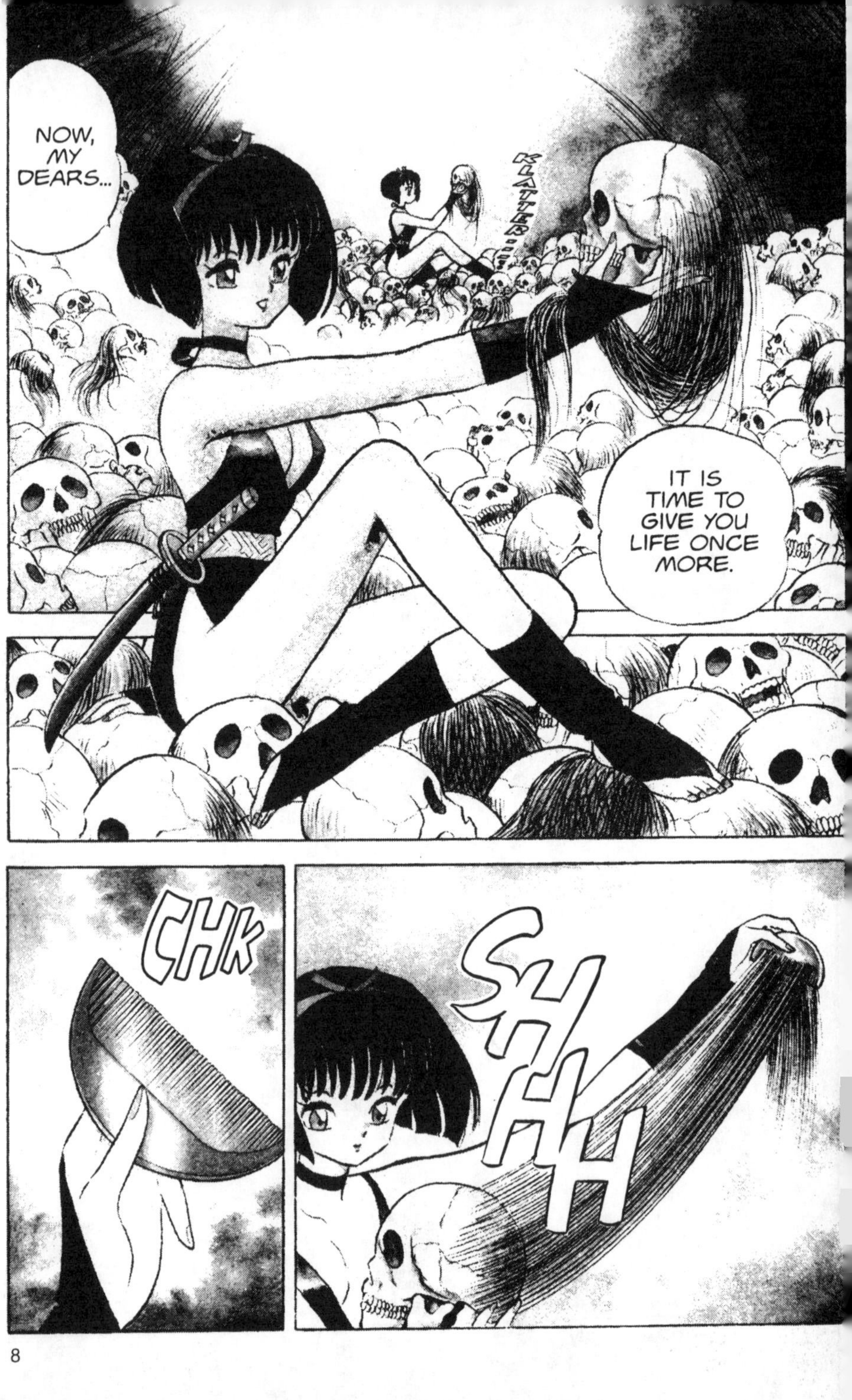
NOW, MY DEARS...
KLATTER...
IT IS TIME TO GIVE YOU LIFE ONCE MORE.
CHK
SHHH

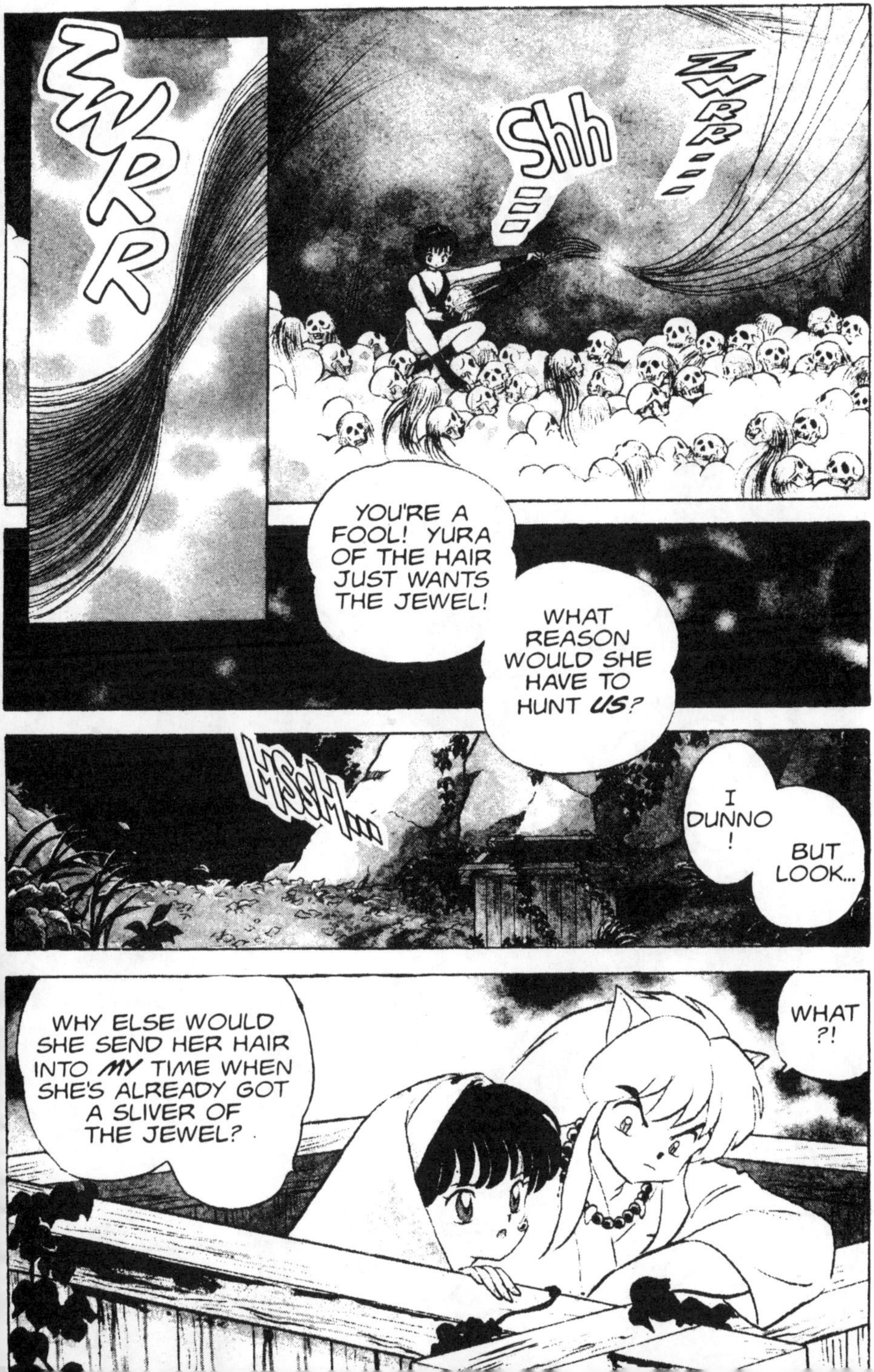
ZWRR
Shh...
ZWRR...
YOU'RE A FOOL! YURA OF THE HAIR JUST WANTS THE JEWEL!
WHAT REASON WOULD SHE HAVE TO HUNT *US*?
HSSH...
I DUNNO!
BUT LOOK...
WHY ELSE WOULD SHE SEND HER HAIR INTO *MY* TIME WHEN SHE'S ALREADY GOT A SLIVER OF THE JEWEL?
WHAT?!

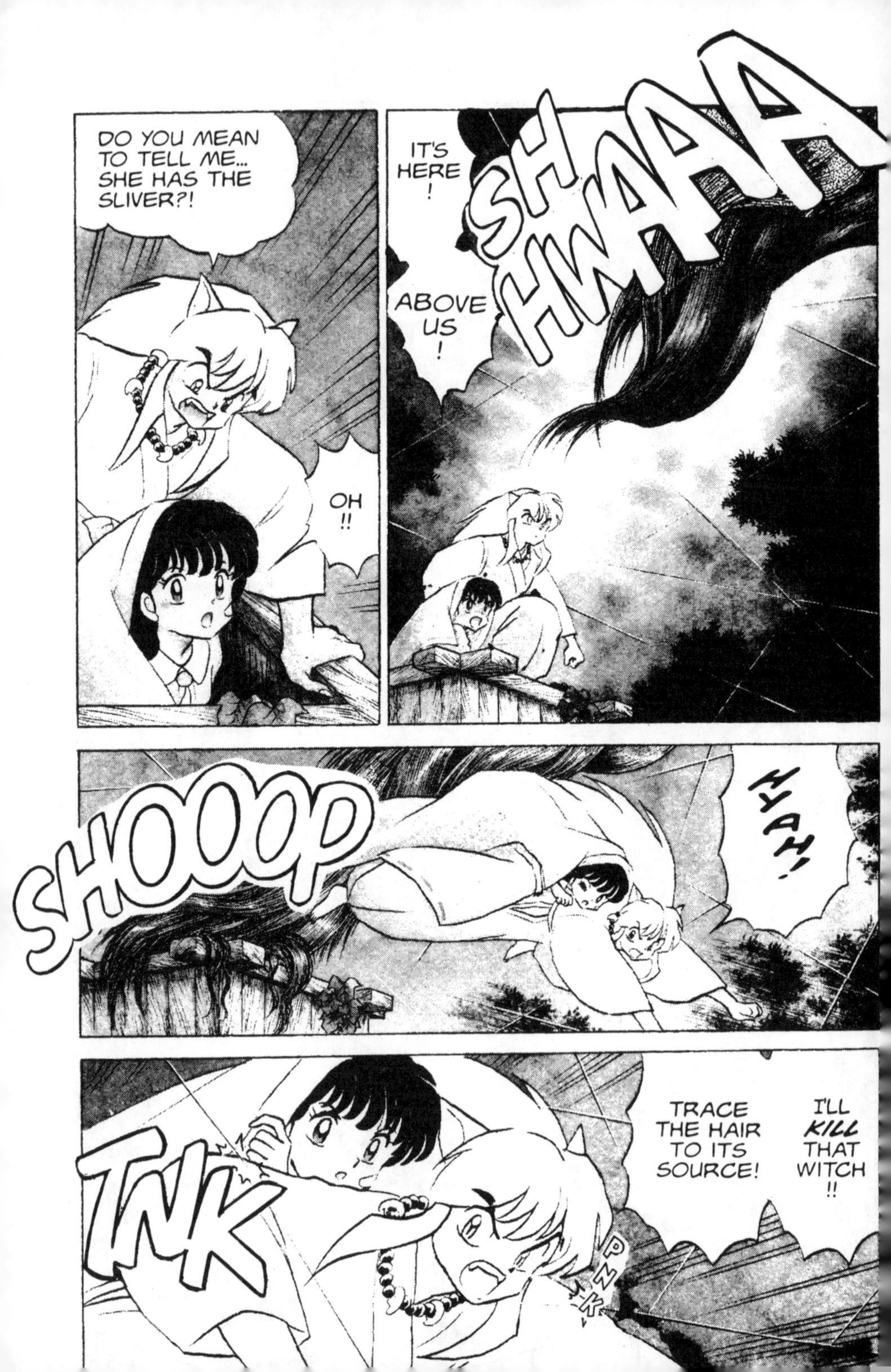

DO YOU MEAN TO TELL ME... SHE HAS THE SLIVER?!
OH!!
IT'S HERE!
ABOVE US!
SH HWAAA
SHOOOP
HYAH!
TNK
TRACE THE HAIR TO ITS SOURCE!
I'LL KILL THAT WITCH!!
PNK

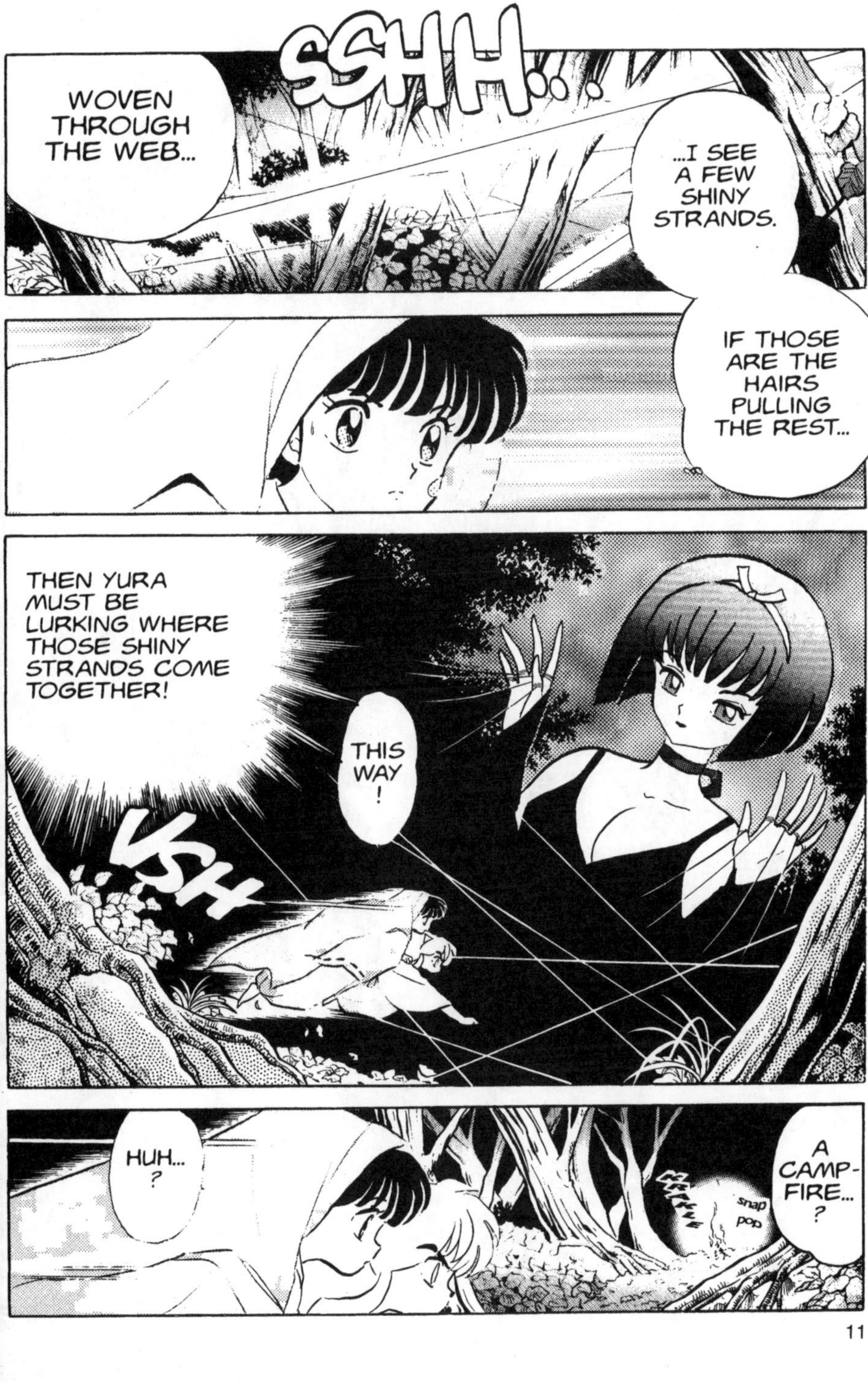
SSHH...
WOVEN THROUGH THE WEB...
...I SEE A FEW SHINY STRANDS.
IF THOSE ARE THE HAIRS PULLING THE REST...
THEN YURA MUST BE LURKING WHERE THOSE SHINY STRANDS COME TOGETHER!
THIS WAY!
VSH
HUH...?
snap
pop
A CAMP-FIRE...?

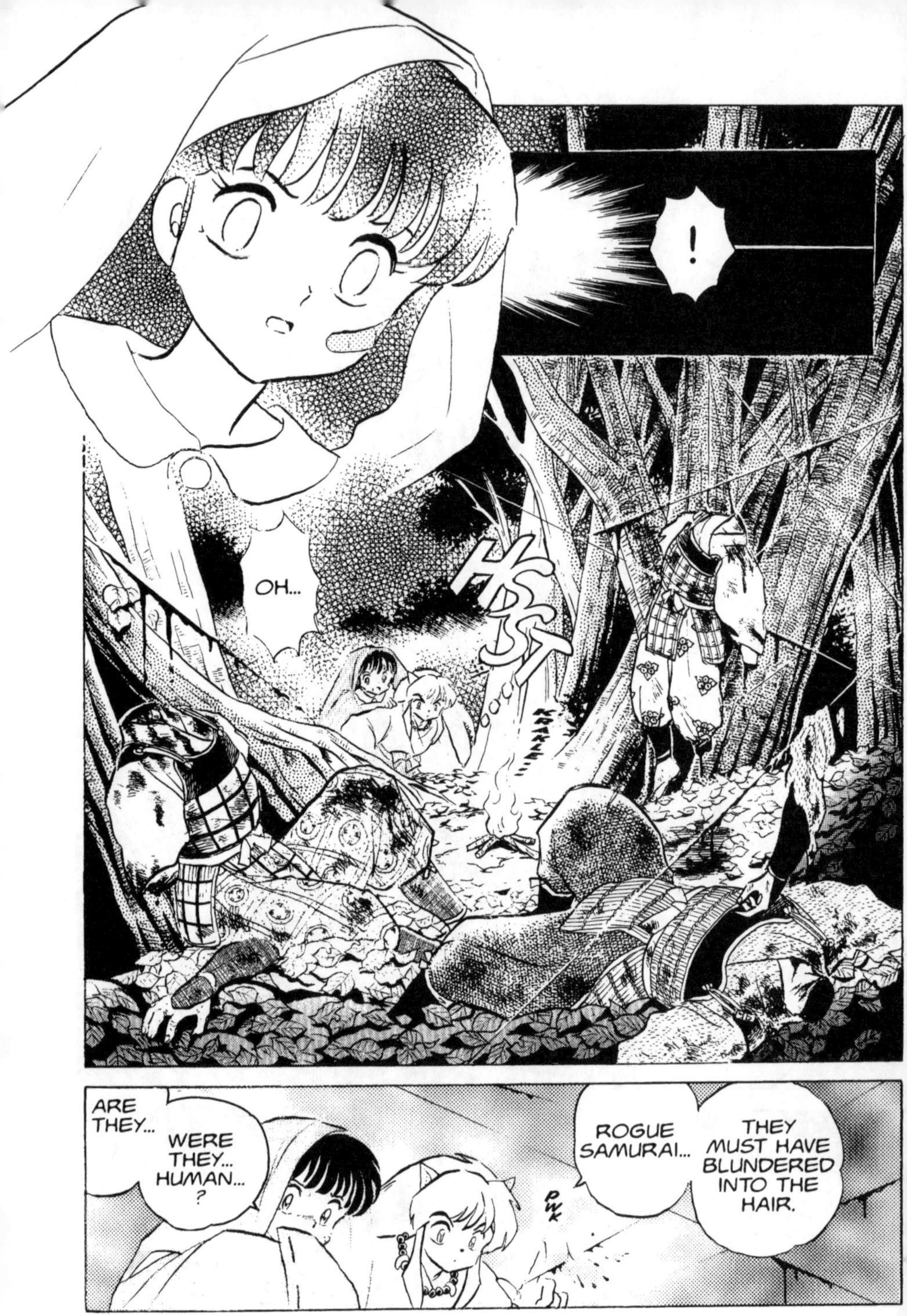
!
OH...
HSST
KRAKKLE...
ARE THEY...
WERE THEY... HUMAN...?
PWK
ROGUE SAMURAI...
THEY MUST HAVE BLUNDERED INTO THE HAIR.

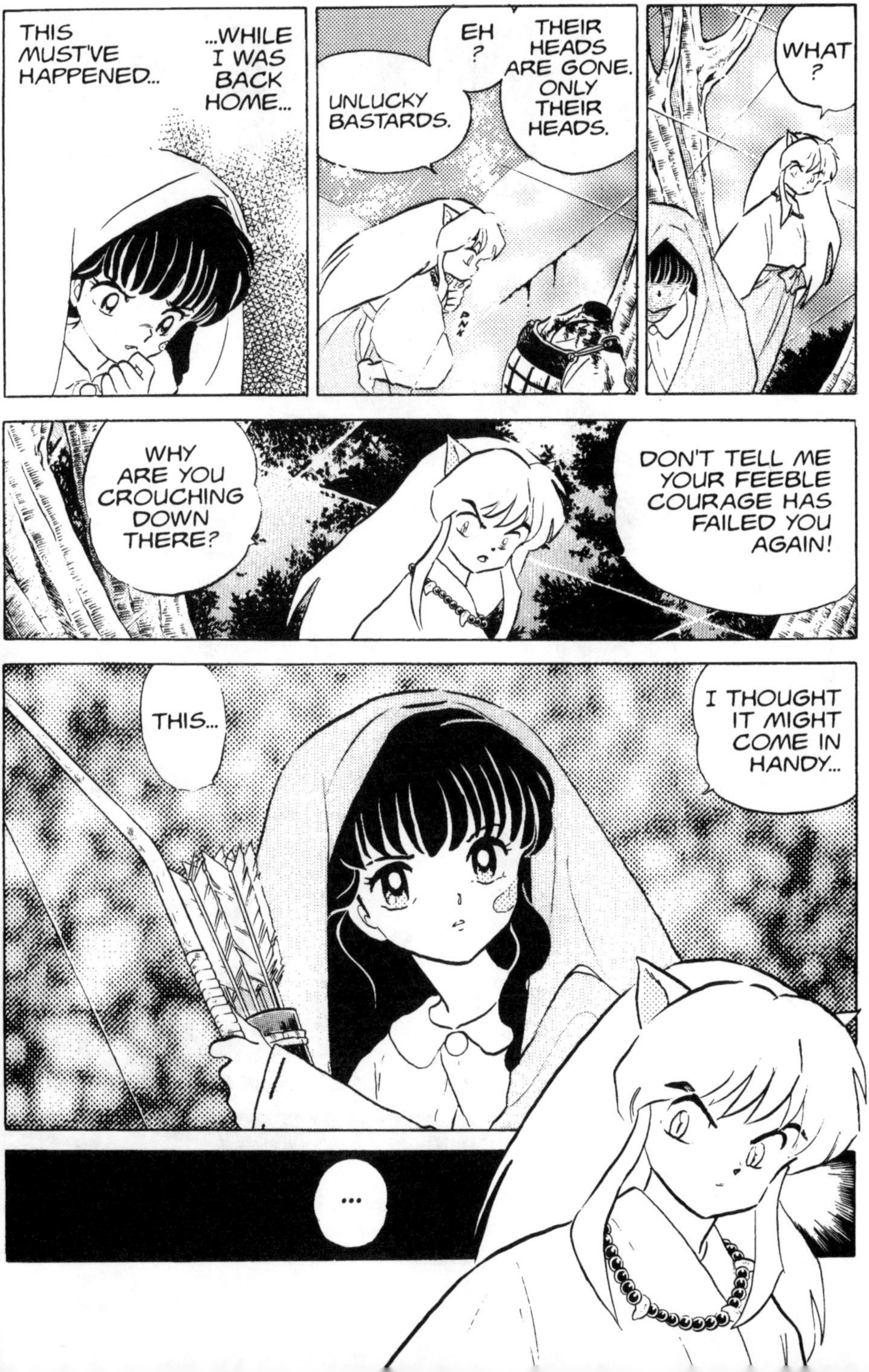
THIS MUST'VE HAPPENED...
...WHILE I WAS BACK HOME...
UNLUCKY BASTARDS.
EH?
THEIR HEADS ARE GONE. ONLY THEIR HEADS.
WHAT?
WHY ARE YOU CROUCHING DOWN THERE?
DON'T TELL ME YOUR FEEBLE COURAGE HAS FAILED YOU AGAIN!
THIS...
I THOUGHT IT MIGHT COME IN HANDY...
...

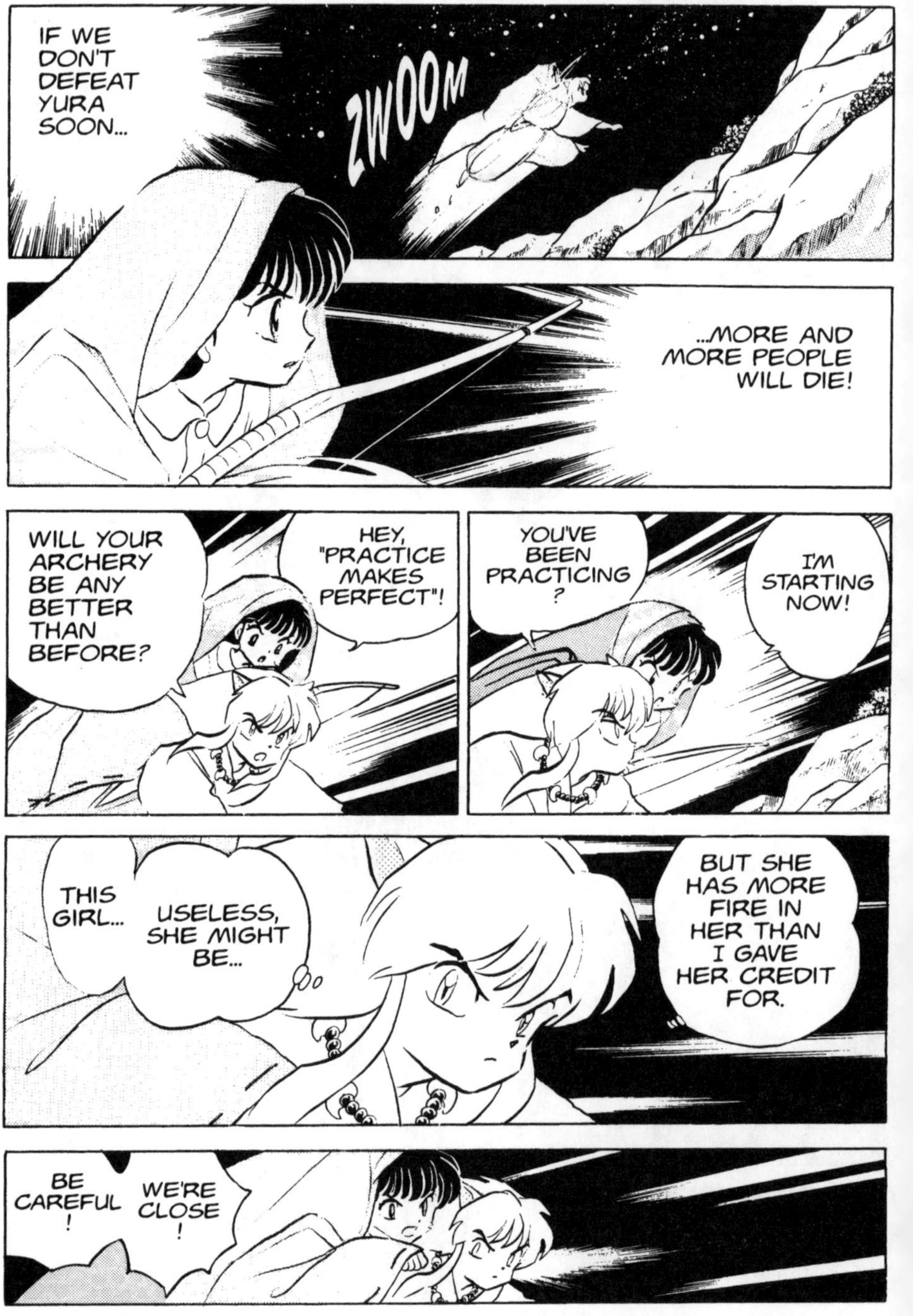
IF WE DON'T DEFEAT YURA SOON...
ZWOOM
...MORE AND MORE PEOPLE WILL DIE!
WILL YOUR ARCHERY BE ANY BETTER THAN BEFORE?
HEY, "PRACTICE MAKES PERFECT"!
YOU'VE BEEN PRACTICING?
I'M STARTING NOW!
THIS GIRL...
USELESS, SHE MIGHT BE...
BUT SHE HAS MORE FIRE IN HER THAN I GAVE HER CREDIT FOR.
BE CAREFUL!
WE'RE CLOSE!

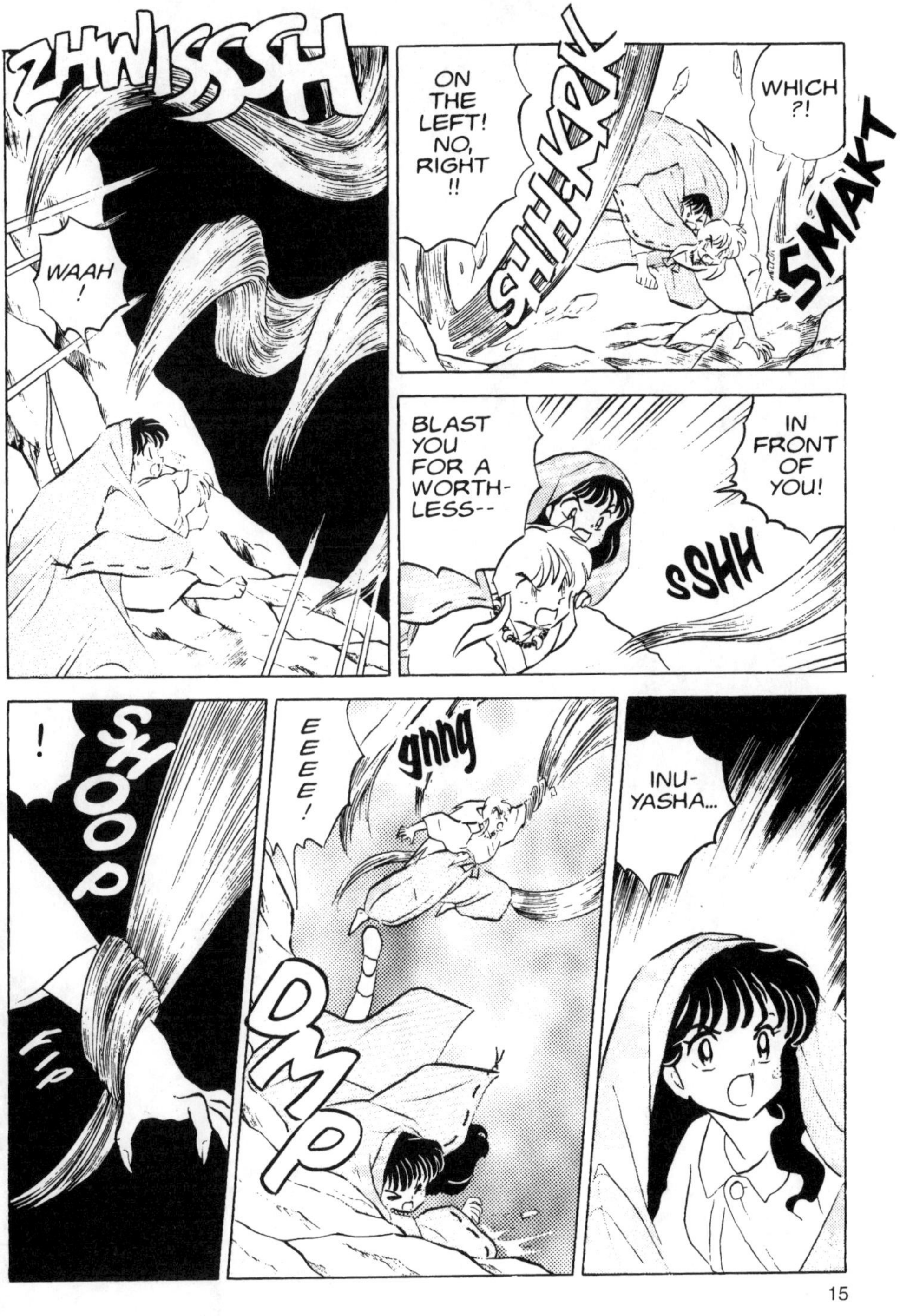
ZHWISSSH
WAAH!
ON THE LEFT! NO, RIGHT!!
SHHKRRK
WHICH?!
SMAKT
BLAST YOU FOR A WORTHLESS--
IN FRONT OF YOU!
SSHH
!
SHOOP
FLIP
EEEE!
gnng
DMP
INU-YASHA...

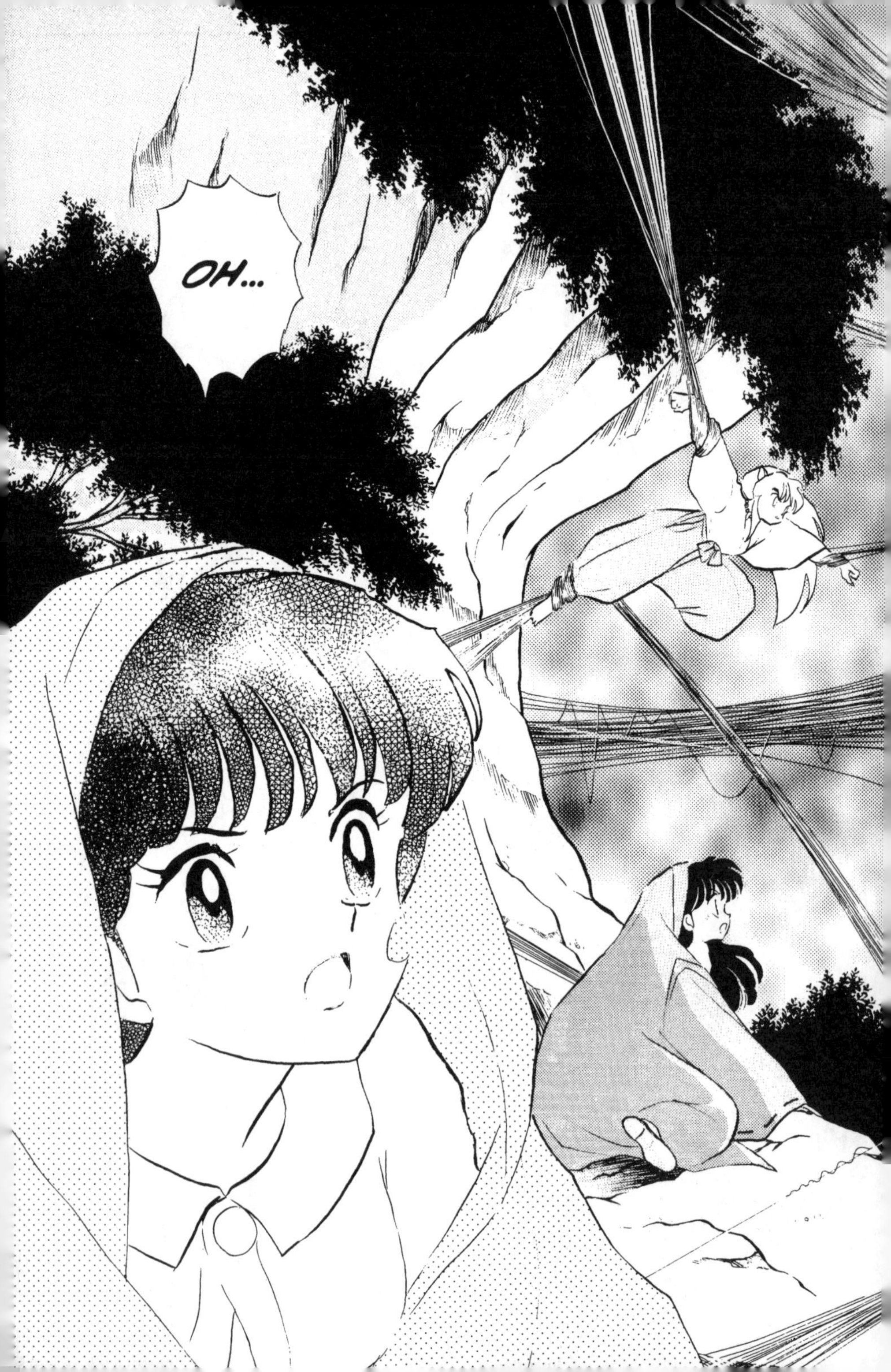
OH...

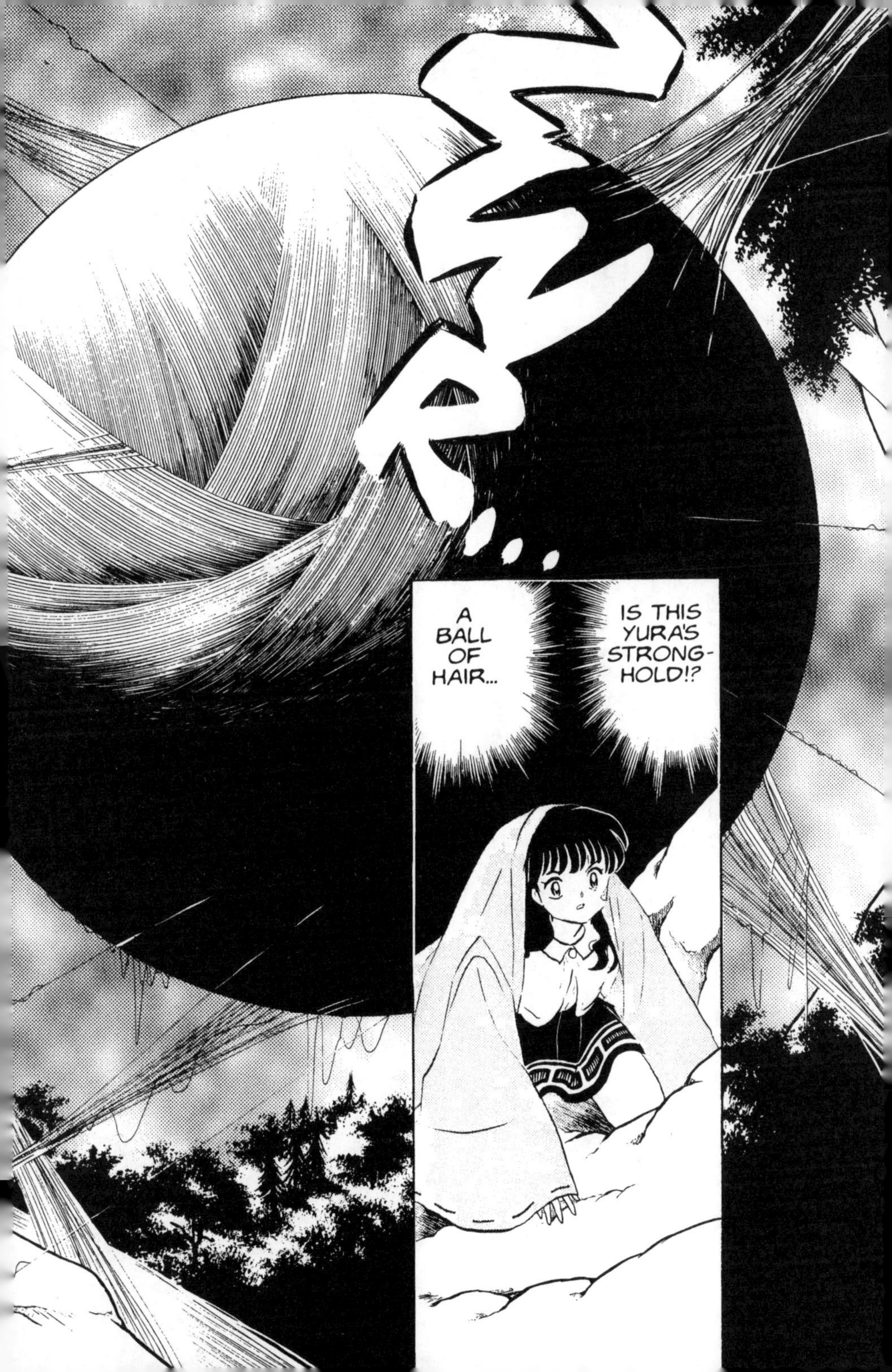
A BALL OF HAIR...
IS THIS YURA'S STRONG-HOLD!?

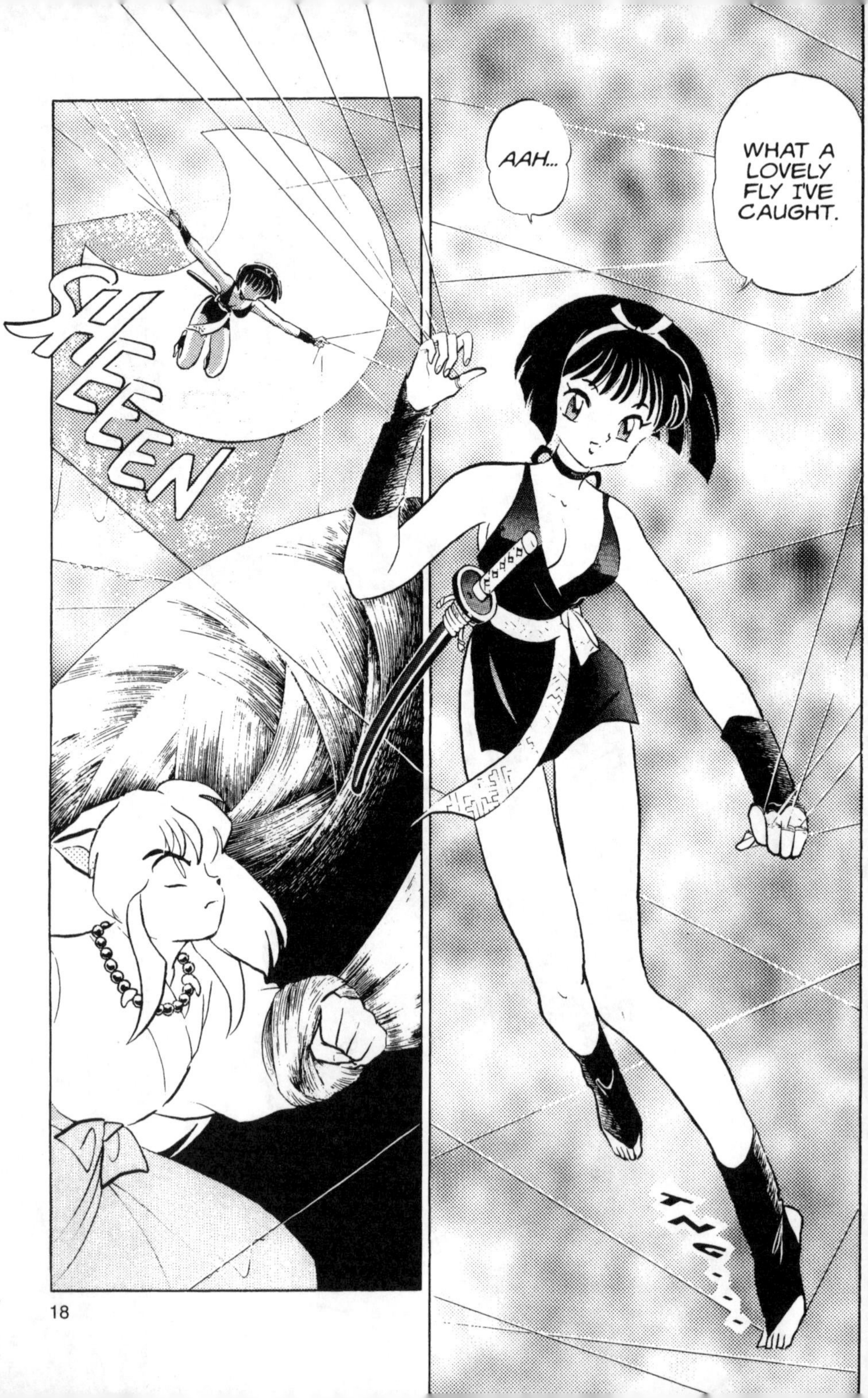
SHEEEN
AAH...
WHAT A LOVELY FLY I'VE CAUGHT.
TNG...

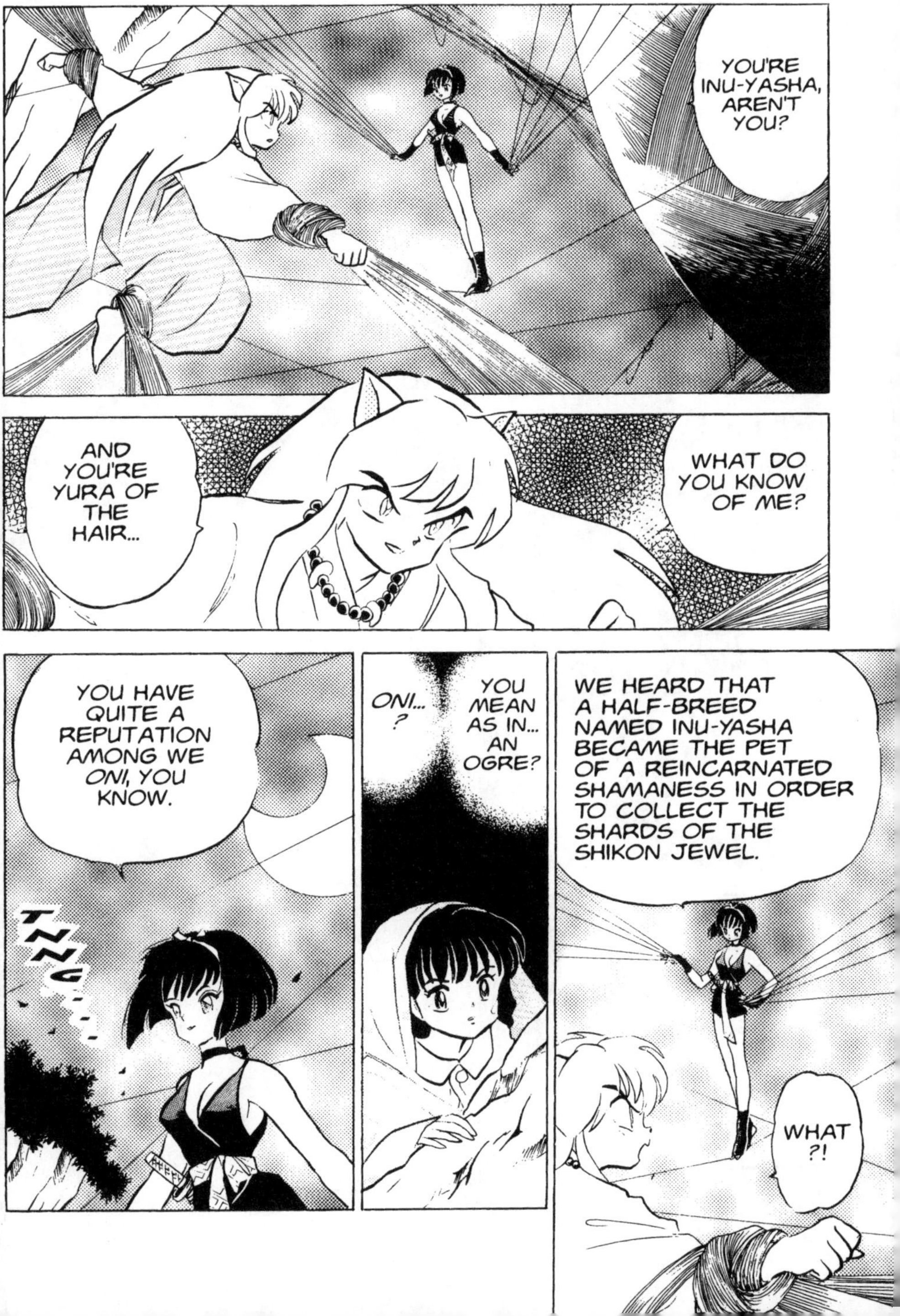
YOU'RE INU-YASHA, AREN'T YOU?
AND YOU'RE YURA OF THE HAIR...
WHAT DO YOU KNOW OF ME?
YOU HAVE QUITE A REPUTATION AMONG WE ONI, YOU KNOW.
TNNG...
ONI...?
YOU MEAN AS IN... AN OGRE?
WE HEARD THAT A HALF-BREED NAMED INU-YASHA BECAME THE PET OF A REINCARNATED SHAMANESS IN ORDER TO COLLECT THE SHARDS OF THE SHIKON JEWEL.
WHAT?!

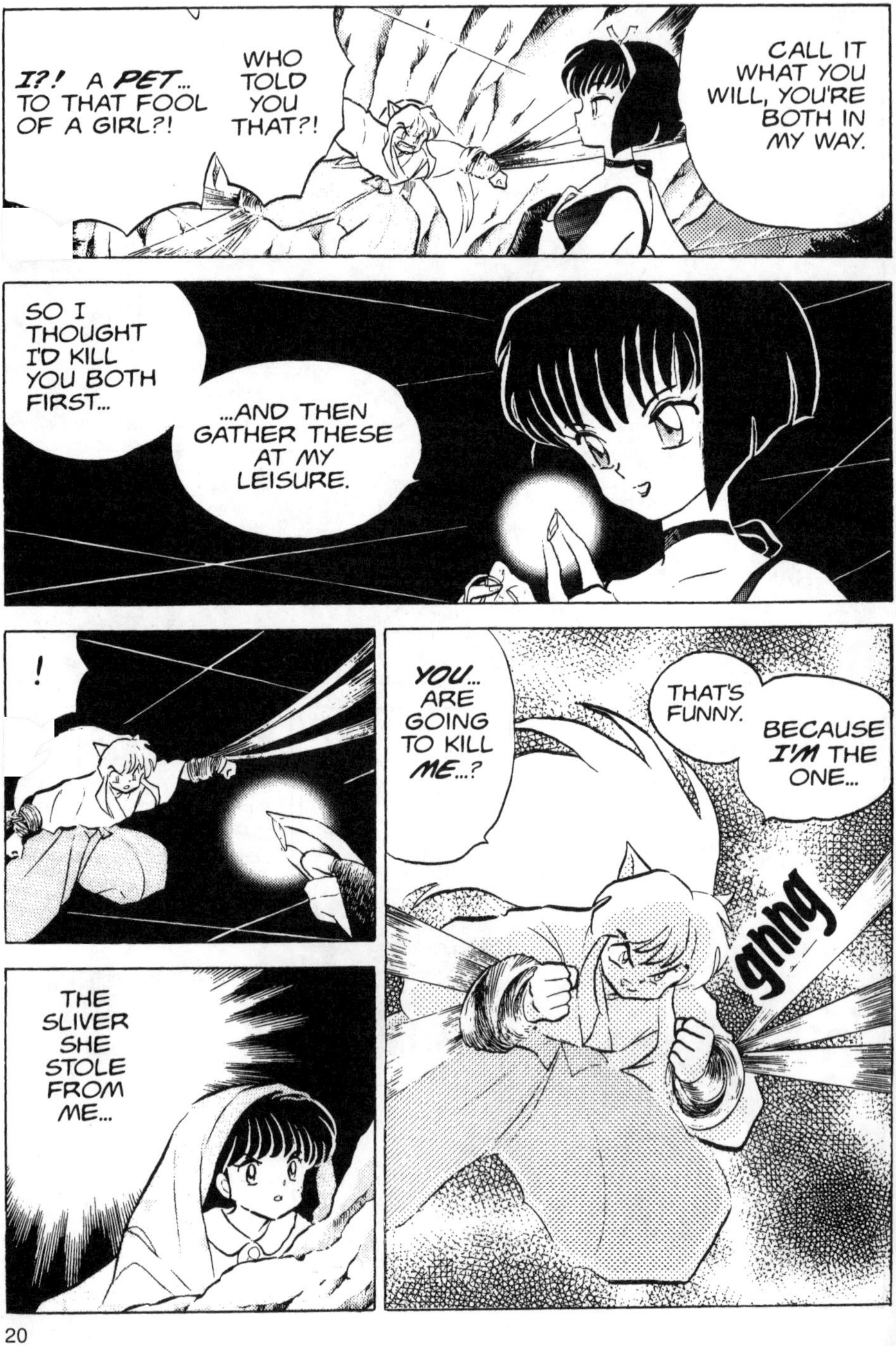
I?! A PET... TO THAT FOOL OF A GIRL?!
WHO TOLD YOU THAT?!
CALL IT WHAT YOU WILL, YOU'RE BOTH IN MY WAY.
SO I THOUGHT I'D KILL YOU BOTH FIRST...
...AND THEN GATHER THESE AT MY LEISURE.
!
THE SLIVER SHE STOLE FROM ME...
YOU... ARE GOING TO KILL ME...?
THAT'S FUNNY.
BECAUSE I'M THE ONE...
gnng

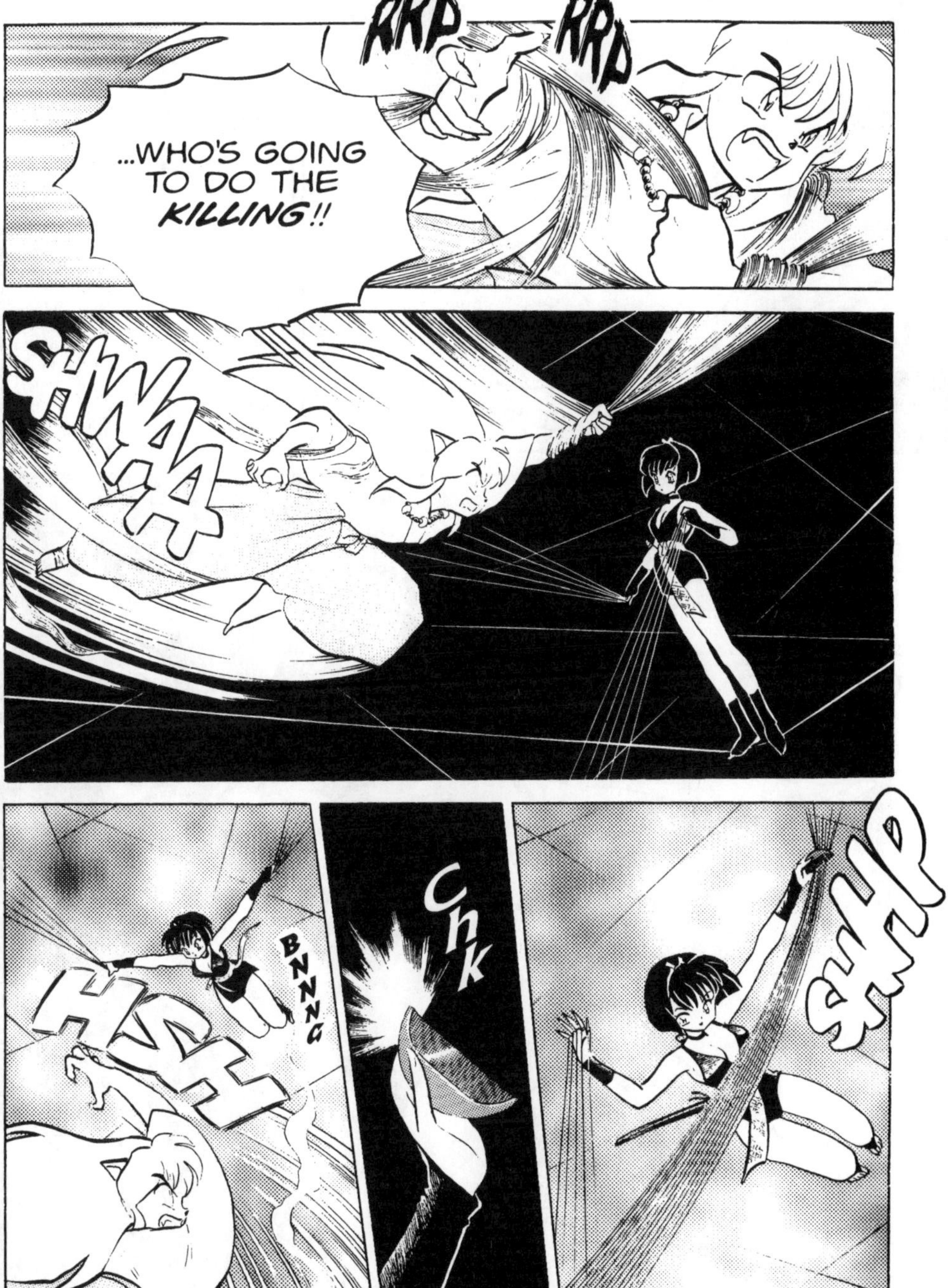
RRP RRP
...WHO'S GOING TO DO THE *KILLING*!!
SHWAA
HSH
BNNNG
Chk
SHIP

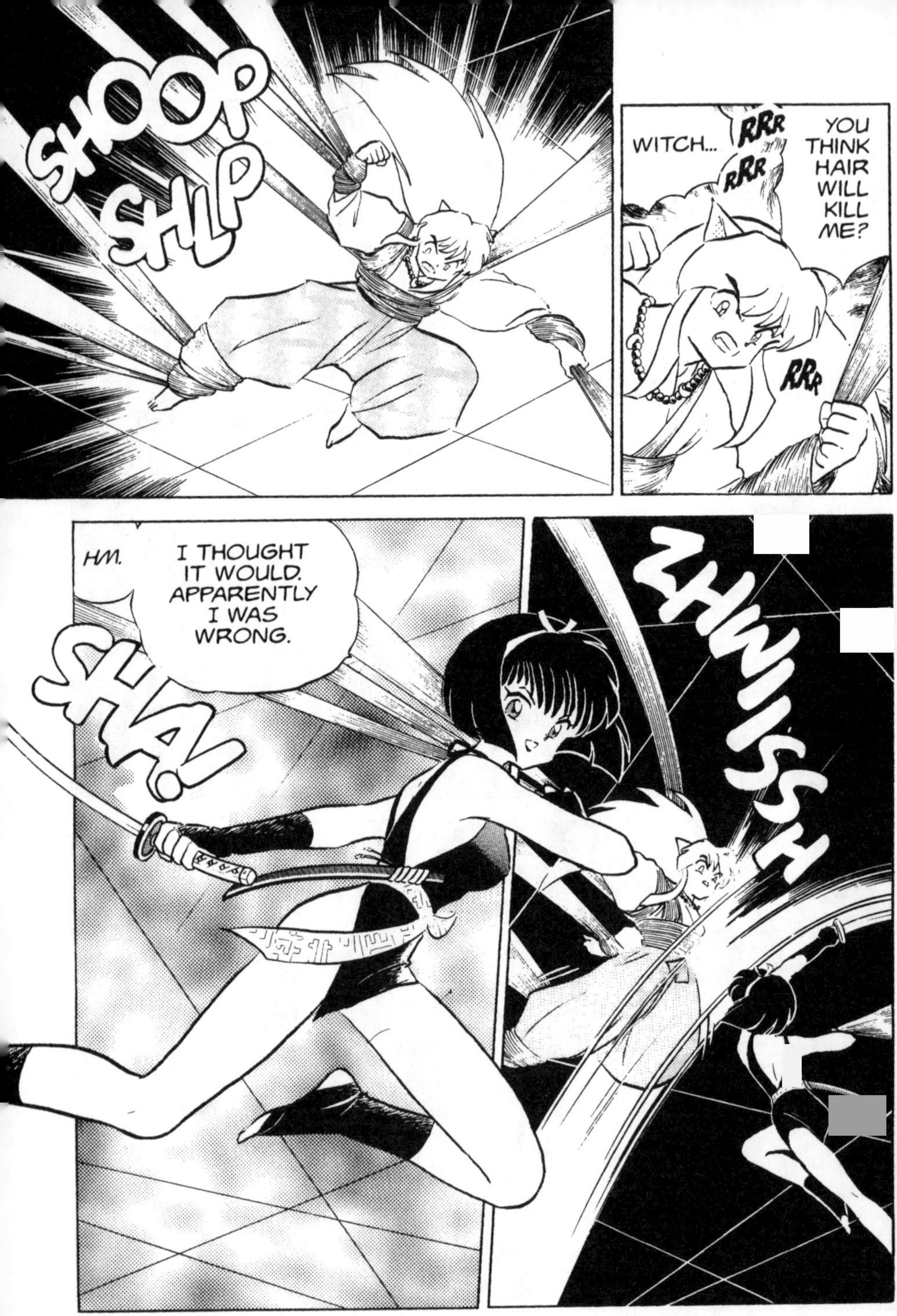
SHOOP
SHLP
WITCH...
RRR
RRR
RRR
YOU THINK HAIR WILL KILL ME?
HM.
I THOUGHT IT WOULD. APPARENTLY I WAS WRONG.
SHA!
ZHWISSH

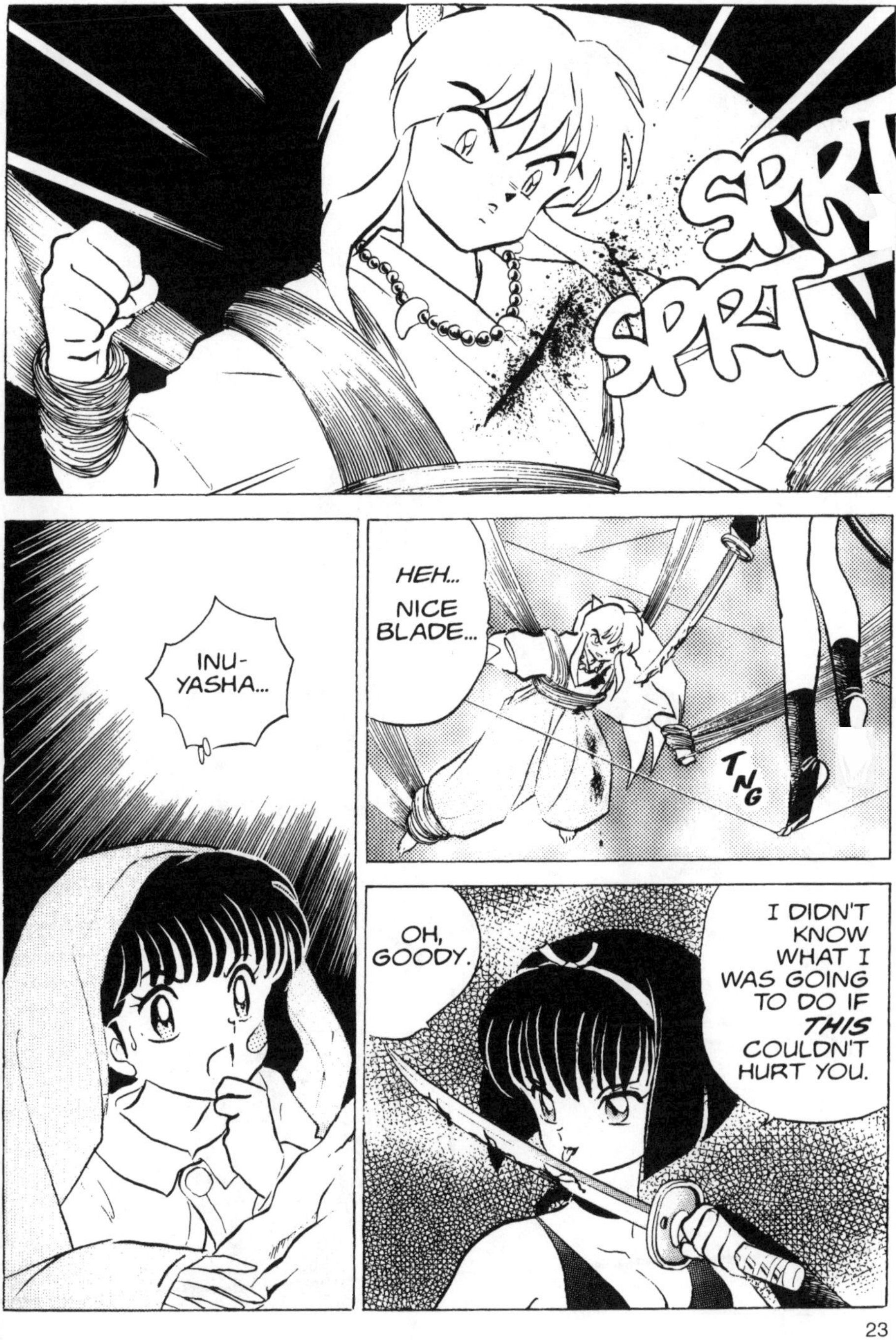
SPRT
SPRT
INU-YASHA...
HEH... NICE BLADE...
TNG
OH, GOODY.
I DIDN'T KNOW WHAT I WAS GOING TO DO IF *THIS* COULDN'T HURT YOU.

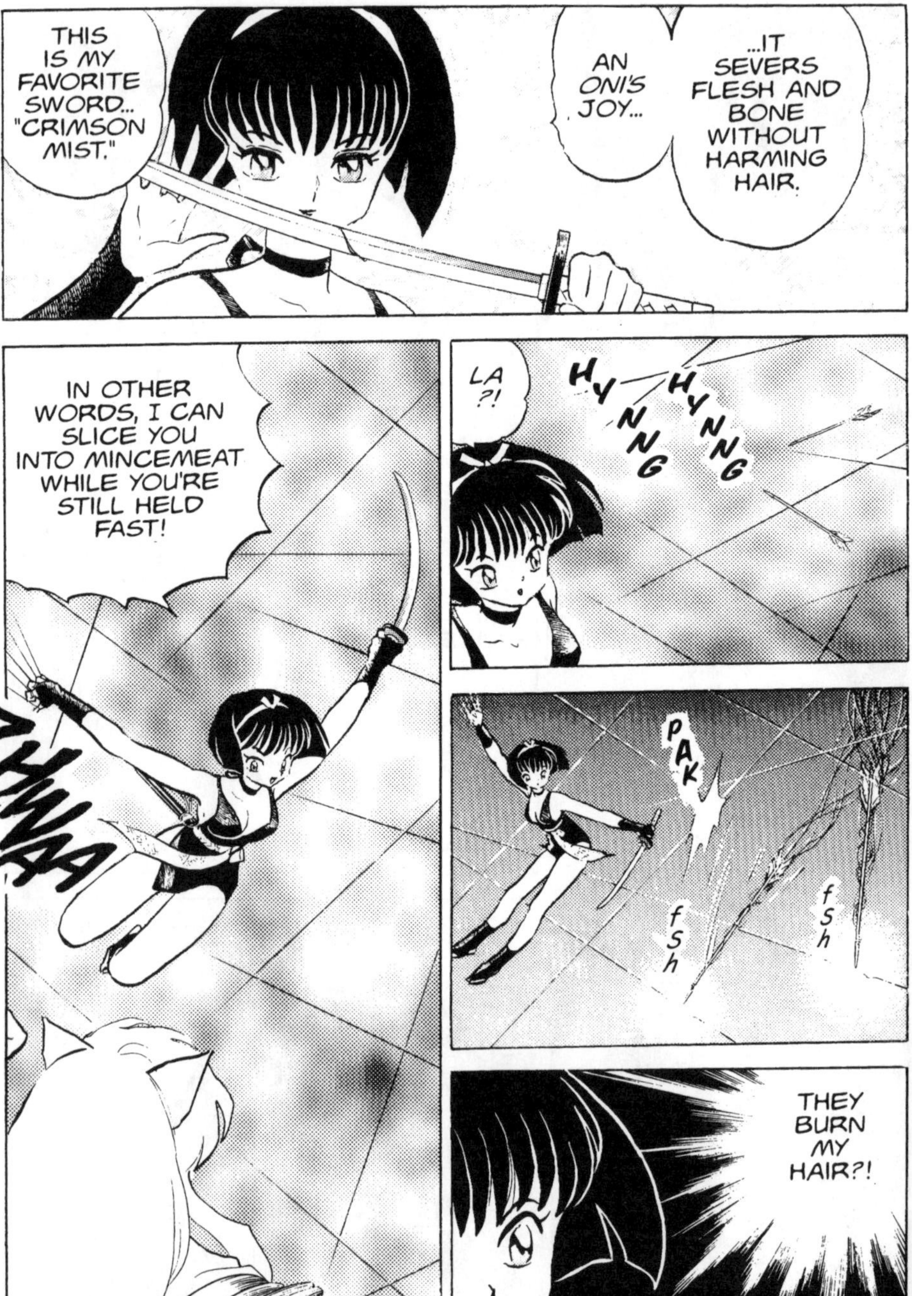
THIS IS MY FAVORITE SWORD... "CRIMSON MIST."
AN ONI'S JOY...
...IT SEVERS FLESH AND BONE WITHOUT HARMING HAIR.
IN OTHER WORDS, I CAN SLICE YOU INTO MINCEMEAT WHILE YOU'RE STILL HELD FAST!
ZHWAA
LA?!
HYNNG
HYNNG
PAK
fsh
fsh
THEY BURN MY HAIR?!

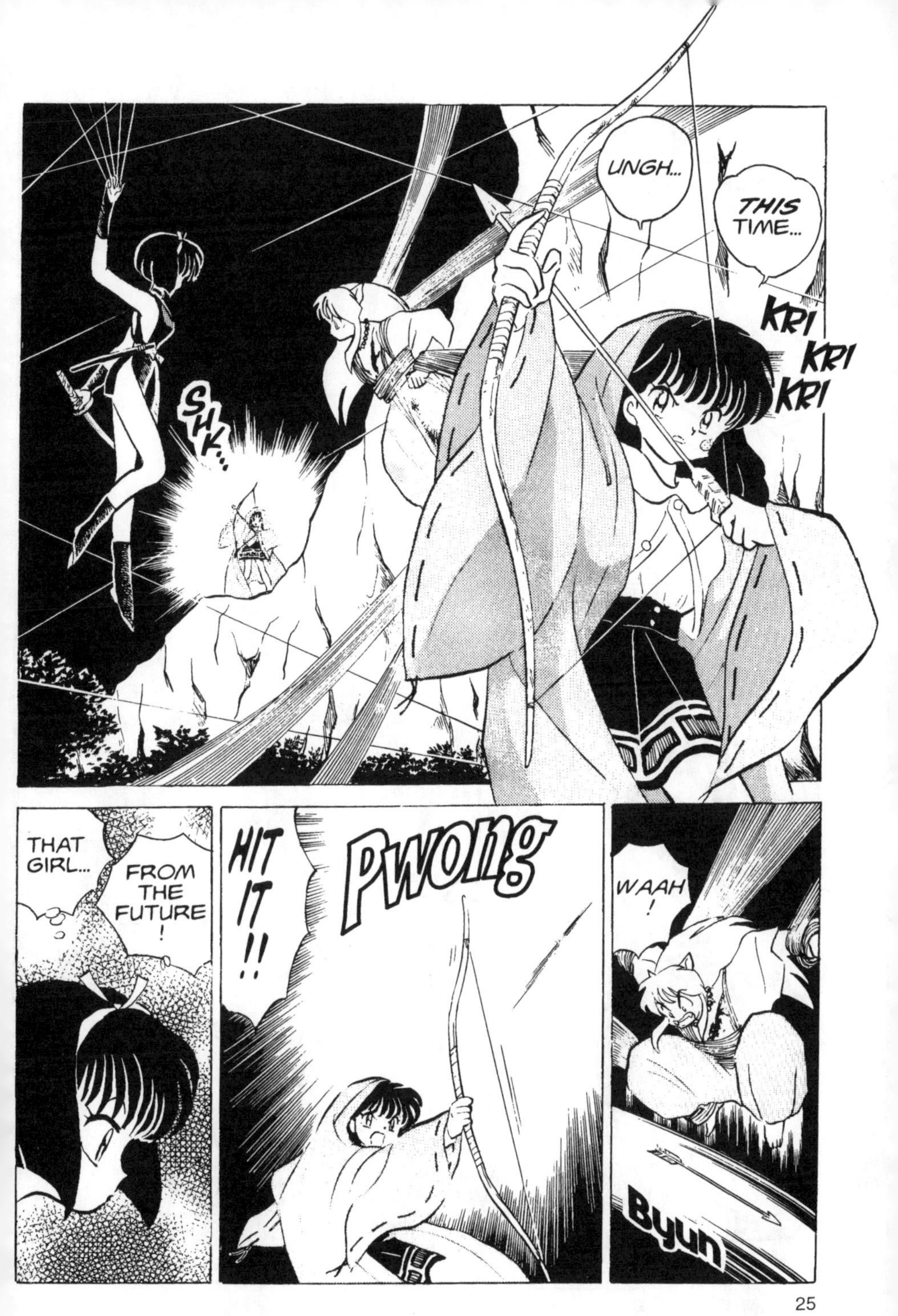
SHK...
UNGH...
THIS TIME...
KRI KRI KRI
THAT GIRL...
FROM THE FUTURE!
HIT IT!!
Pwong
WAAH!
Byun

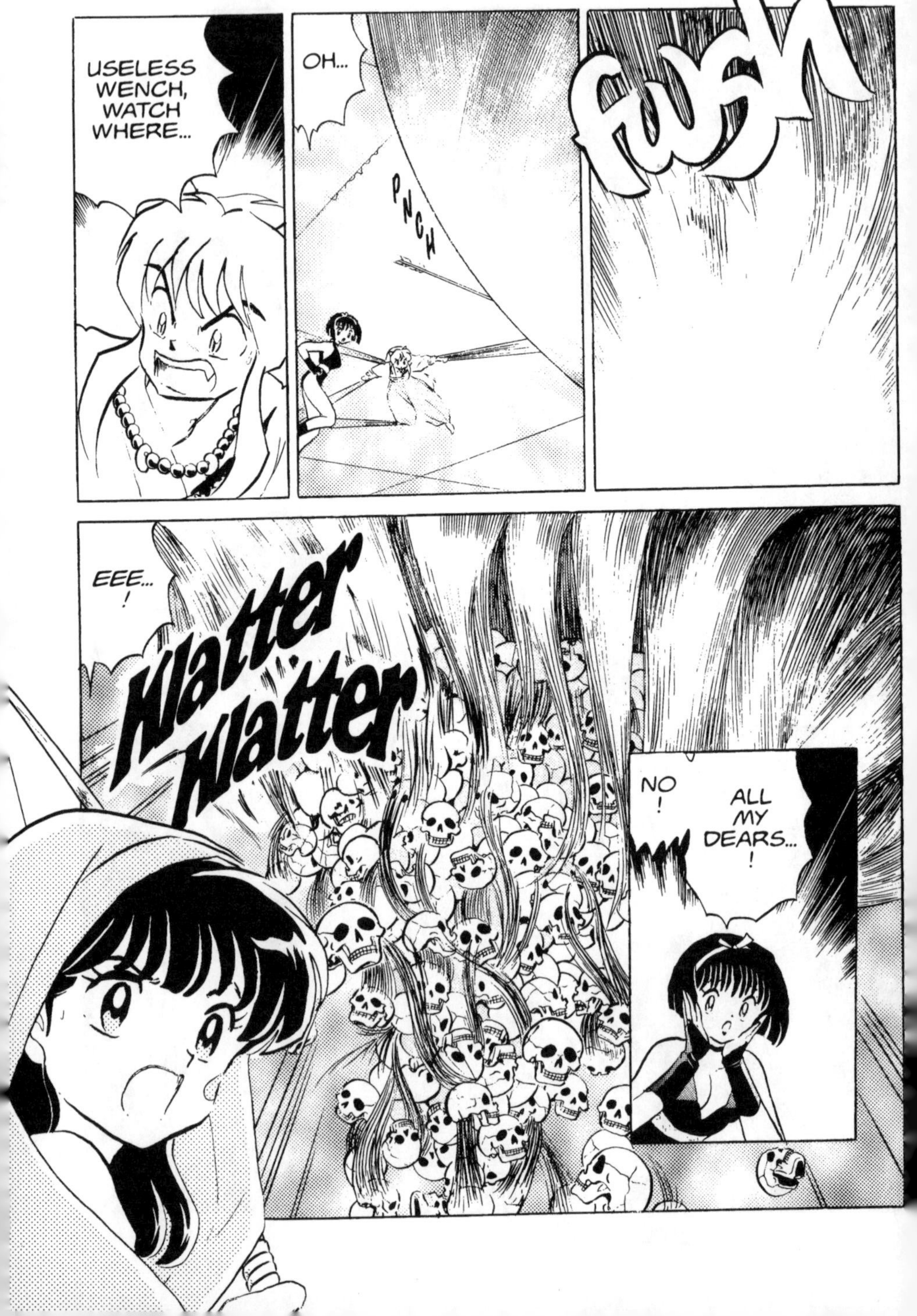
USELESS WENCH, WATCH WHERE...
OH...
PNCH
FWSH
EEE...!
KLATTER KLATTER
NO!
ALL MY DEARS...!

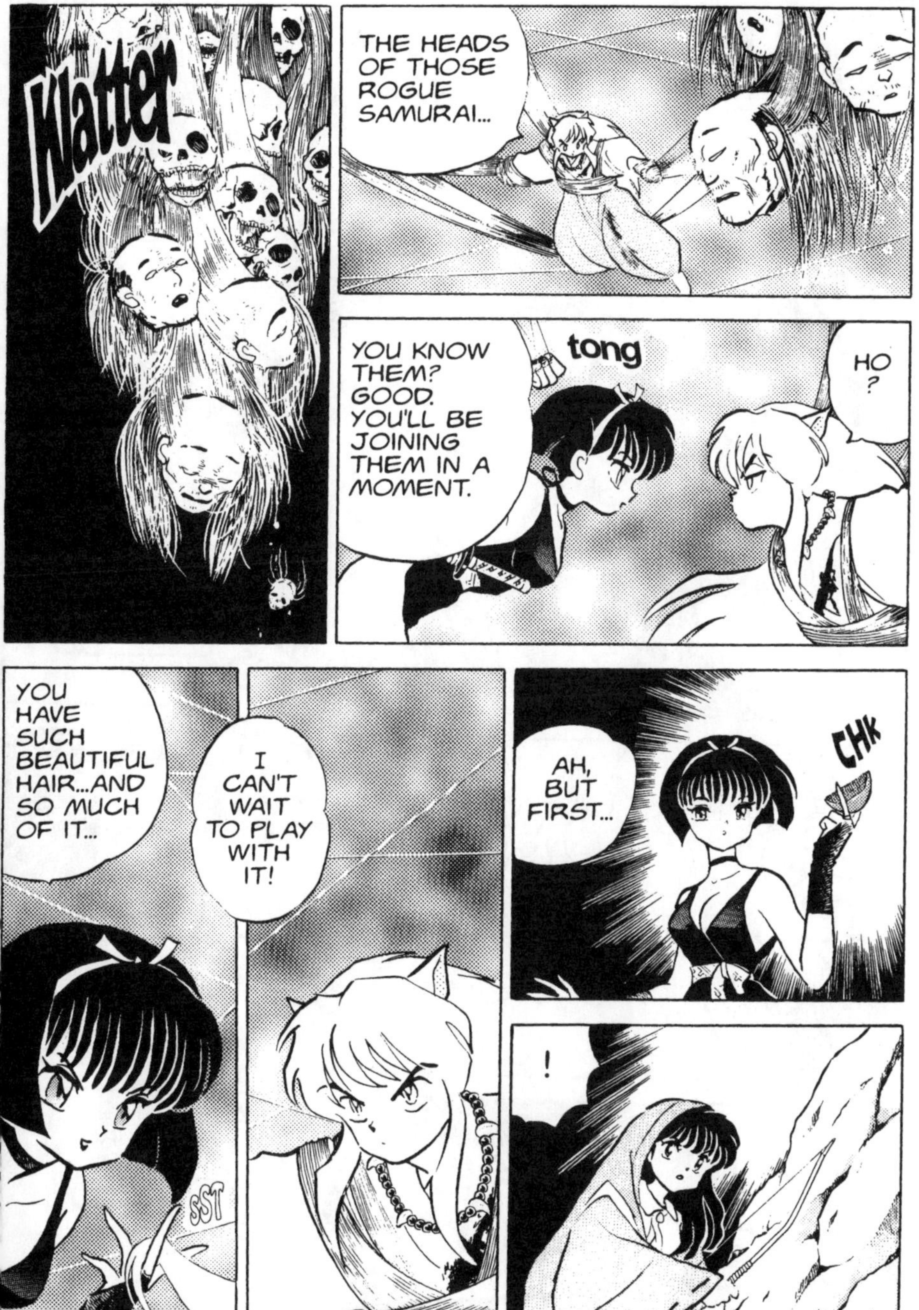
Klatter
THE HEADS OF THOSE ROGUE SAMURAI...
YOU KNOW THEM? GOOD. YOU'LL BE JOINING THEM IN A MOMENT.
tong
HO?
YOU HAVE SUCH BEAUTIFUL HAIR...AND SO MUCH OF IT...
SST
I CAN'T WAIT TO PLAY WITH IT!
AH, BUT FIRST...
CHK
!

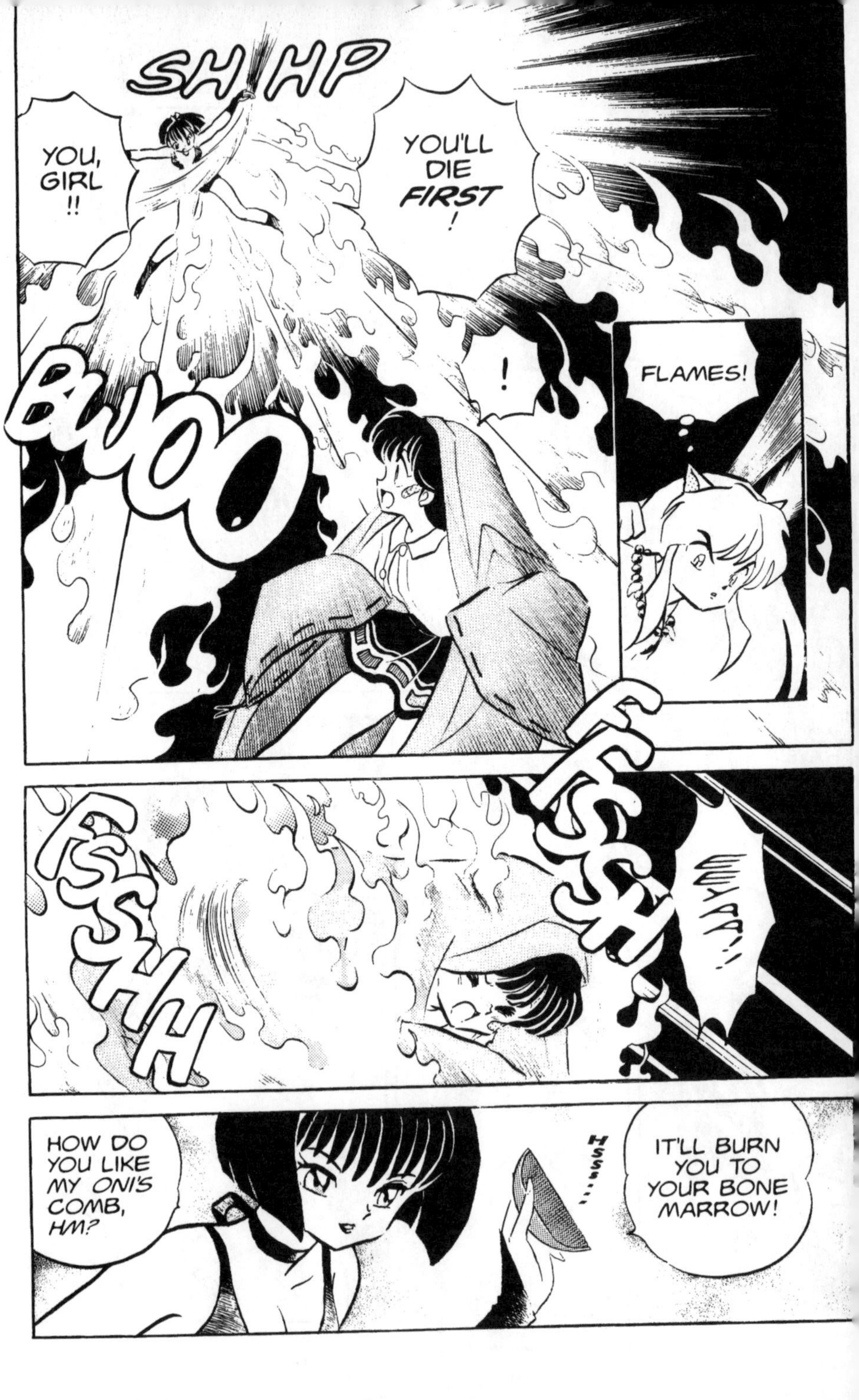
SHHP
YOU, GIRL !!
YOU'LL DIE FIRST !
BUOO
!
FLAMES!
FSSHH
FSSH
EEYAA!!
HOW DO YOU LIKE MY ONI'S COMB, HM?
HSSS...
IT'LL BURN YOU TO YOUR BONE MARROW!

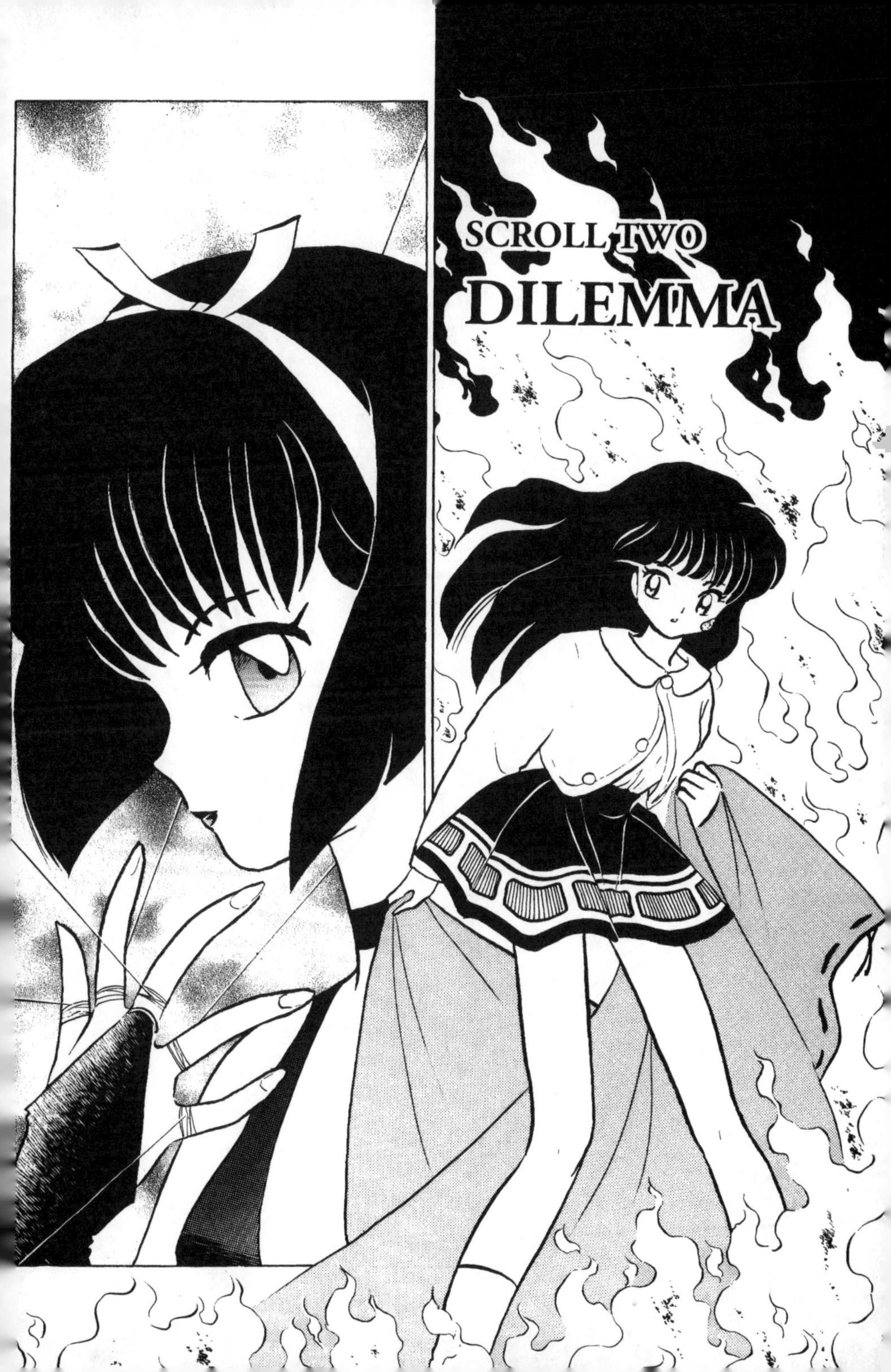
SCROLL TWO
DILEMMA

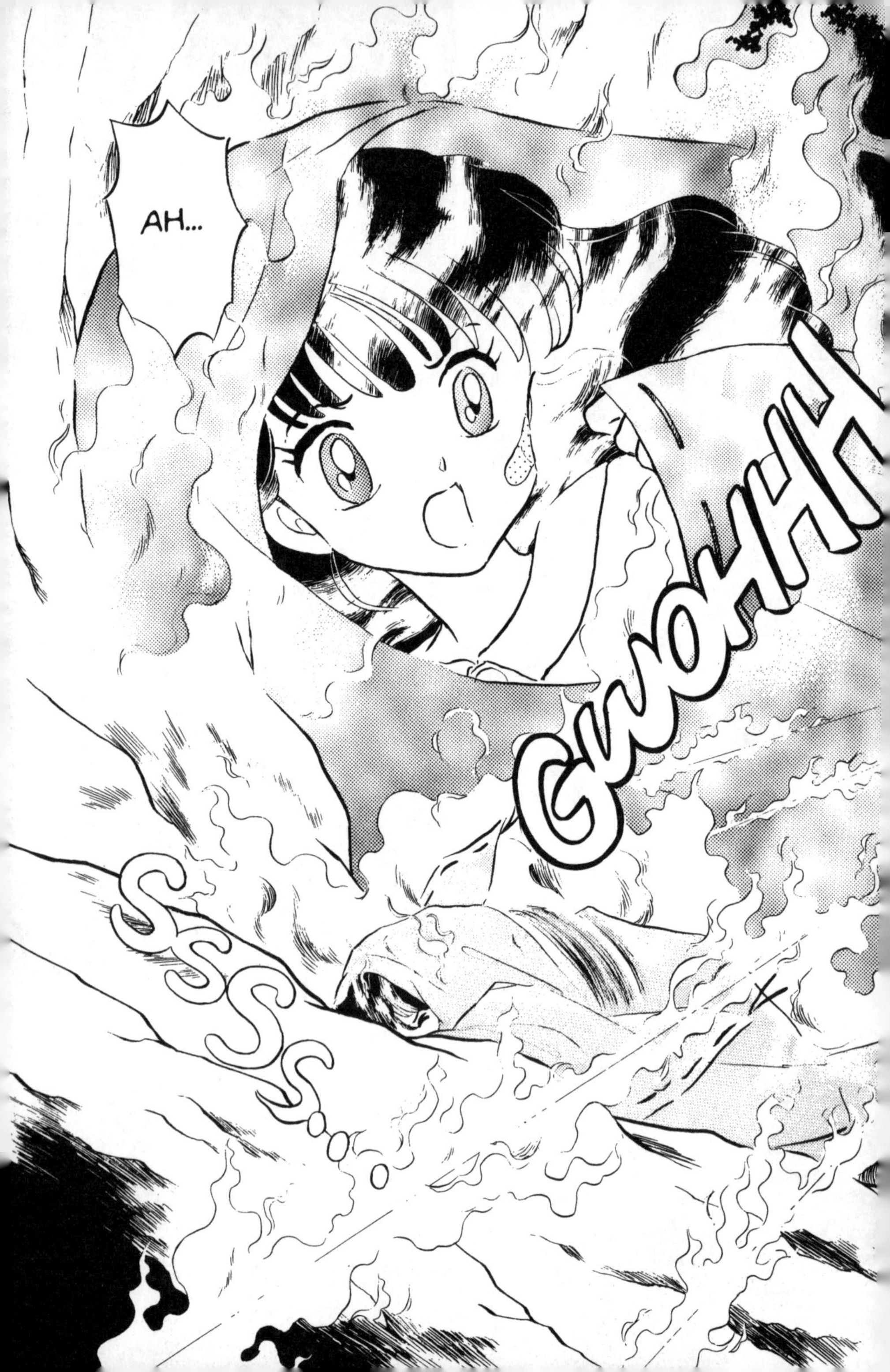
AH...
GWOHH
SSSS...

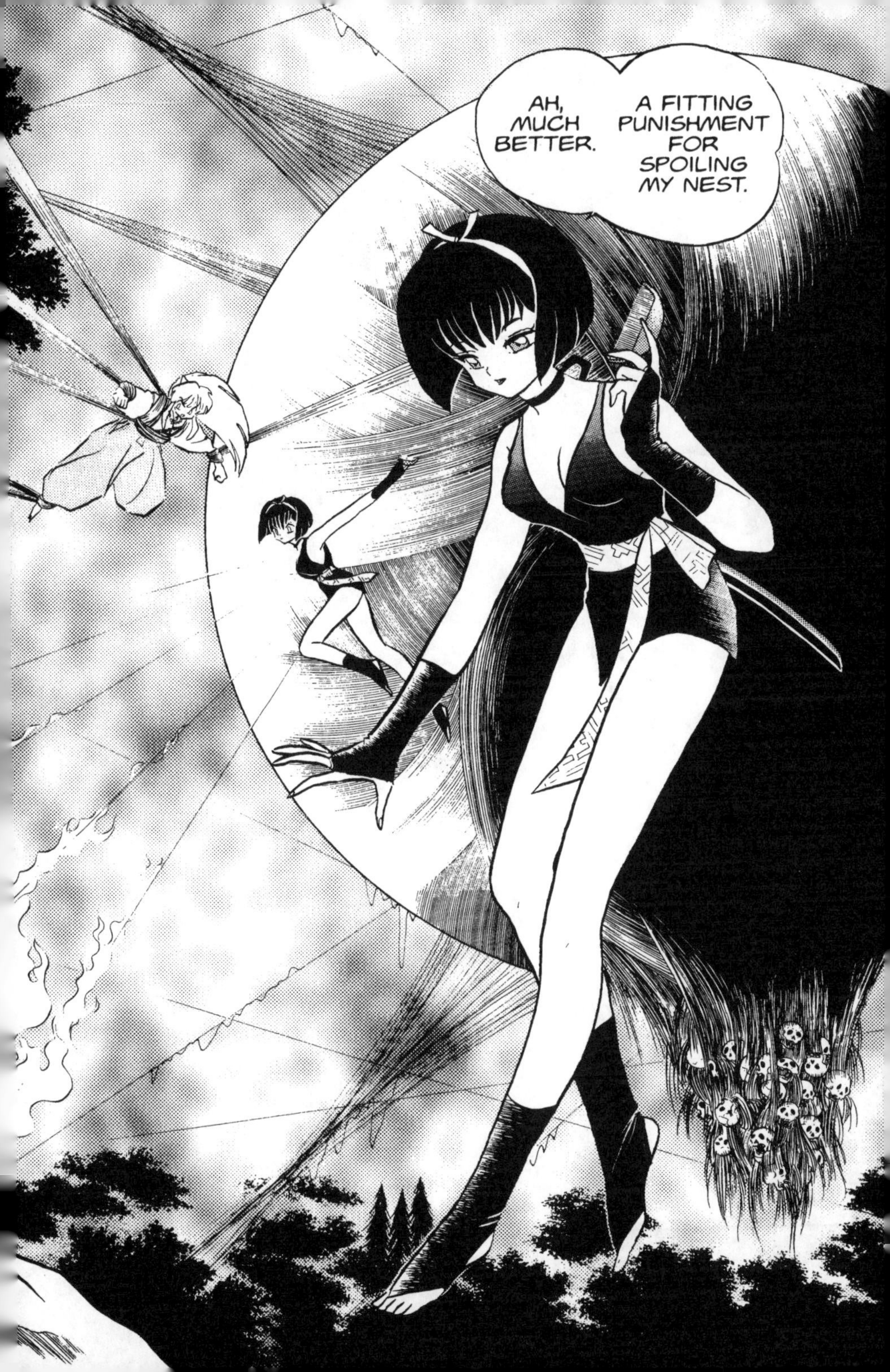
AH, MUCH BETTER.
A FITTING PUNISHMENT FOR SPOILING MY NEST.

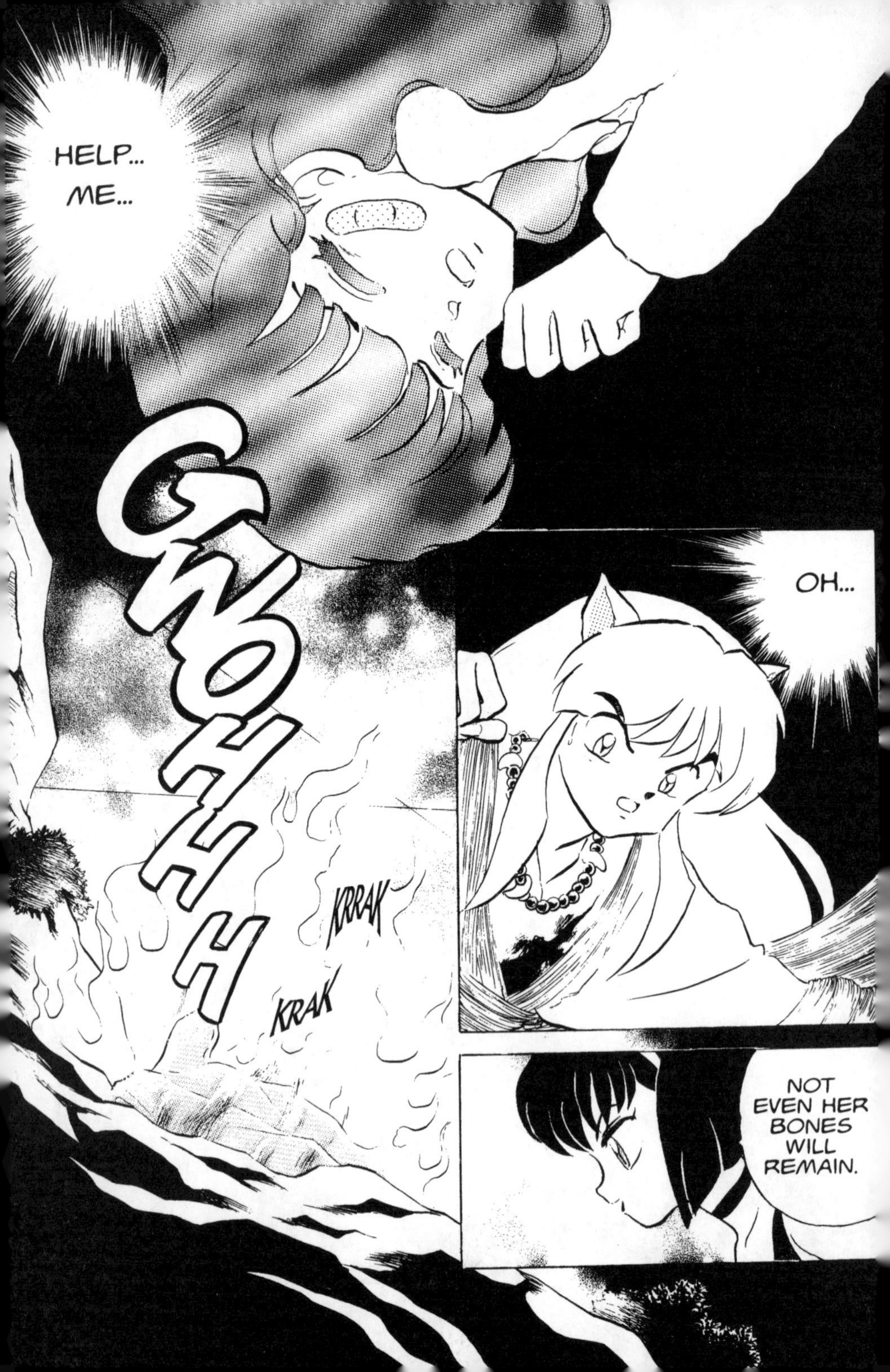
HELP... ME...
GWOHHHH
KRRAK
KRAK
OH...
NOT EVEN HER BONES WILL REMAIN.

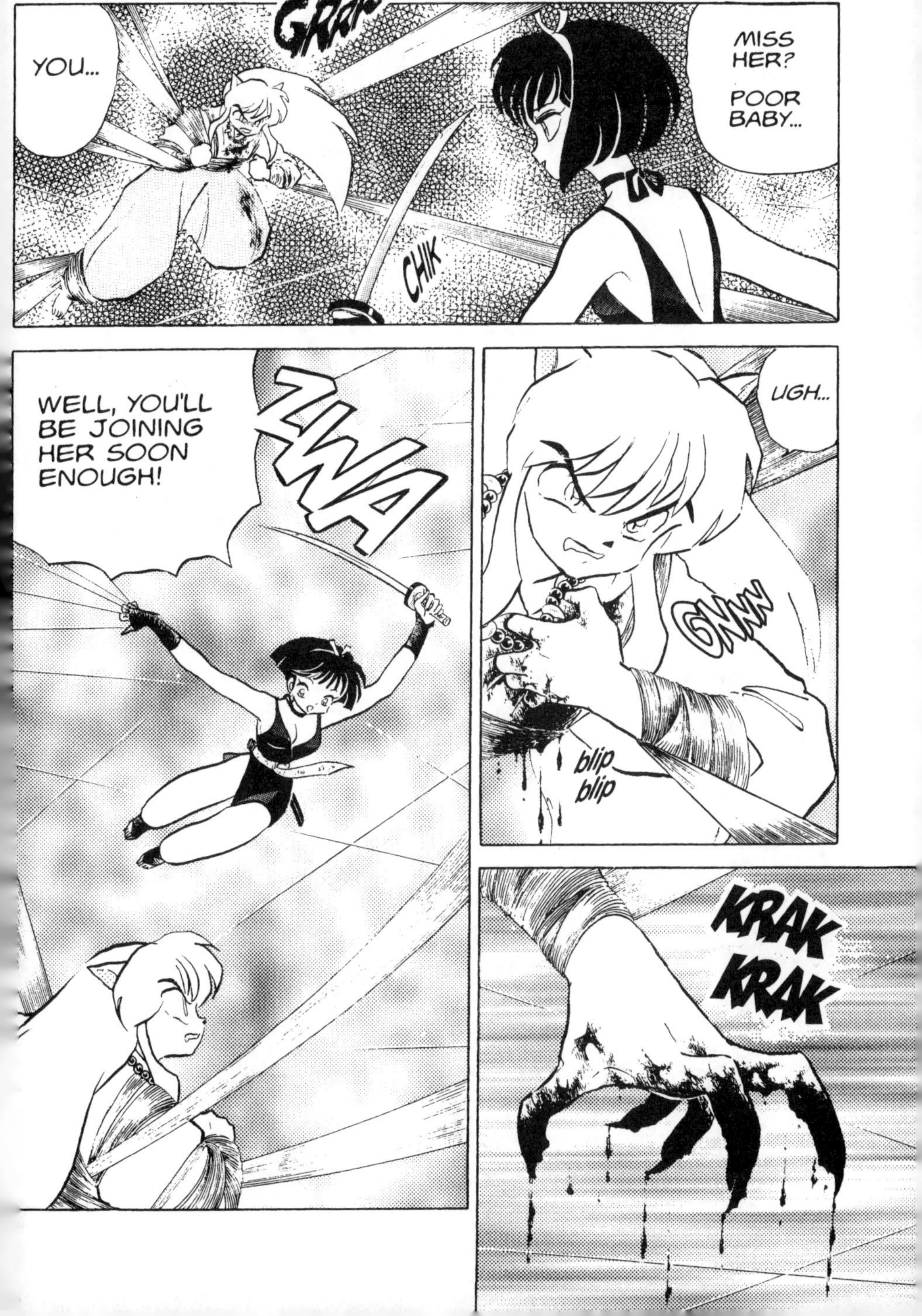
YOU...
GRRR...
MISS HER?
POOR BABY...
CHIK
WELL, YOU'LL BE JOINING HER SOON ENOUGH!
ZWA
UGH...
GNNN
blip blip
KRAK KRAK

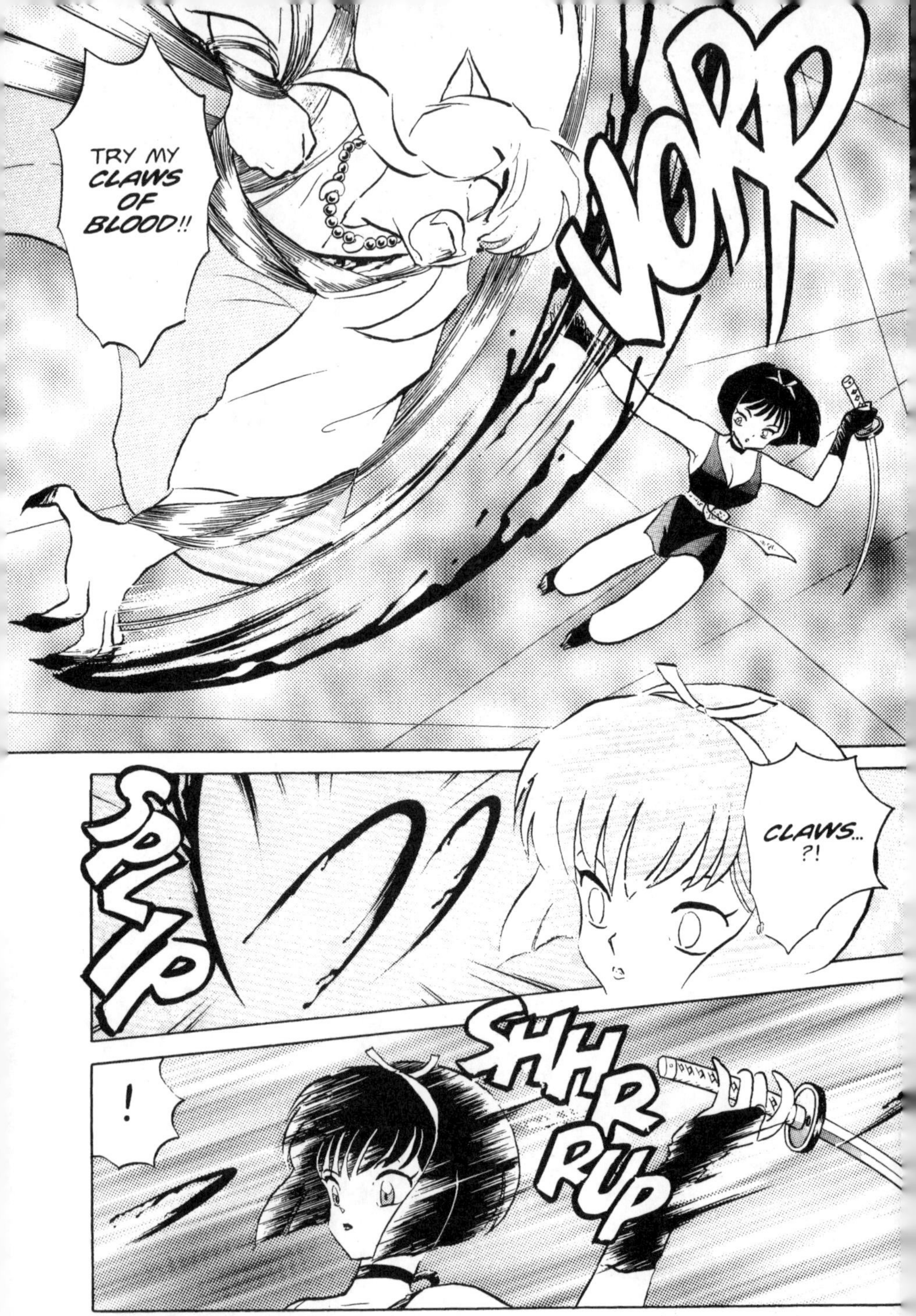
TRY MY CLAWS OF BLOOD!!
VOPP
SPLIP
CLAWS... ?!
SHHRRUP
!

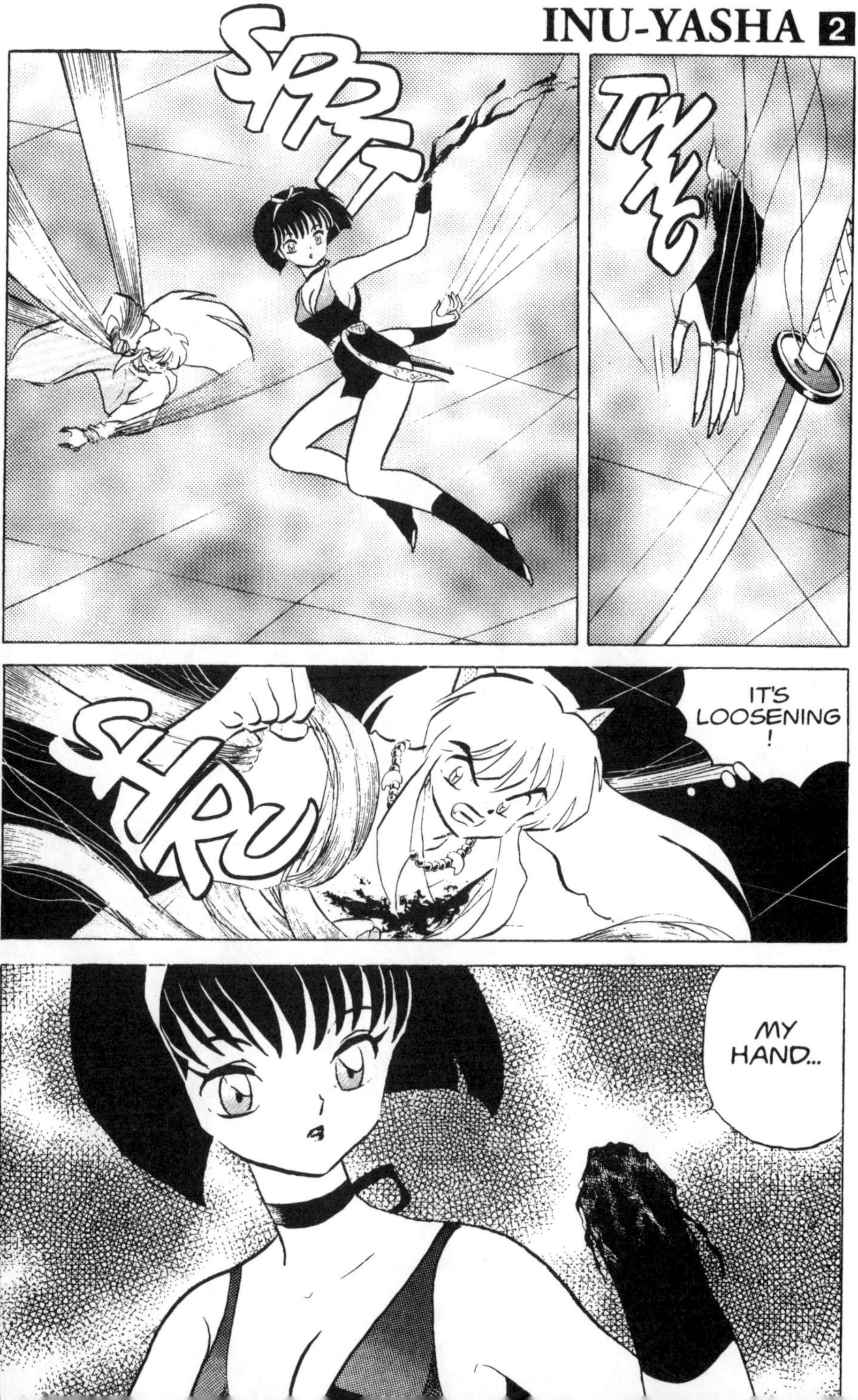
SPRIT
TWING
SHRU
IT'S LOOSENING!
MY HAND...

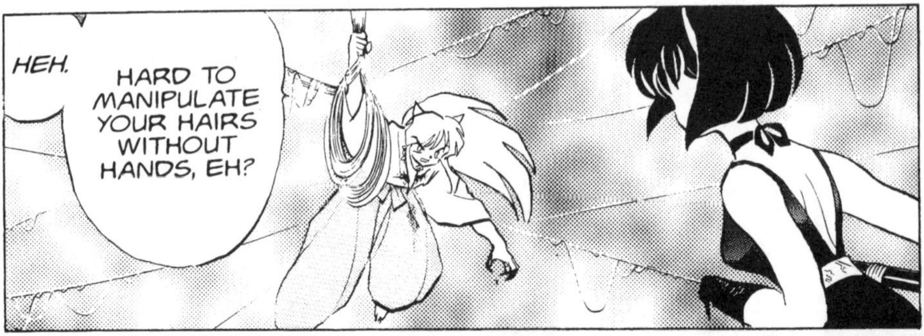
HEH.
HARD TO MANIPULATE YOUR HAIRS WITHOUT HANDS, EH?
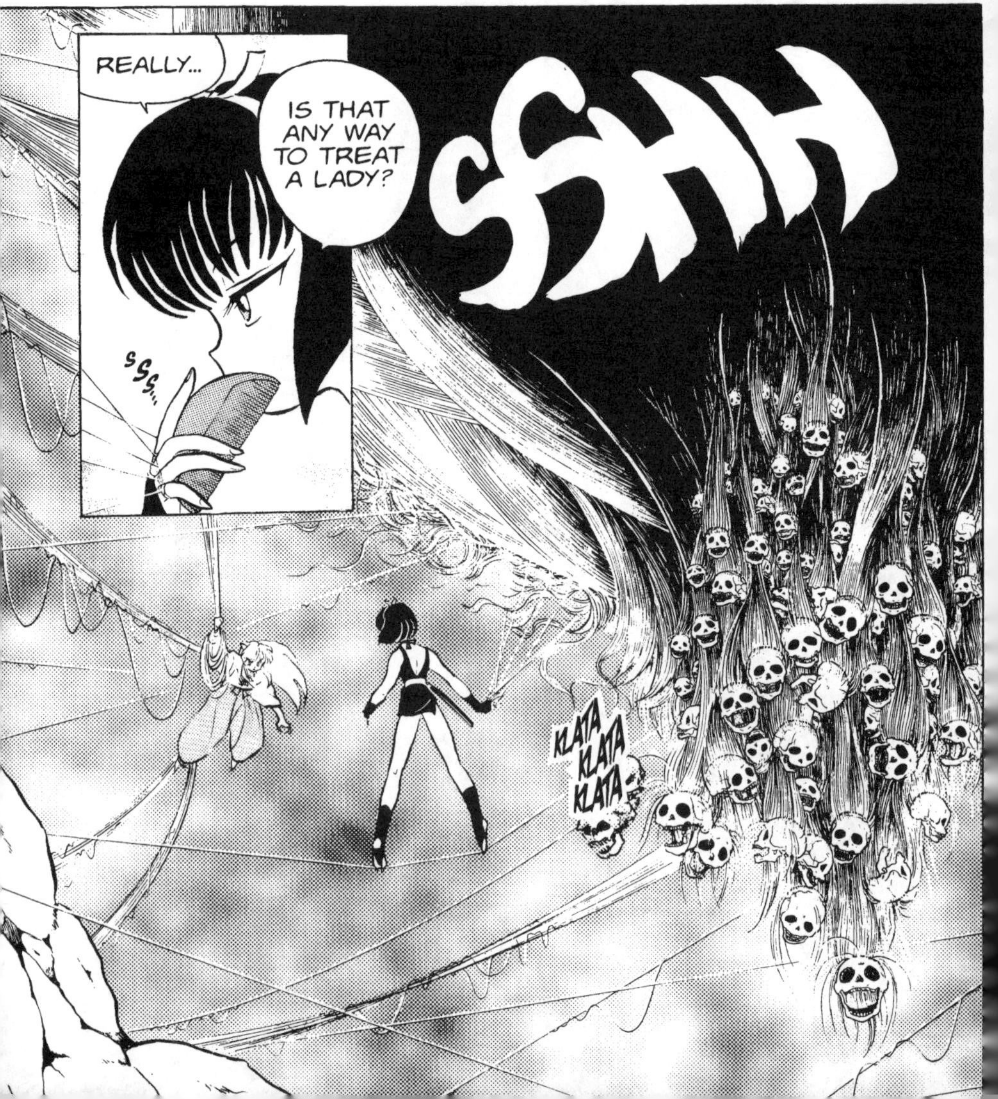
REALLY...
IS THAT ANY WAY TO TREAT A LADY?
SSS...
SSHH
KLATA KLATA KLATA

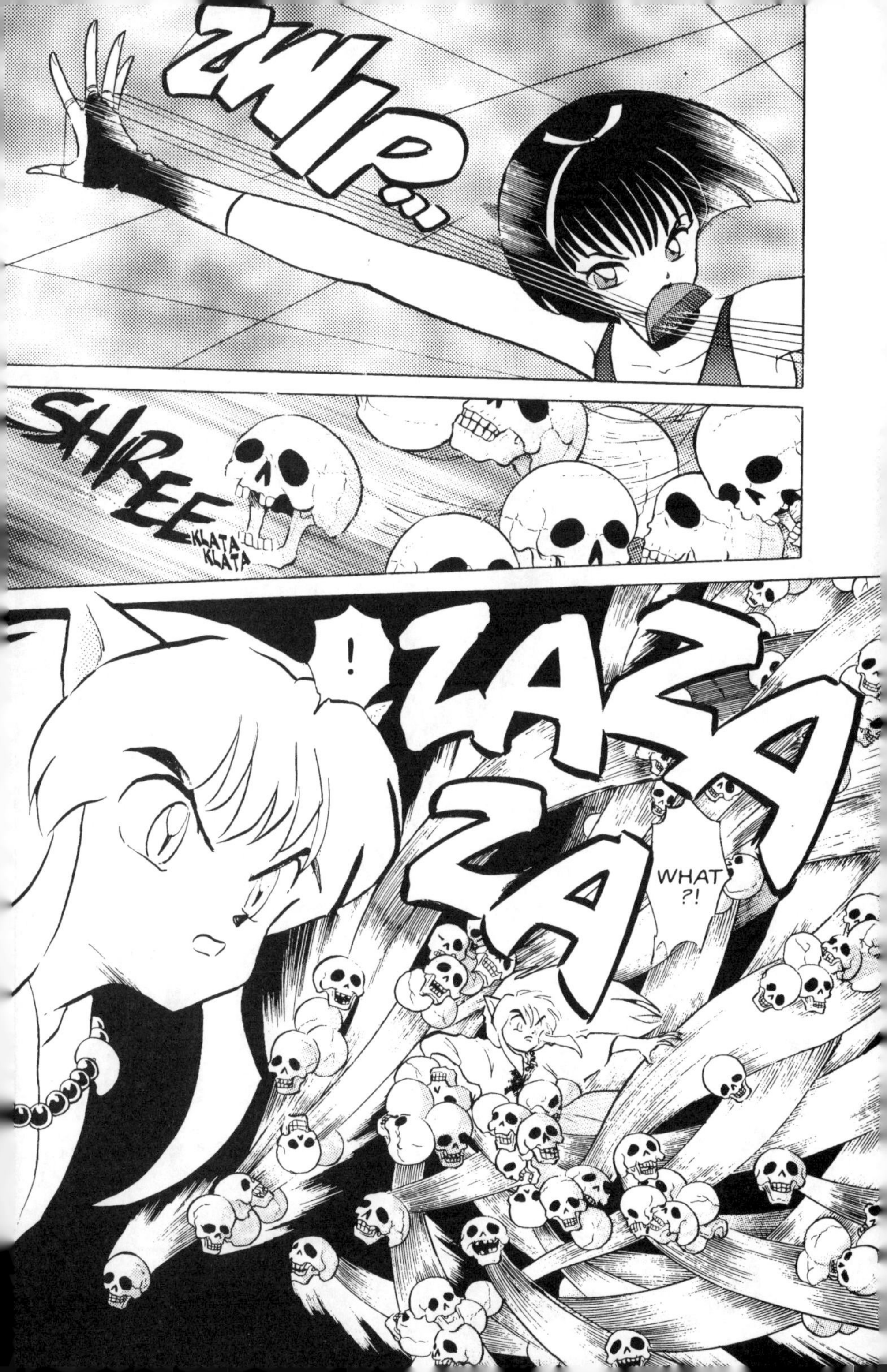
ZWIP...
SHREE
KLATA KLATA
!
ZAZAZA
WHAT ?!

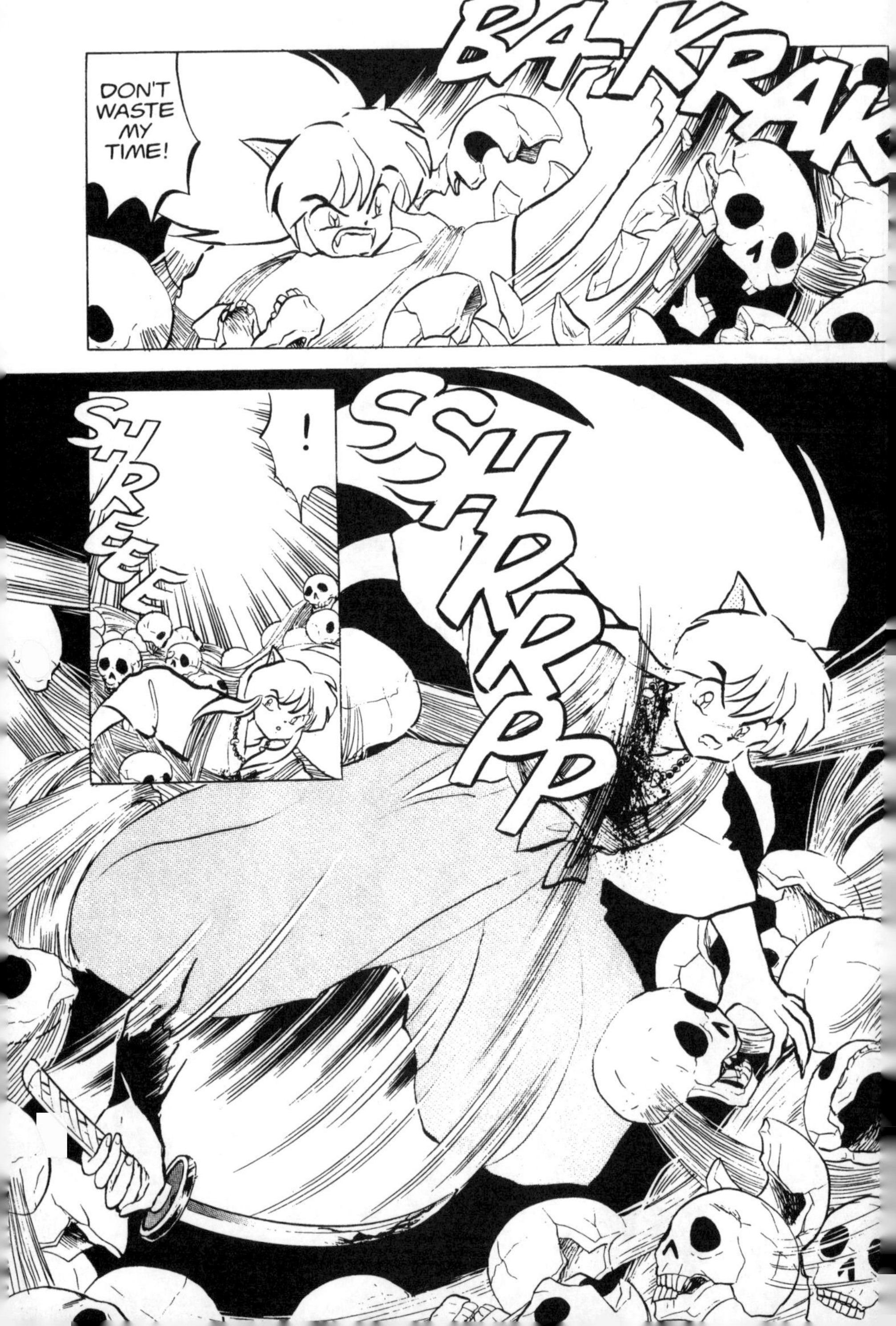
DON'T WASTE MY TIME!
BA-KRAK
SHREEE
!
SSHRRPPP

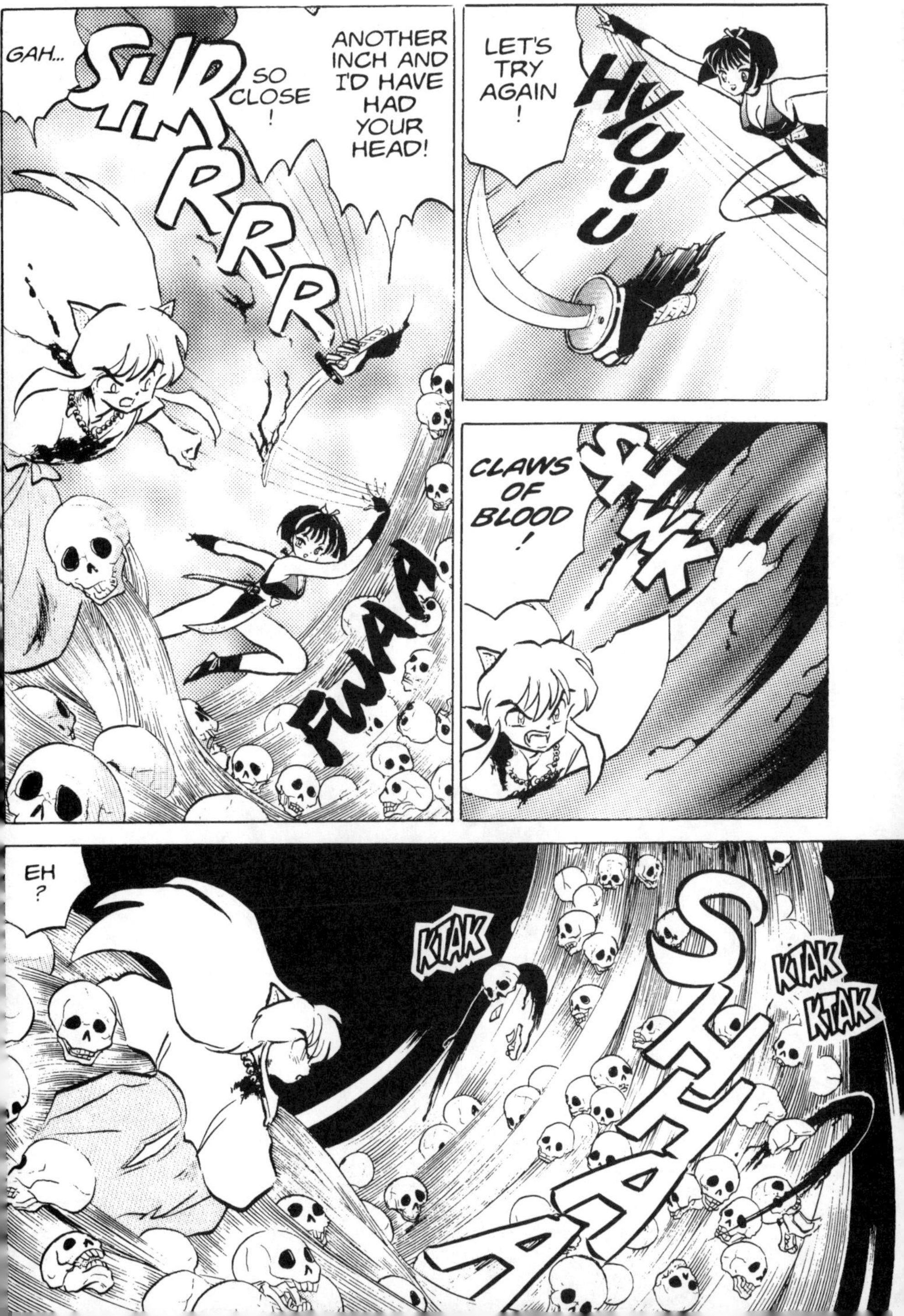
GAH...
SHRRRRR
SO CLOSE!
ANOTHER INCH AND I'D HAVE HAD YOUR HEAD!
FWAA
LET'S TRY AGAIN!
HYUUU
CLAWS OF BLOOD!
SHWK
EH?
KTAK
S
KTAK KTAK
SHHAA

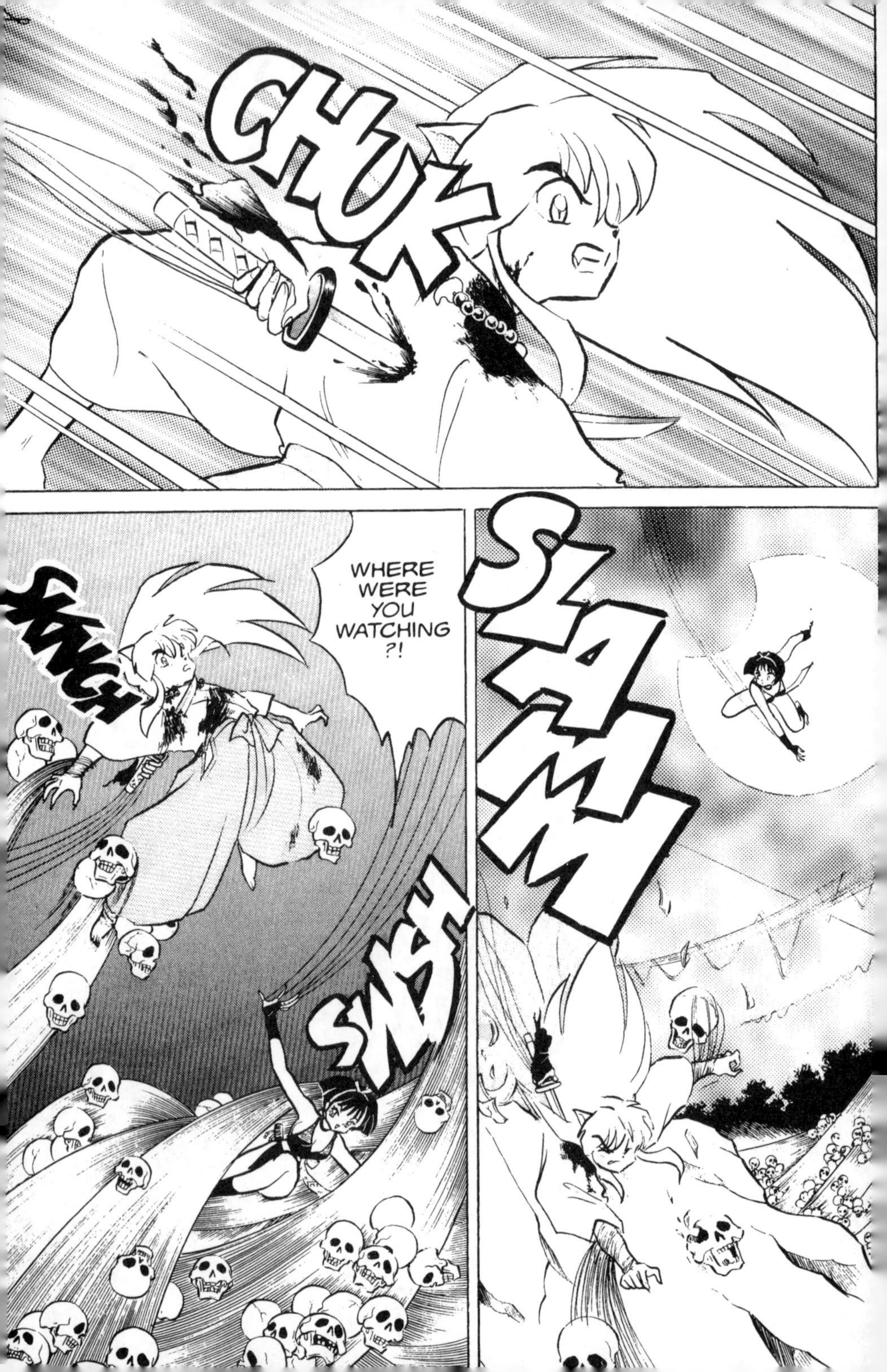
CHUK
SKNCH
WHERE WERE YOU WATCHING ?!
SWSH
SLAMM

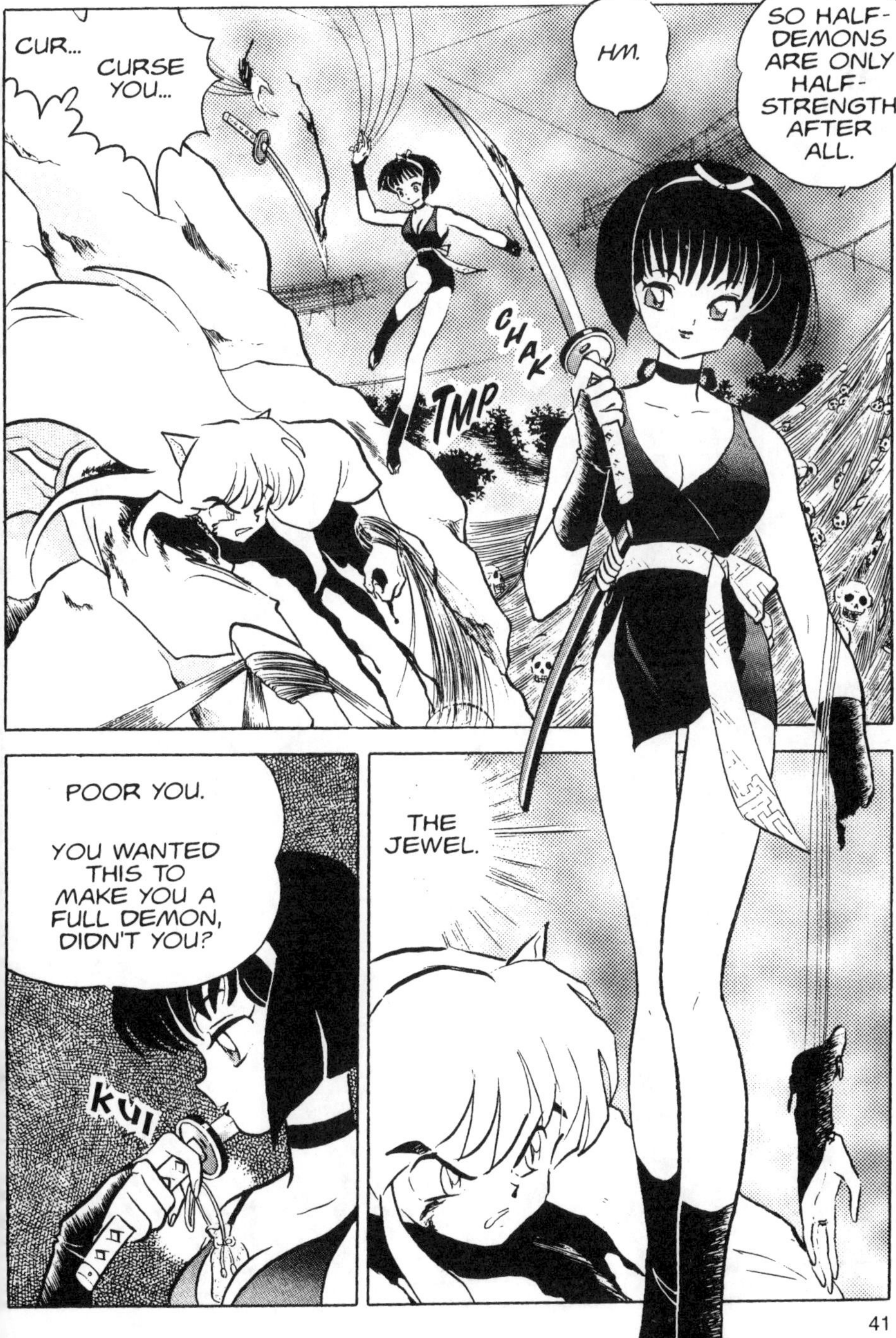
SO HALF-DEMONS ARE ONLY HALF-STRENGTH AFTER ALL.
HM.
CUR... CURSE YOU...
CHAK
TMP
THE JEWEL.
POOR YOU.
YOU WANTED THIS TO MAKE YOU A FULL DEMON, DIDN'T YOU?
KUI

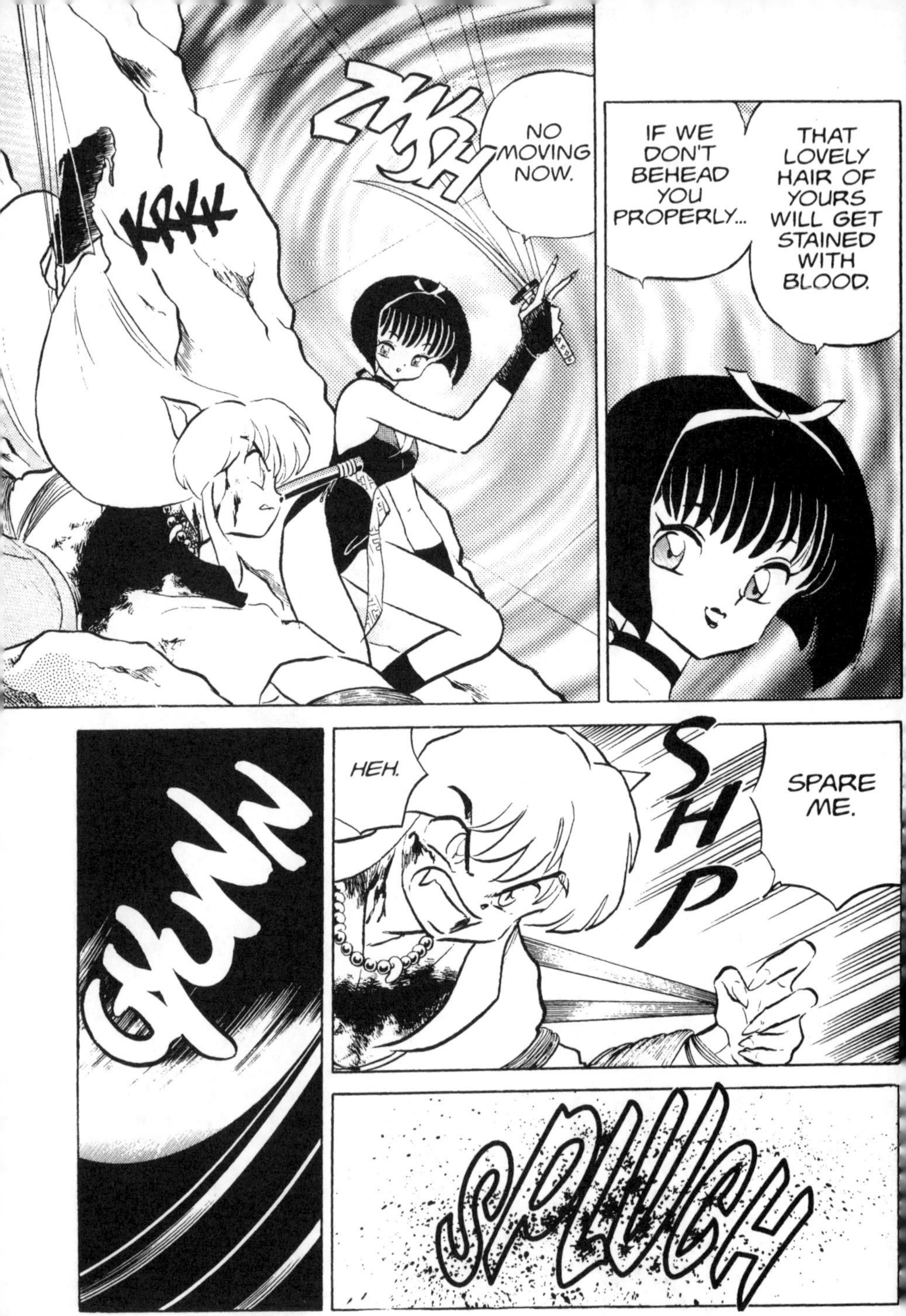
NO MOVING NOW.
KRKK
IF WE DON'T BEHEAD YOU PROPERLY...
THAT LOVELY HAIR OF YOURS WILL GET STAINED WITH BLOOD.
HEH.
SHP
SPARE ME.

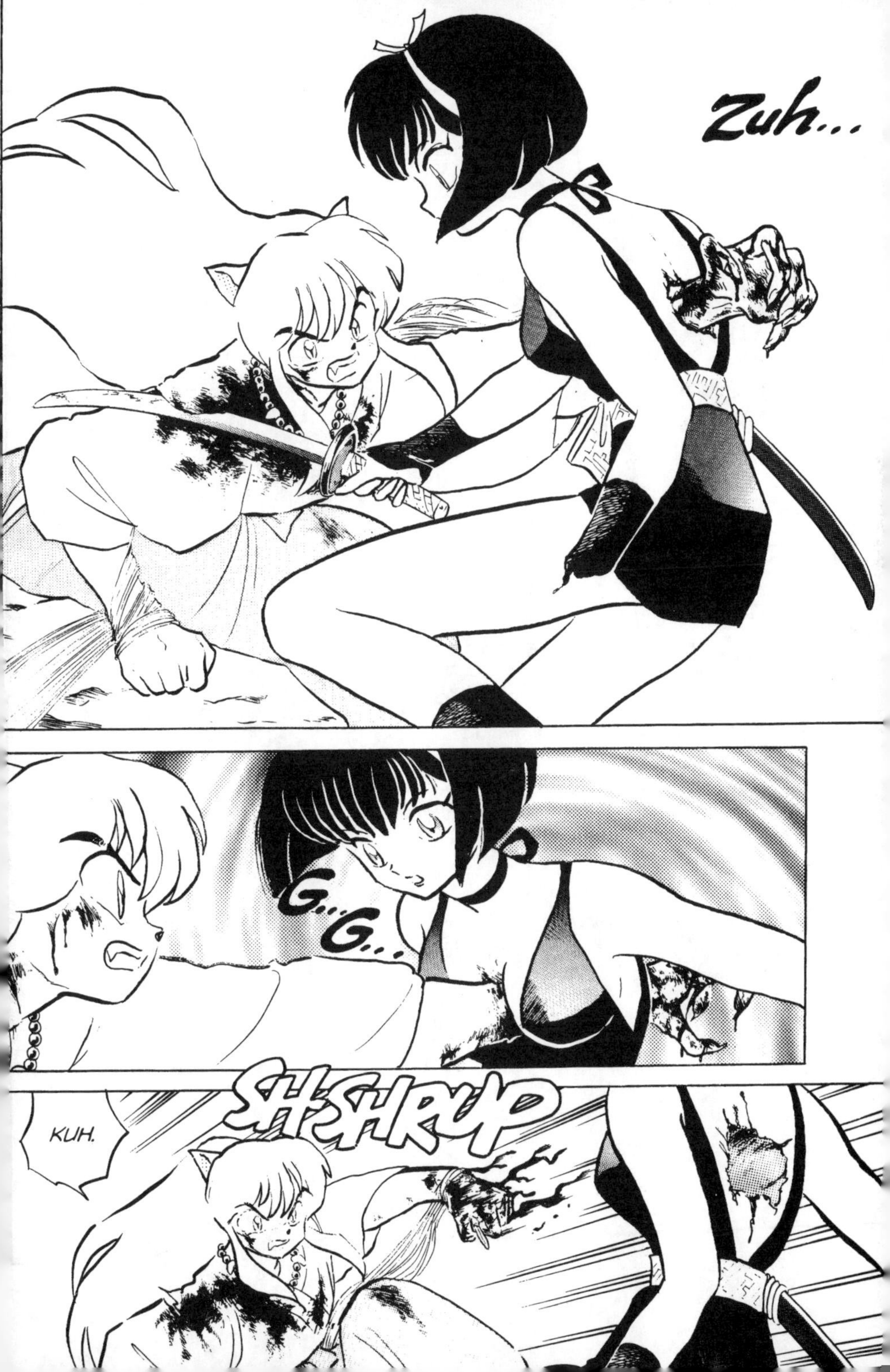

Zuh...
G... G...
SHSHRUP
KUH.

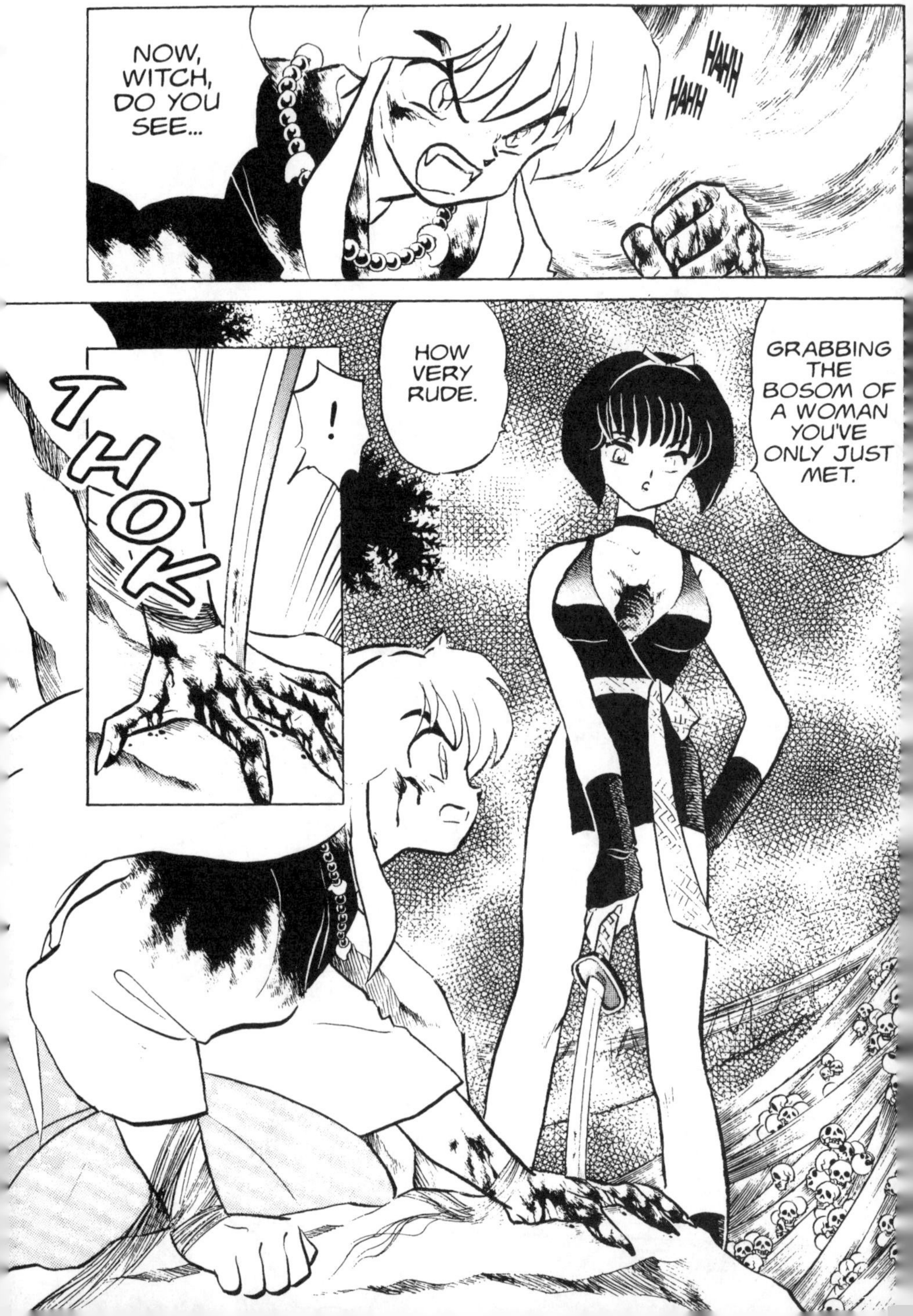
NOW, WITCH, DO YOU SEE...
HAHH HAHH
THOK
!
HOW VERY RUDE.
GRABBING THE BOSOM OF A WOMAN YOU'VE ONLY JUST MET.

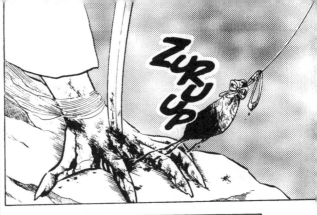

ZURU UP

SHE...
SHE'S...

STILL
STANDING...
?!

HMPH.

pch

AND TO
HAVE TAKEN
MY SHIKON
JEWEL WHILE
YOU WERE
AT IT.

STUBBORN,
AREN'T
YOU?

WHERE
?!

WHERE
IS YURA'S
WEAKNESS...
?

LA
?!

KUI

!

bata
bata

KATA
KATA

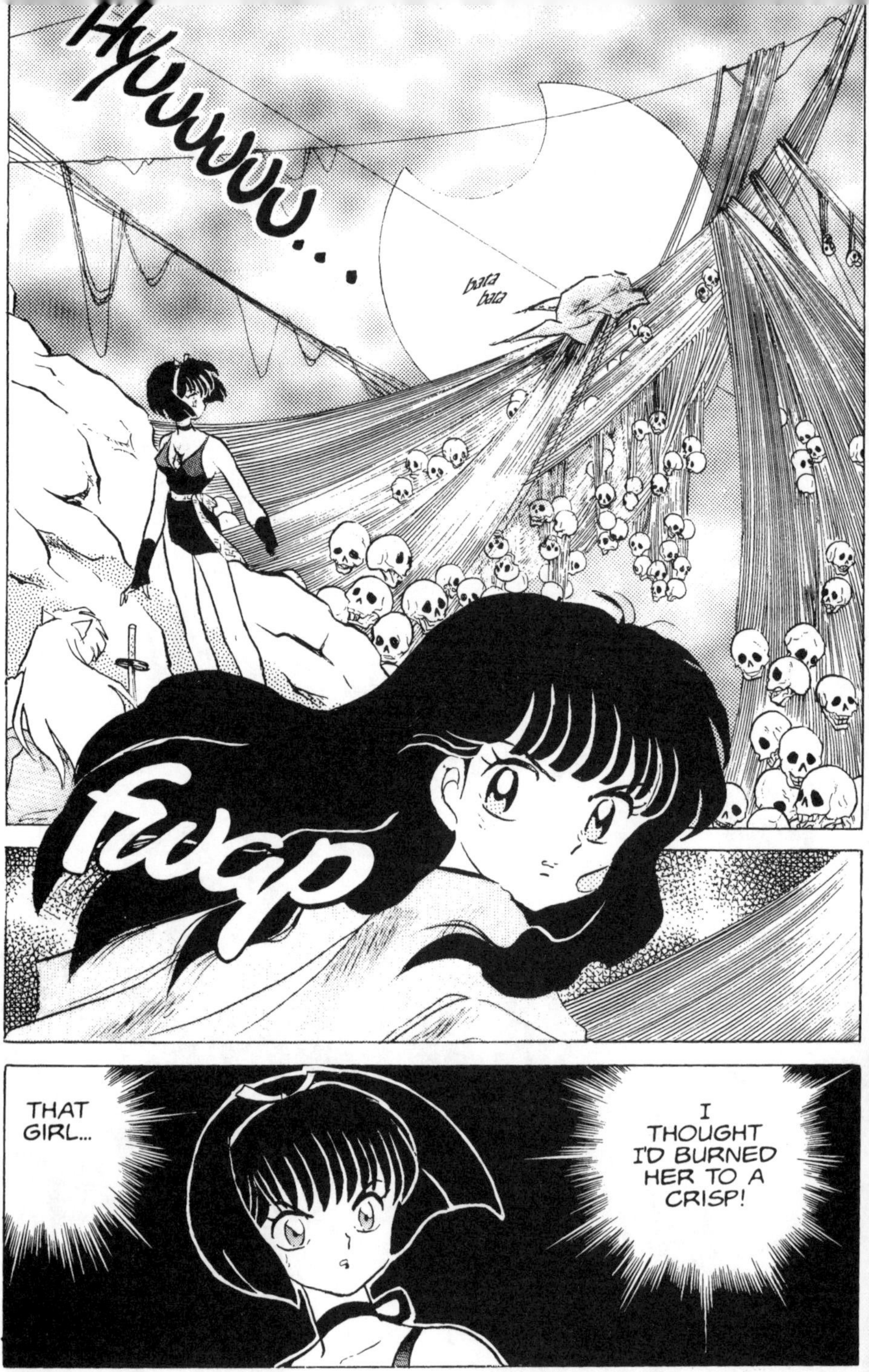
HYUUUUUU...
bata bata
fwap
THAT GIRL...
I THOUGHT I'D BURNED HER TO A CRISP!

SCROLL THREE
SOUL TRANSFER

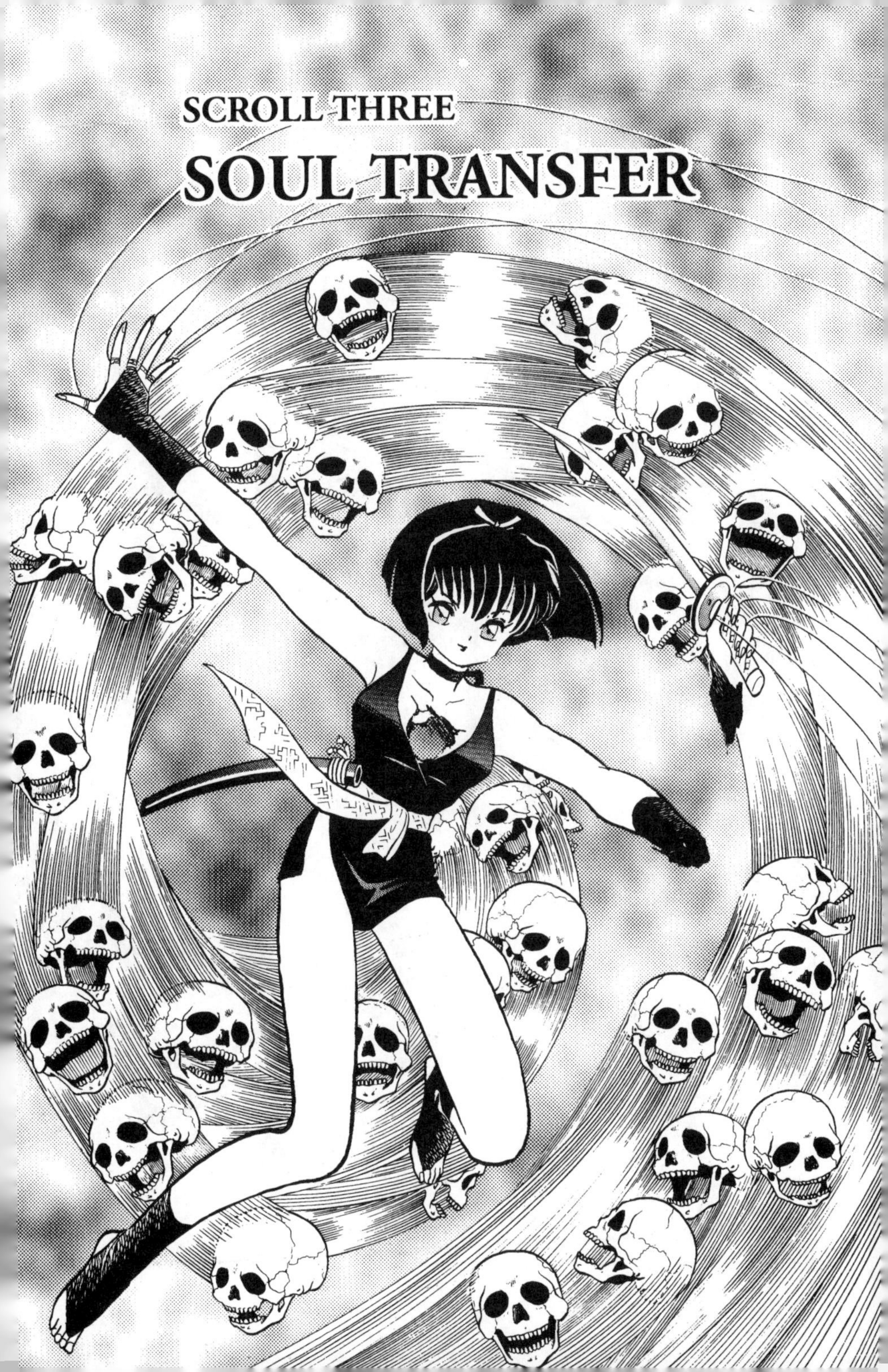

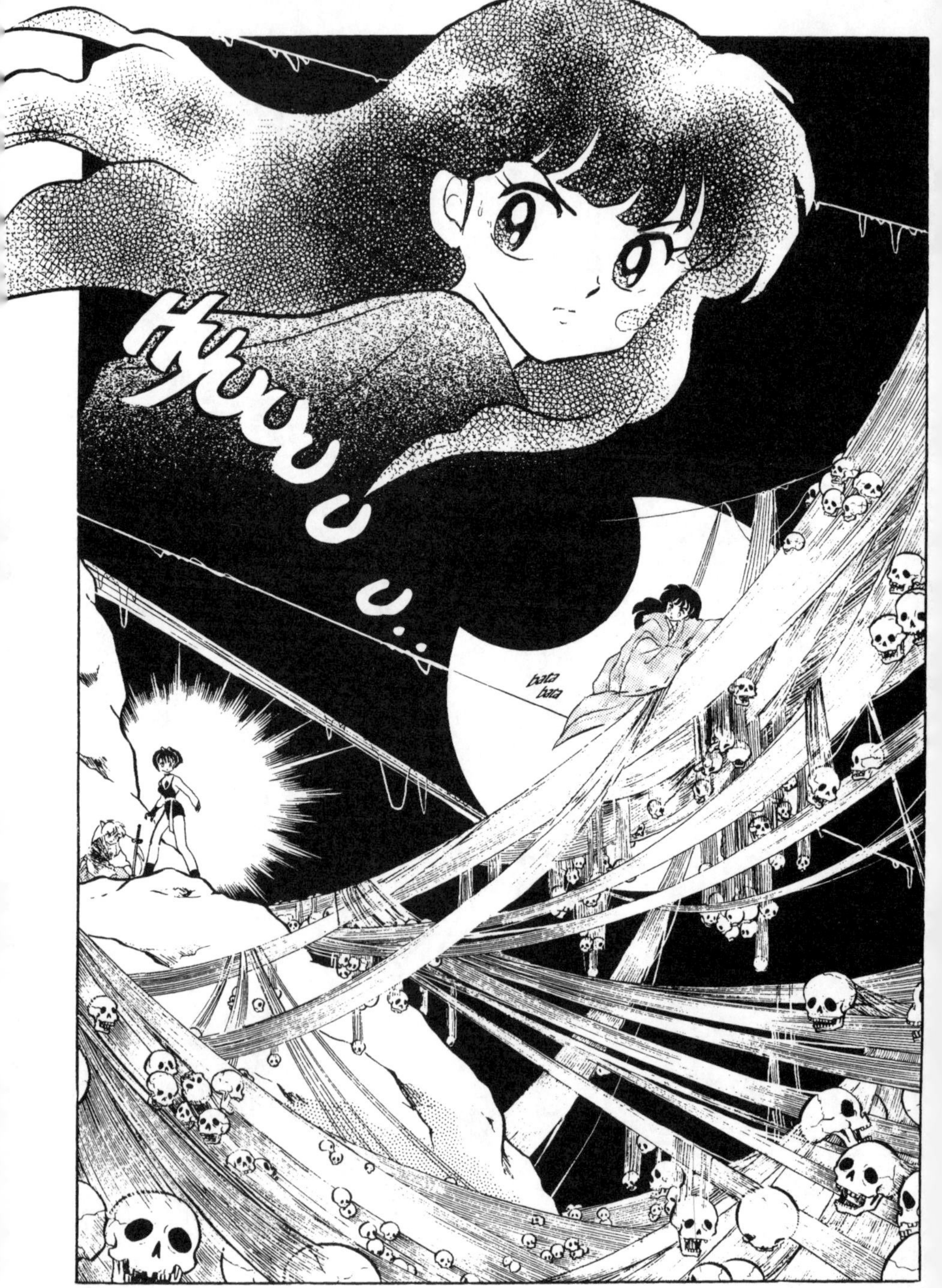
Hyuuu u..
bata bata

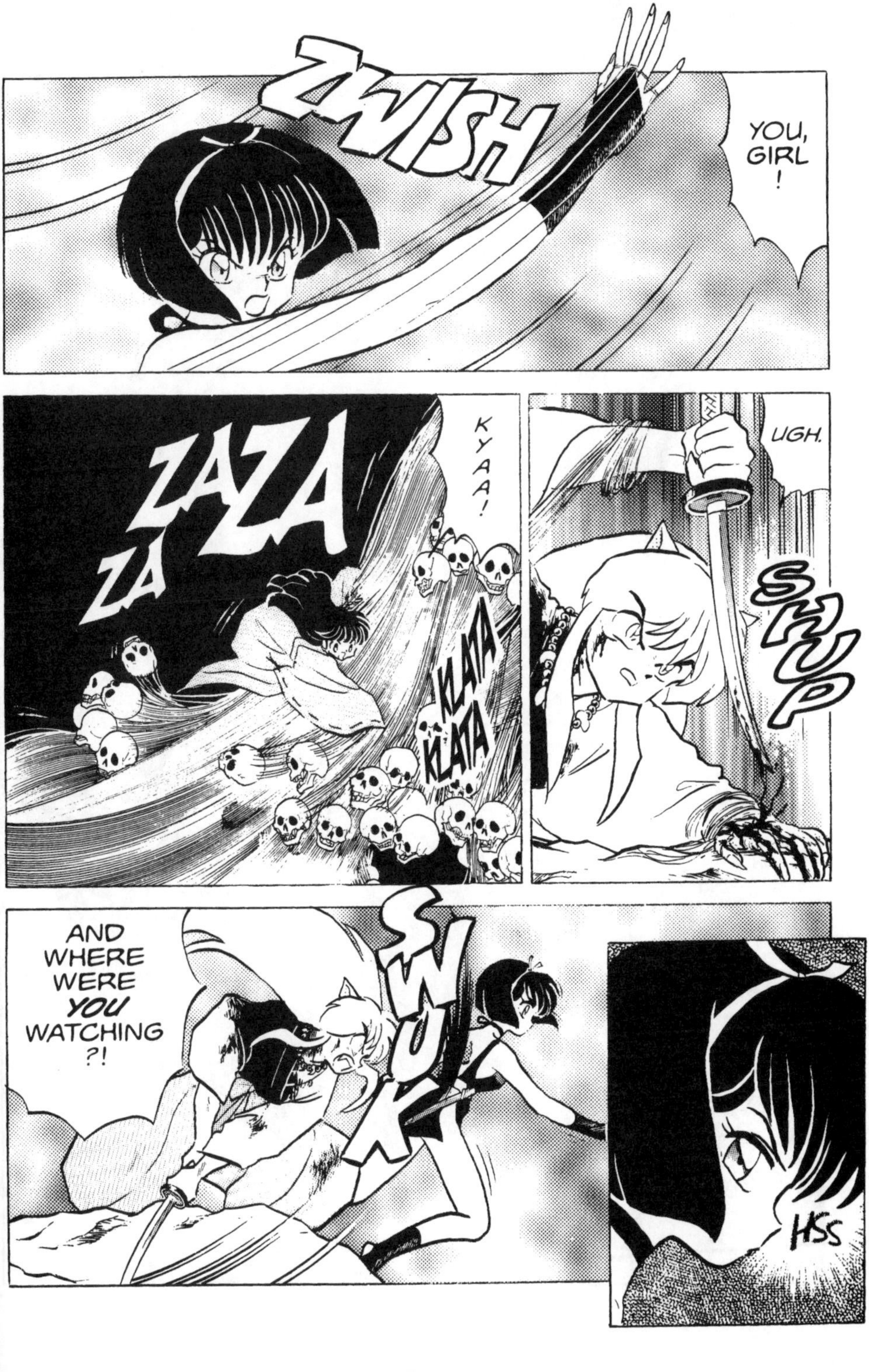
ZWISH
YOU, GIRL!
ZAZAZA
KYAAA!
KLATA KLATA
UGH.
SHUP
AND WHERE WERE *YOU* WATCHING?!
SWUK
HSS

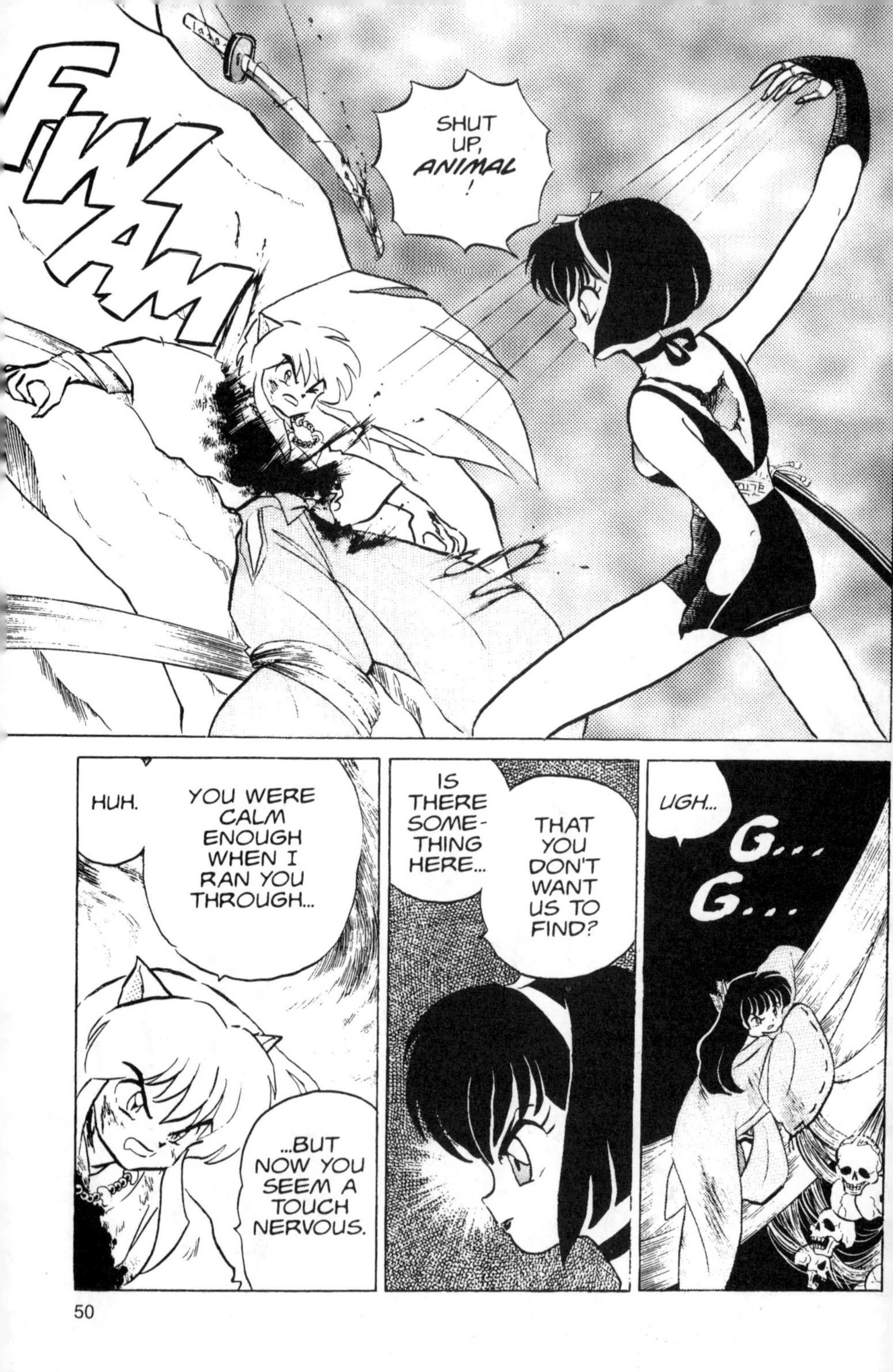
FWAM
SHUT UP, ANIMAL!
HUH.
YOU WERE CALM ENOUGH WHEN I RAN YOU THROUGH...
...BUT NOW YOU SEEM A TOUCH NERVOUS.
IS THERE SOMETHING HERE...
THAT YOU DON'T WANT US TO FIND?
UGH...
G... G...

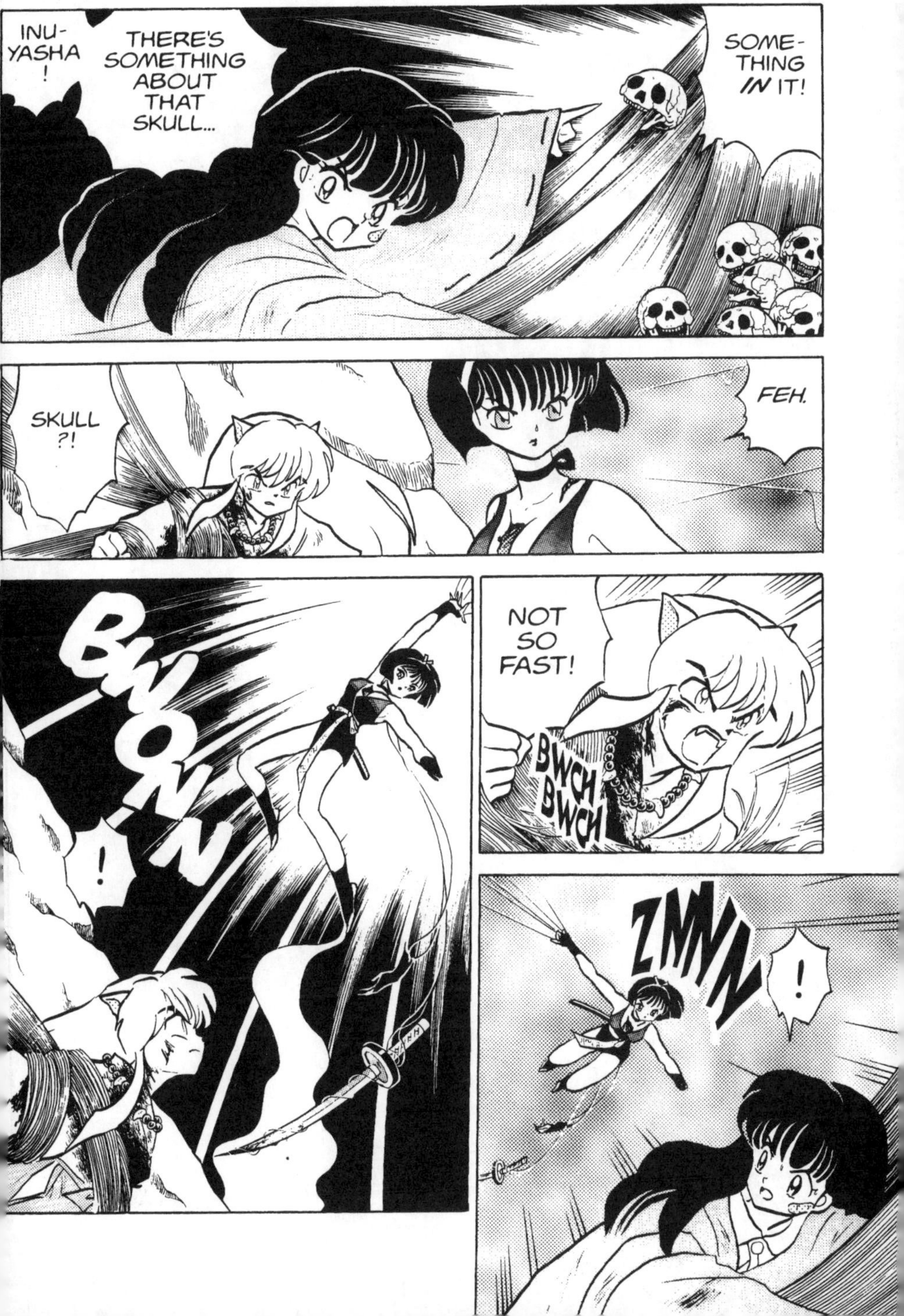
INU-YASHA!
THERE'S SOMETHING ABOUT THAT SKULL...
SOME-THING *IN* IT!
SKULL?!
FEH.
BWONNN
!
NOT SO FAST!
BWCH BWCH
ZMNN
!

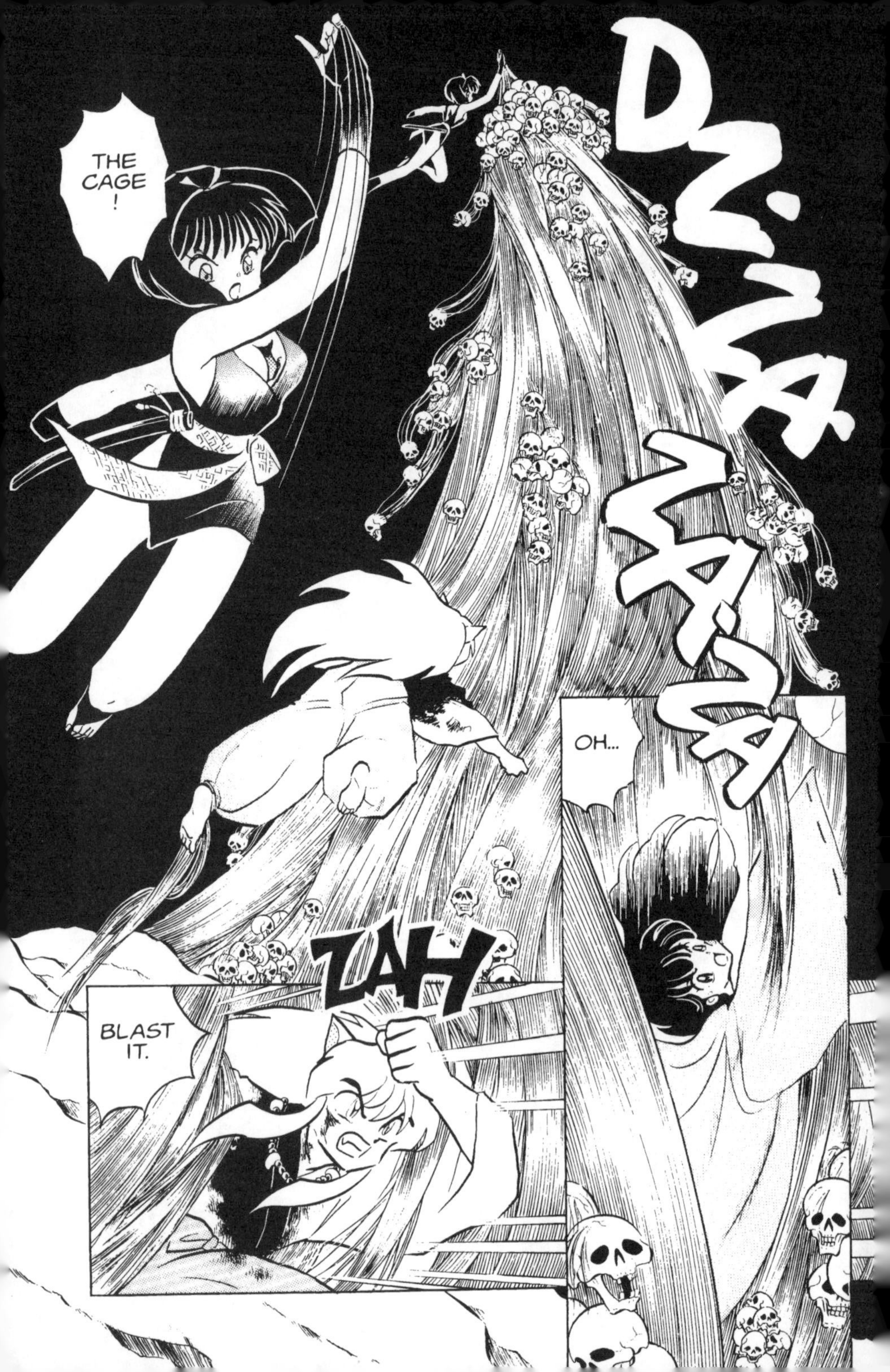
THE CAGE !
ZAH
BLAST IT.
OH...

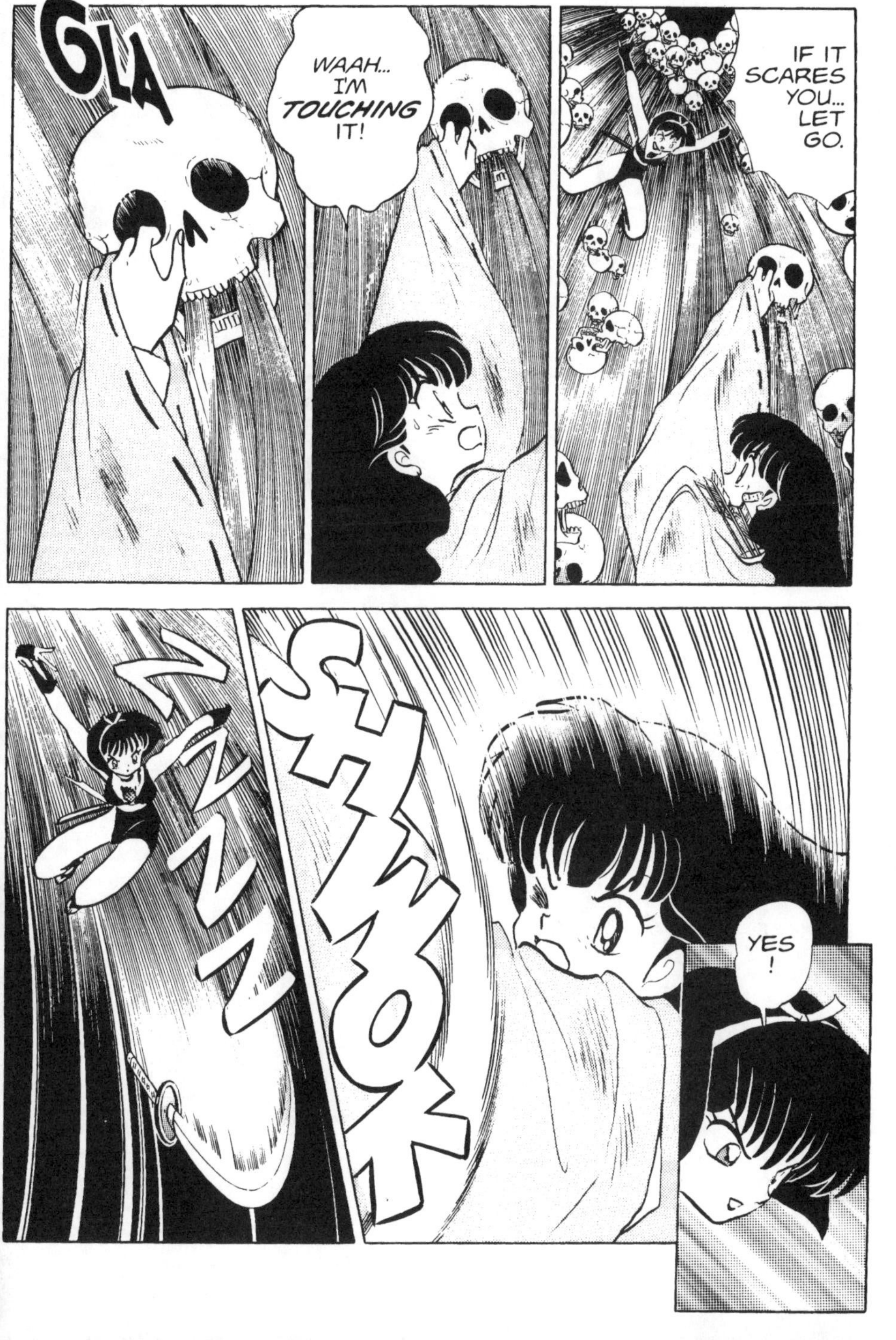
GLA
WAAH... I'M *TOUCHING* IT!
IF IT SCARES YOU... LET GO.
ZNNN
SHWOK
YES!

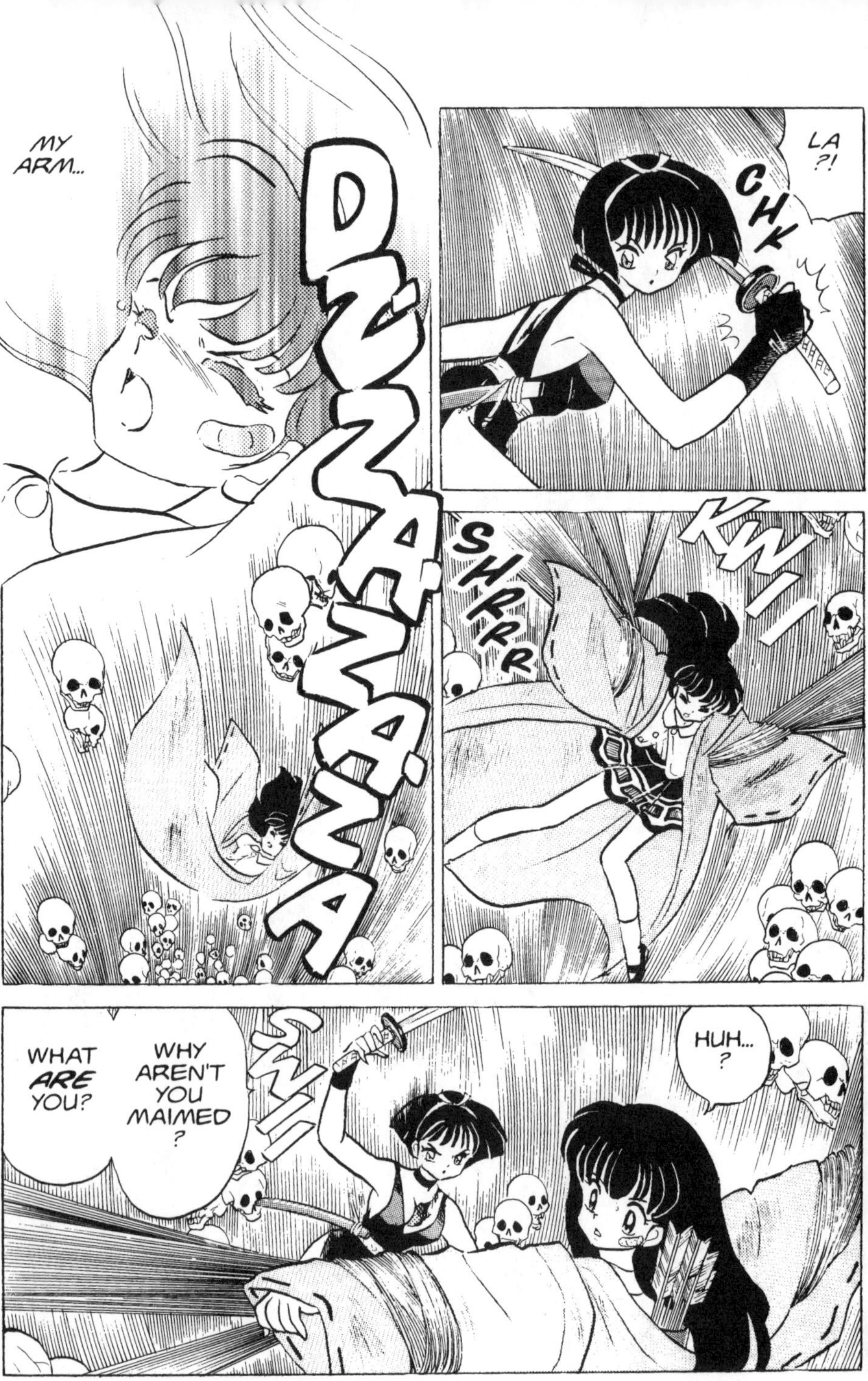
MY ARM...
LA ?!
CHK
SHRRR
KWIII
WHAT ARE YOU?
WHY AREN'T YOU MAIMED?
SWIII
HUH... ?

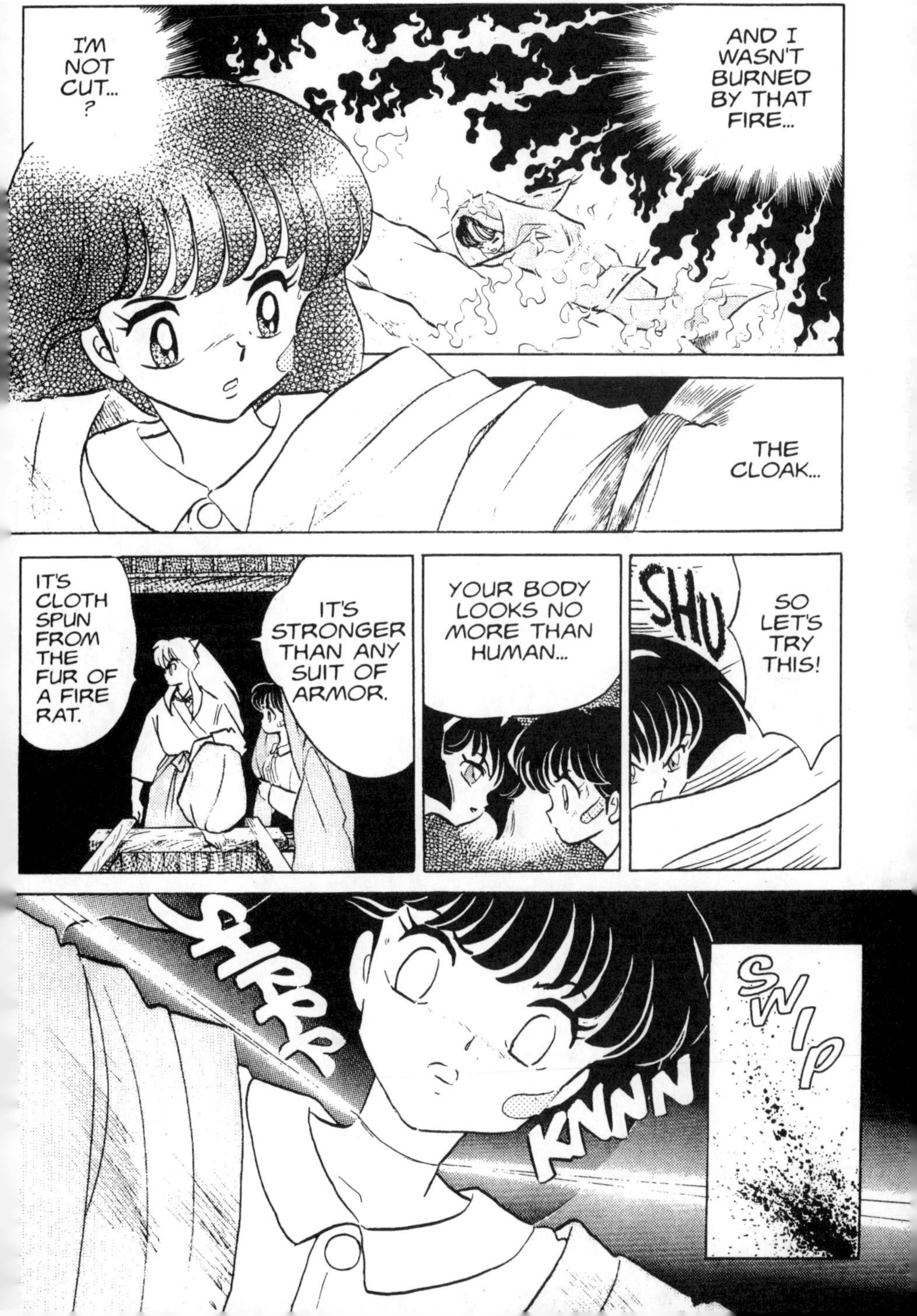
I'M NOT CUT... ?
AND I WASN'T BURNED BY THAT FIRE...
THE CLOAK...
IT'S CLOTH SPUN FROM THE FUR OF A FIRE RAT.
IT'S STRONGER THAN ANY SUIT OF ARMOR.
YOUR BODY LOOKS NO MORE THAN HUMAN...
SHU
SO LET'S TRY THIS!
SHRRR
KNNN
SWIP

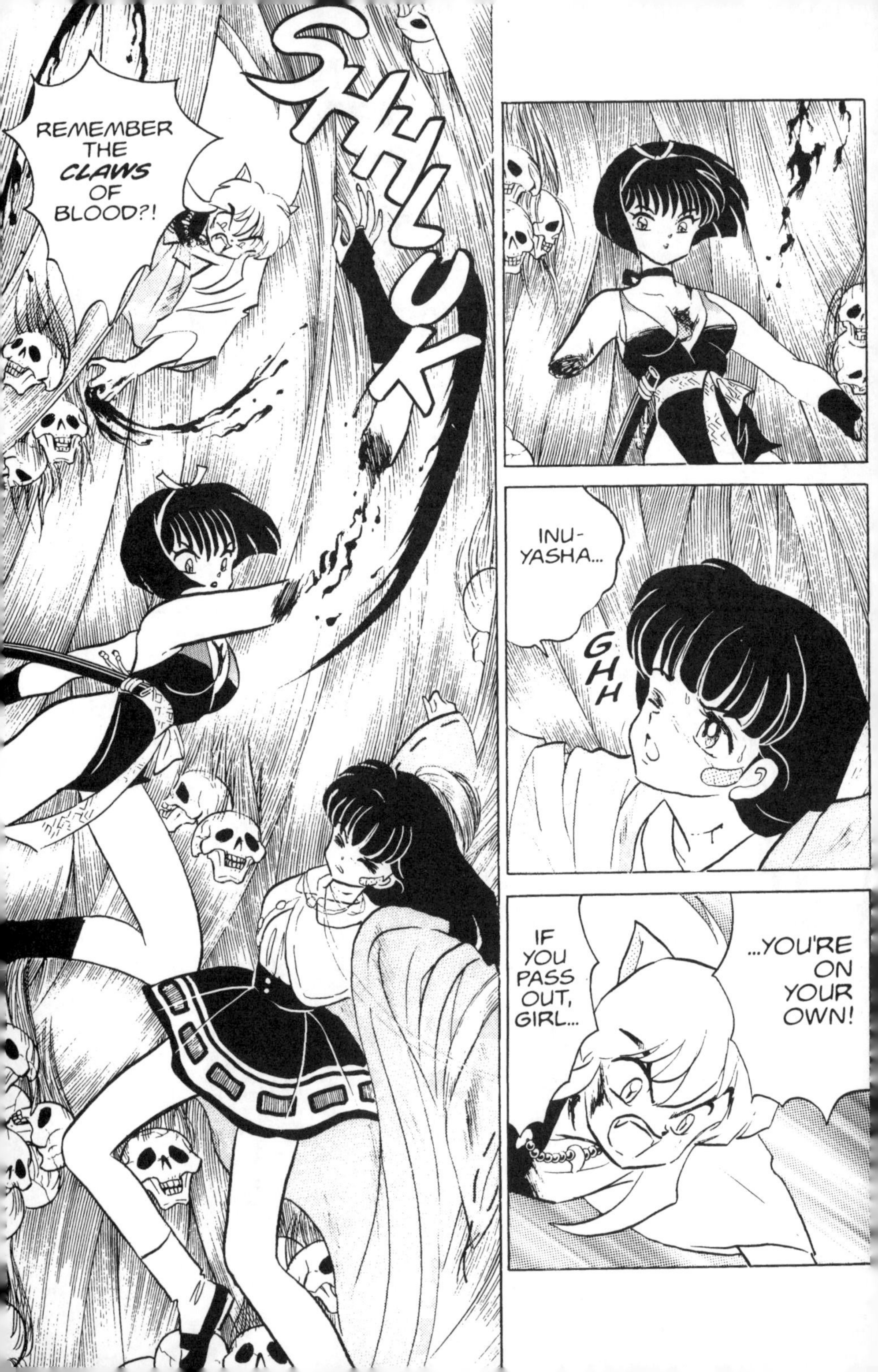
REMEMBER THE *CLAWS* OF BLOOD?!
SHHLUK
INU-YASHA...
GHH
IF YOU PASS OUT, GIRL...
...YOU'RE ON YOUR OWN!

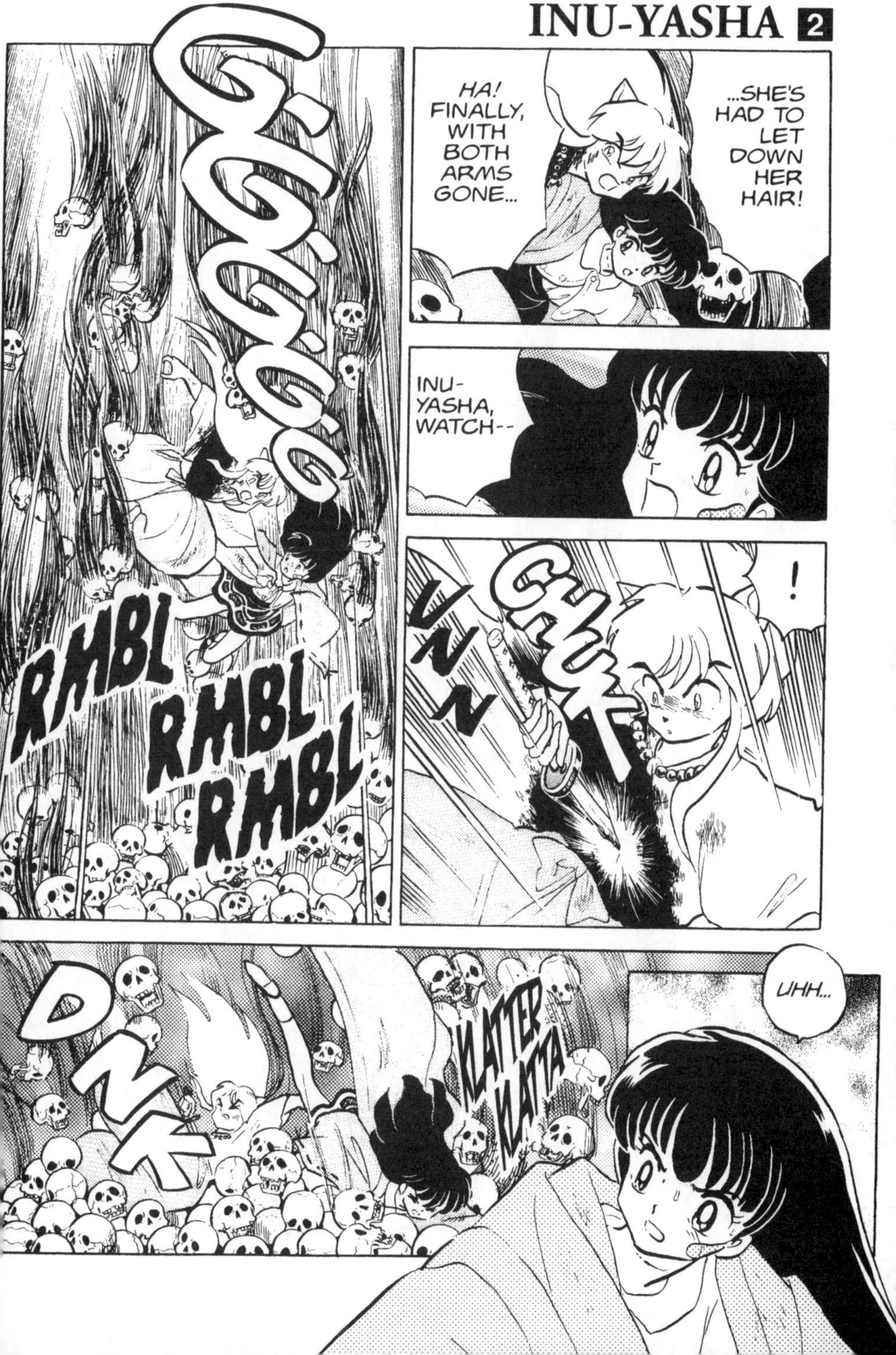
GGGGGG
RMBL RMBL RMBL RMBL
HA! FINALLY, WITH BOTH ARMS GONE...
...SHE'S HAD TO LET DOWN HER HAIR!
INU-YASHA, WATCH--
CHUK
UNN
!
DNK
KLATTER KLATTA
UHH...

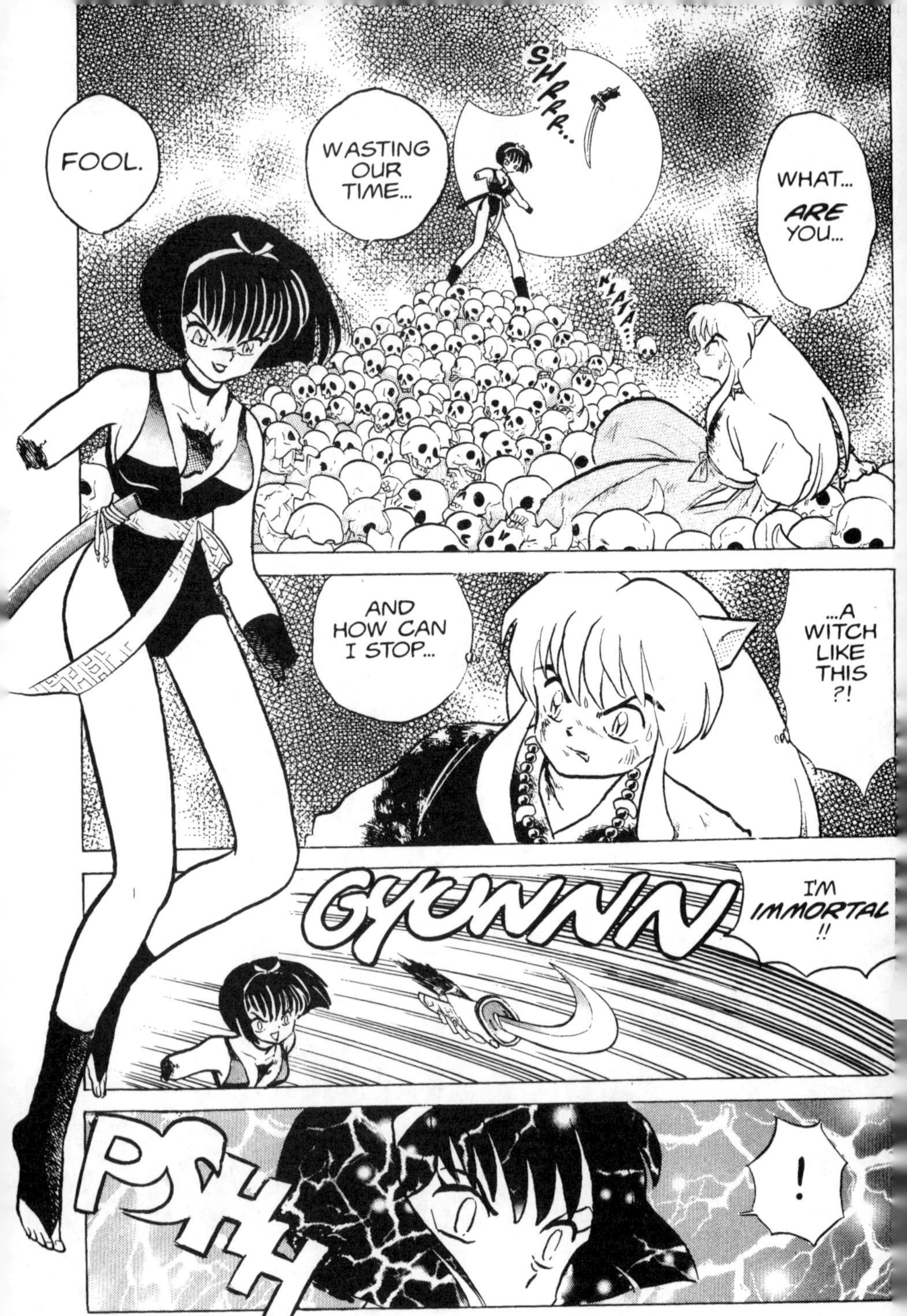
FOOL.
WASTING OUR TIME...
SHRRR...
WHAT... ARE YOU...
AND HOW CAN I STOP...
...A WITCH LIKE THIS ?!
GYUNNN
I'M IMMORTAL !!
PSH
!

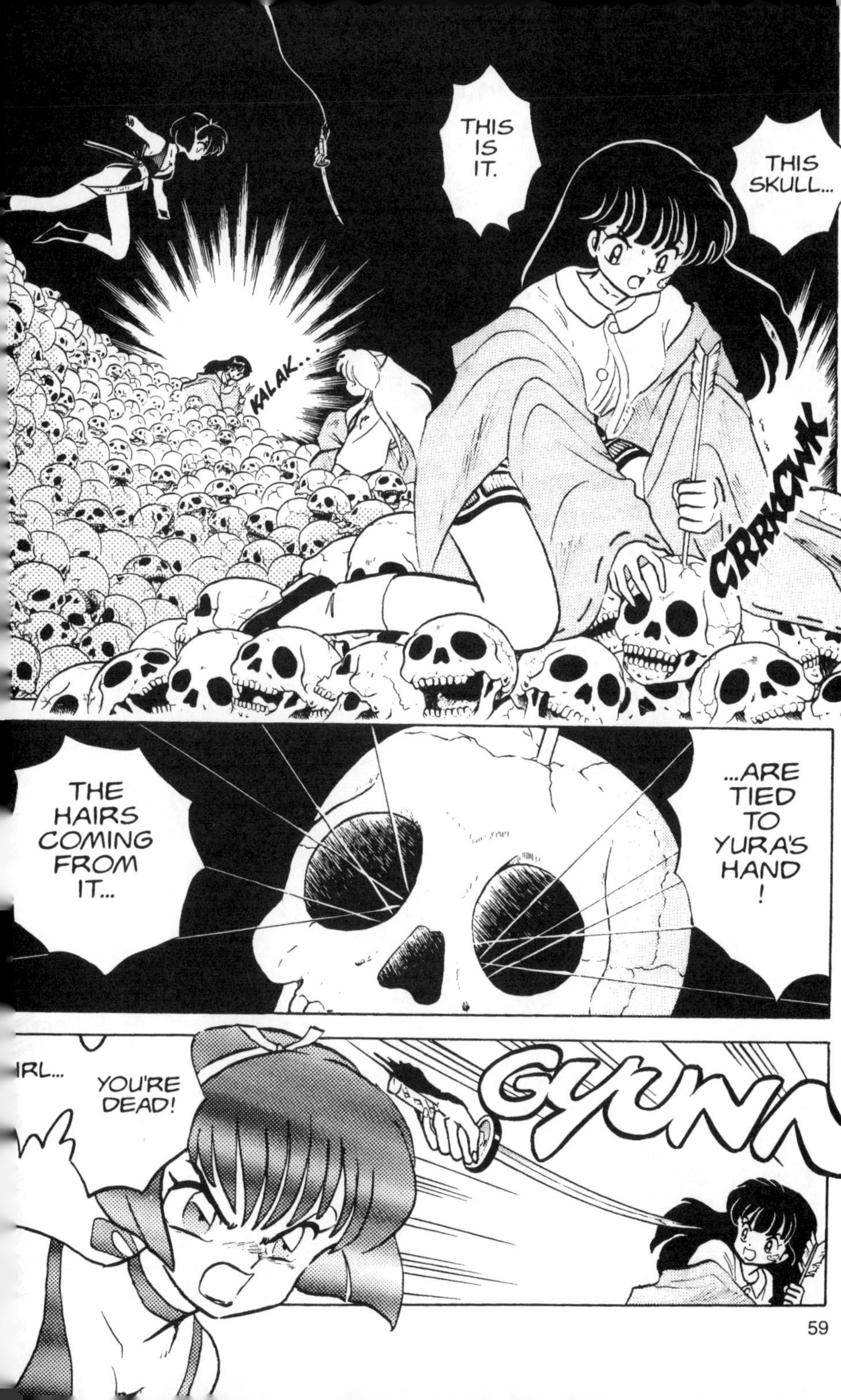
KALAK...
THIS IS IT.
THIS SKULL...
CRRKOWK
THE HAIRS COMING FROM IT...
...ARE TIED TO YURA'S HAND!
IRL...
YOU'RE DEAD!
GYUNN

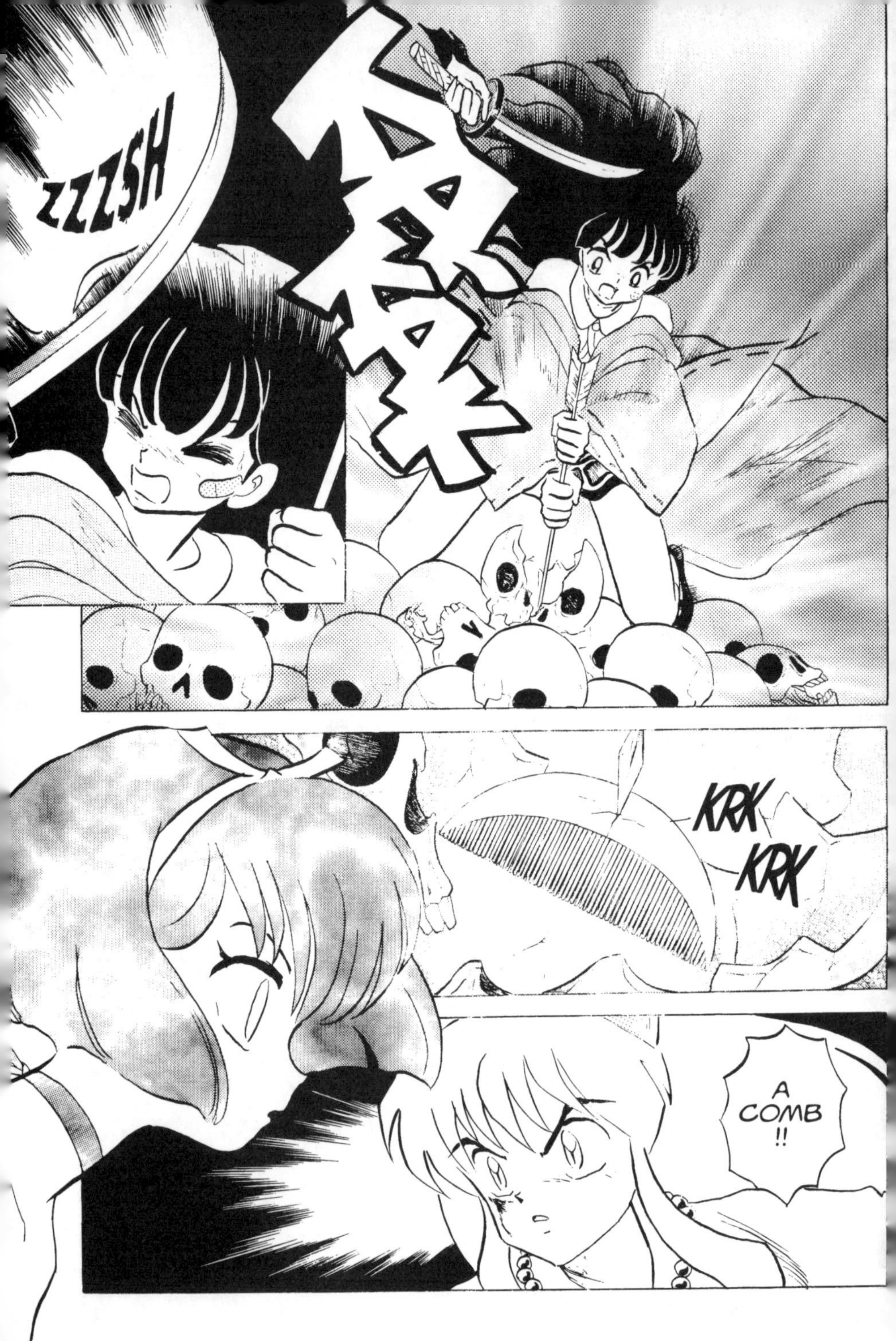
ZZZSH
KRK
KRK
A COMB !!

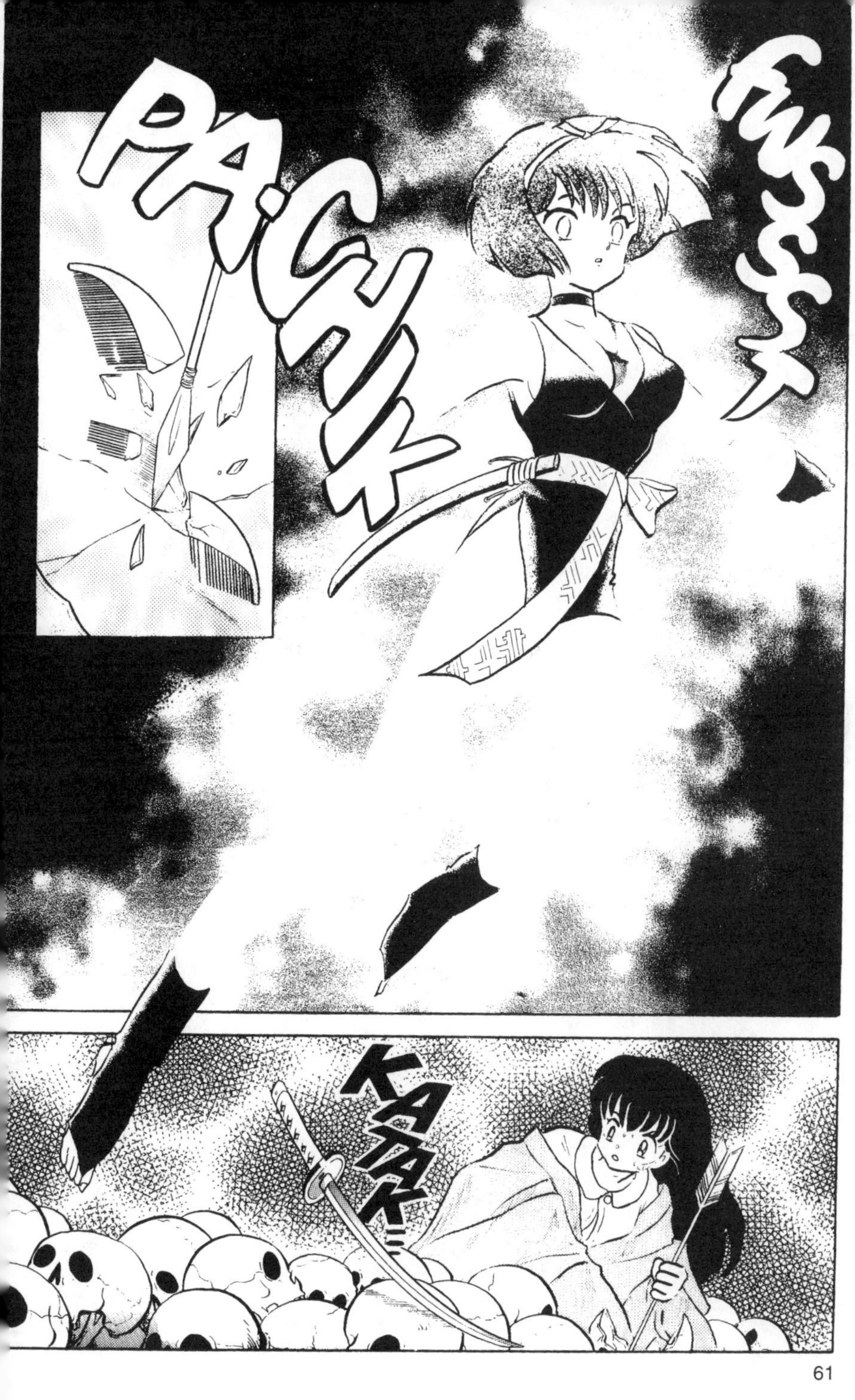
PA-CHIK
FWSSSSST
KATAK...

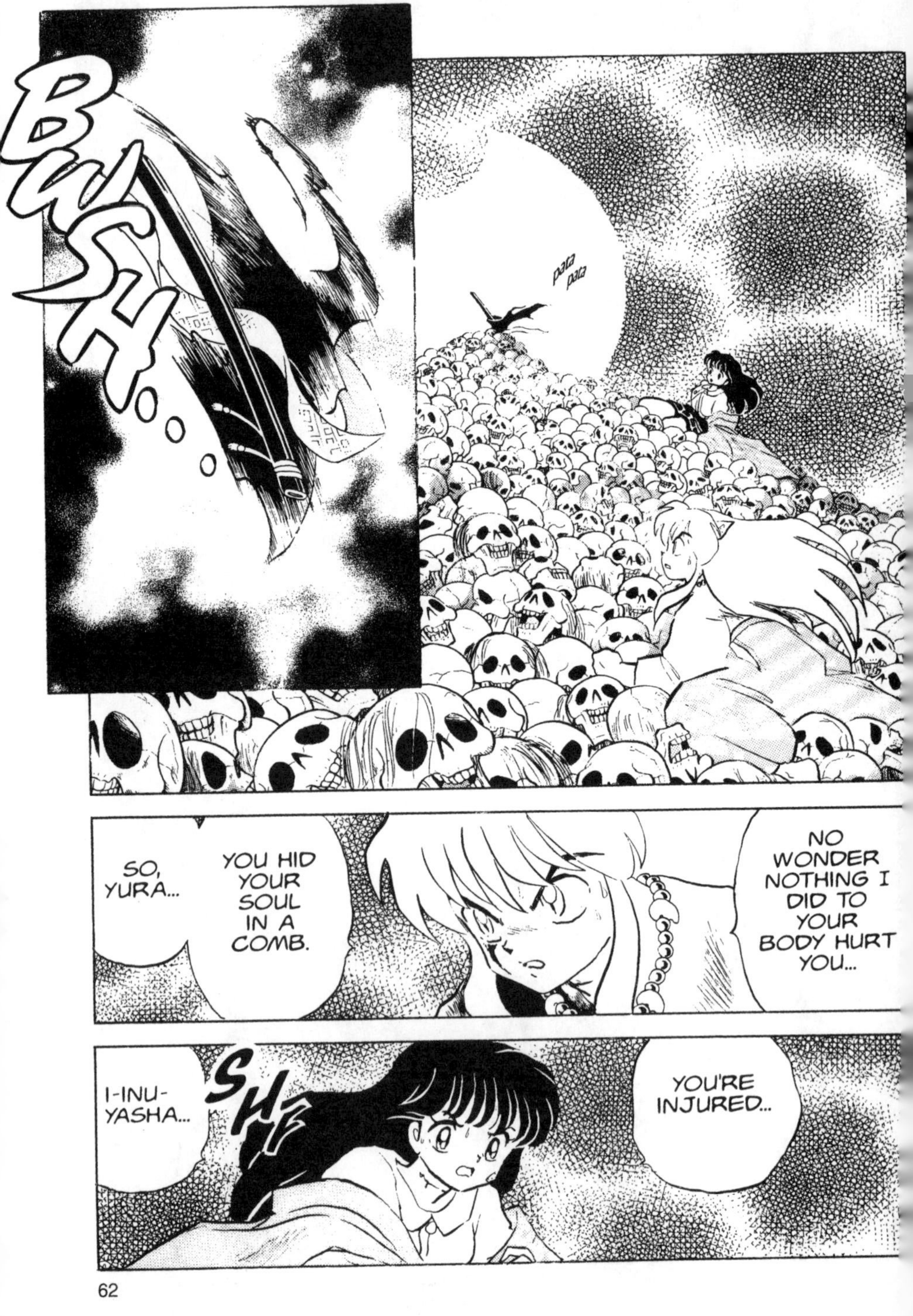
BUSH...
pata pata
SO, YURA...
YOU HID YOUR SOUL IN A COMB.
NO WONDER NOTHING I DID TO YOUR BODY HURT YOU...
I-INU-YASHA...
SHF
YOU'RE INJURED...

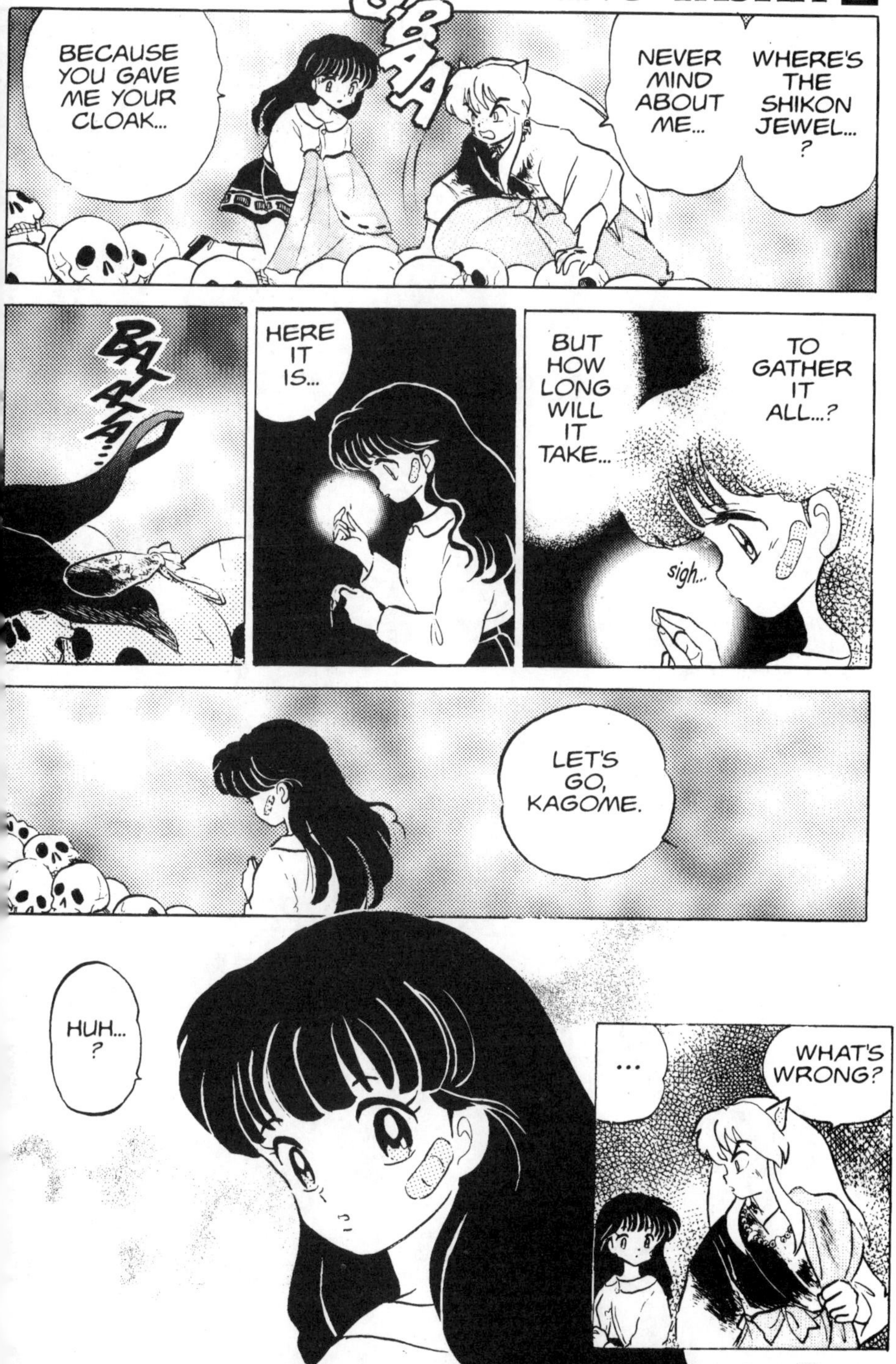
BECAUSE YOU GAVE ME YOUR CLOAK...
GBAA
NEVER MIND ABOUT ME...
WHERE'S THE SHIKON JEWEL...?
BATATA...
HERE IT IS...
BUT HOW LONG WILL IT TAKE...
TO GATHER IT ALL...?
sigh...
LET'S GO, KAGOME.
HUH...?
...
WHAT'S WRONG?

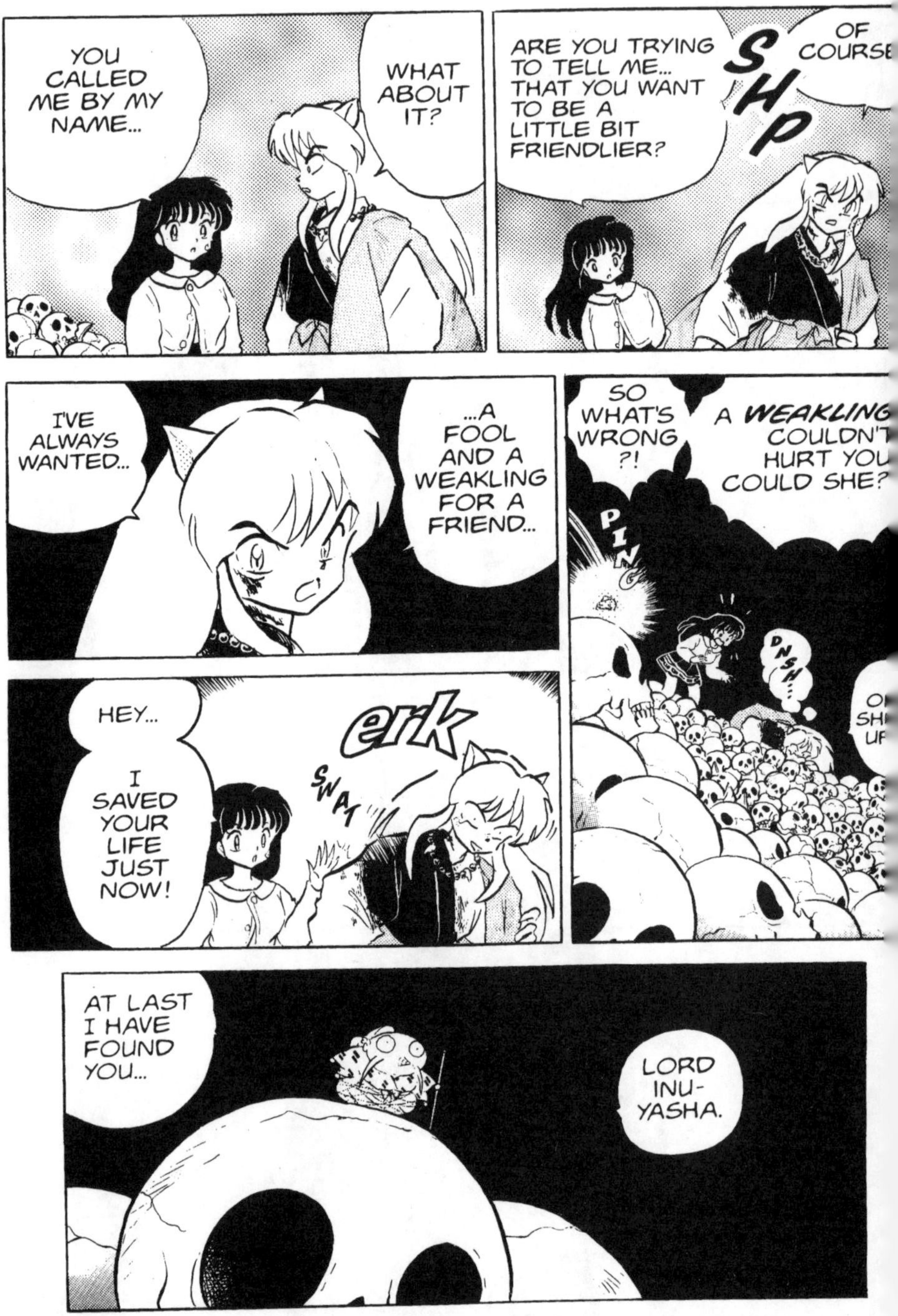
YOU CALLED ME BY MY NAME...
WHAT ABOUT IT?
ARE YOU TRYING TO TELL ME... THAT YOU WANT TO BE A LITTLE BIT FRIENDLIER?
SHP
OF COURSE
I'VE ALWAYS WANTED...
...A FOOL AND A WEAKLING FOR A FRIEND...
HEY...
I SAVED YOUR LIFE JUST NOW!
erk
SWAT
SO WHAT'S WRONG ?!
A WEAKLING COULDN'T HURT YOU COULD SHE?
PING
DNSH...
AT LAST I HAVE FOUND YOU...
LORD INU-YASHA.

SCROLL FOUR
HALF-BREED

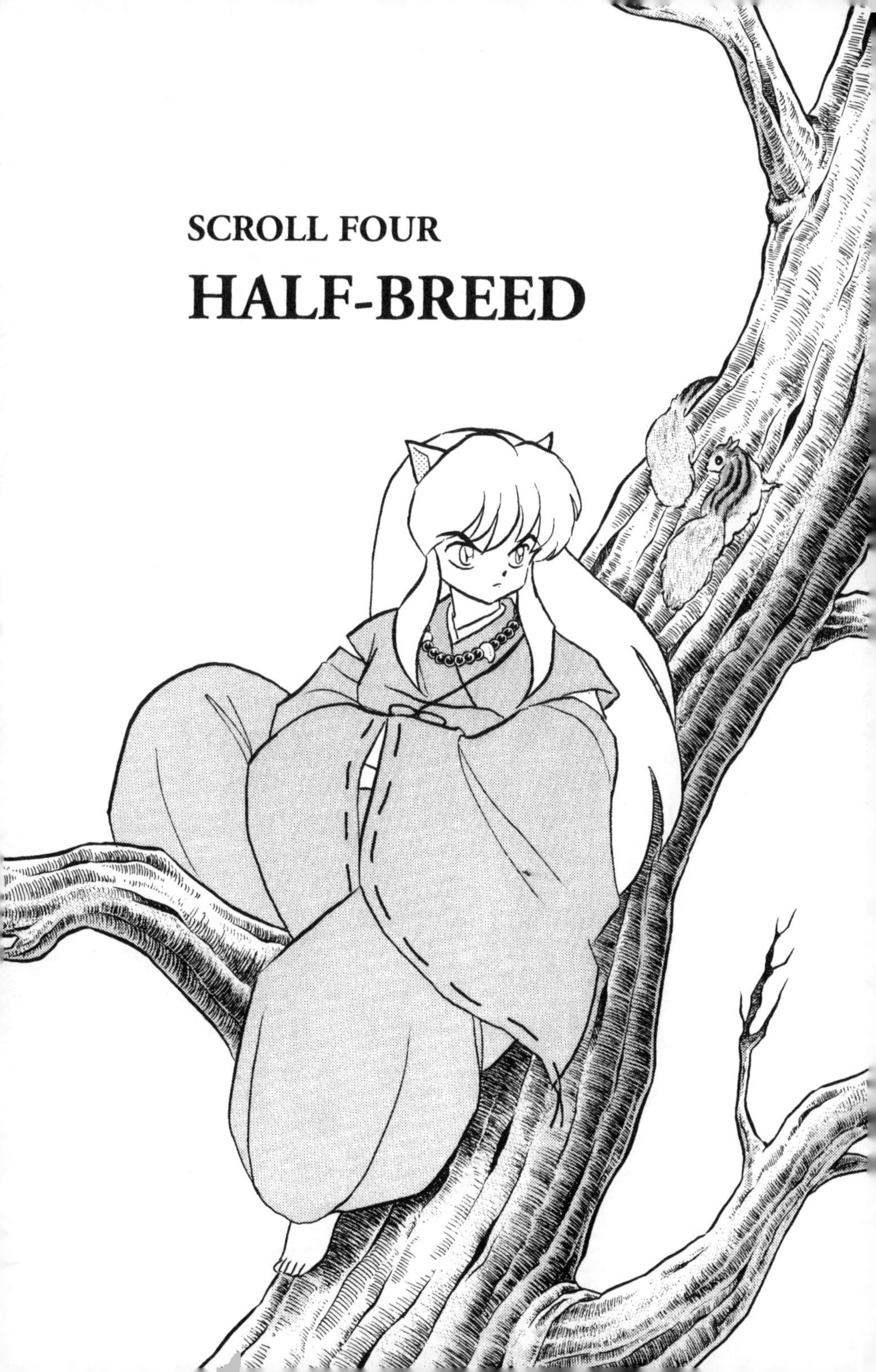

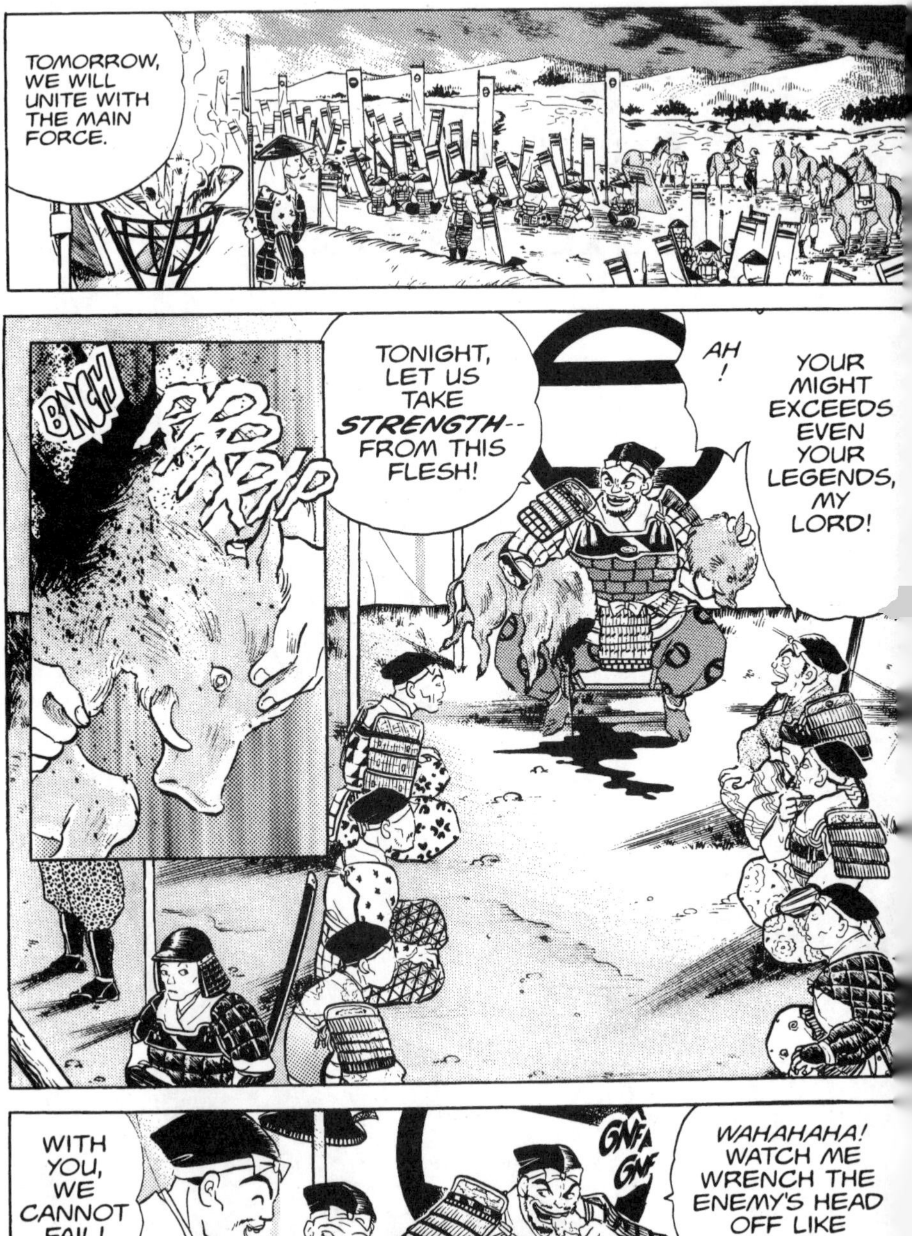
TOMORROW, WE WILL UNITE WITH THE MAIN FORCE.
BNCH
TONIGHT, LET US TAKE *STRENGTH*-- FROM THIS FLESH!
AH!
YOUR MIGHT EXCEEDS EVEN YOUR LEGENDS, MY LORD!
WITH YOU, WE CANNOT FAIL!
GNF GNF
WAHAHAHA! WATCH ME WRENCH THE ENEMY'S HEAD OFF LIKE THIS PIG'S!

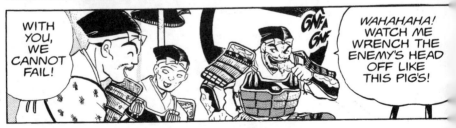

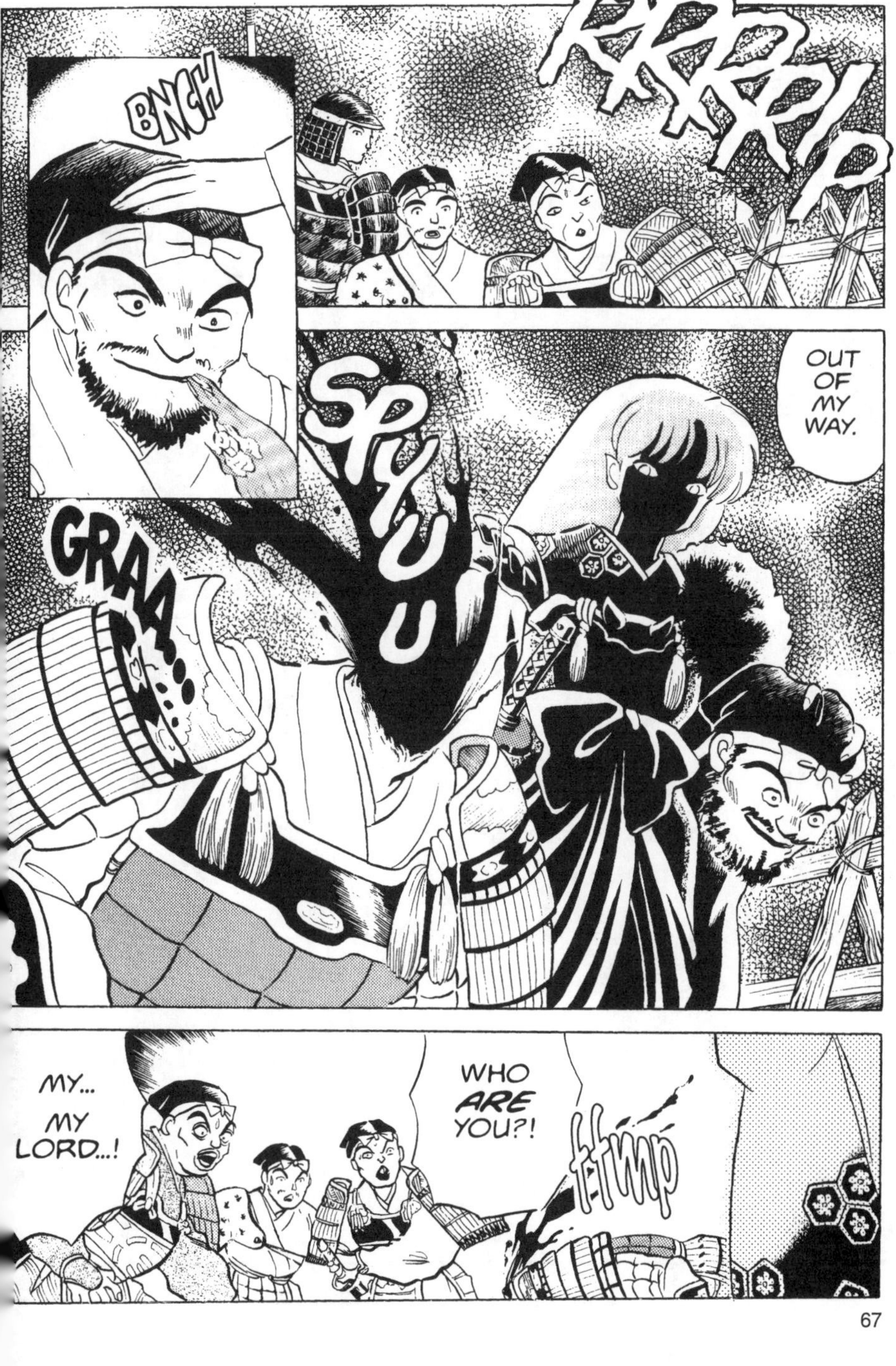
BNCH
OUT OF MY WAY.
GRAA...
MY... MY LORD...!
WHO ARE YOU?!

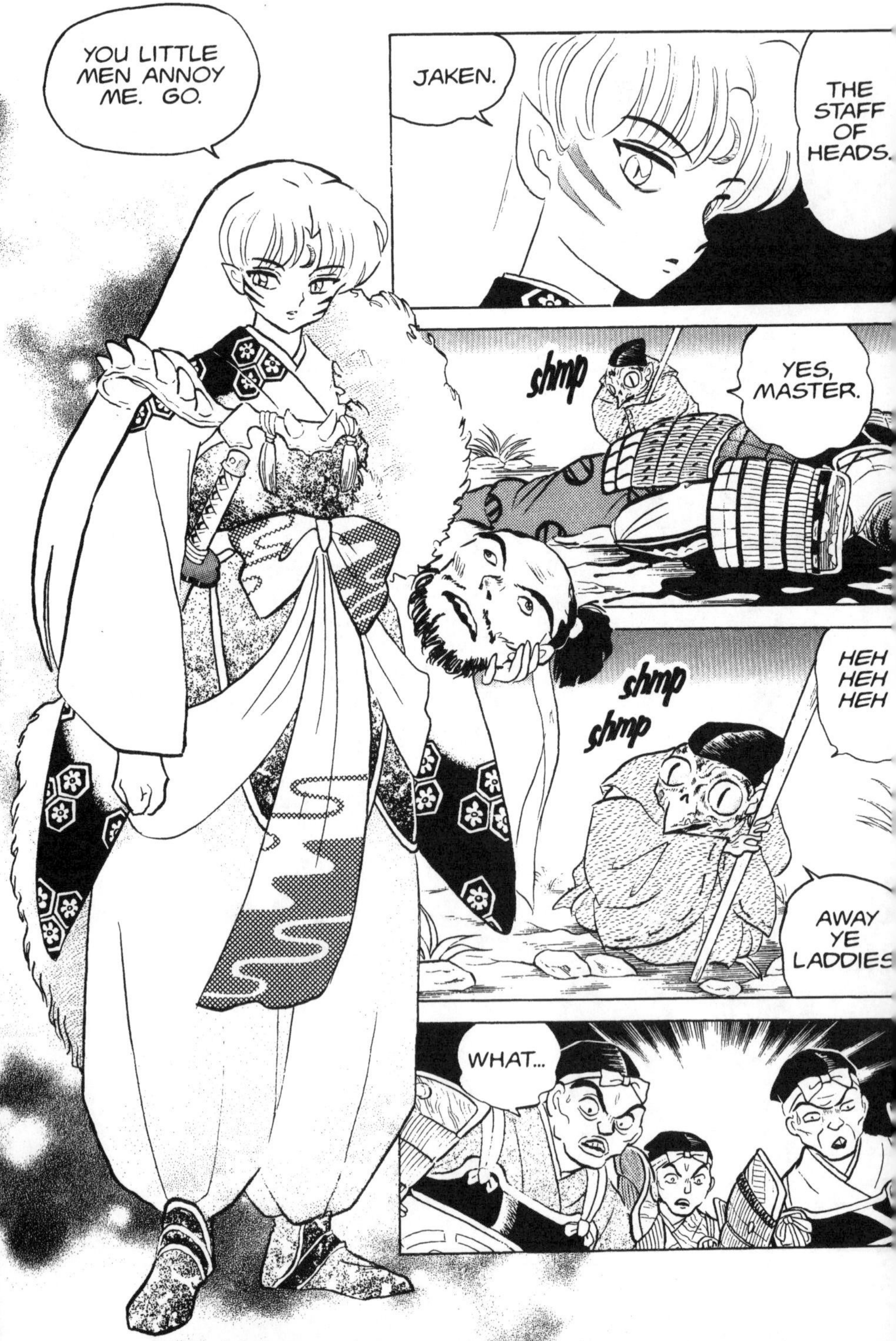
YOU LITTLE MEN ANNOY ME. GO.
JAKEN.
THE STAFF OF HEADS.
shmp
YES, MASTER.
shmp
shmp
HEH HEH HEH
AWAY YE LADDIES
WHAT...

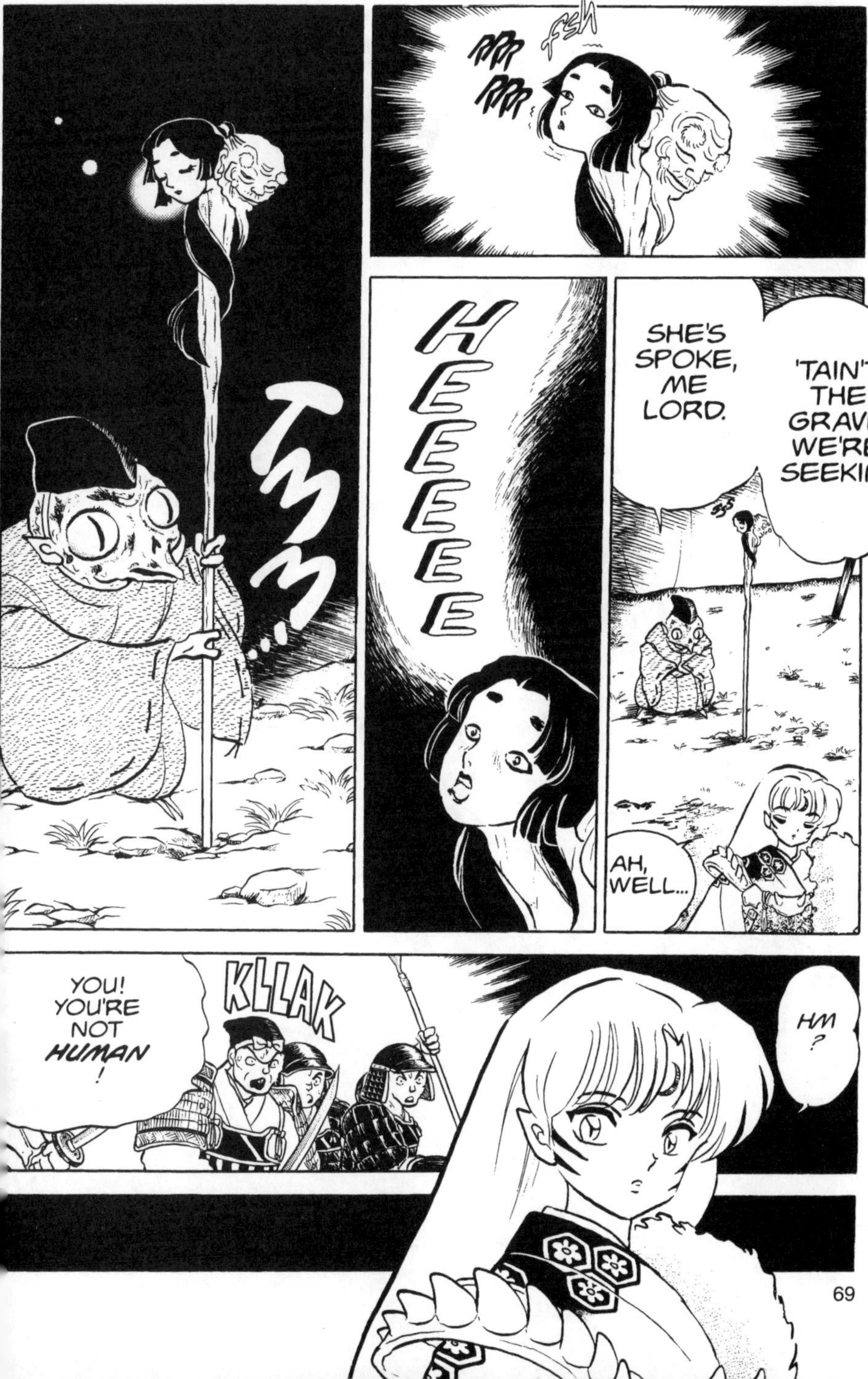
TMM...
PPPR PPPR
fsh
HEEEEEE
SHE'S SPOKE, ME LORD.
'TAIN'T THE GRAVE WE'RE SEEKIN'.
AH, WELL...
YOU! YOU'RE NOT HUMAN!
KLLAK
HM?

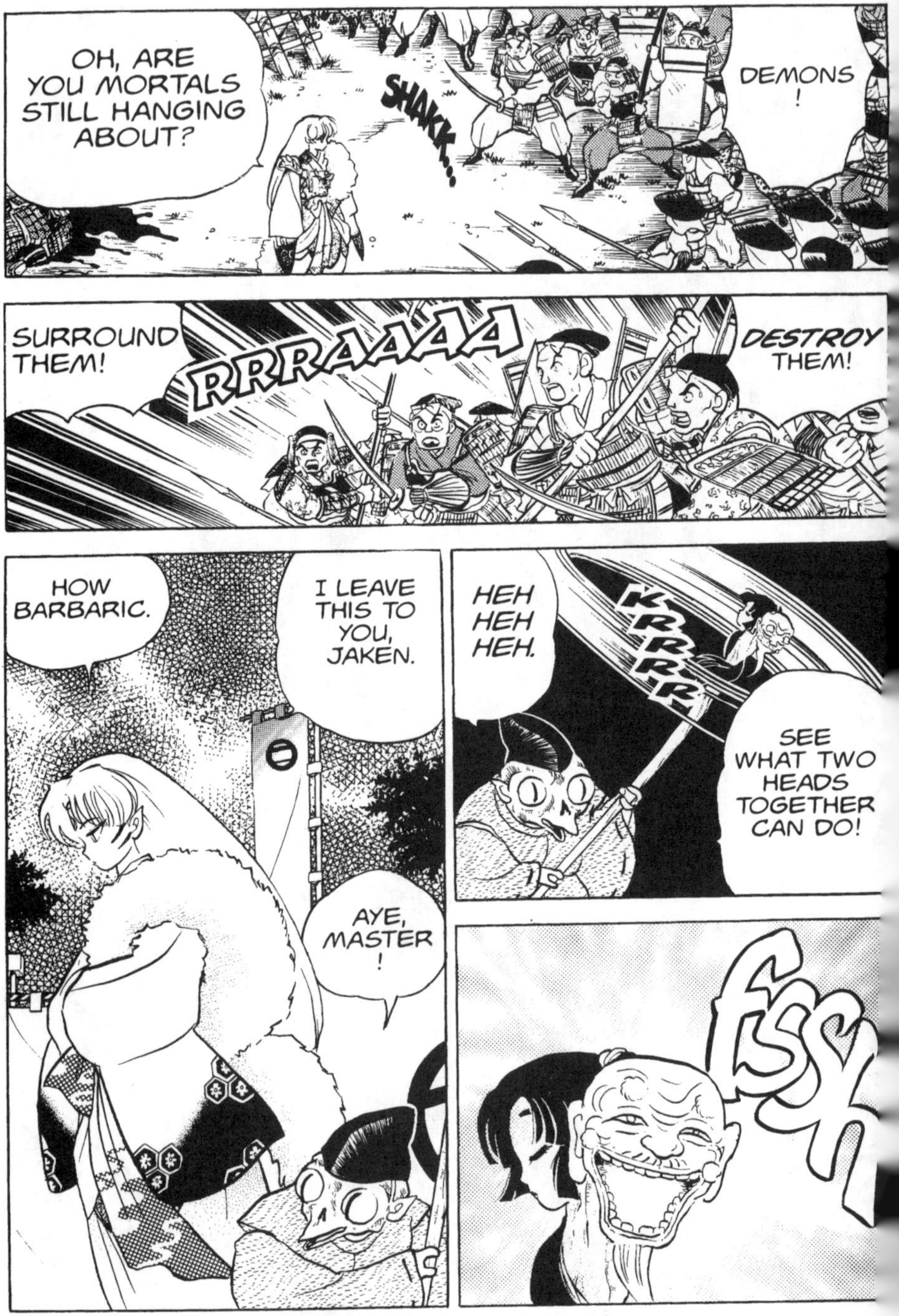
OH, ARE YOU MORTALS STILL HANGING ABOUT?
SHAKK...
DEMONS!
SURROUND THEM!
RRRAAAAA
DESTROY THEM!
HOW BARBARIC.
I LEAVE THIS TO YOU, JAKEN.
AYE, MASTER!
HEH HEH HEH.
KRRRRR
SEE WHAT TWO HEADS TOGETHER CAN DO!
fssh

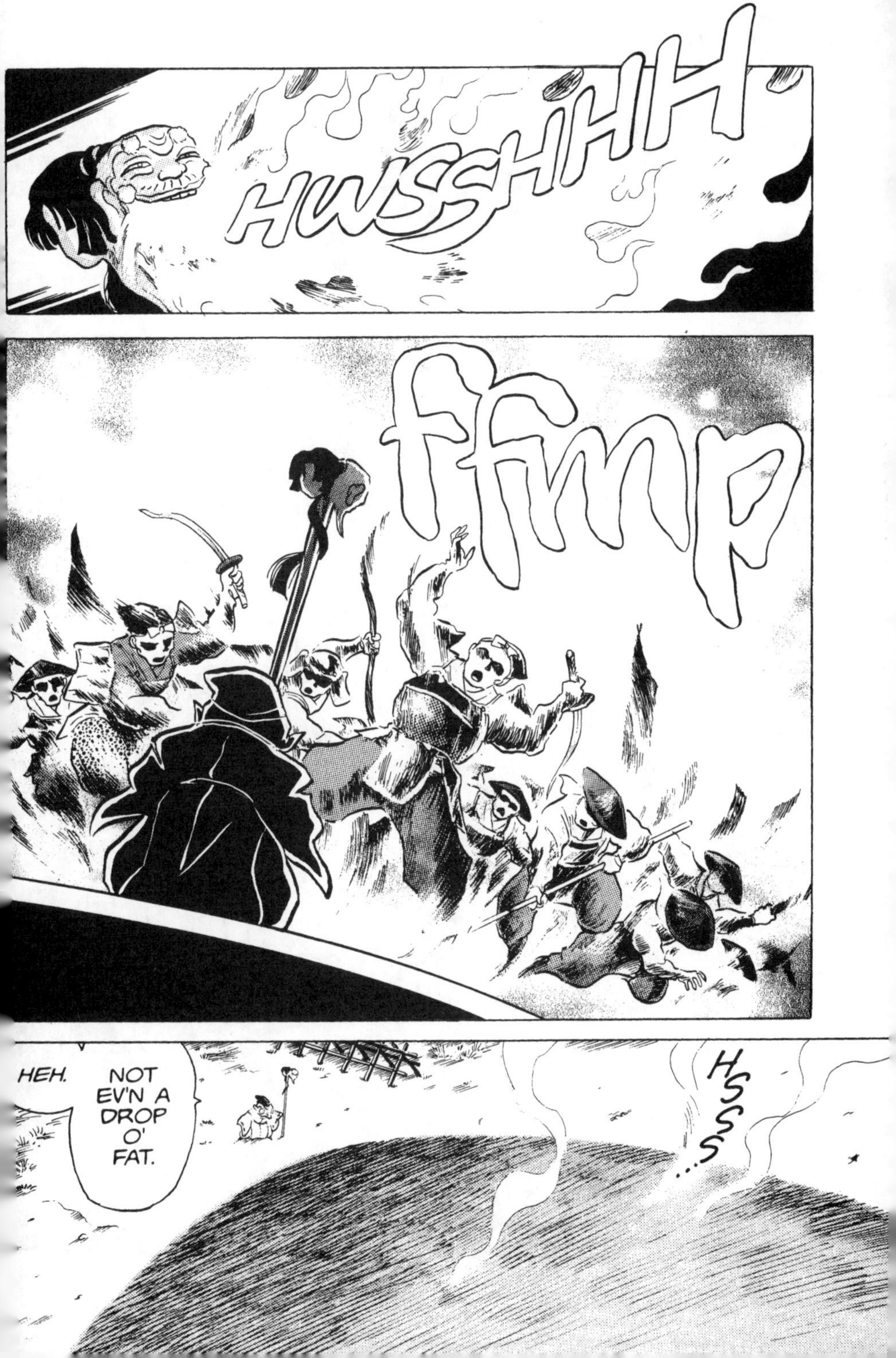
HWSSHHHH
ffmp
HEH.
NOT EV'N A DROP O' FAT.
HSSS...

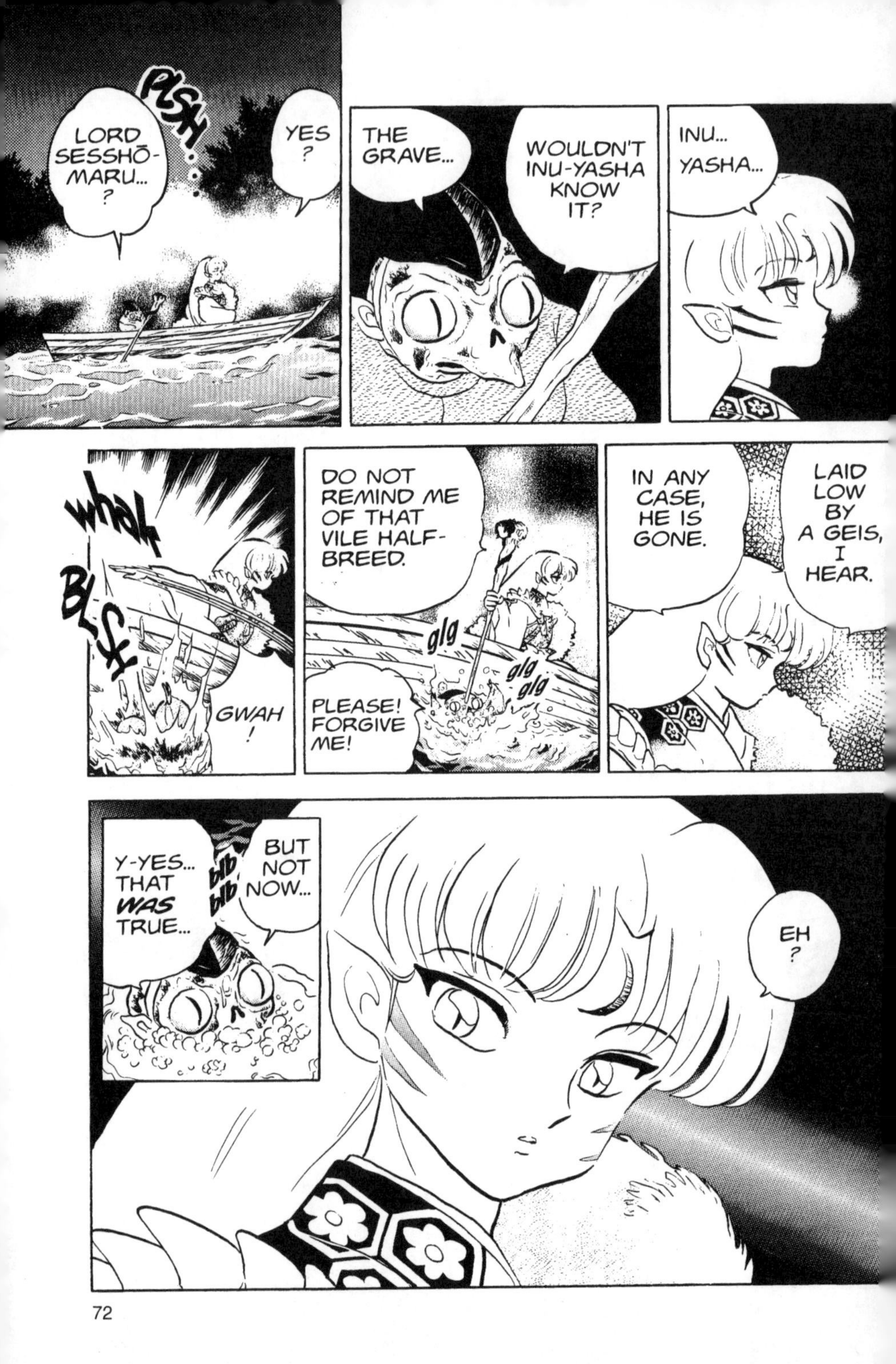
PLSH
LORD SESSHŌ-MARU...?
YES?
THE GRAVE...
WOULDN'T INU-YASHA KNOW IT?
INU... YASHA...
whak
BLSH
GWAH!
DO NOT REMIND ME OF THAT VILE HALF-BREED.
glg
glg glg
PLEASE! FORGIVE ME!
IN ANY CASE, HE IS GONE.
LAID LOW BY A GEIS, I HEAR.
Y-YES... THAT *WAS* TRUE...
blb, blb
BUT NOT NOW...
EH?

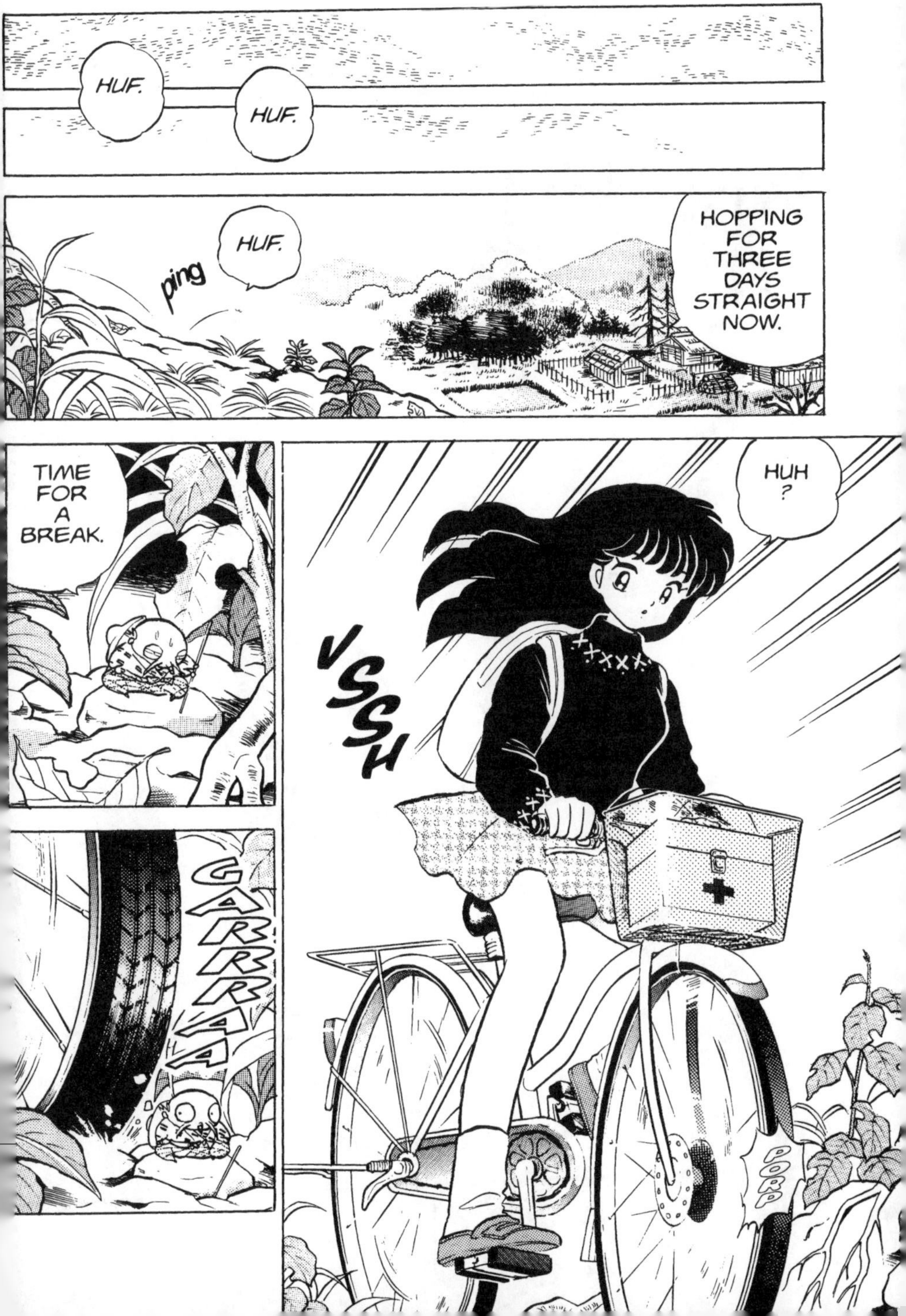
HUF.
HUF.
HUF.
ping
HOPPING FOR THREE DAYS STRAIGHT NOW.
TIME FOR A BREAK.
GARRRAAA
HUH ?
VSSH
DORP

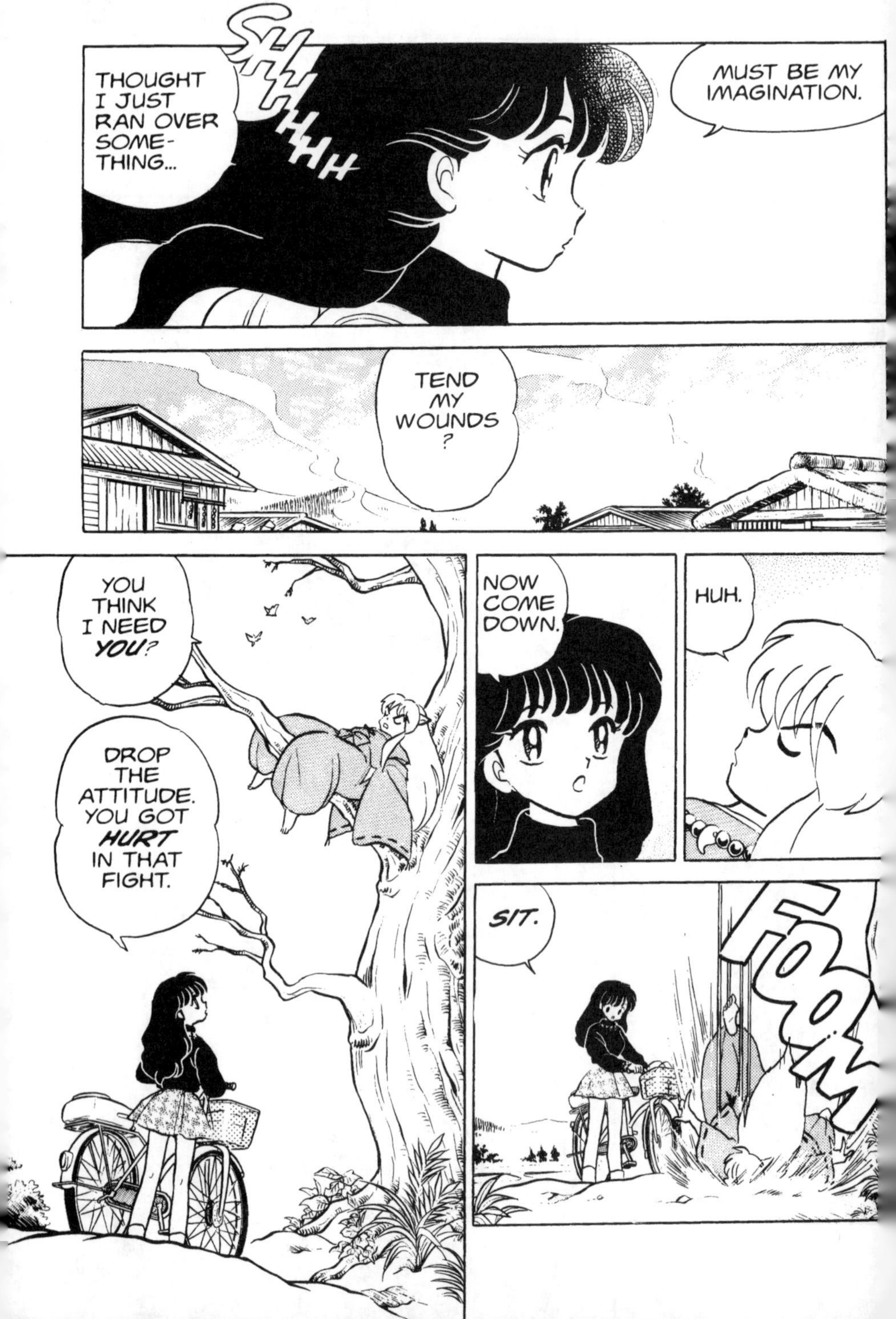
SHHHHH
THOUGHT I JUST RAN OVER SOME-THING...
MUST BE MY IMAGINATION.
TEND MY WOUNDS?
YOU THINK I NEED *YOU*?
DROP THE ATTITUDE. YOU GOT *HURT* IN THAT FIGHT.
NOW COME DOWN.
HUH.
SIT.
FOOM

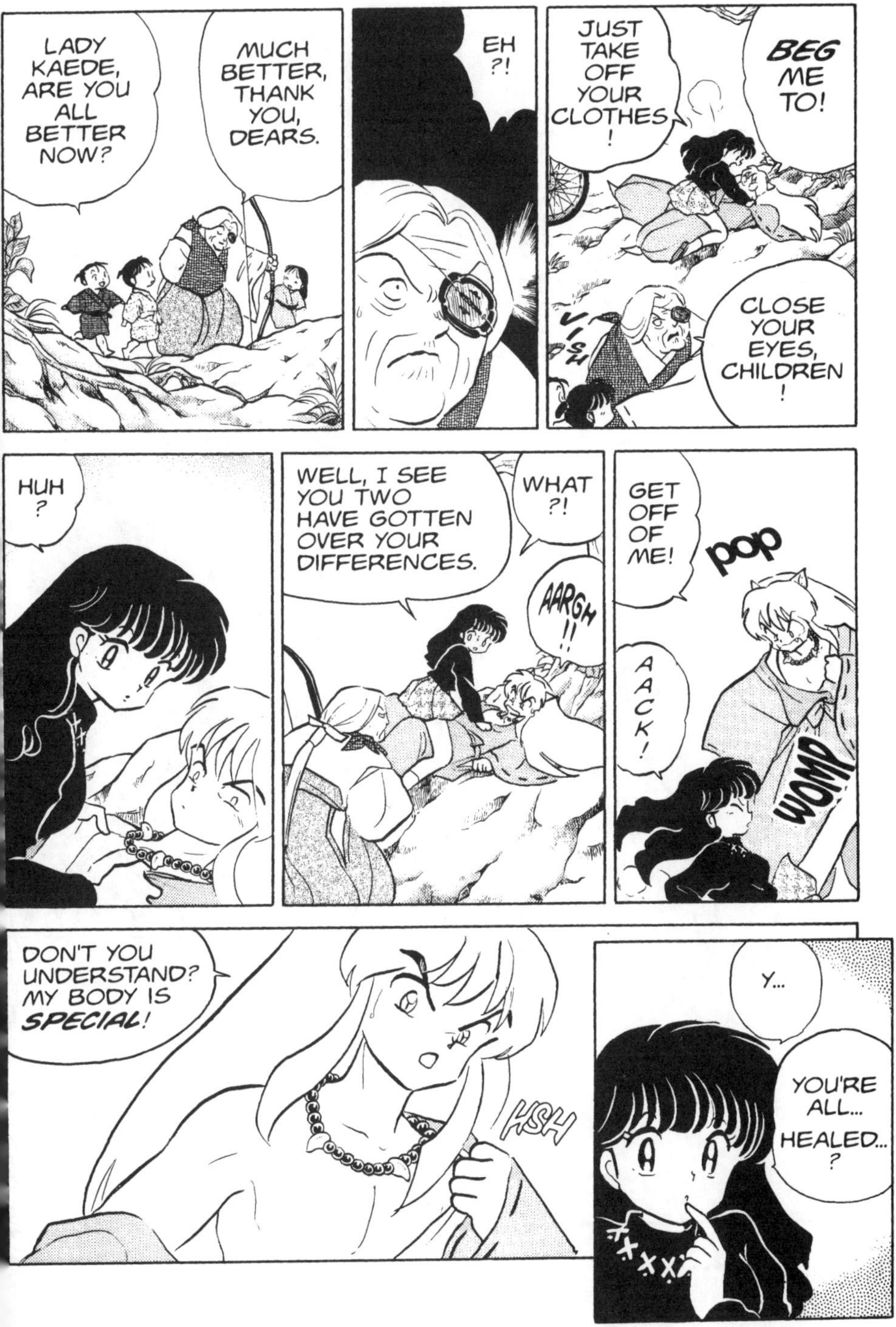
LADY KAEDE, ARE YOU ALL BETTER NOW?
MUCH BETTER, THANK YOU, DEARS.
EH ?!
JUST TAKE OFF YOUR CLOTHES !
BEG ME TO!
VISH
CLOSE YOUR EYES, CHILDREN !
HUH ?
WELL, I SEE YOU TWO HAVE GOTTEN OVER YOUR DIFFERENCES.
WHAT ?!
AARGH !!
GET OFF OF ME!
pop
AACK!
WOMP
DON'T YOU UNDERSTAND? MY BODY IS SPECIAL!
HSH
Y...
YOU'RE ALL... HEALED... ?

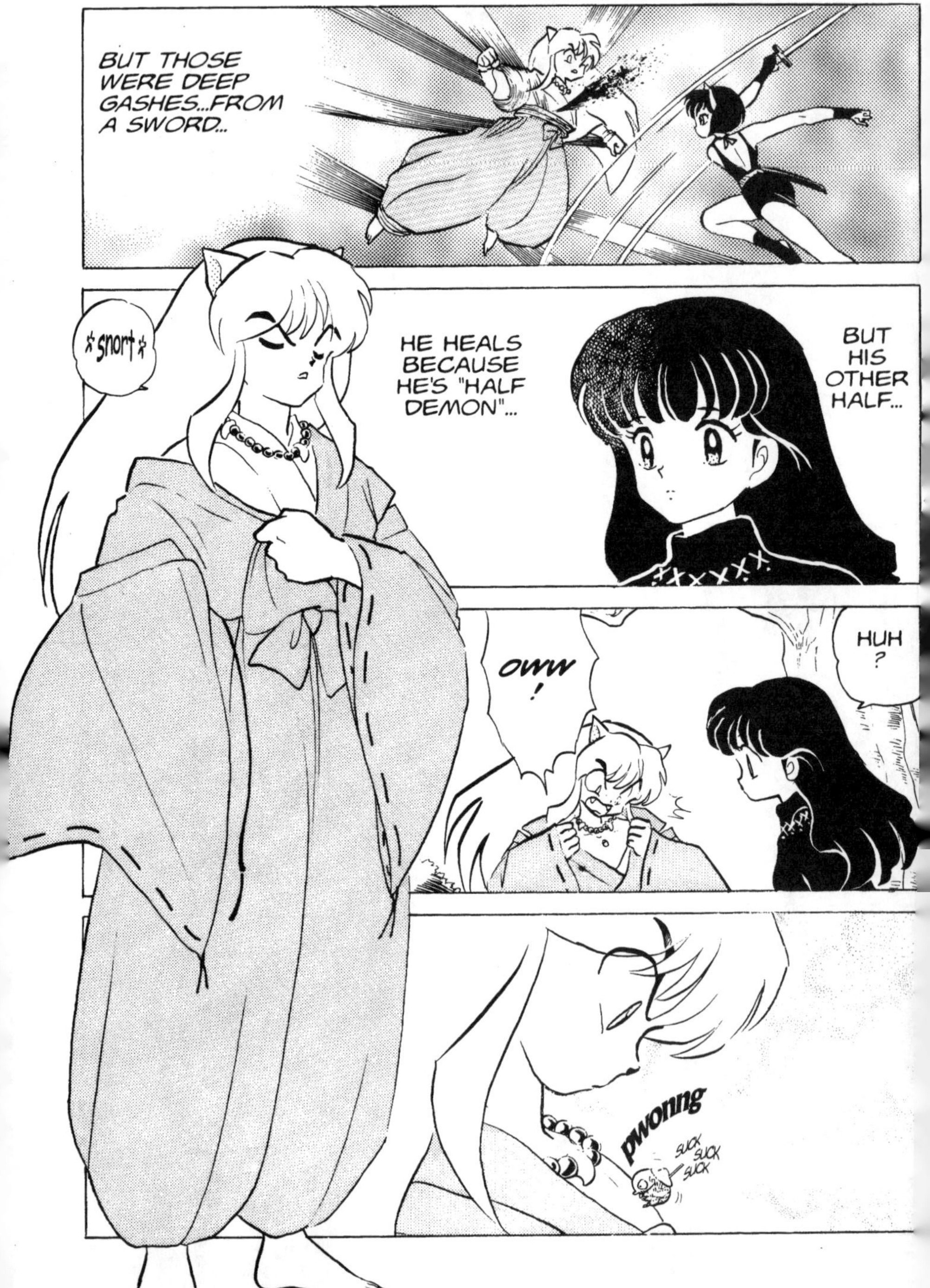
BUT THOSE WERE DEEP GASHES...FROM A SWORD...
snort
HE HEALS BECAUSE HE'S "HALF DEMON"...
BUT HIS OTHER HALF...
OWW!
HUH?
pwonng
SUCK SUCK SUCK

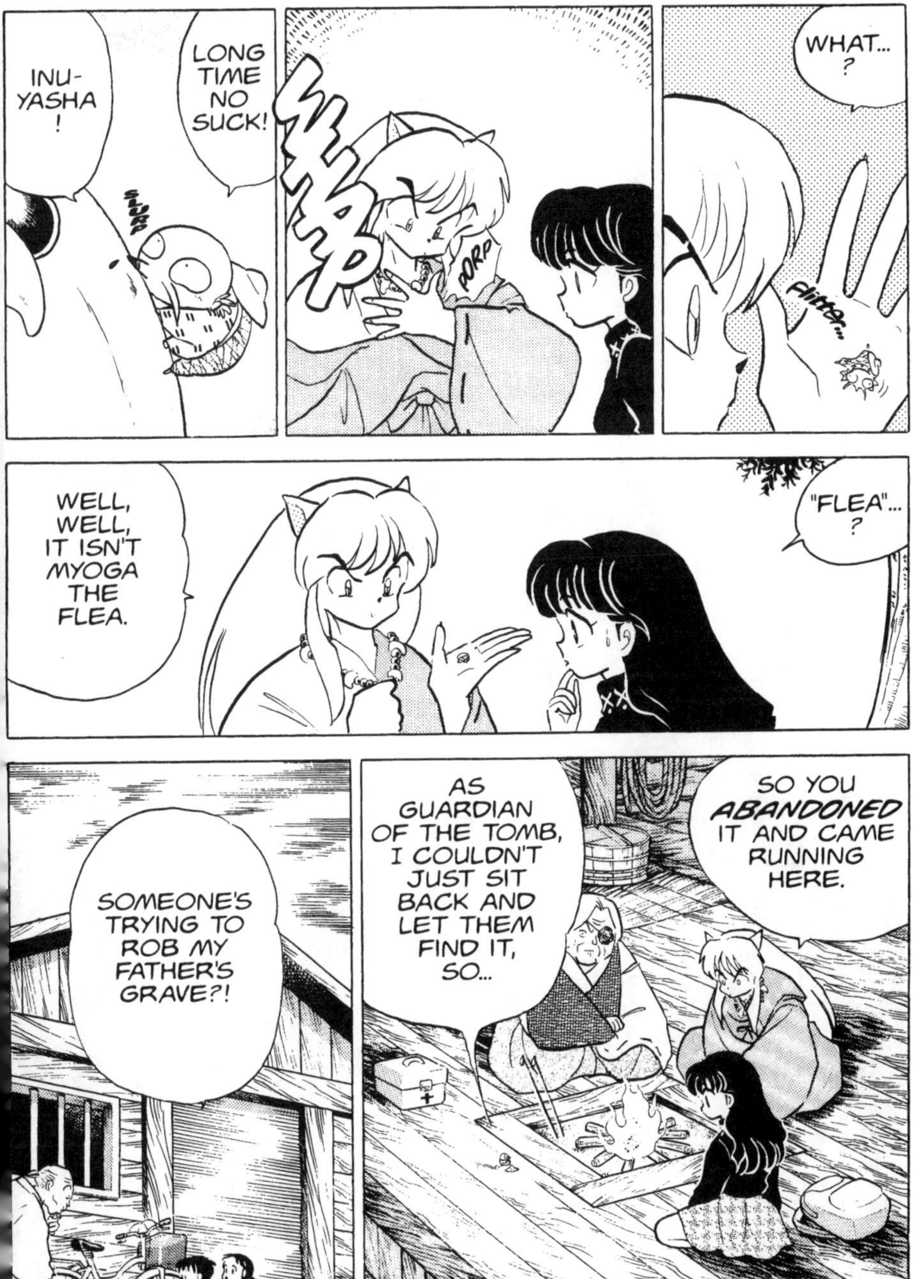
INU-YASHA!
LONG TIME NO SUCK!
SLURP
WHAP
PORP
WHAT...?
Flitter...
WELL, WELL, IT ISN'T MYOGA THE FLEA.
"FLEA"...?
SOMEONE'S TRYING TO ROB MY FATHER'S GRAVE?!
AS GUARDIAN OF THE TOMB, I COULDN'T JUST SIT BACK AND LET THEM FIND IT, SO...
SO YOU *ABANDONED* IT AND CAME RUNNING HERE.

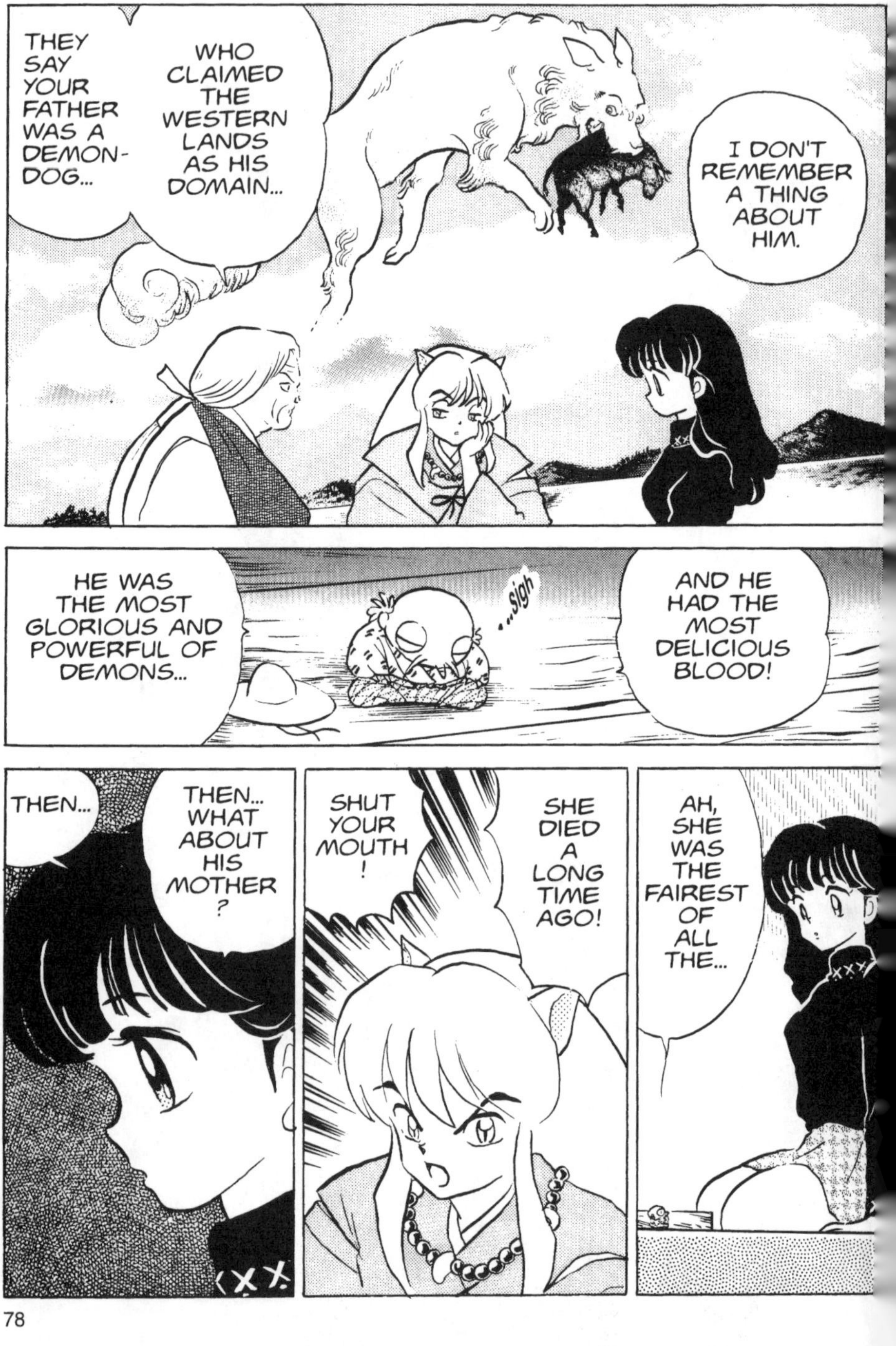
THEY SAY YOUR FATHER WAS A DEMON-DOG...
WHO CLAIMED THE WESTERN LANDS AS HIS DOMAIN...
I DON'T REMEMBER A THING ABOUT HIM.
HE WAS THE MOST GLORIOUS AND POWERFUL OF DEMONS...
...sigh
AND HE HAD THE MOST DELICIOUS BLOOD!
THEN...
THEN... WHAT ABOUT HIS MOTHER?
SHUT YOUR MOUTH!
SHE DIED A LONG TIME AGO!
AH, SHE WAS THE FAIREST OF ALL THE...

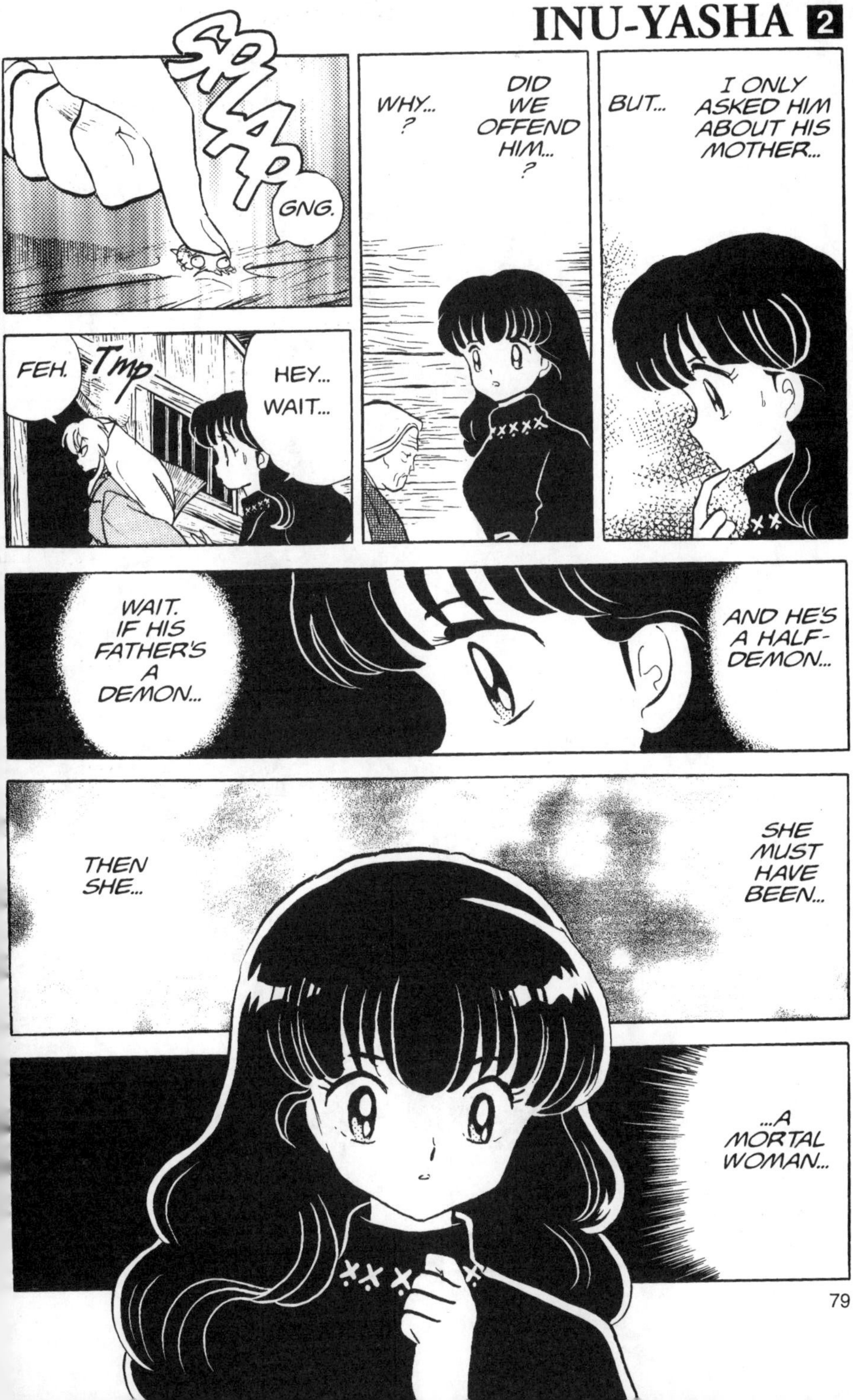
SPLAP
GNG.
FEH.
Tmp
HEY... WAIT...
WHY...?
DID WE OFFEND HIM...?
BUT...
I ONLY ASKED HIM ABOUT HIS MOTHER...
WAIT. IF HIS FATHER'S A DEMON...
AND HE'S A HALF-DEMON...
THEN SHE...
SHE MUST HAVE BEEN...
...A MORTAL WOMAN...

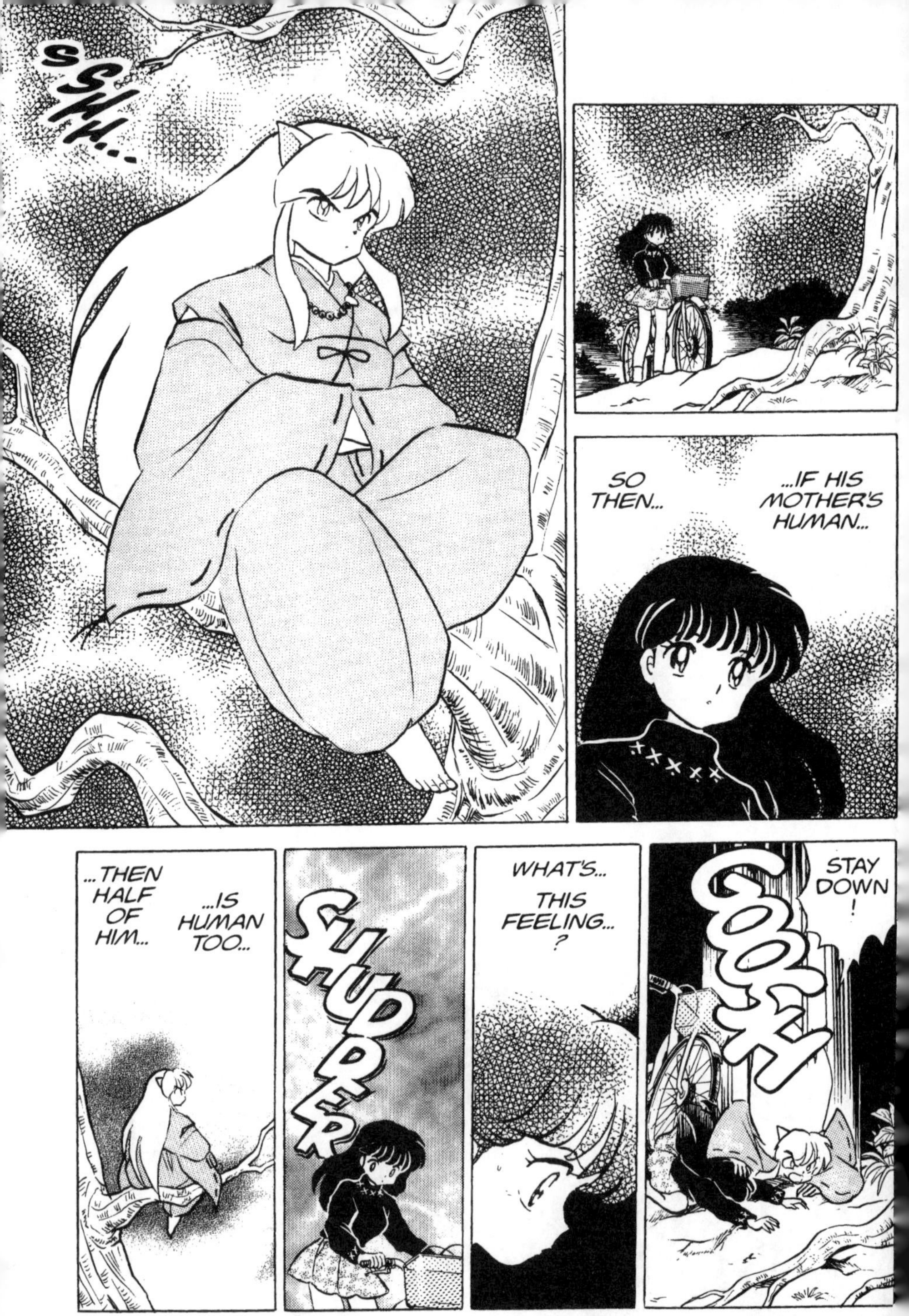
SSHH...
SO THEN...
...IF HIS MOTHER'S HUMAN...
...THEN HALF OF HIM...
...IS HUMAN TOO...
SHUDDER
WHAT'S...
THIS FEELING...?
GOOSH
STAY DOWN!

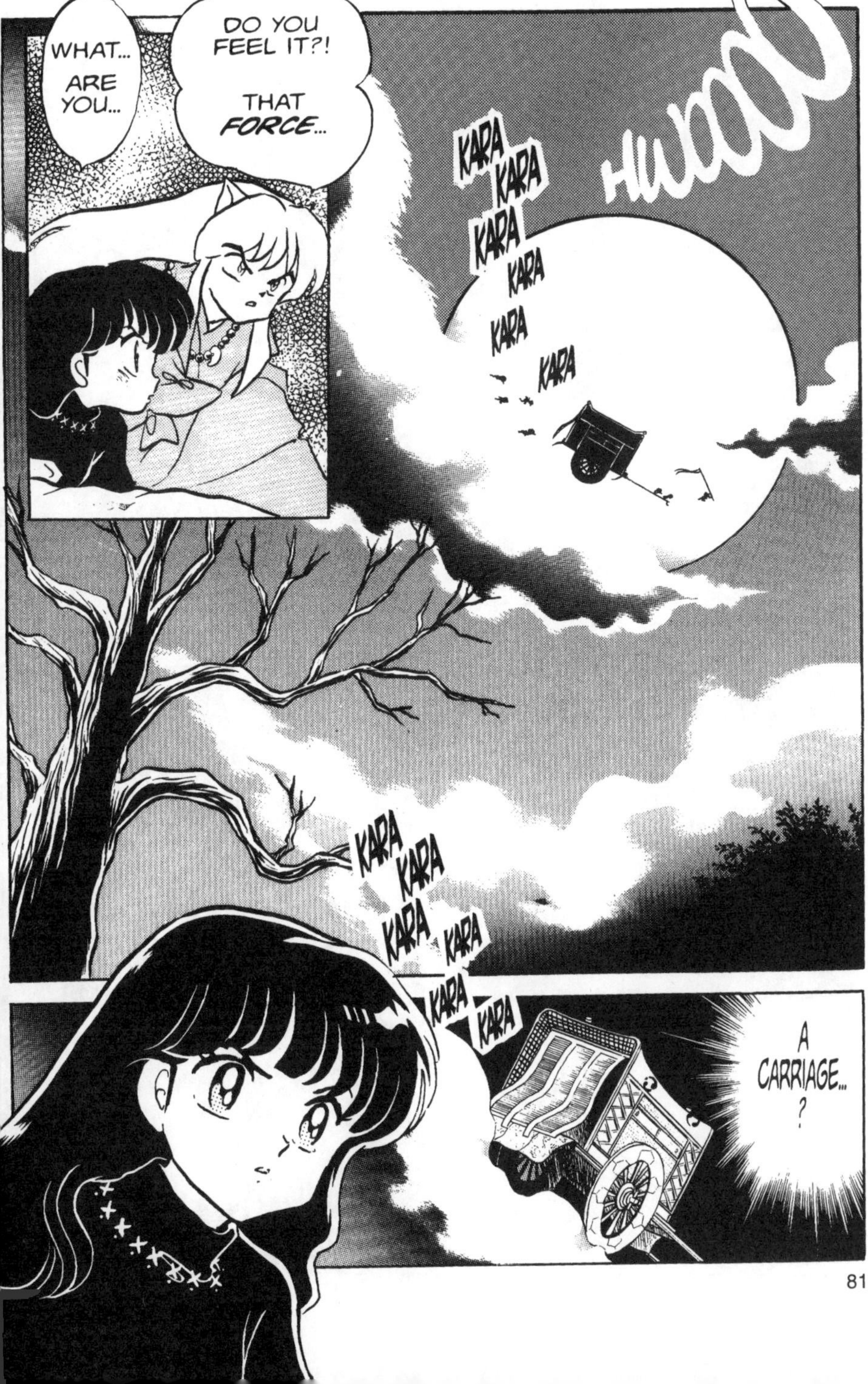
WHAT... ARE YOU...
DO YOU FEEL IT?! THAT FORCE...
HWOOOO
KARA KARA KARA KARA KARA KARA
KARA KARA KARA KARA KARA KARA
A CARRIAGE...?

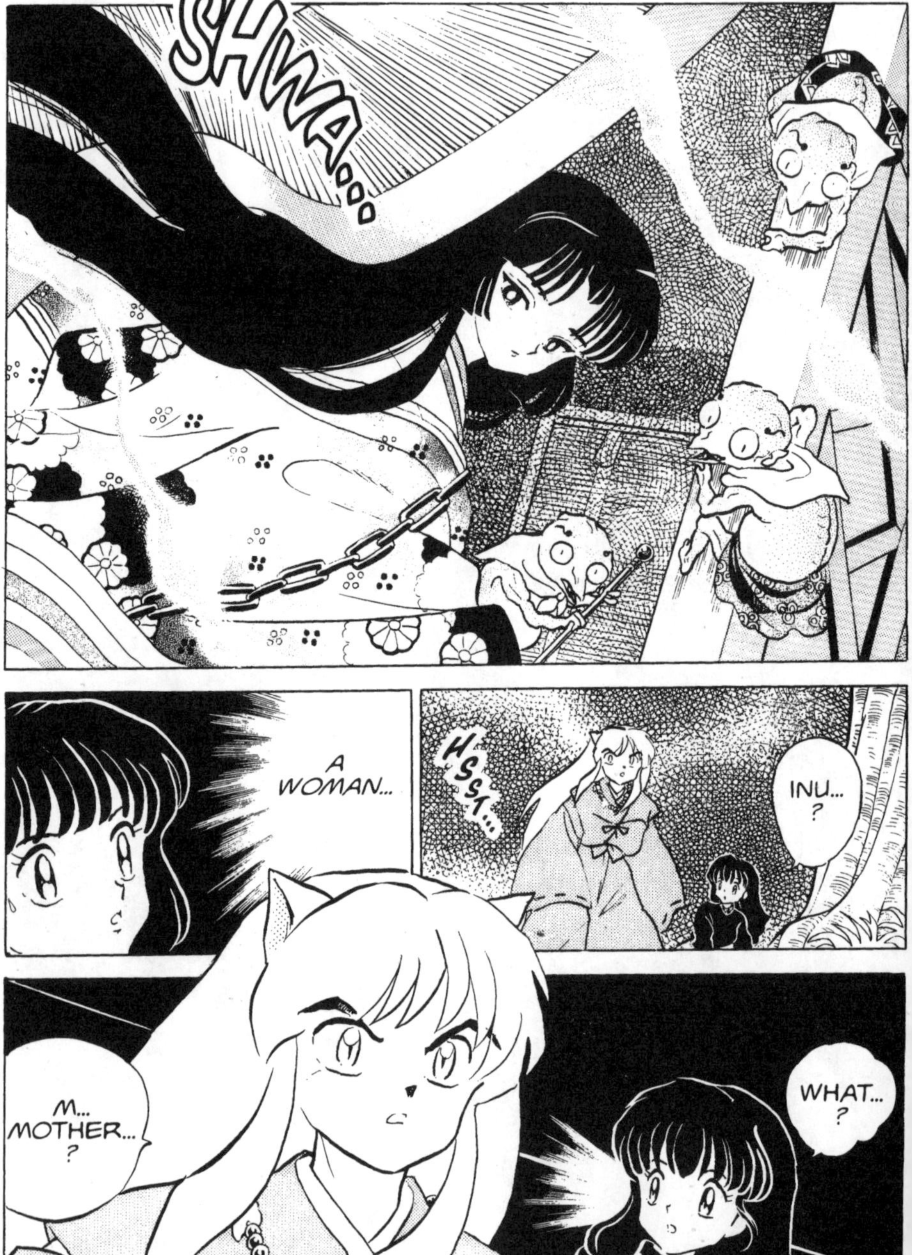
SHWA...
A WOMAN...
HSS1...
INU...?
M... MOTHER...?
WHAT...?

SCROLL FIVE

A MOTHER'S FACE

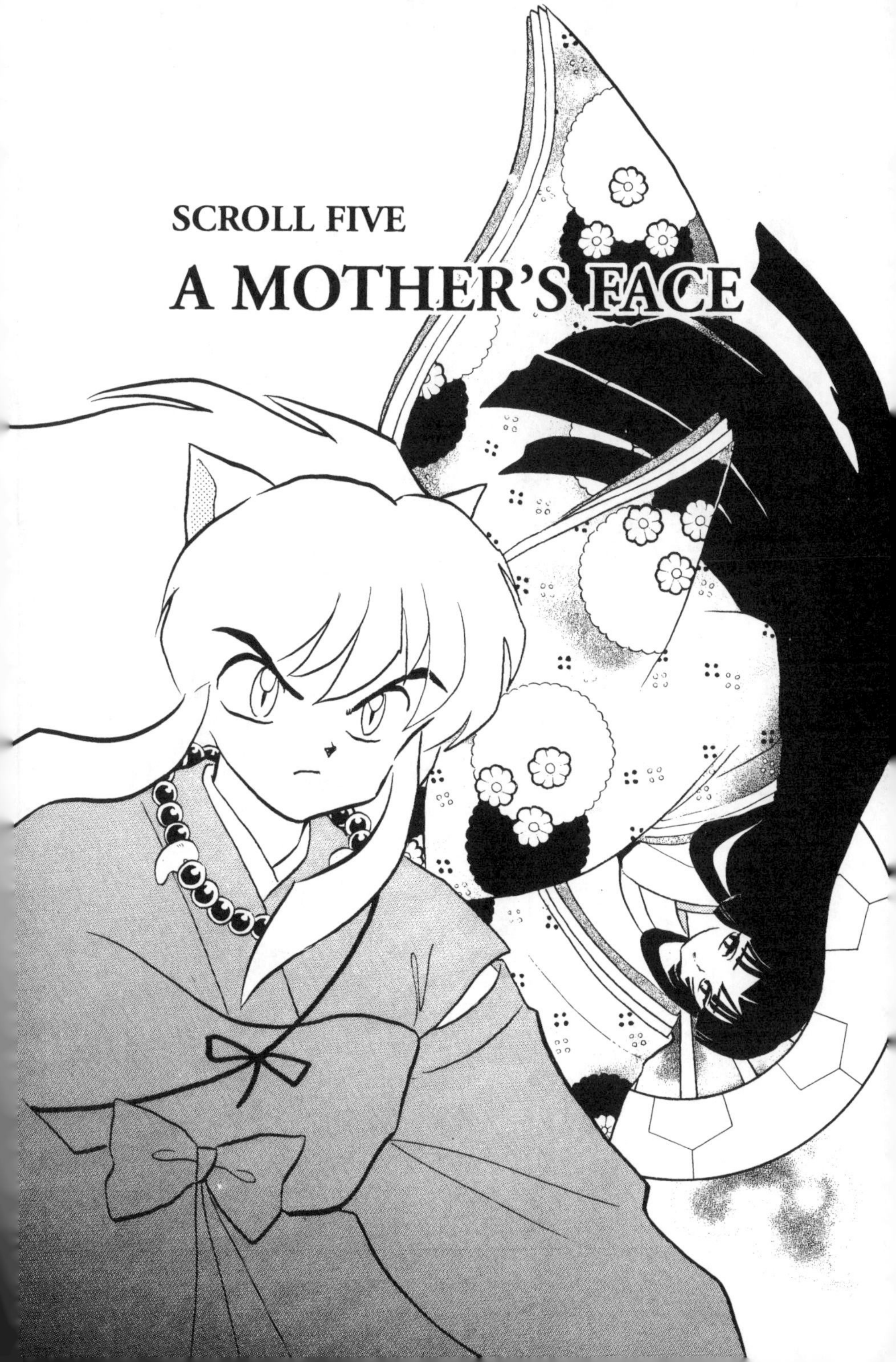

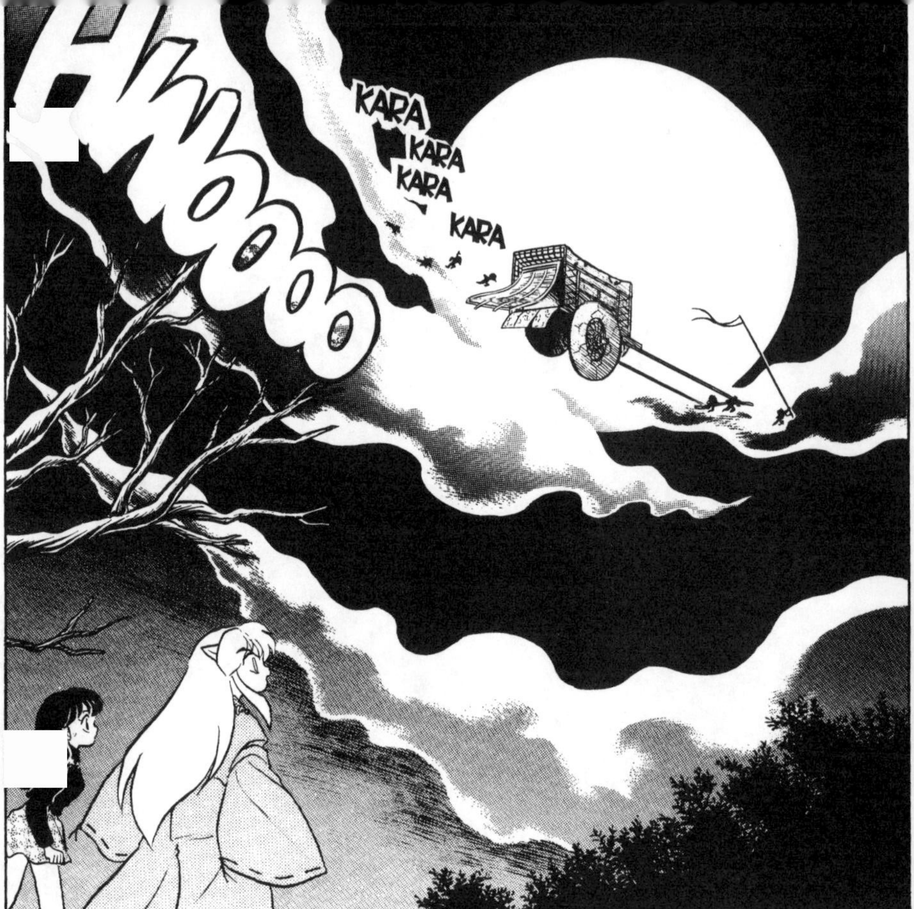
HWOOOO
KARA
KARA
KARA
KARA

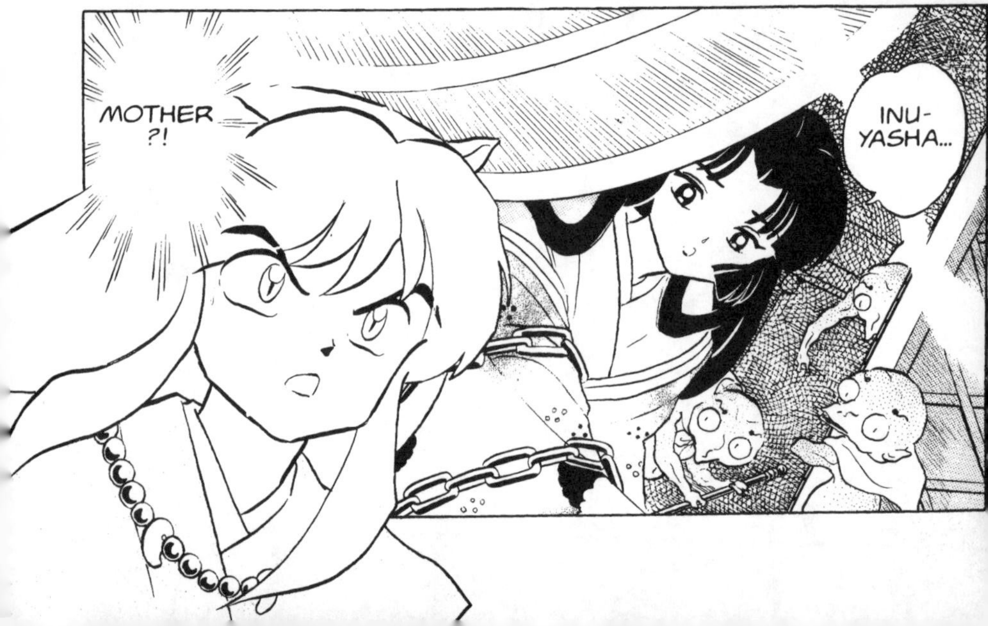
MOTHER ?!
INU-YASHA...

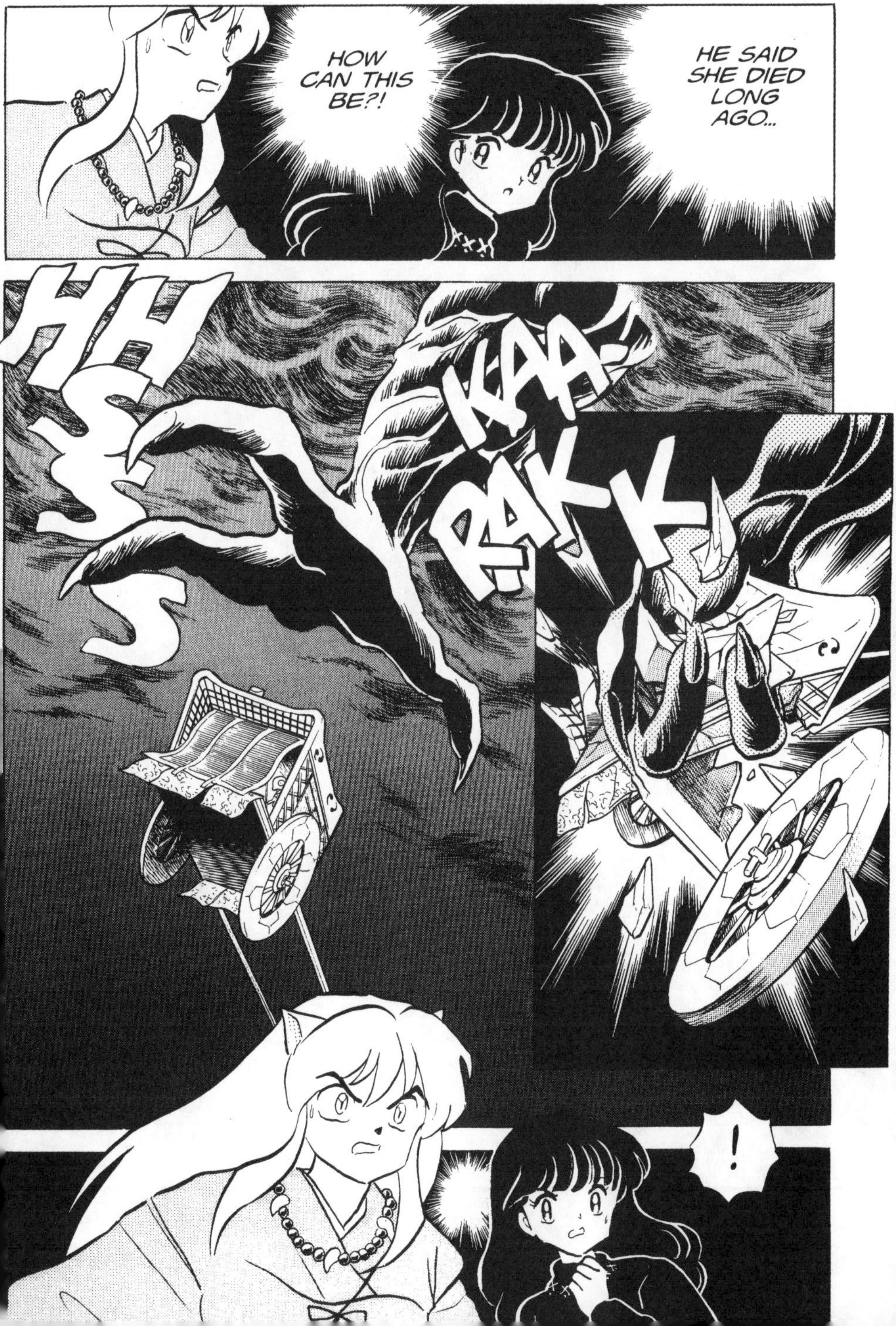
HOW CAN THIS BE?!
HE SAID SHE DIED LONG AGO...
HHSSS
KAA-RAK-K
!

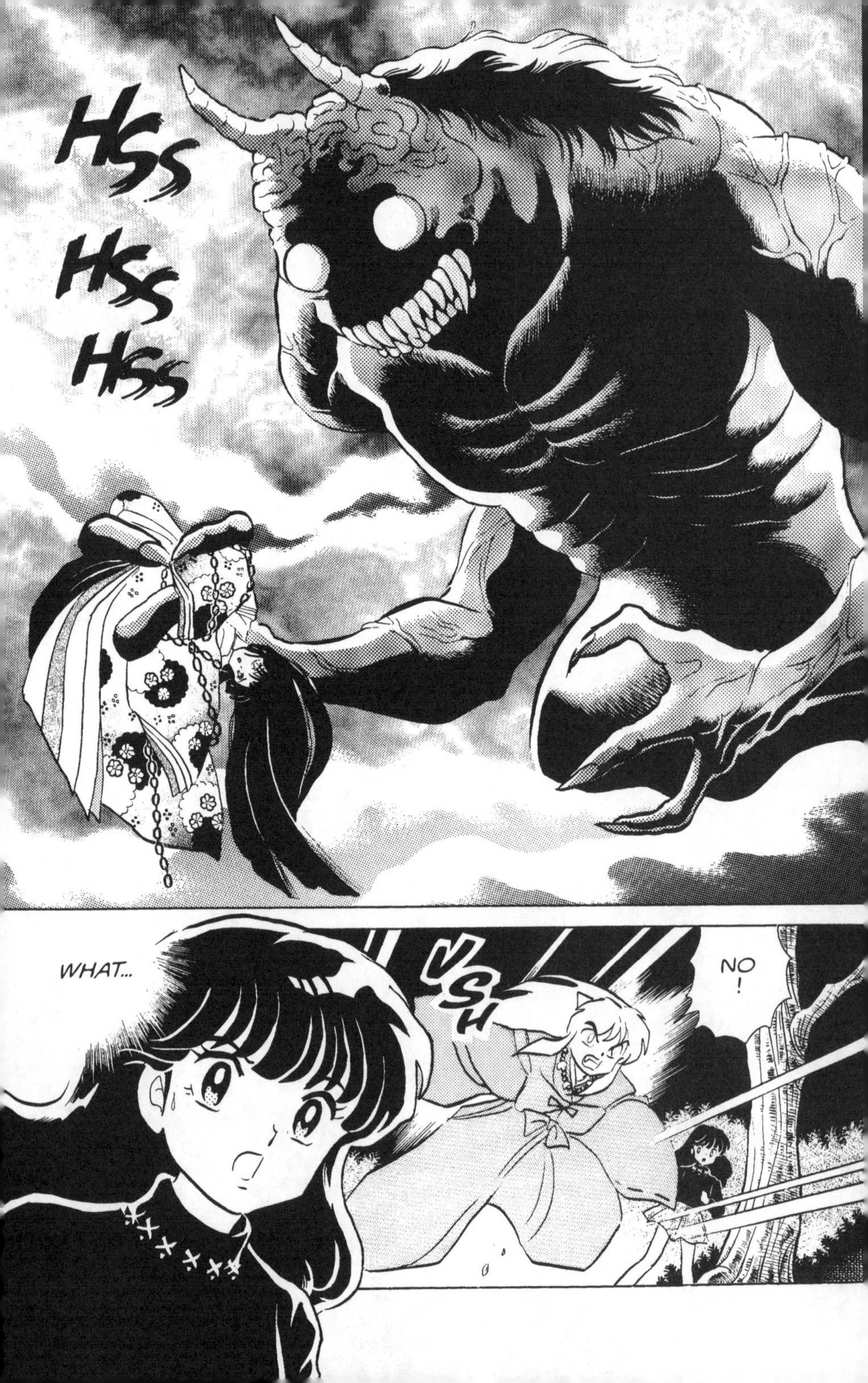
HSS
HSS
HSS
WHAT...
VSH
NO!

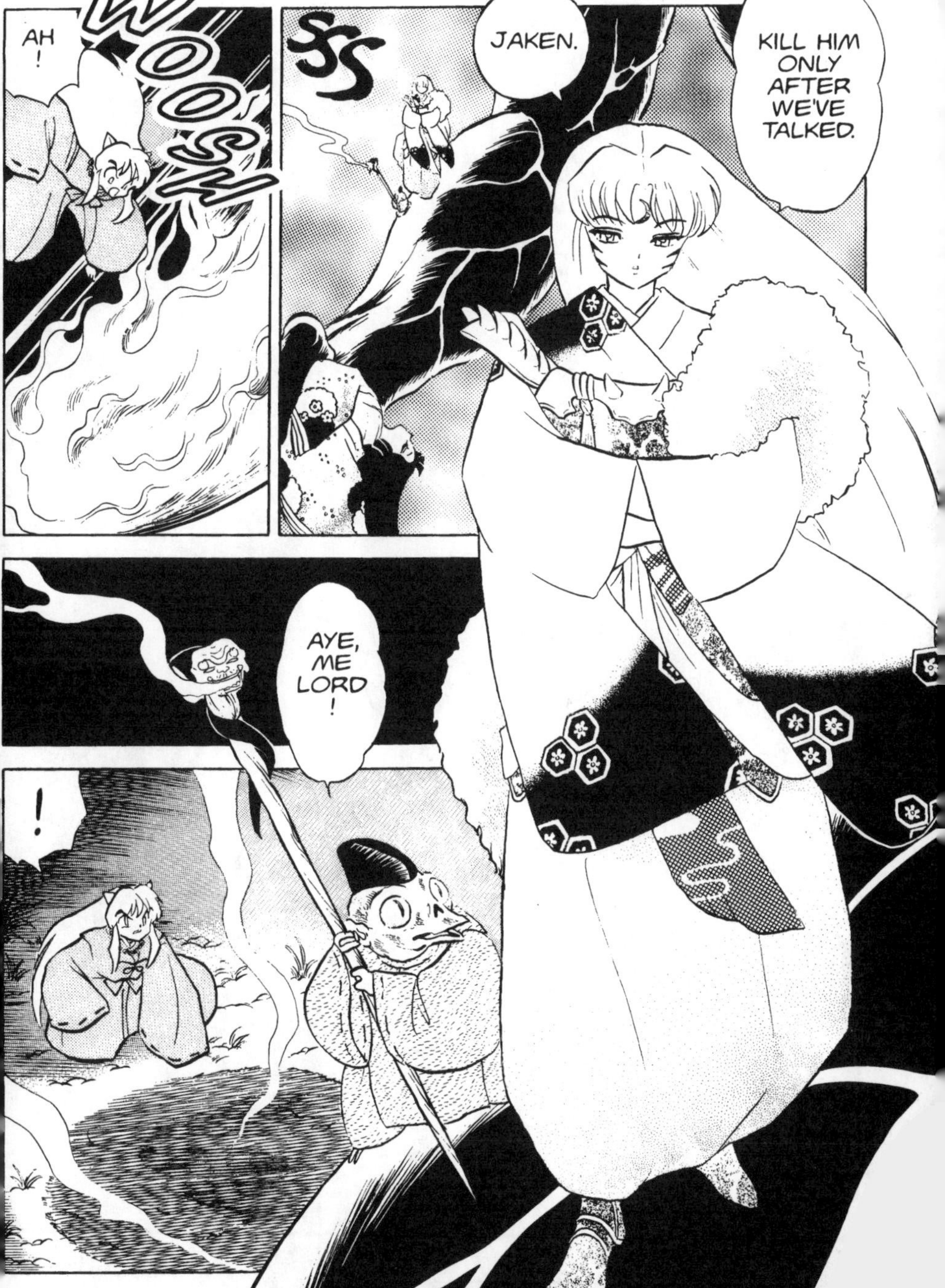
AH!
WOOSH
SSS
AYE, ME LORD!
!
JAKEN.
KILL HIM ONLY AFTER WE'VE TALKED.

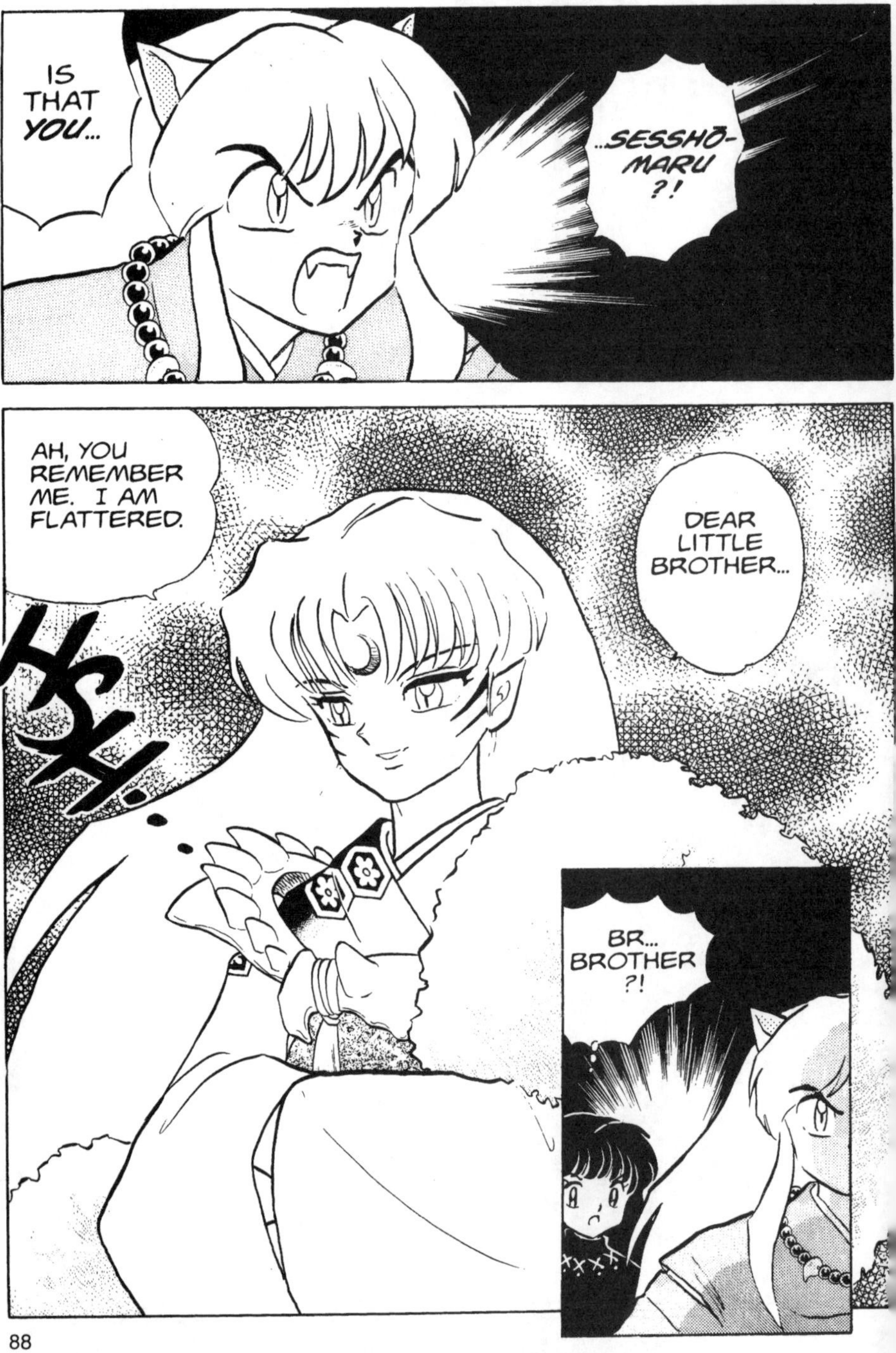
IS THAT YOU...
...SESSHŌ-MARU?!
AH, YOU REMEMBER ME. I AM FLATTERED.
DEAR LITTLE BROTHER...
HSH!
BR... BROTHER?!

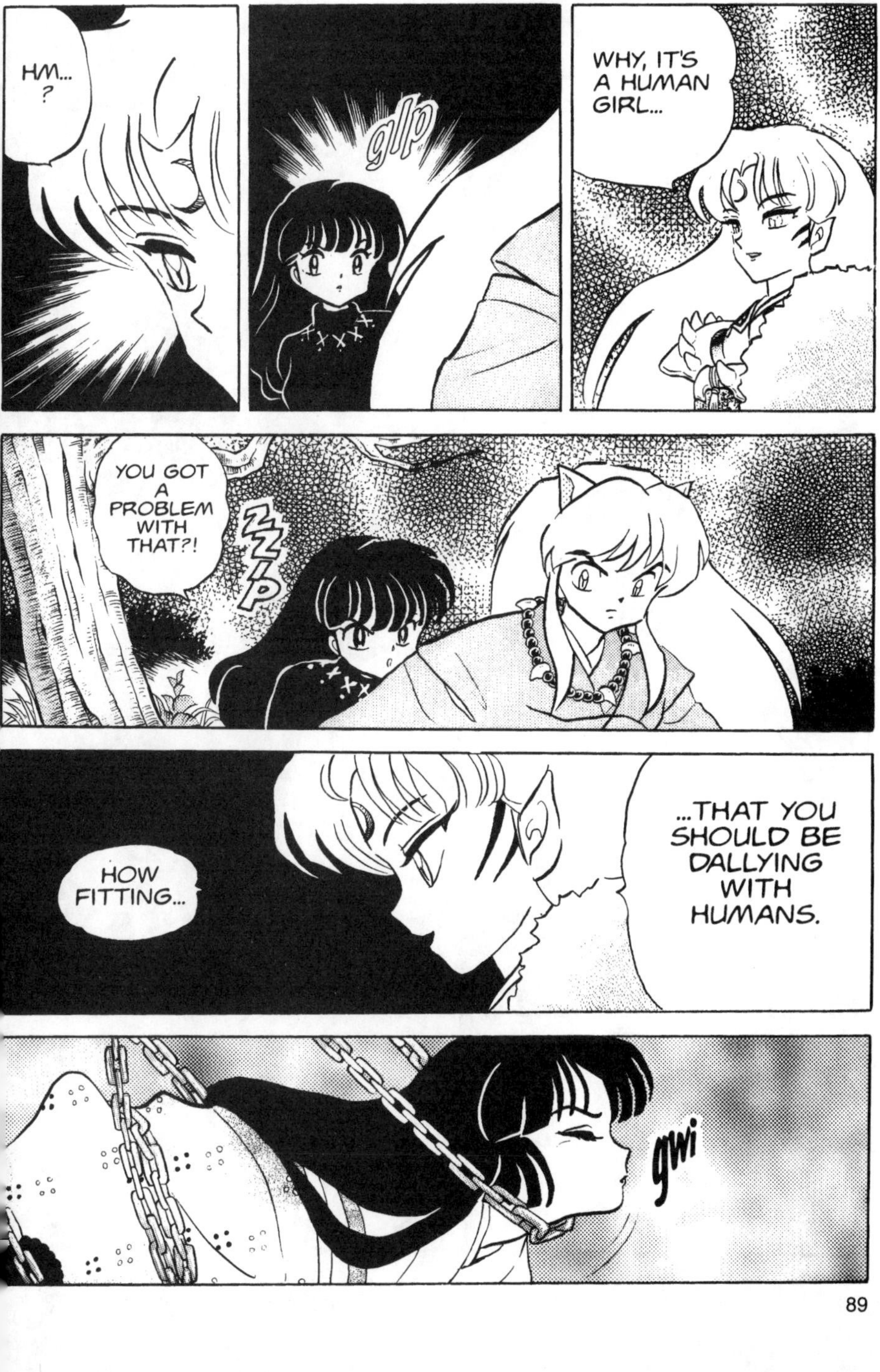
HM... ?
glp
WHY, IT'S A HUMAN GIRL...
YOU GOT A PROBLEM WITH THAT?!
ZZIP
HOW FITTING...
...THAT YOU SHOULD BE DALLYING WITH HUMANS.
gwi

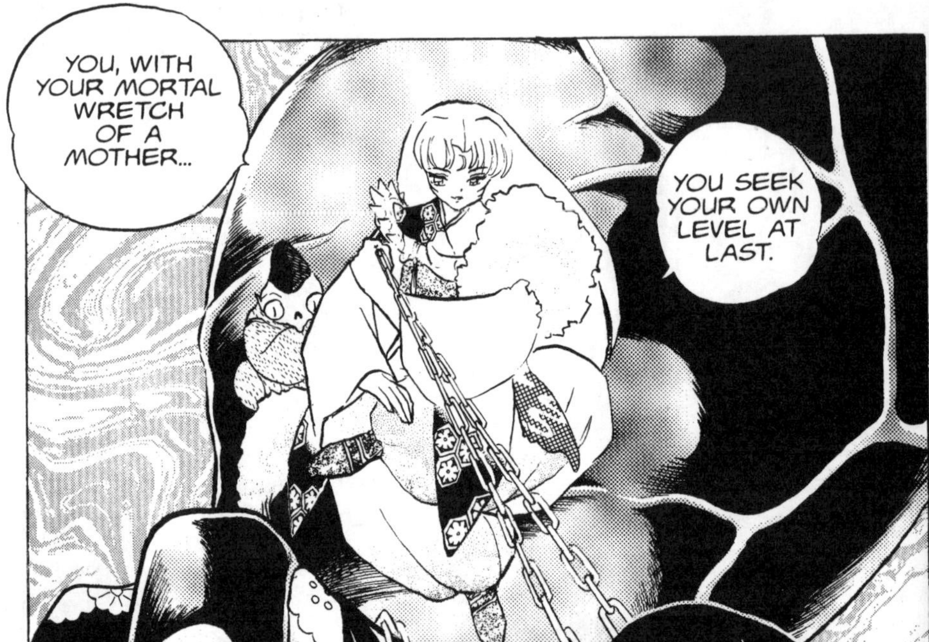
YOU, WITH YOUR MORTAL WRETCH OF A MOTHER...
YOU SEEK YOUR OWN LEVEL AT LAST.
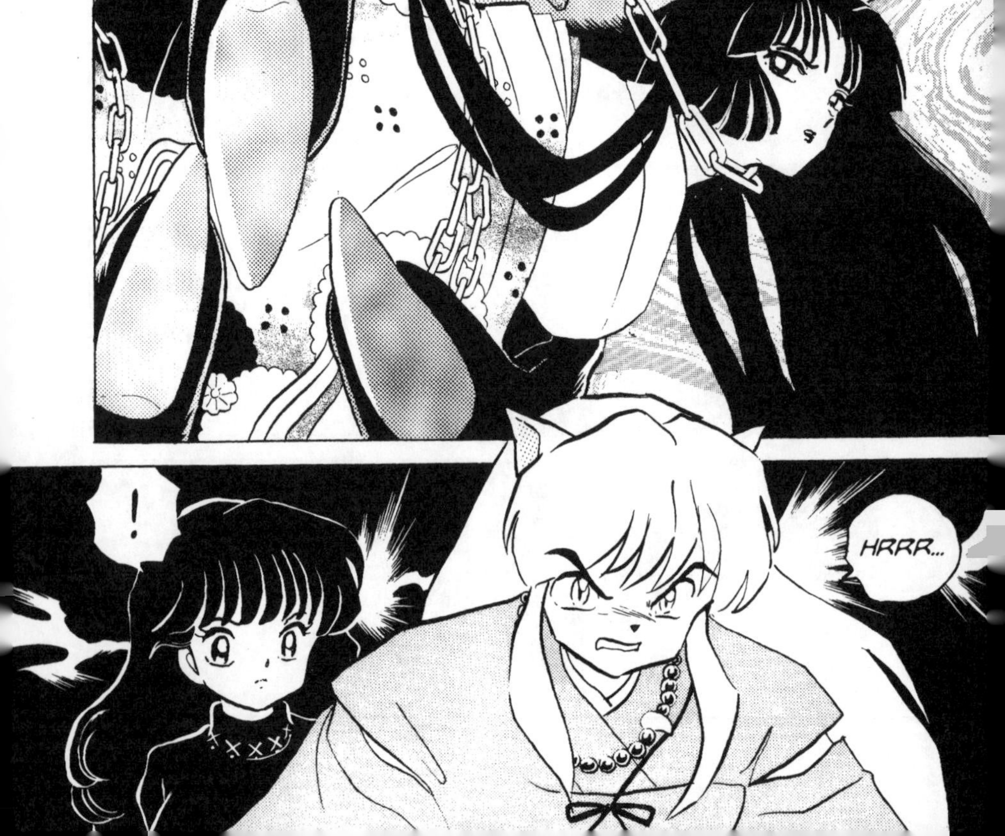
!
HRRR...

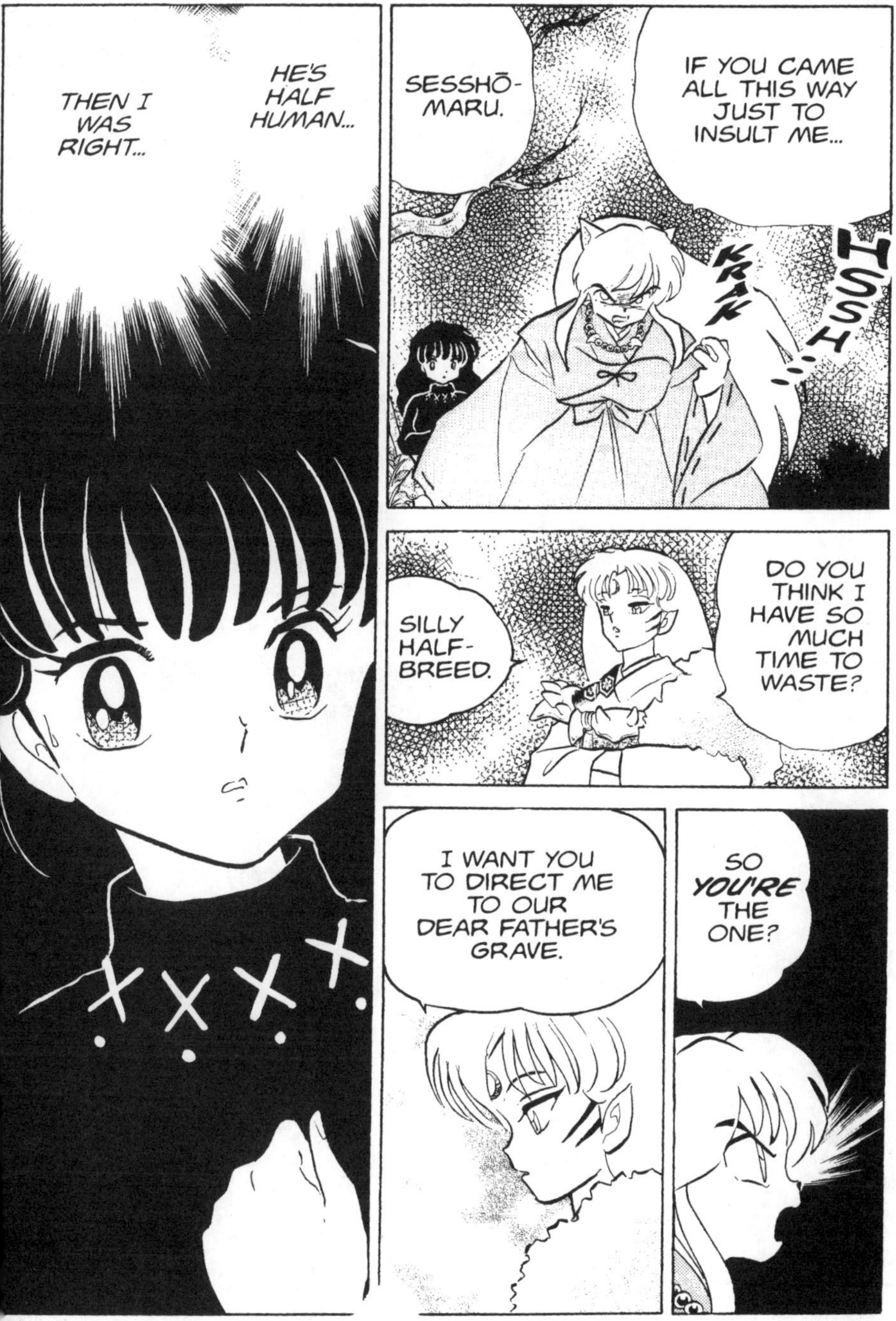
THEN I WAS RIGHT...
HE'S HALF HUMAN...
SESSHŌ-MARU.
IF YOU CAME ALL THIS WAY JUST TO INSULT ME...
KRAK
HSSH!!
SILLY HALF-BREED.
DO YOU THINK I HAVE SO MUCH TIME TO WASTE?
I WANT YOU TO DIRECT ME TO OUR DEAR FATHER'S GRAVE.
SO *YOU'RE* THE ONE?

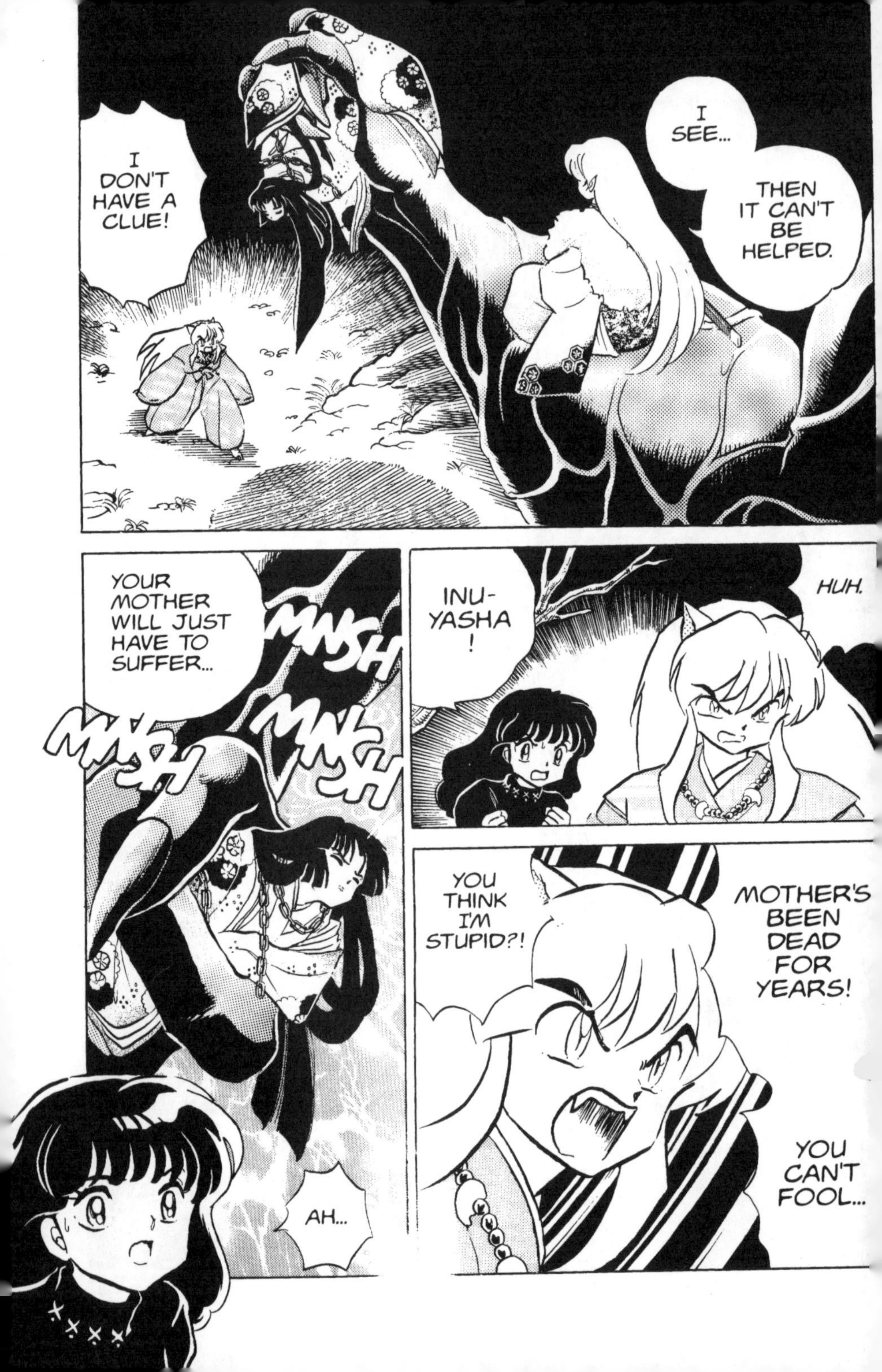
I DON'T HAVE A CLUE!
I SEE...
THEN IT CAN'T BE HELPED.
YOUR MOTHER WILL JUST HAVE TO SUFFER...
MNSH
MNSH
MNSH
AH...
INU-YASHA!
HUH.
YOU THINK I'M STUPID?!
MOTHER'S BEEN DEAD FOR YEARS!
YOU CAN'T FOOL...

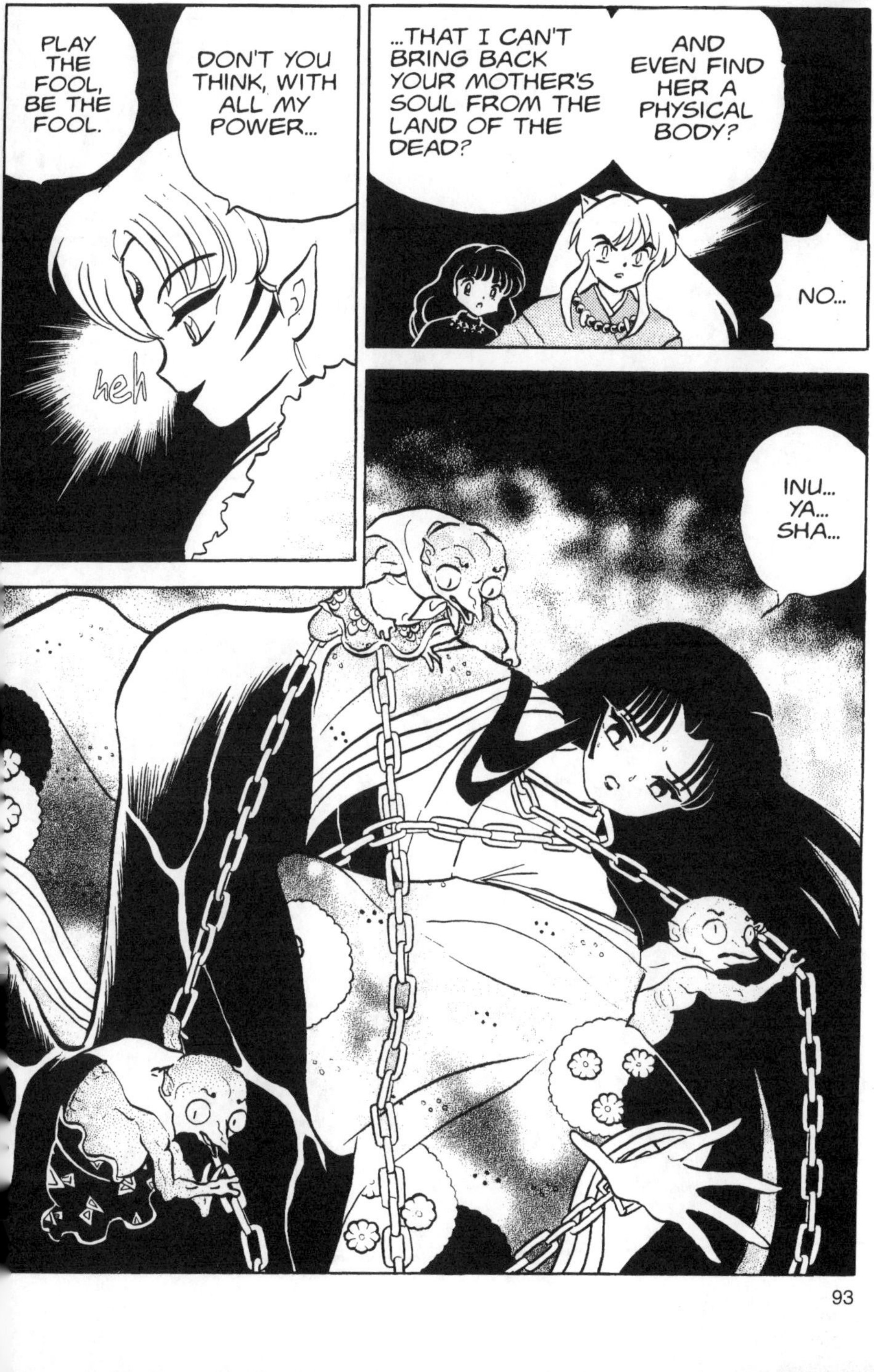
PLAY THE FOOL, BE THE FOOL.
DON'T YOU THINK, WITH ALL MY POWER...
heh
...THAT I CAN'T BRING BACK YOUR MOTHER'S SOUL FROM THE LAND OF THE DEAD?
AND EVEN FIND HER A PHYSICAL BODY?
NO...
INU... YA... SHA...

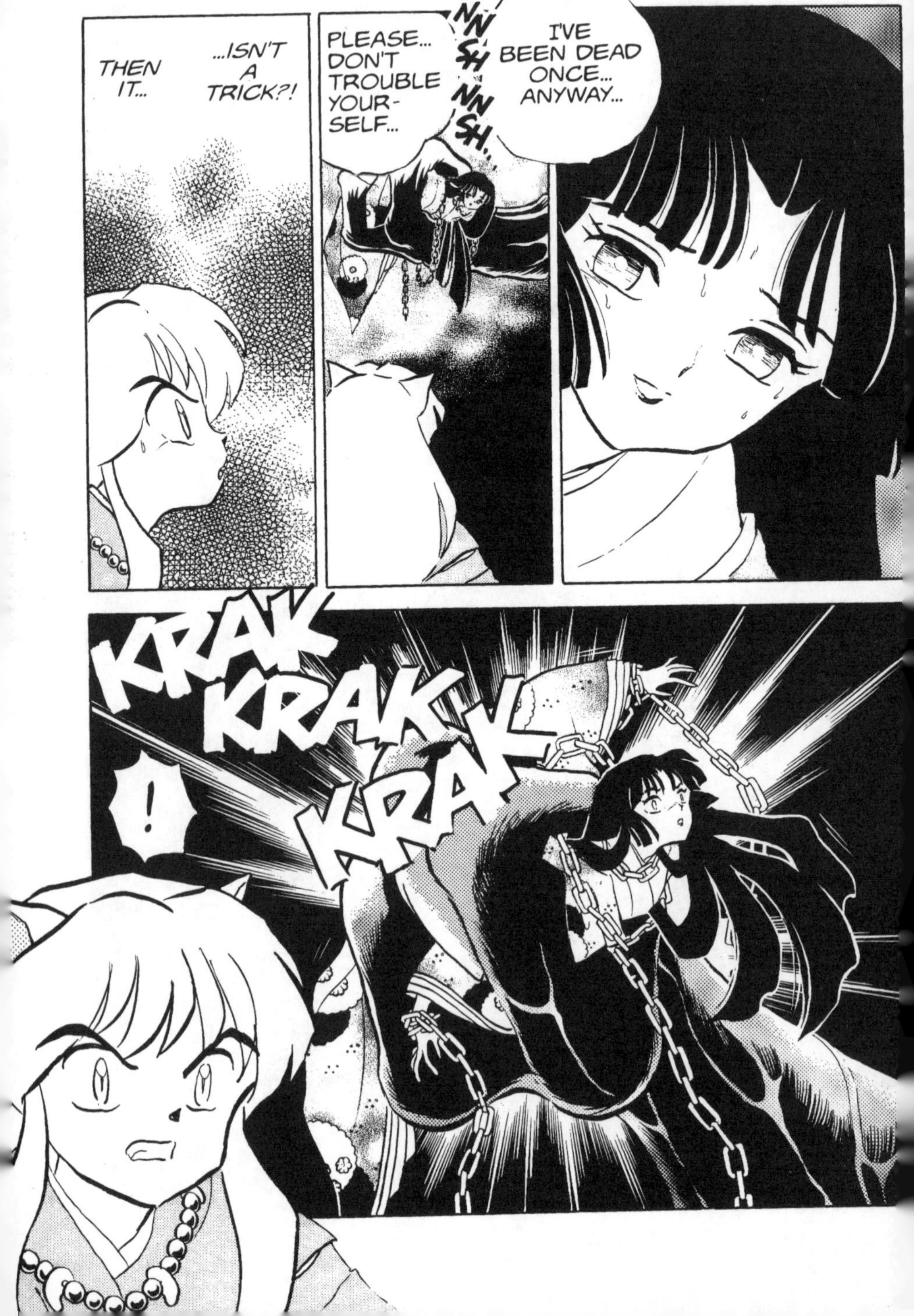
THEN IT...
...ISN'T A TRICK?!
PLEASE... DON'T TROUBLE YOURSELF...
NNSH NNSH...
I'VE BEEN DEAD ONCE... ANYWAY...
KRAK KRAK KRAK KRAK
!

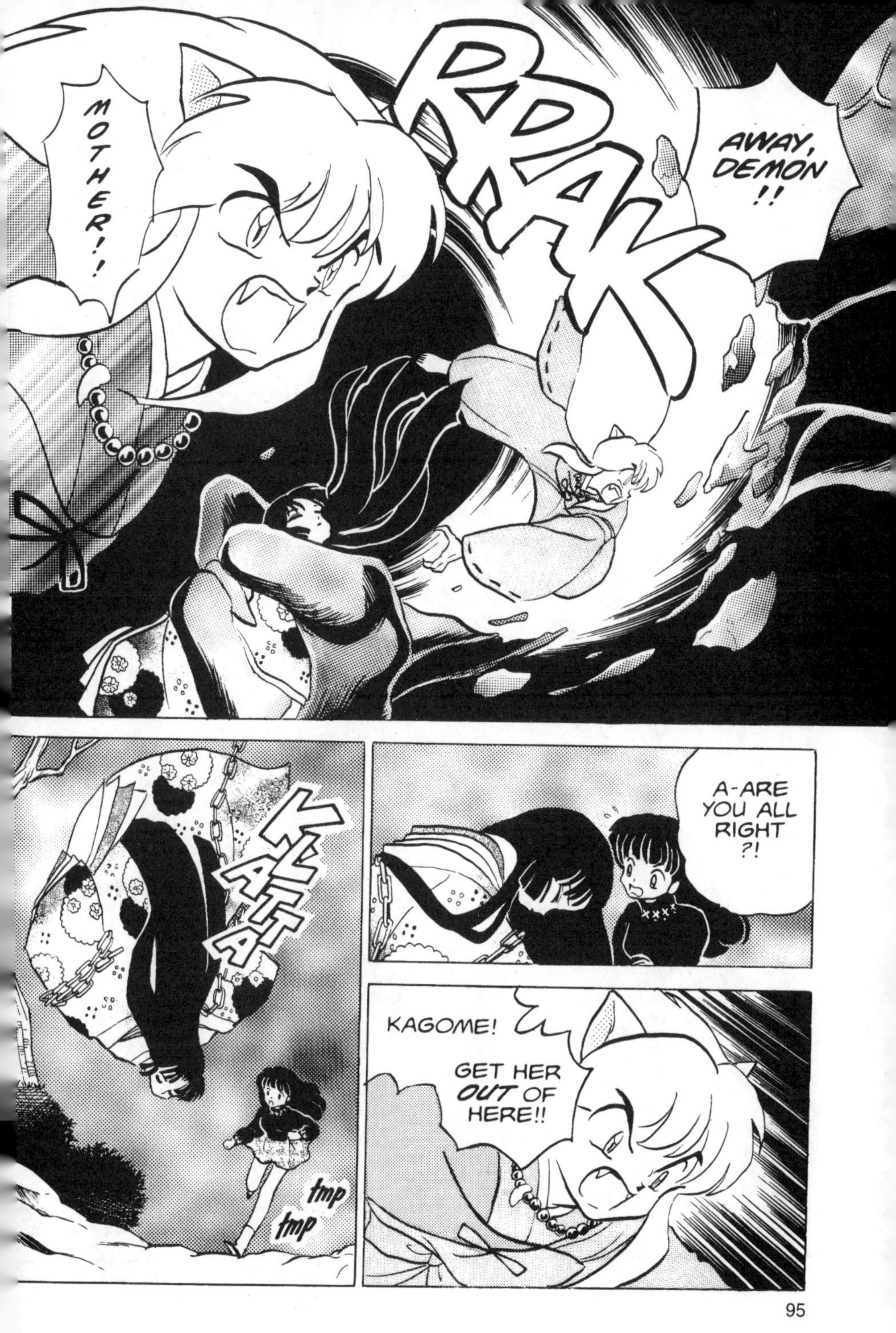
MOTHER!!
BRAK
AWAY, DEMON!!
KLATTA
tmp tmp
A-ARE YOU ALL RIGHT?!
KAGOME!
GET HER OUT OF HERE!!

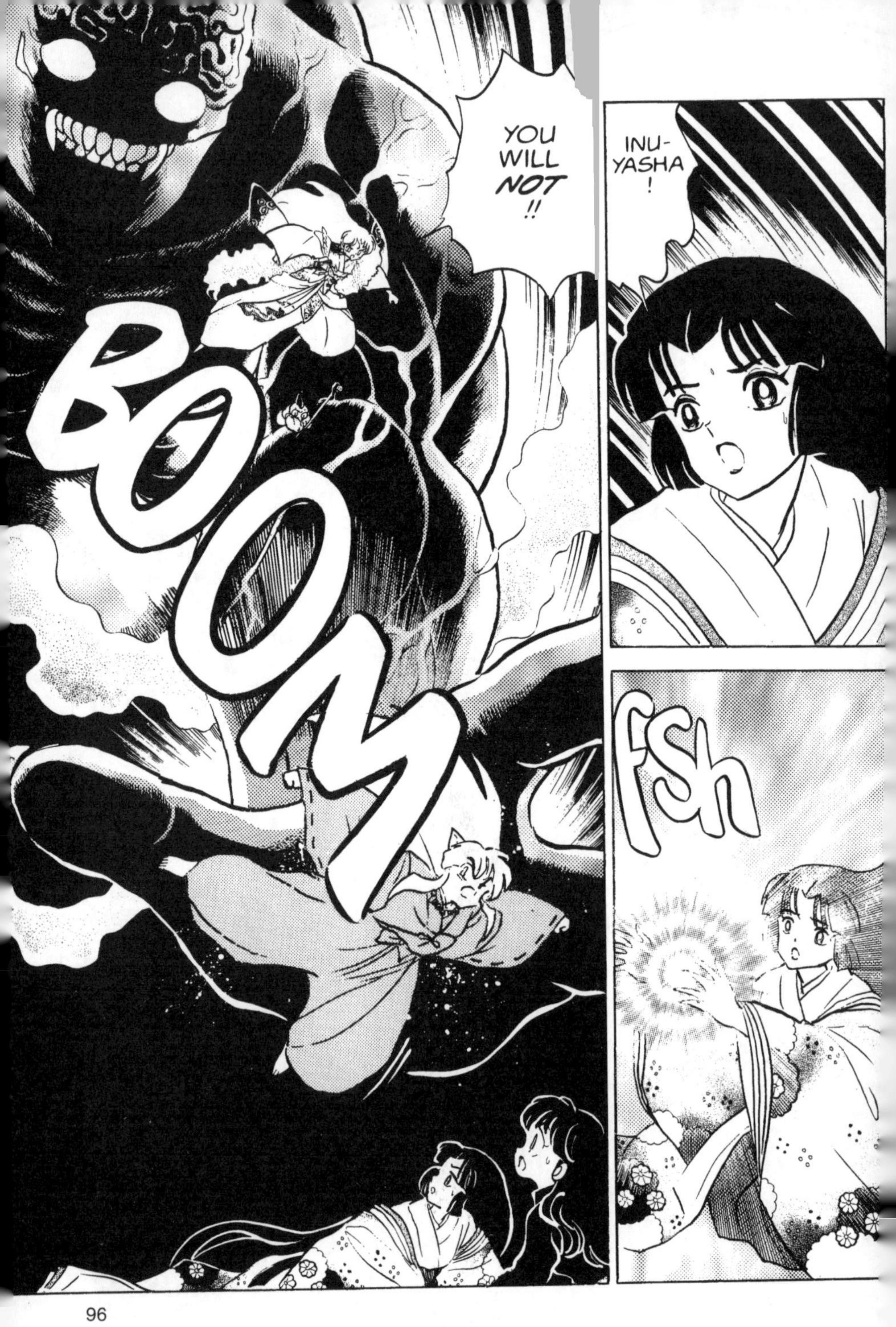
INU-YASHA!
FSH
YOU WILL NOT!!
BOOM

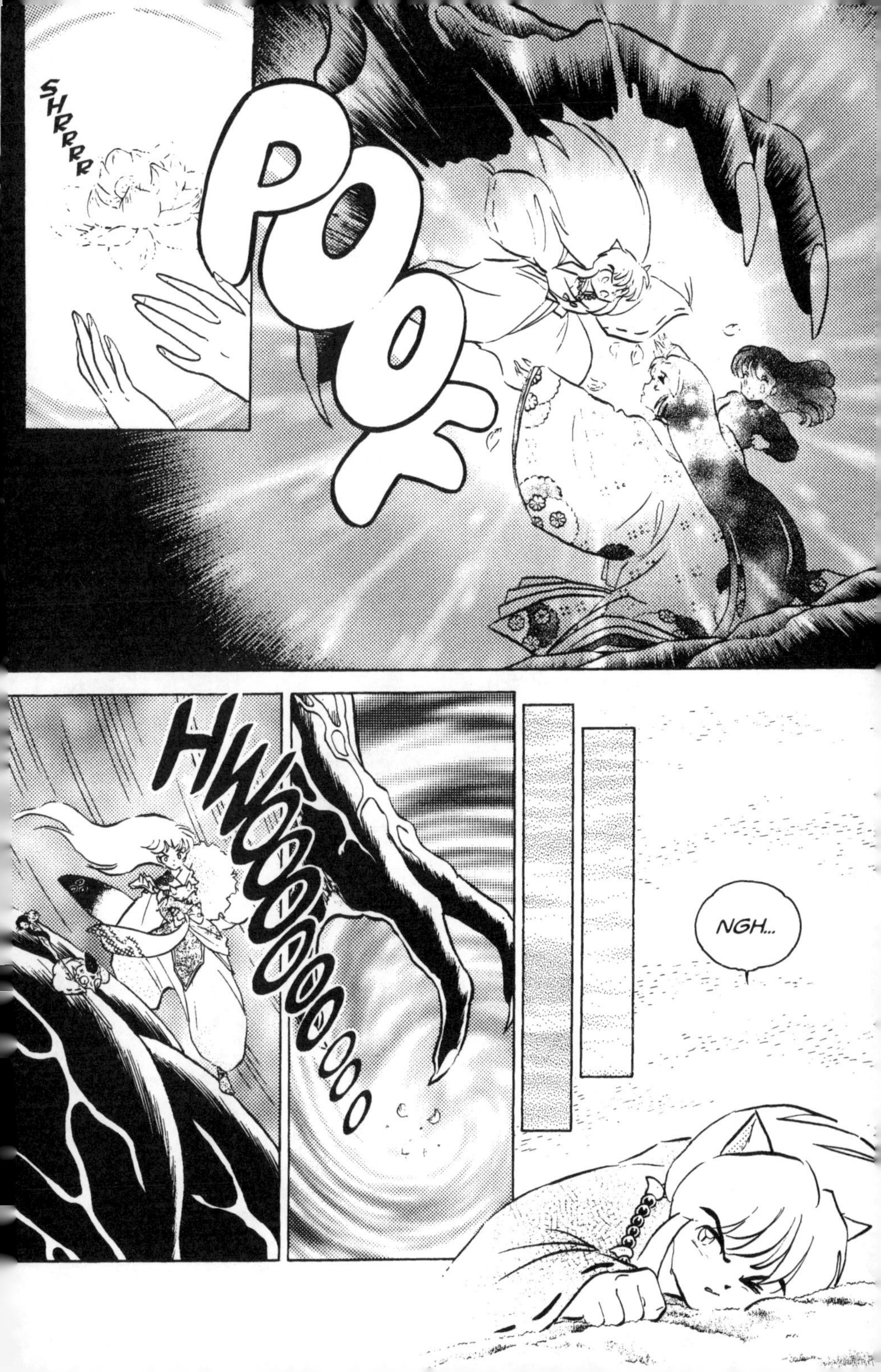
SHRRRR
POOF
HWOOOOOOOO...
NGH...

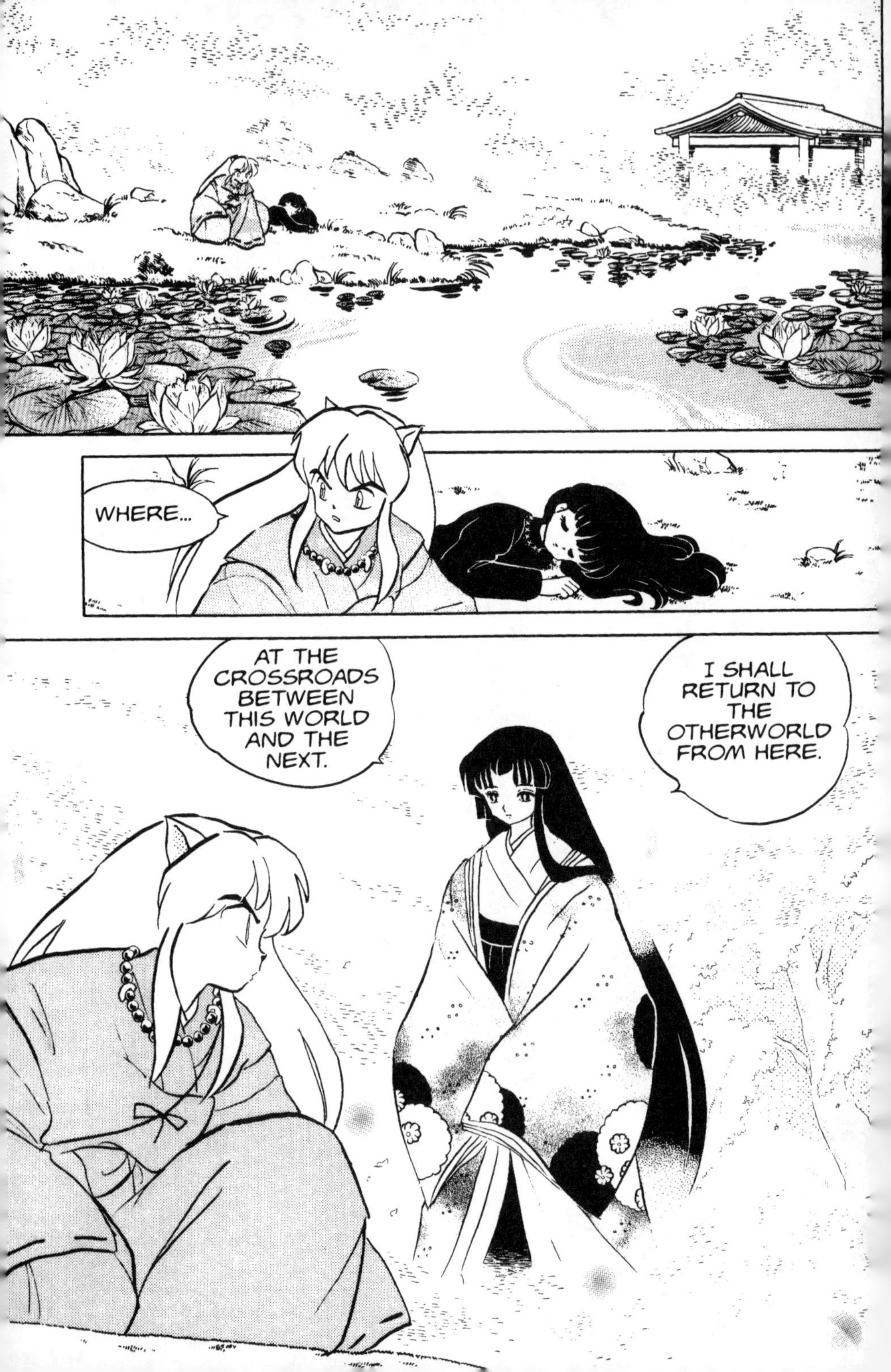
WHERE...
AT THE CROSSROADS BETWEEN THIS WORLD AND THE NEXT.
I SHALL RETURN TO THE OTHERWORLD FROM HERE.

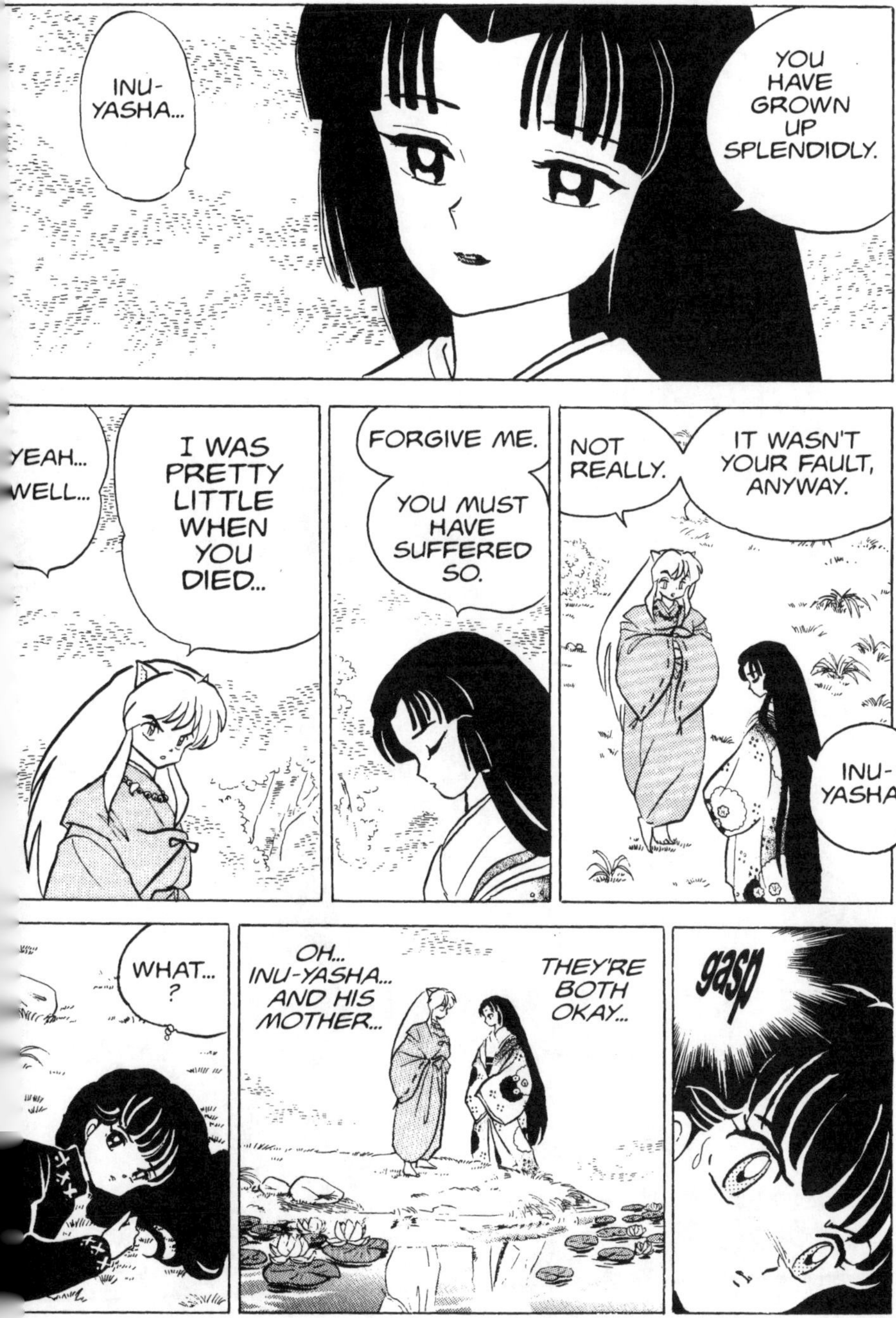

INU-YASHA...
YOU HAVE GROWN UP SPLENDIDLY.
YEAH... WELL...
I WAS PRETTY LITTLE WHEN YOU DIED...
FORGIVE ME.
YOU MUST HAVE SUFFERED SO.
NOT REALLY.
IT WASN'T YOUR FAULT, ANYWAY.
INU-YASHA...
WHAT... ?
OH... INU-YASHA... AND HIS MOTHER...
THEY'RE BOTH OKAY...
gasp

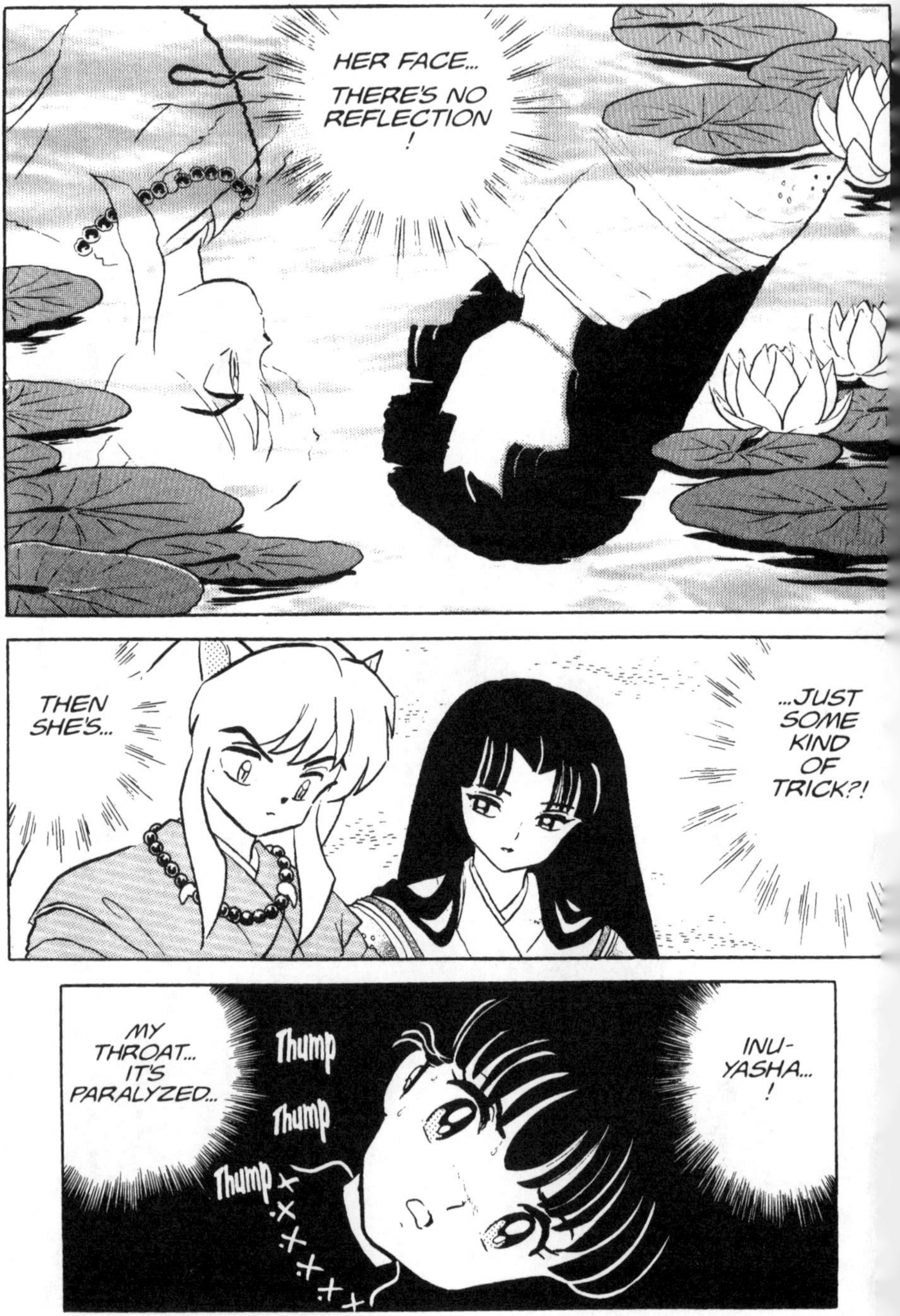
HER FACE... THERE'S NO REFLECTION !
THEN SHE'S...
...JUST SOME KIND OF TRICK?!
MY THROAT... IT'S PARALYZED...
Thump
Thump
Thump
INU-YASHA... !

SCROLL SIX

THE NOTHING WOMAN

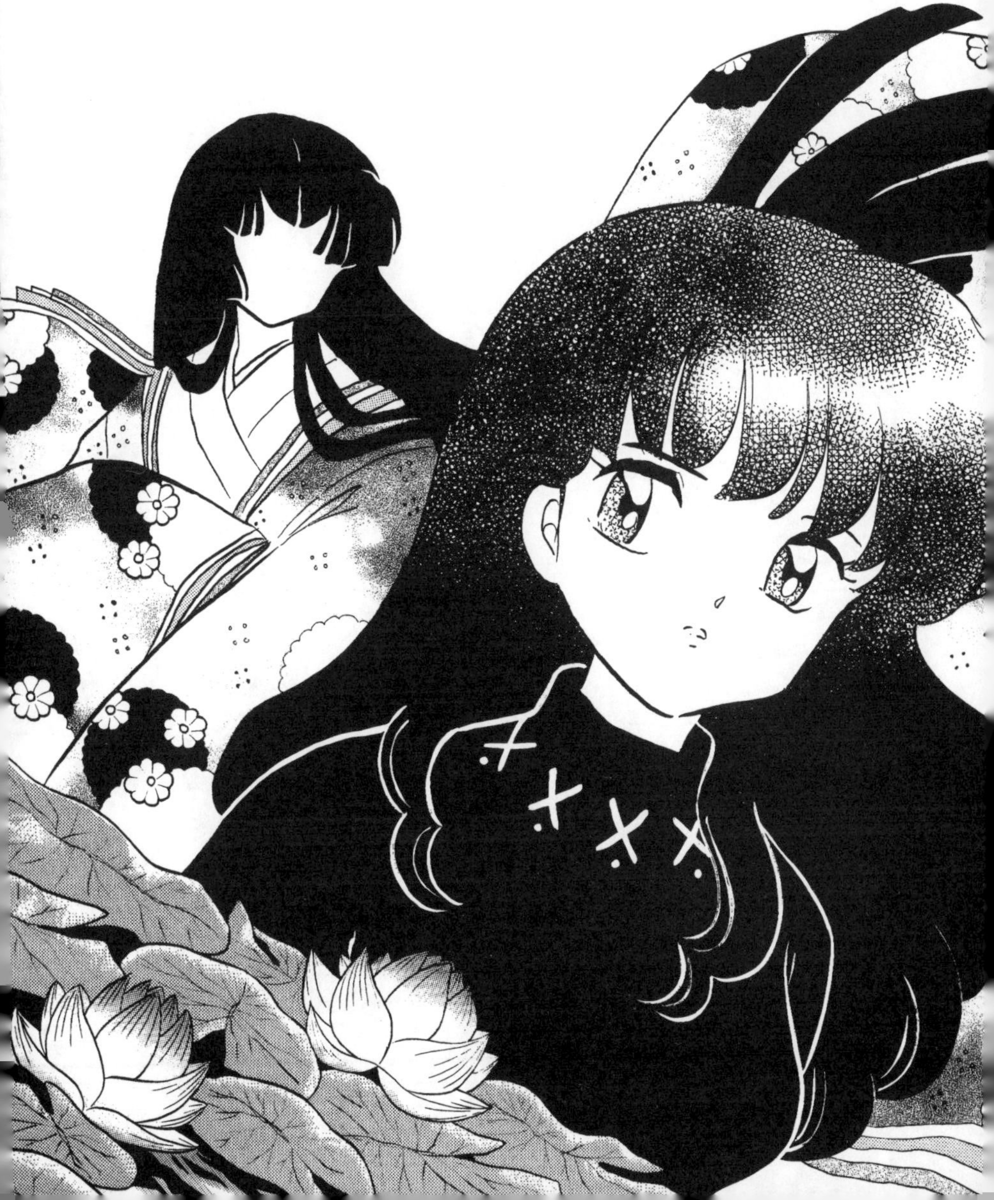

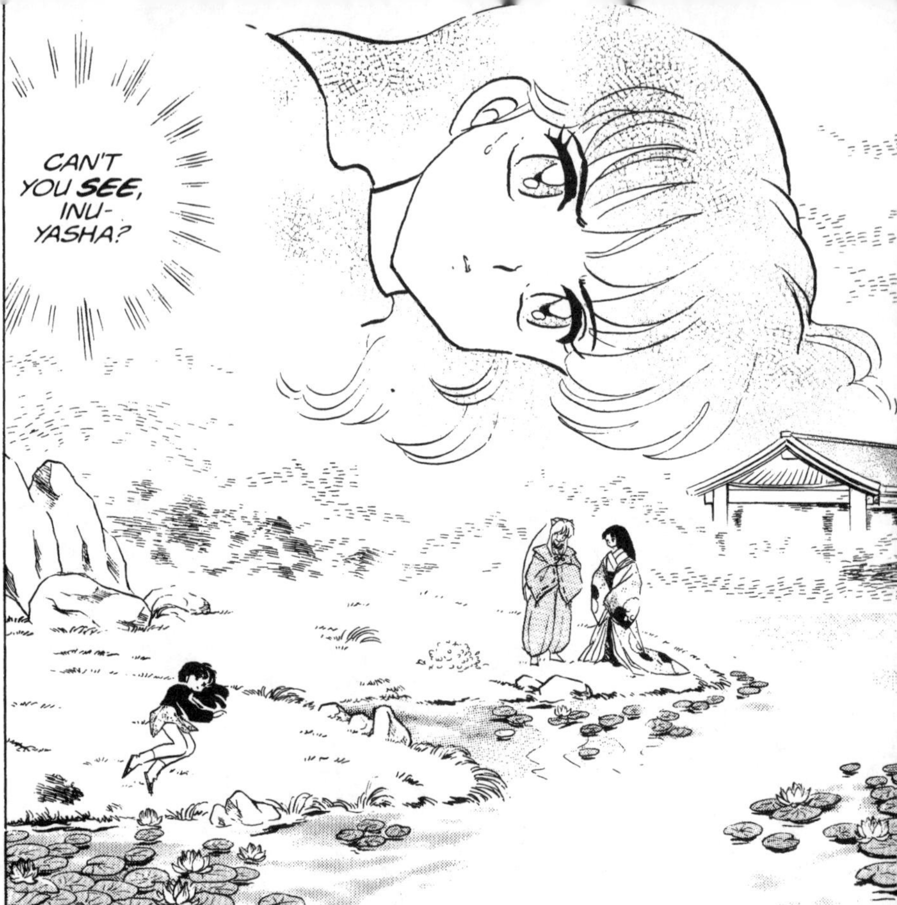
CAN'T YOU SEE, INU-YASHA?
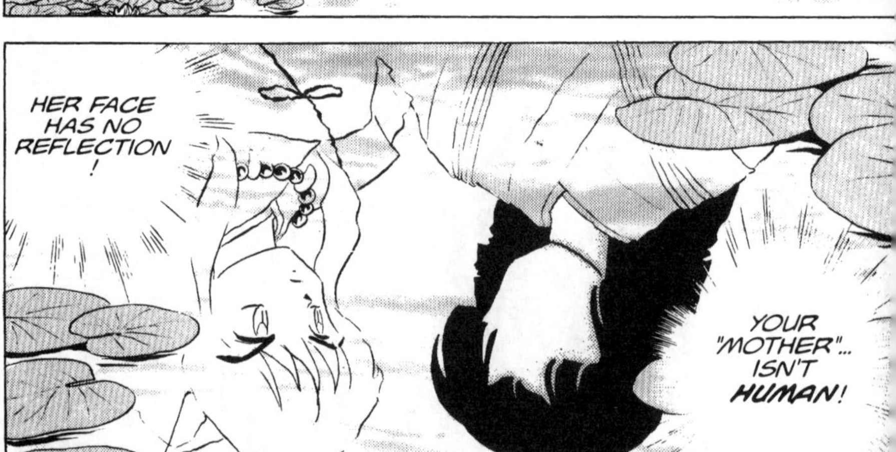
HER FACE HAS NO REFLECTION!
YOUR "MOTHER"... ISN'T HUMAN!

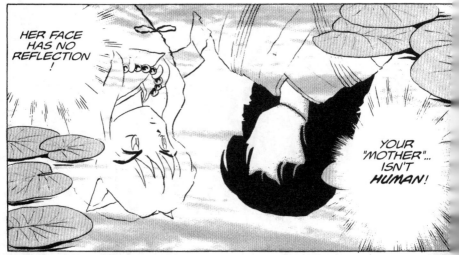

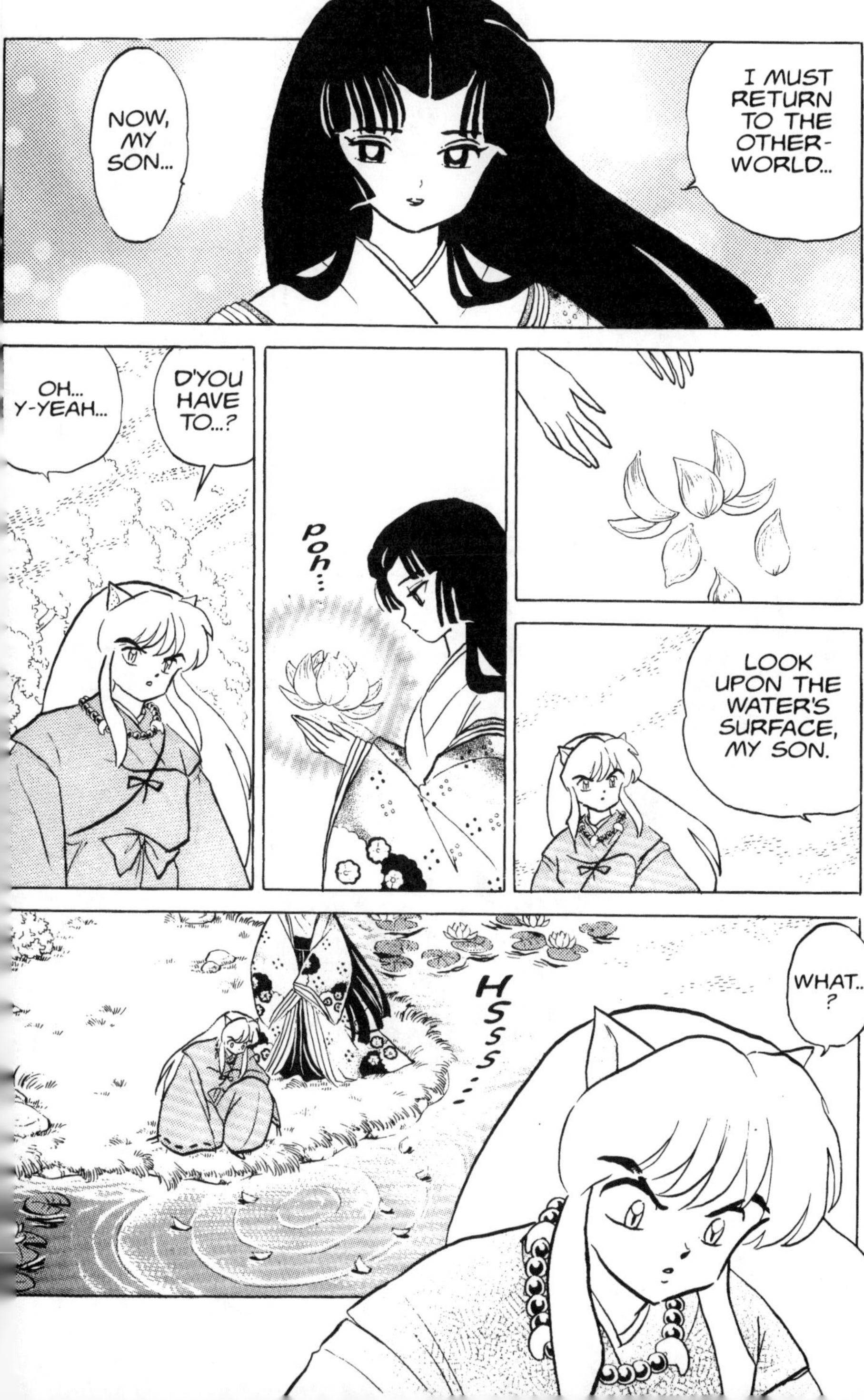
NOW, MY SON...
I MUST RETURN TO THE OTHER-WORLD...
OH... Y-YEAH...
D'YOU HAVE TO...?
poh...
LOOK UPON THE WATER'S SURFACE, MY SON.
HSSS...
WHAT...?

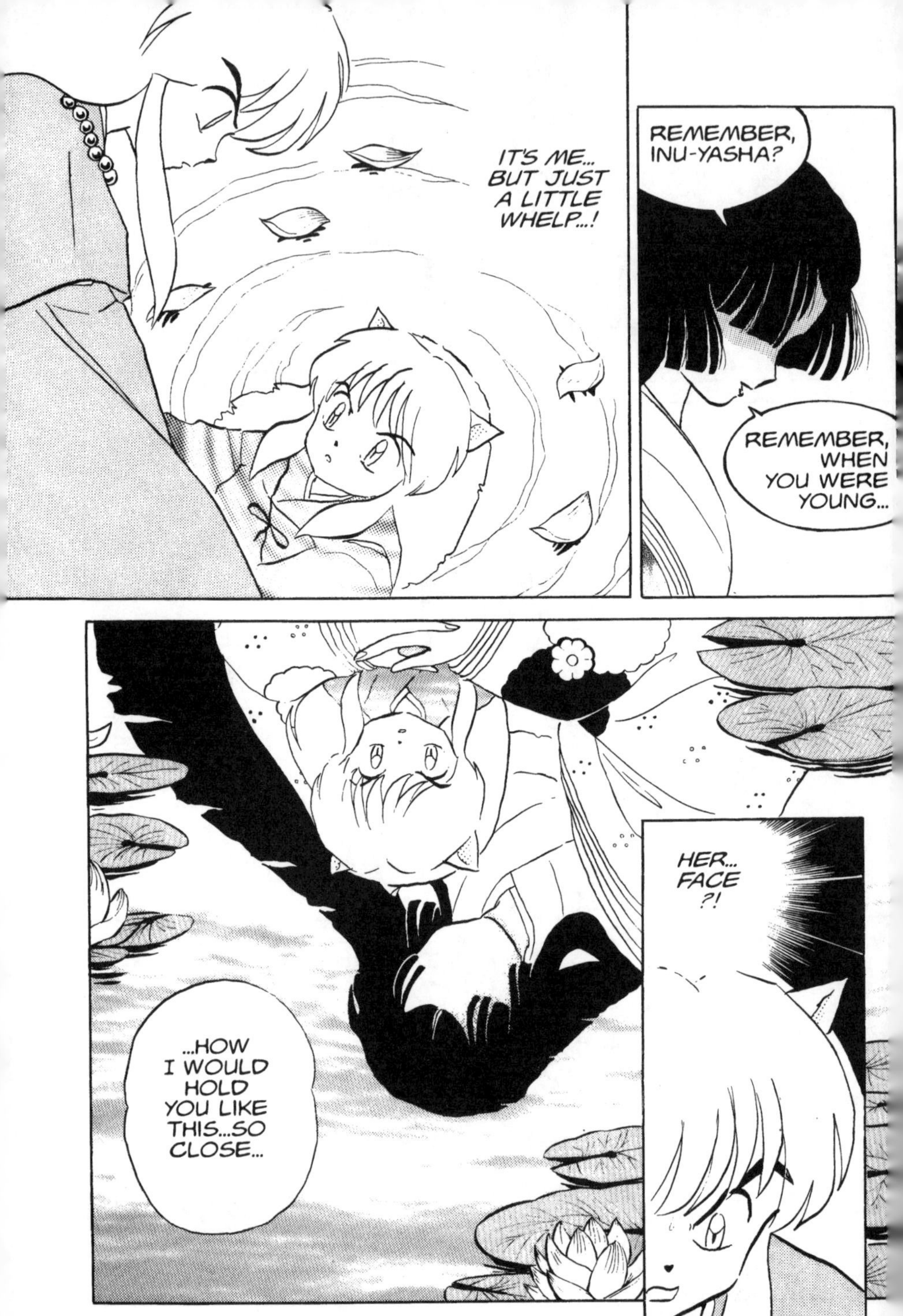
IT'S ME... BUT JUST A LITTLE WHELP...!
REMEMBER, INU-YASHA?
REMEMBER, WHEN YOU WERE YOUNG...
...HOW I WOULD HOLD YOU LIKE THIS...SO CLOSE...
HER... FACE ?!

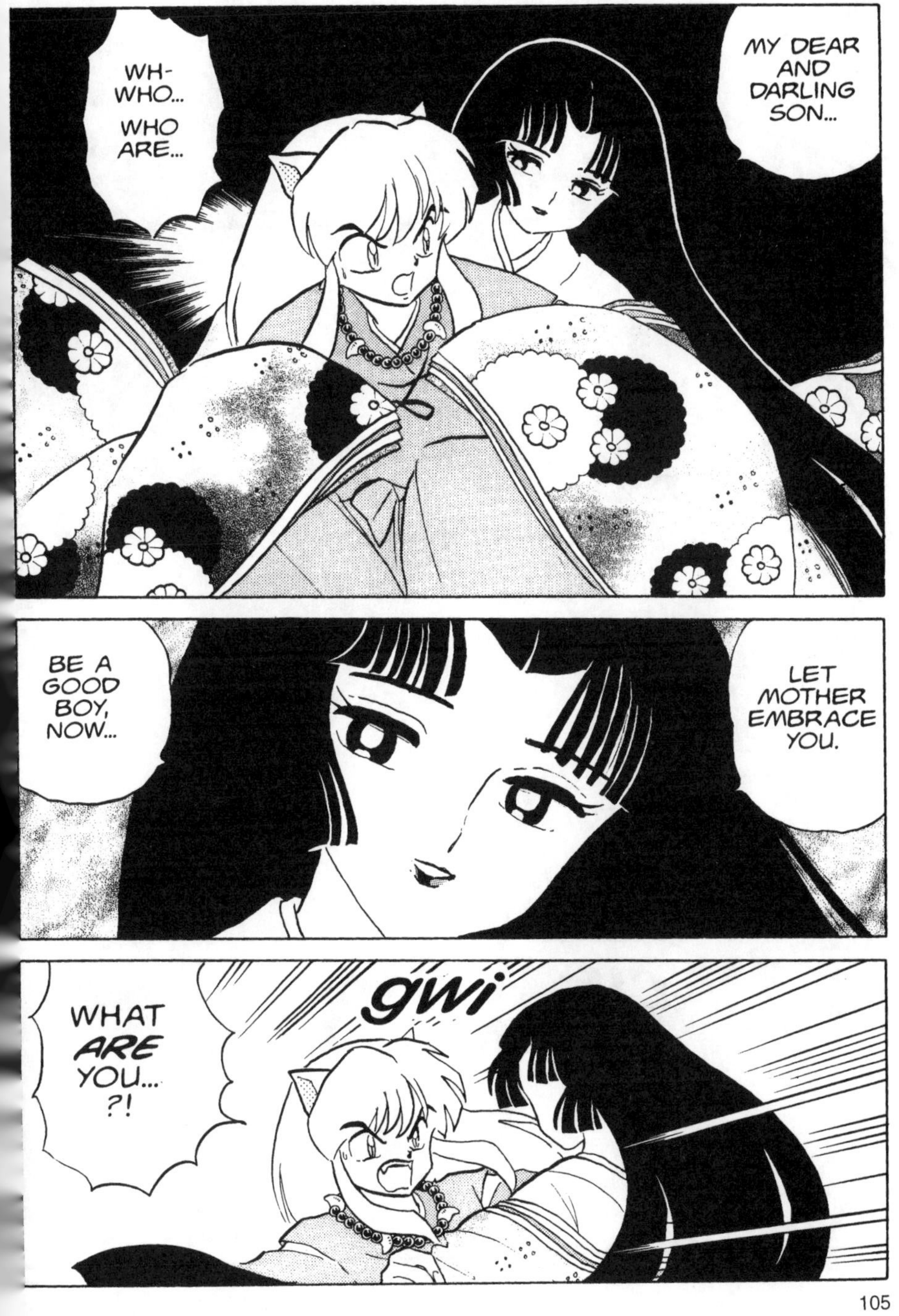
WH- WHO... WHO ARE...
MY DEAR AND DARLING SON...
BE A GOOD BOY, NOW...
LET MOTHER EMBRACE YOU.
WHAT ARE YOU... ?!
gwi

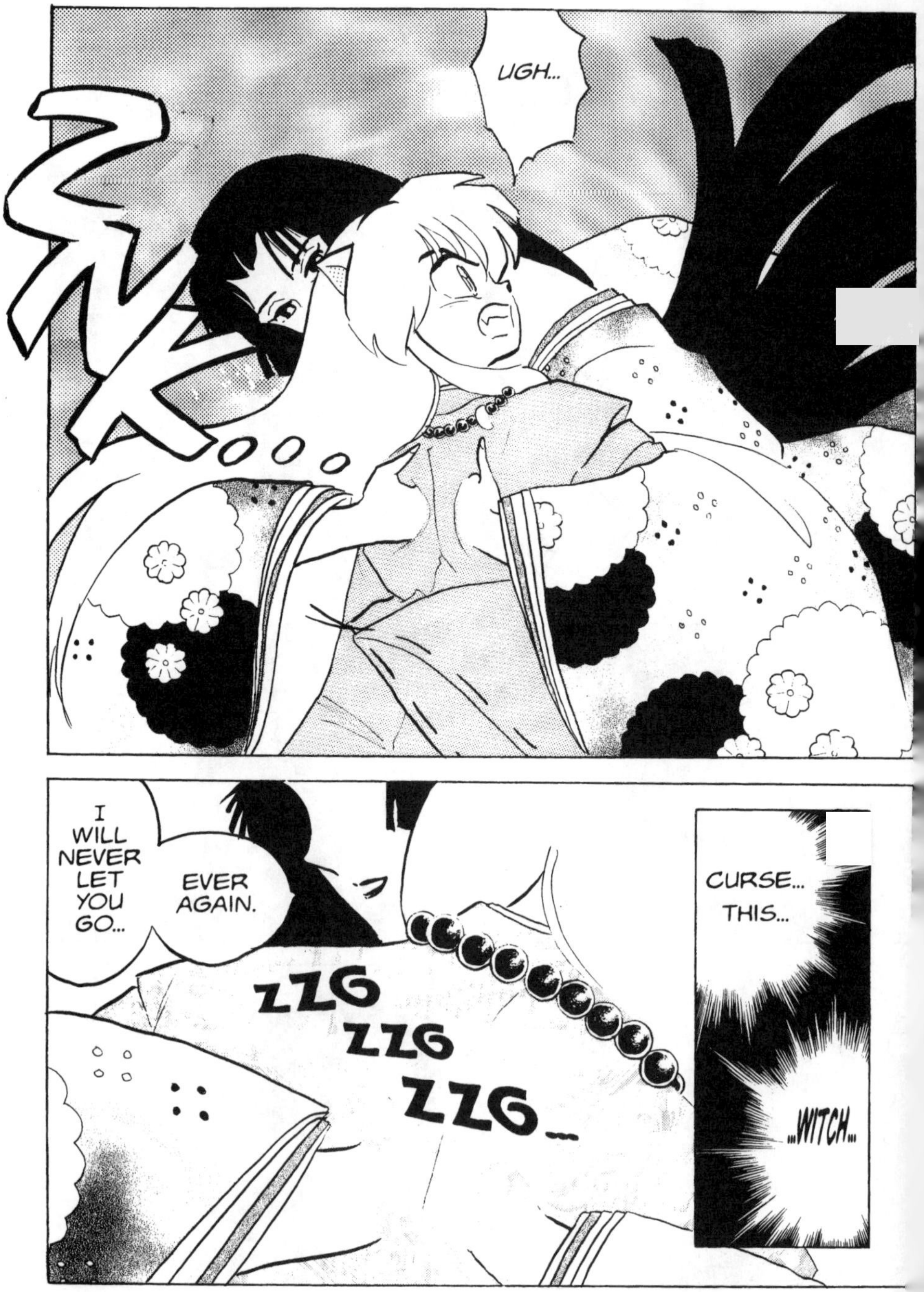
UGH...
I WILL NEVER LET YOU GO...
EVER AGAIN.
ZZG ZZG ZZG...
CURSE... THIS...
...WITCH...

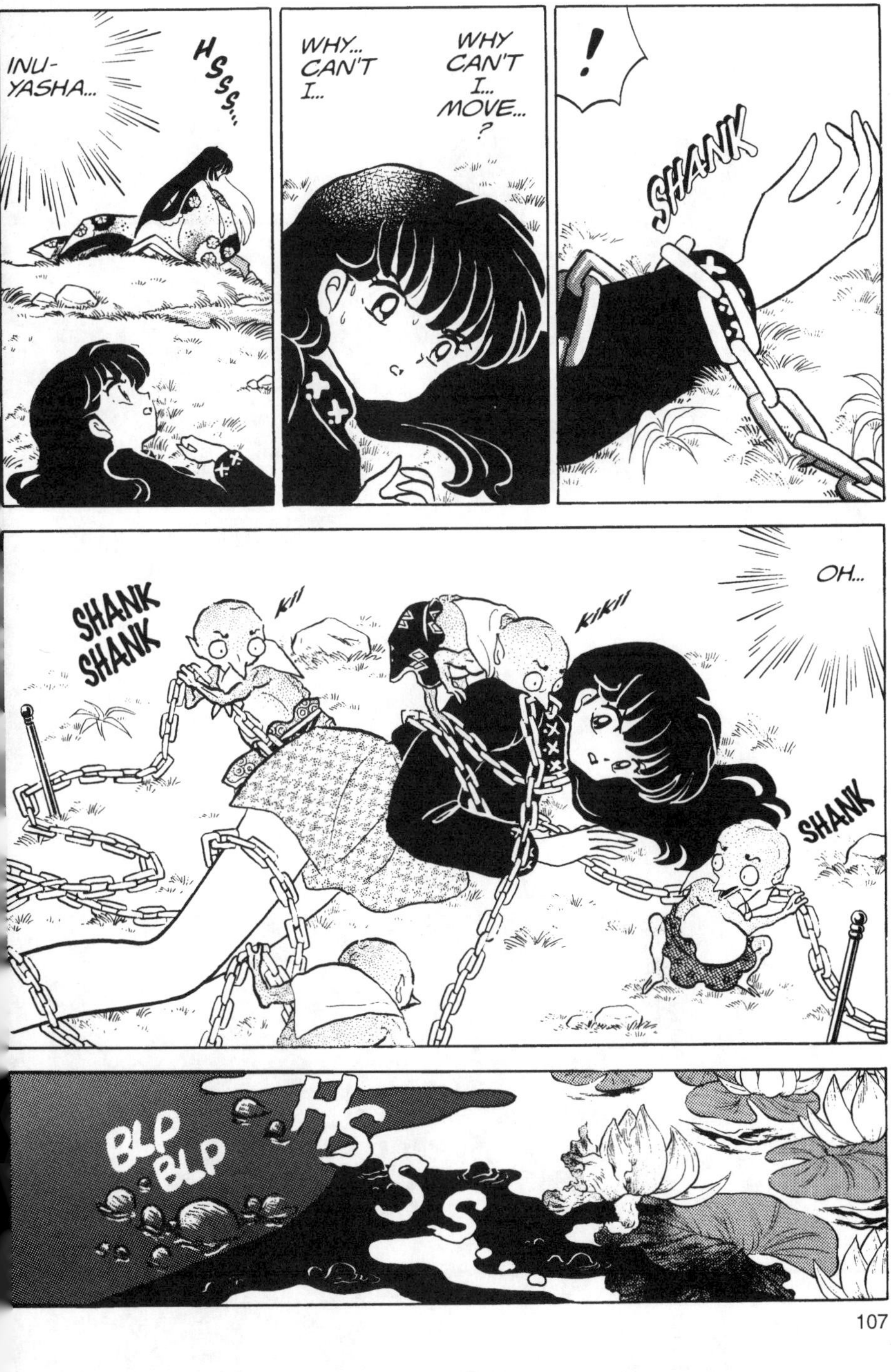
INU-YASHA...
HSSS...
WHY... CAN'T I...
WHY CAN'T I... MOVE...?
!
SHANK
SHANK SHANK
KII
KIKII
OH...
SHANK
BLP BLP
HSSS

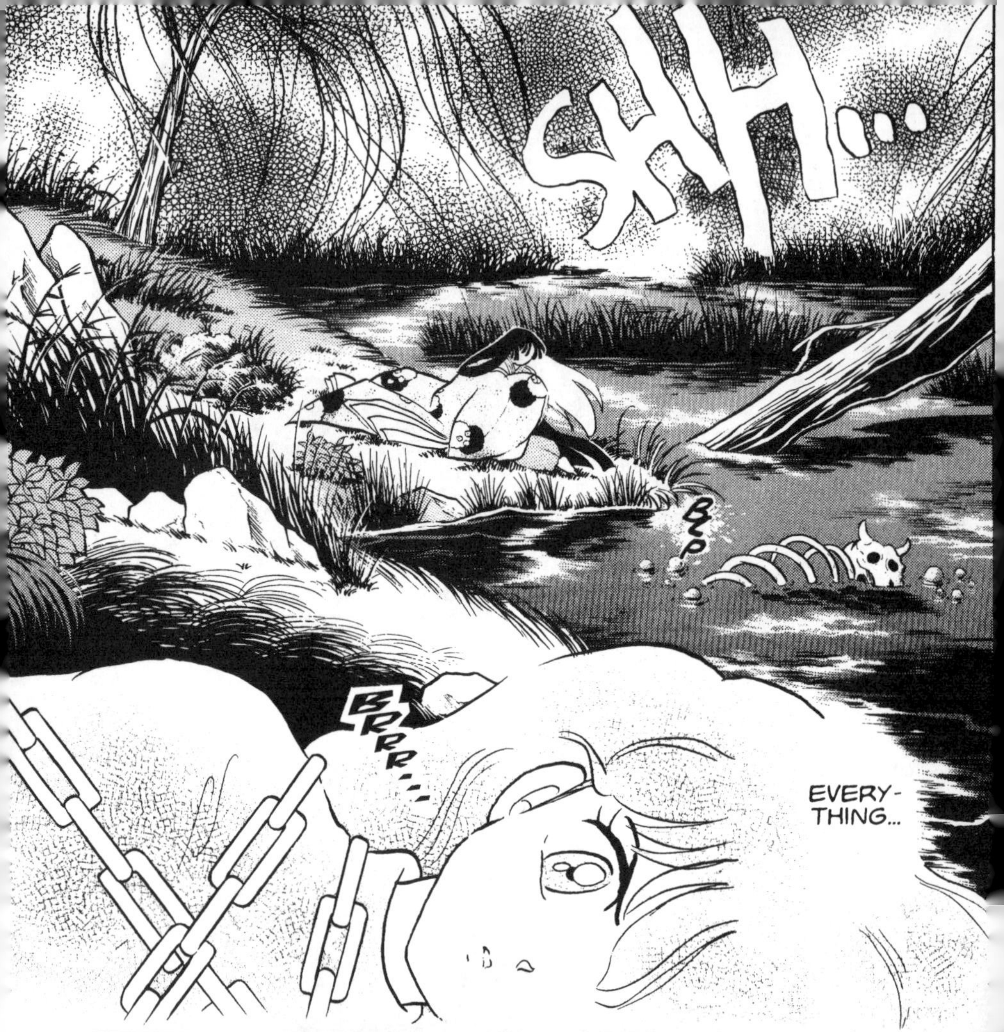
SHH...
BLP
BRRR...
EVERY-THING...
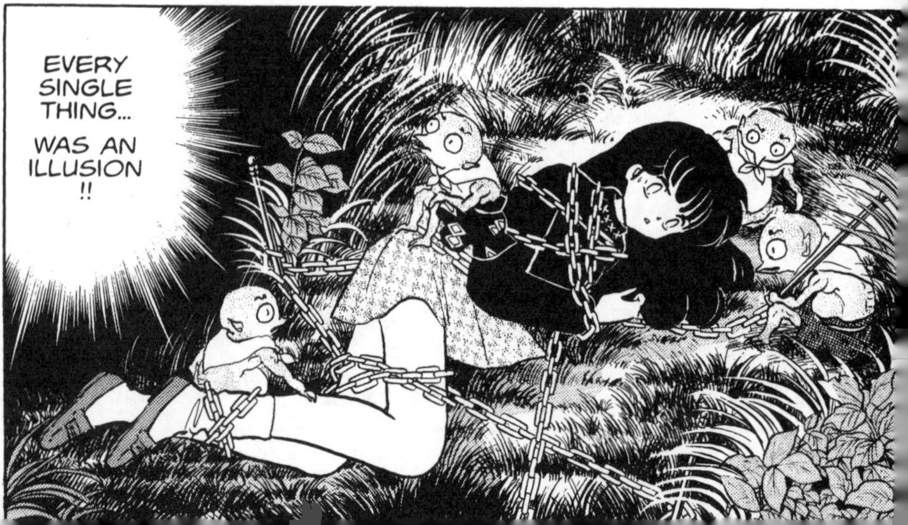
EVERY SINGLE THING... WAS AN ILLUSION !!

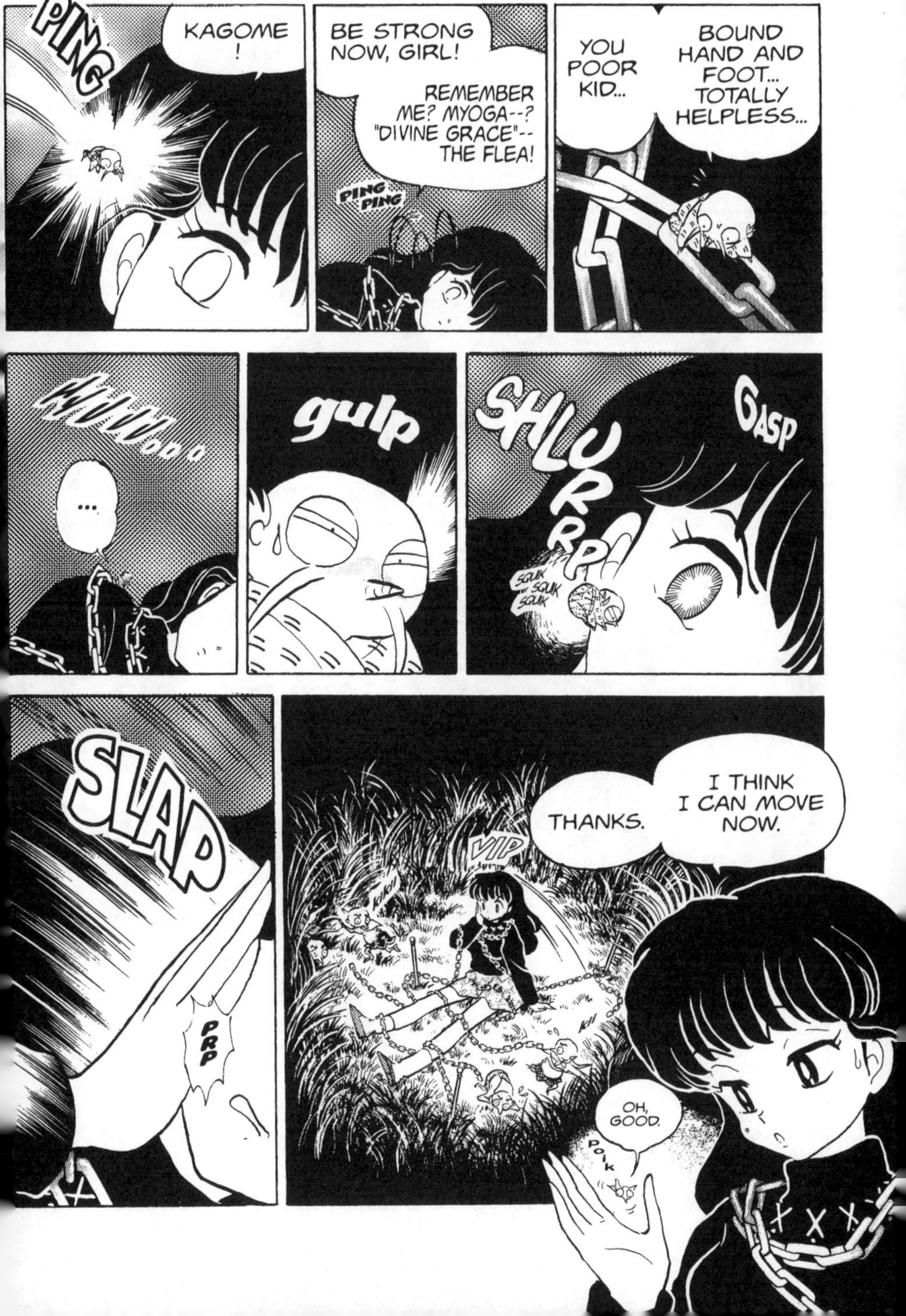
PING
KAGOME !
BE STRONG NOW, GIRL!
REMEMBER ME? MYOGA--? "DIVINE GRACE"-- THE FLEA!
PING PING
YOU POOR KID...
BOUND HAND AND FOOT... TOTALLY HELPLESS...
...
gulp
SHLURRP
GASP
SQUIK SQUIK SQUIK
SLAP
PRP
VIP
THANKS.
I THINK I CAN MOVE NOW.
OH, GOOD.
POIK

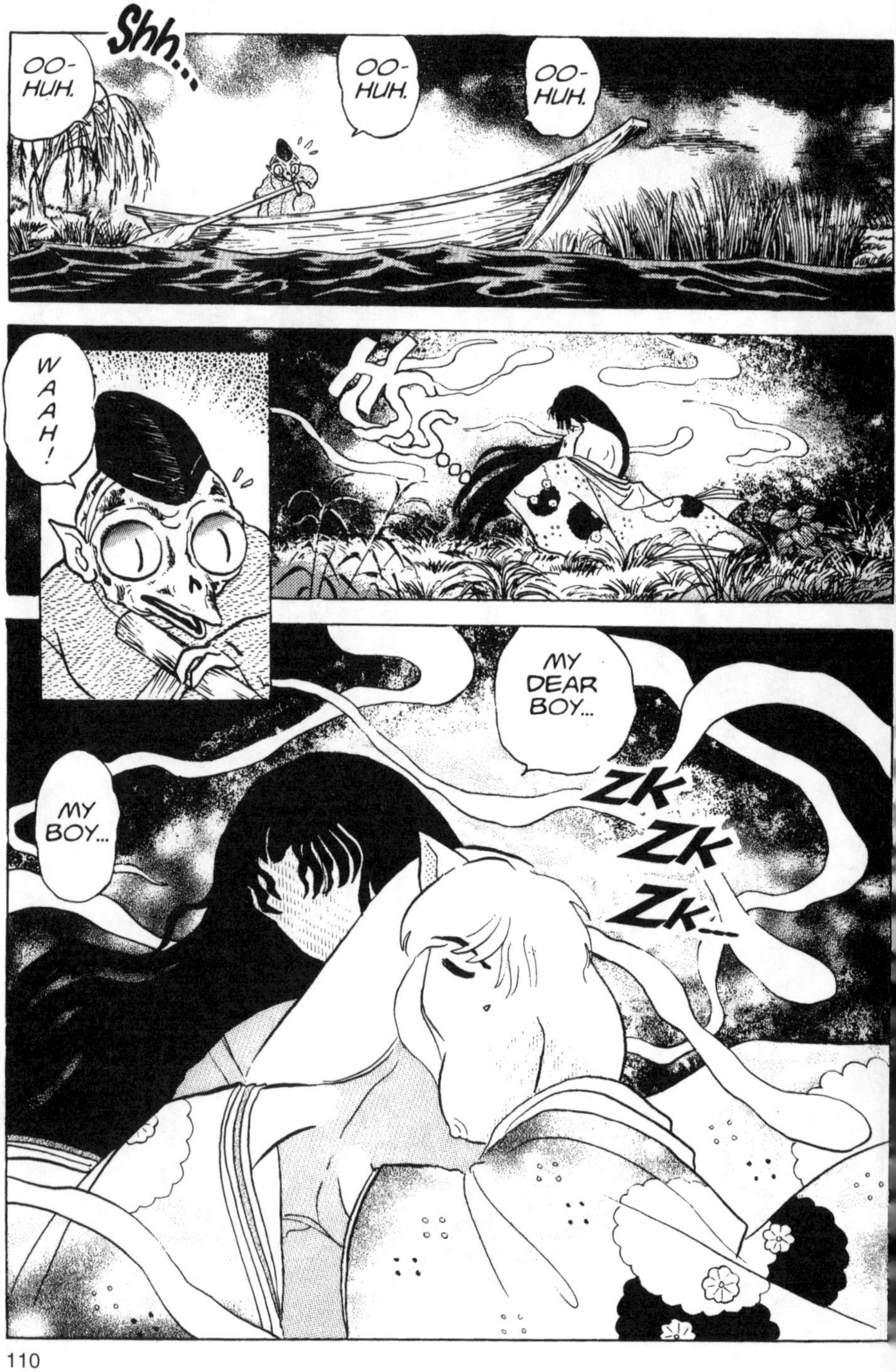
Shh...
OO-HUH.
OO-HUH.
OO-HUH.
WAAAH!
MY DEAR BOY...
MY BOY...
ZK ZK ZK...

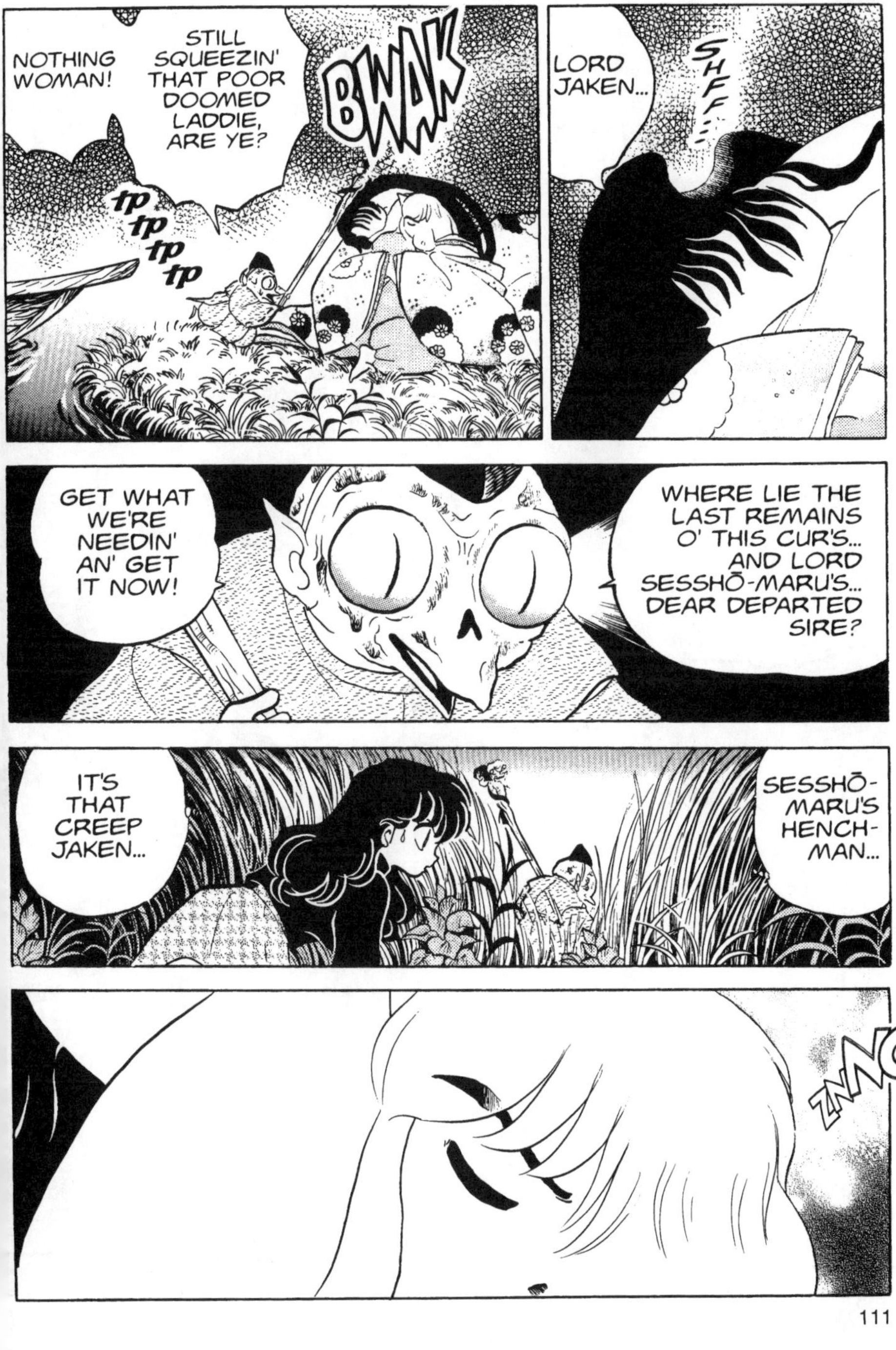
NOTHING WOMAN!
STILL SQUEEZIN' THAT POOR DOOMED LADDIE, ARE YE?
BWAK
tp tp tp tp
LORD JAKEN...
SHFF...
GET WHAT WE'RE NEEDIN' AN' GET IT NOW!
WHERE LIE THE LAST REMAINS O' THIS CUR'S... AND LORD SESSHŌ-MARU'S... DEAR DEPARTED SIRE?
IT'S THAT CREEP JAKEN...
SESSHŌ-MARU'S HENCHMAN...
ZNNG...

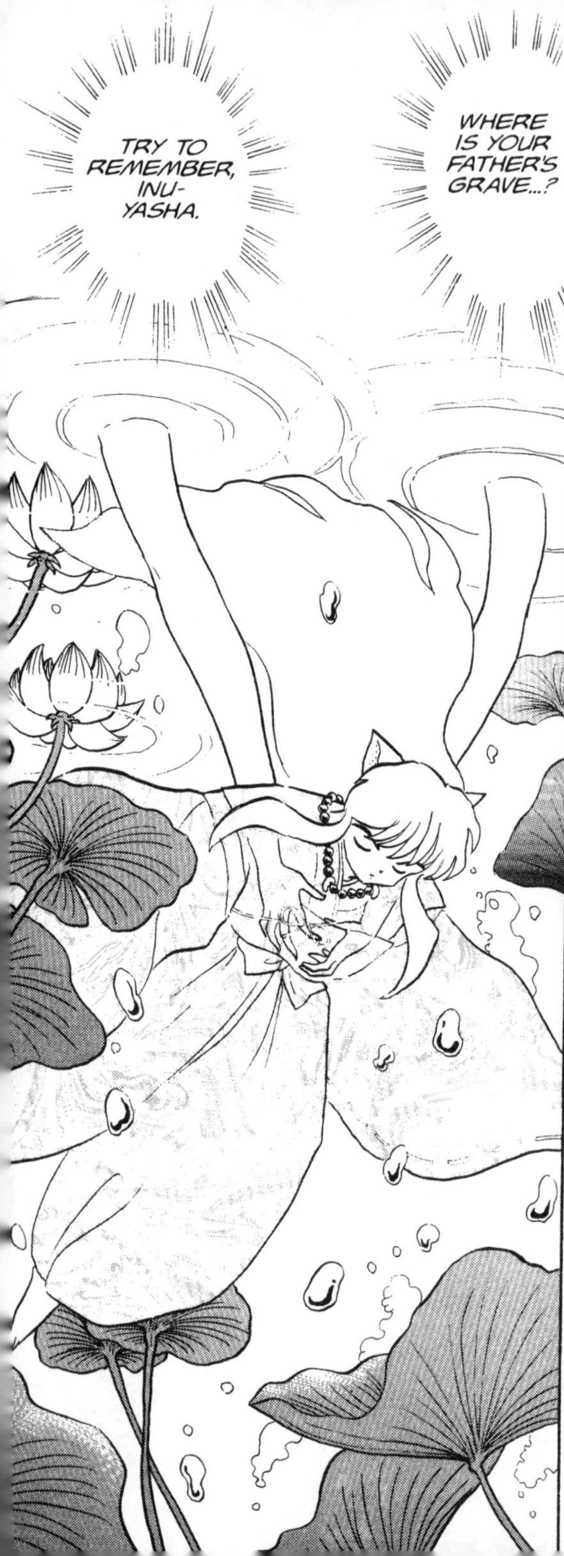
TRY TO REMEMBER, INU-YASHA.
WHERE IS YOUR FATHER'S GRAVE...?
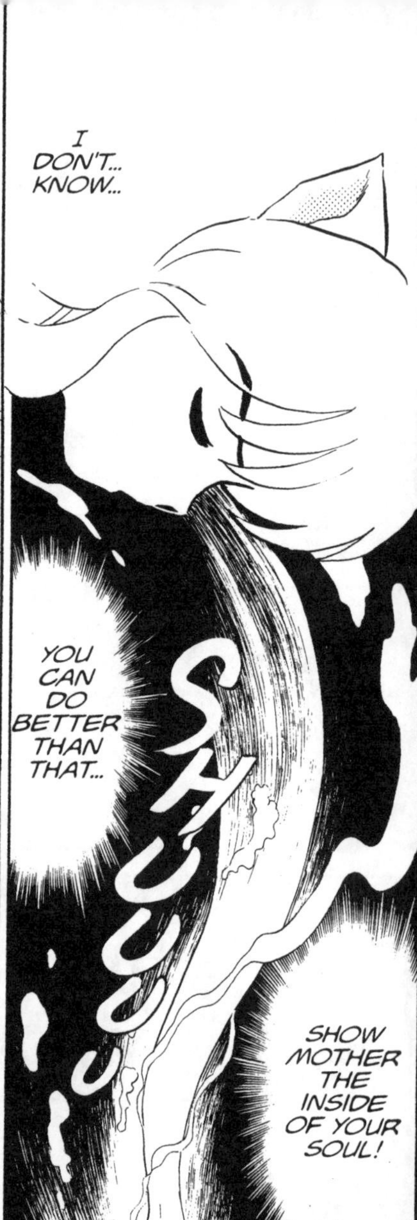
I DON'T... KNOW...
YOU CAN DO BETTER THAN THAT...
SHUUUU
SHOW MOTHER THE INSIDE OF YOUR SOUL!

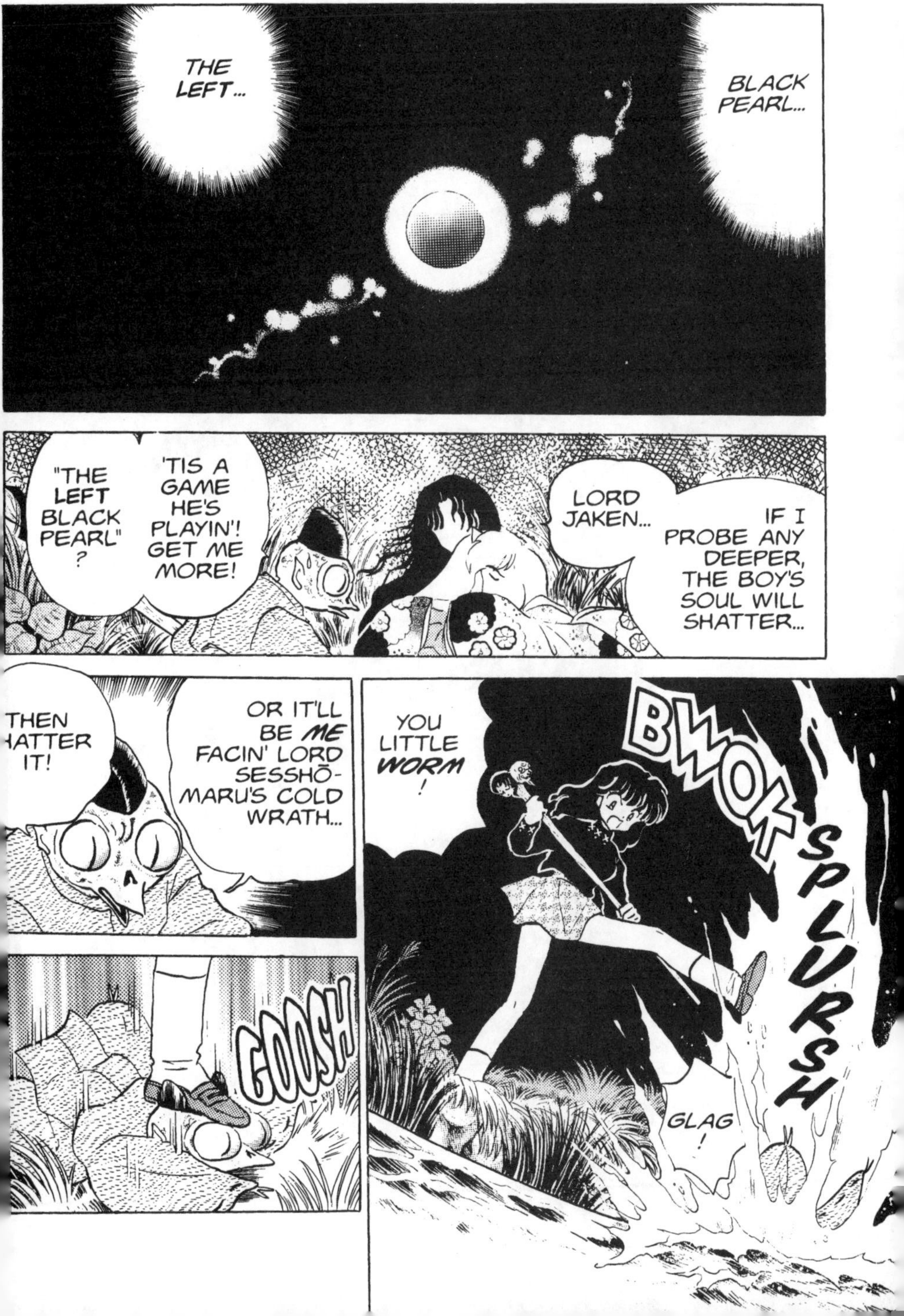
THE LEFT...
BLACK PEARL...
"THE LEFT BLACK PEARL"?
'TIS A GAME HE'S PLAYIN'! GET ME MORE!
LORD JAKEN...
IF I PROBE ANY DEEPER, THE BOY'S SOUL WILL SHATTER...
THEN HATTER IT!
OR IT'LL BE ME FACIN' LORD SESSHŌ-MARU'S COLD WRATH...
GOOSH
YOU LITTLE WORM!
BWOK
SPLURSH
GLAG!

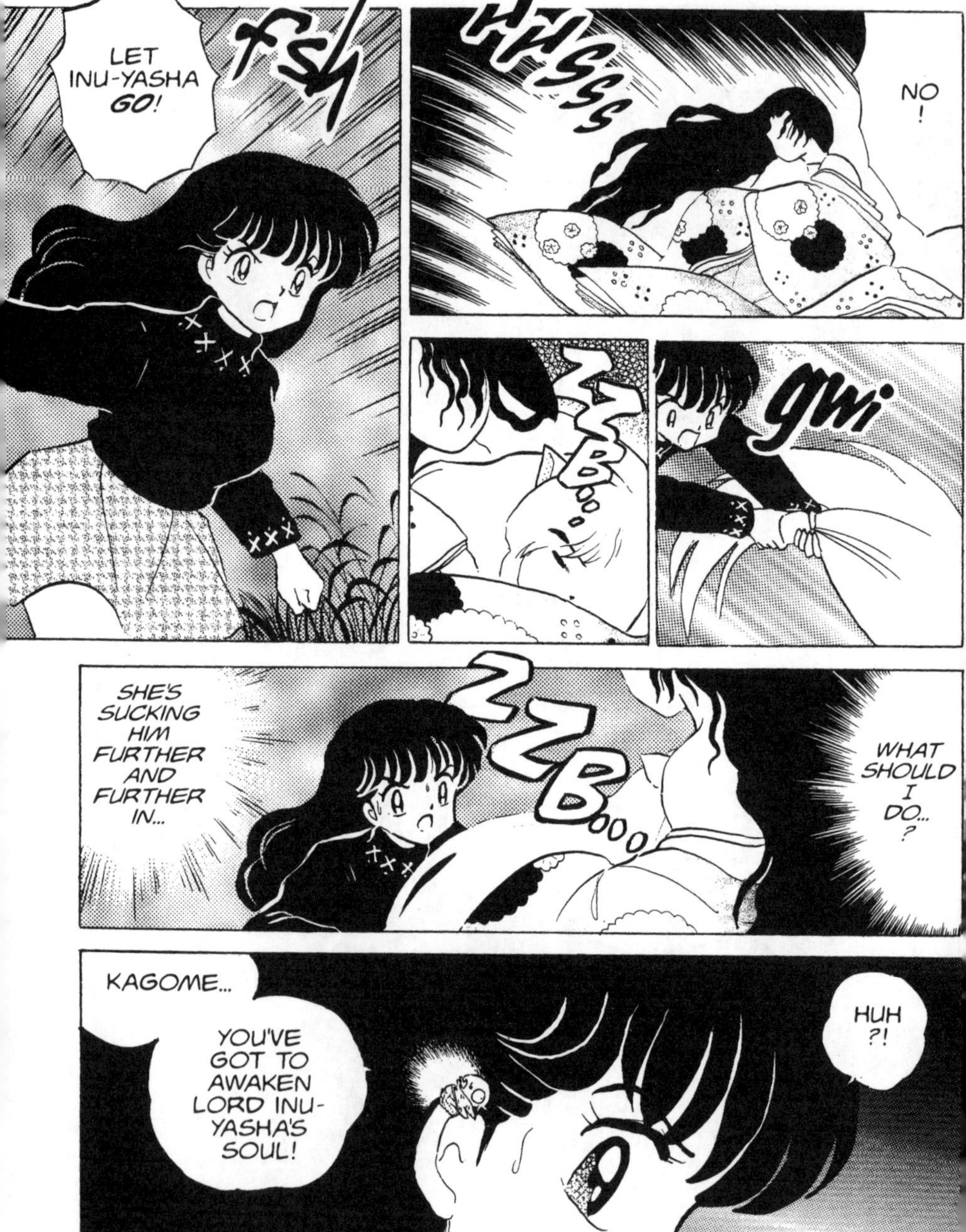
LET INU-YASHA GO!
fsh
hhsss
NO!
ZZBooo
gwi
SHE'S SUCKING HIM FURTHER AND FURTHER IN...
ZZBooo
WHAT SHOULD I DO...?
KAGOME...
YOU'VE GOT TO AWAKEN LORD INU-YASHA'S SOUL!
HUH?!

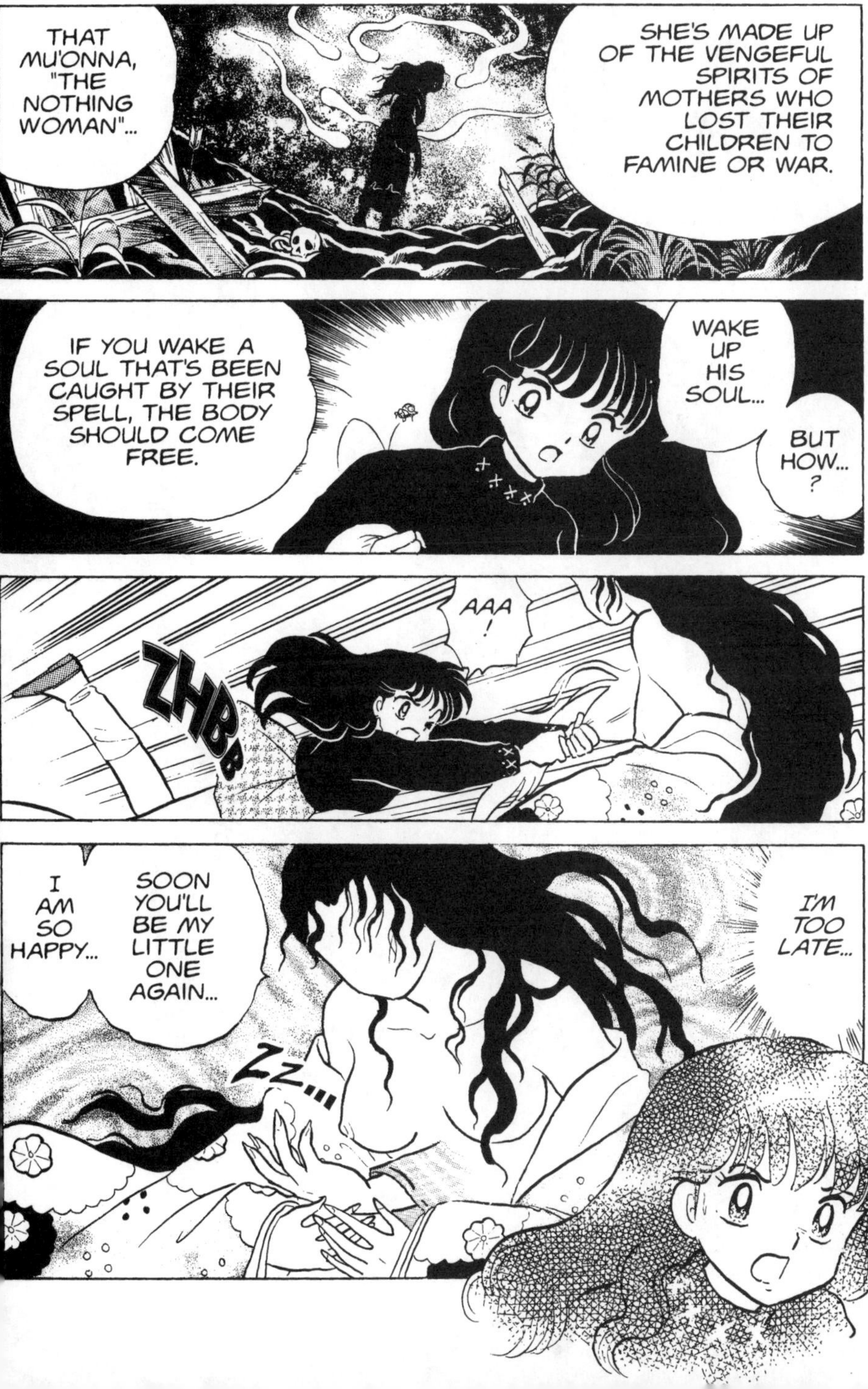
THAT MU'ONNA, "THE NOTHING WOMAN"...
SHE'S MADE UP OF THE VENGEFUL SPIRITS OF MOTHERS WHO LOST THEIR CHILDREN TO FAMINE OR WAR.
IF YOU WAKE A SOUL THAT'S BEEN CAUGHT BY THEIR SPELL, THE BODY SHOULD COME FREE.
WAKE UP HIS SOUL...
BUT HOW... ?
ZHBB
AAA!
I AM SO HAPPY...
SOON YOU'LL BE MY LITTLE ONE AGAIN...
ZZ...
I'M TOO LATE...

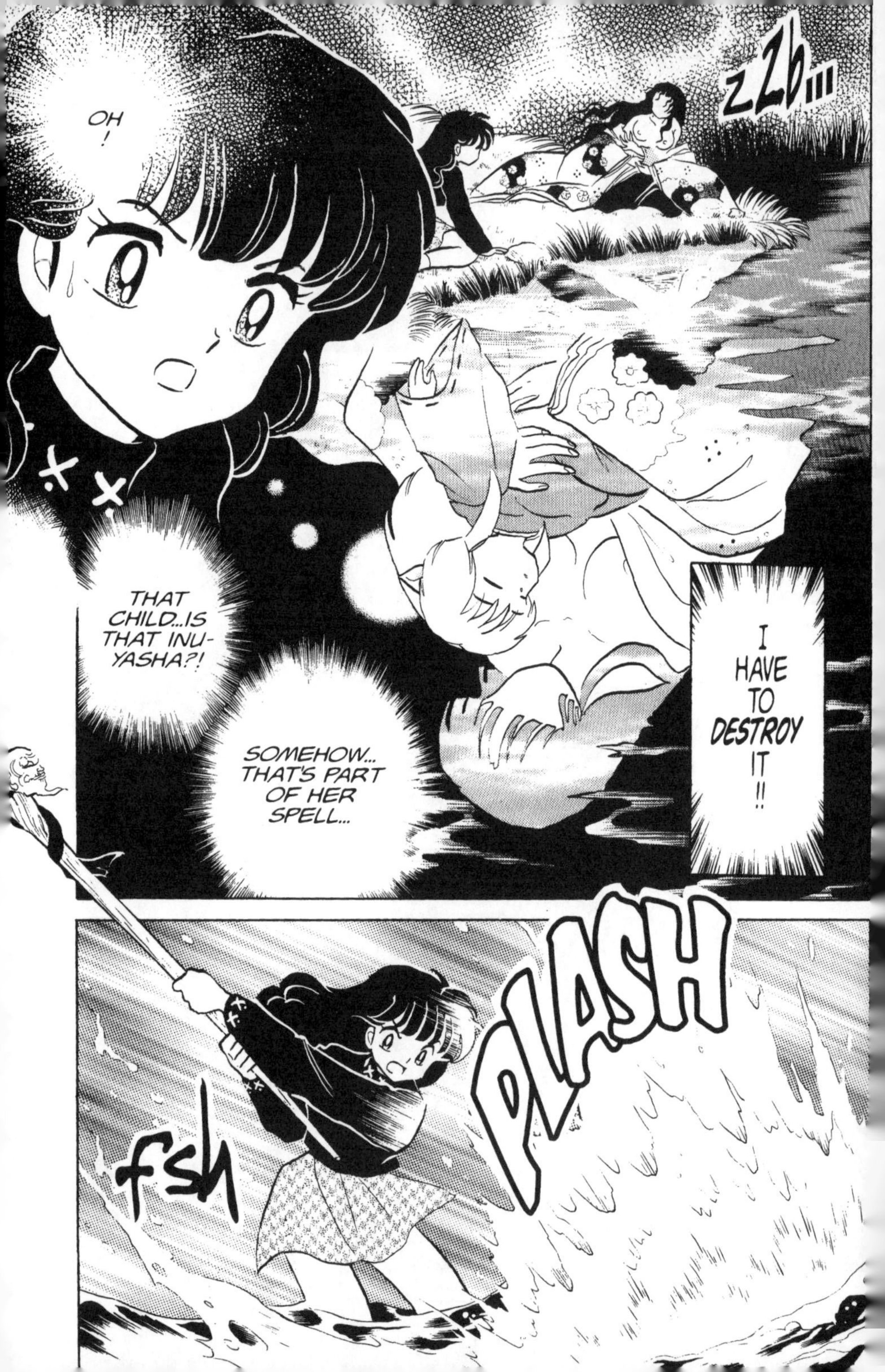
OH!
zzb...
THAT CHILD...IS THAT INU-YASHA?!
SOMEHOW... THAT'S PART OF HER SPELL...
I HAVE TO DESTROY IT!!
fsh
PLASH

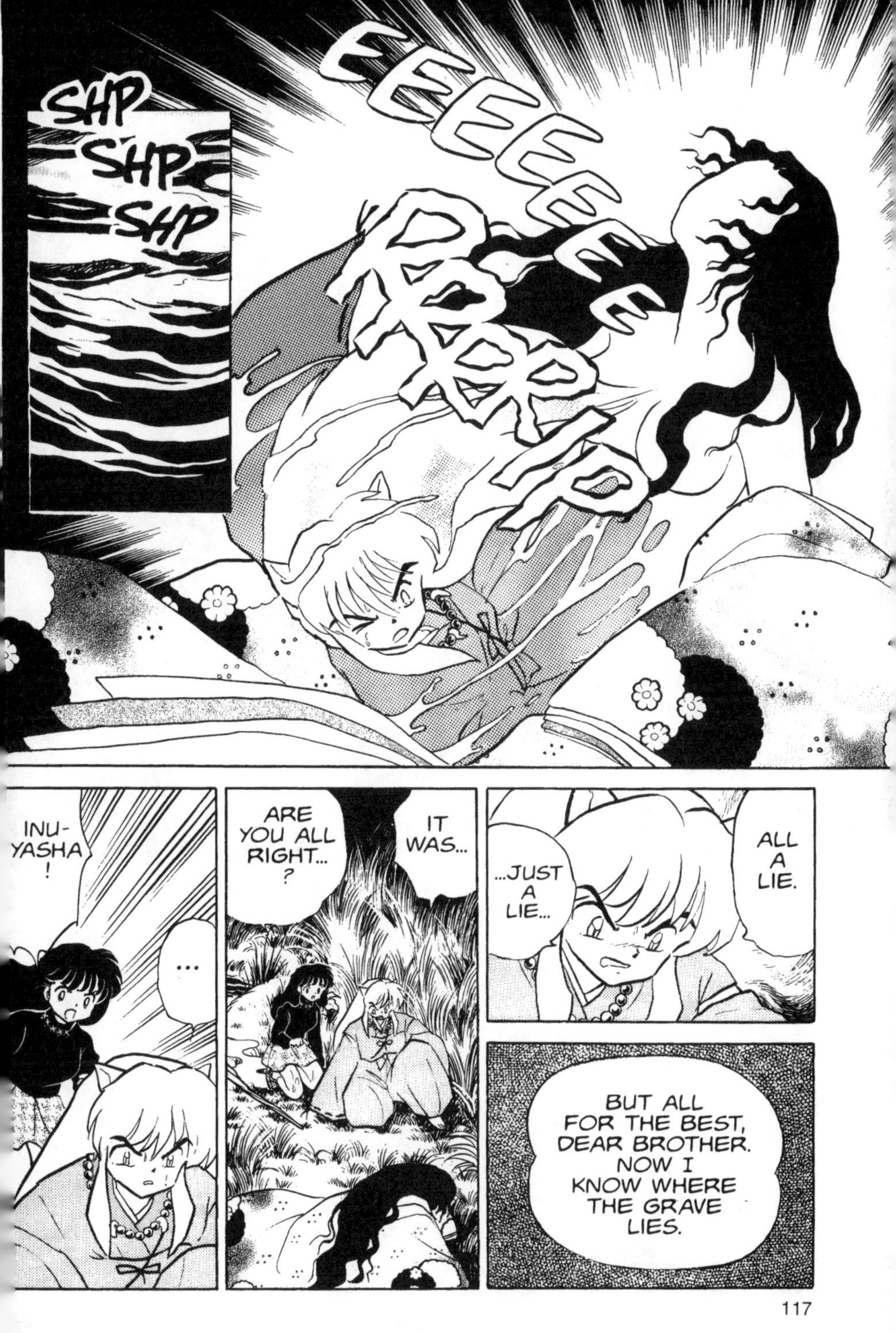

SHP
SHP
SHP
EEEEEEE
DRRRIP
INU-YASHA!
...
ARE YOU ALL RIGHT...?
IT WAS...
...JUST A LIE...
ALL A LIE.
BUT ALL FOR THE BEST, DEAR BROTHER. NOW I KNOW WHERE THE GRAVE LIES.

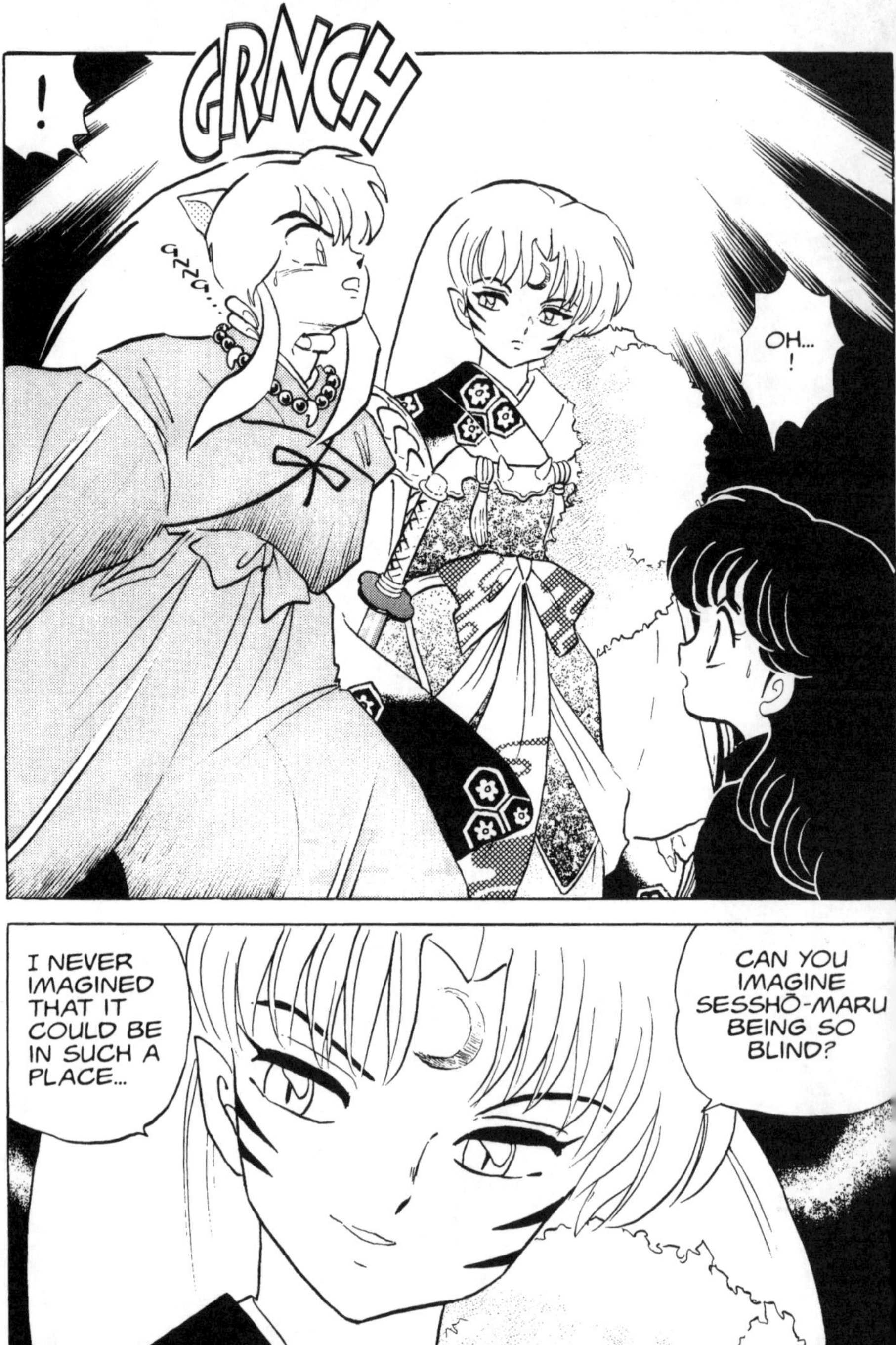
!
GRNCH
GNNG...
OH... !
I NEVER IMAGINED THAT IT COULD BE IN SUCH A PLACE...
CAN YOU IMAGINE SESSHŌ-MARU BEING SO BLIND?

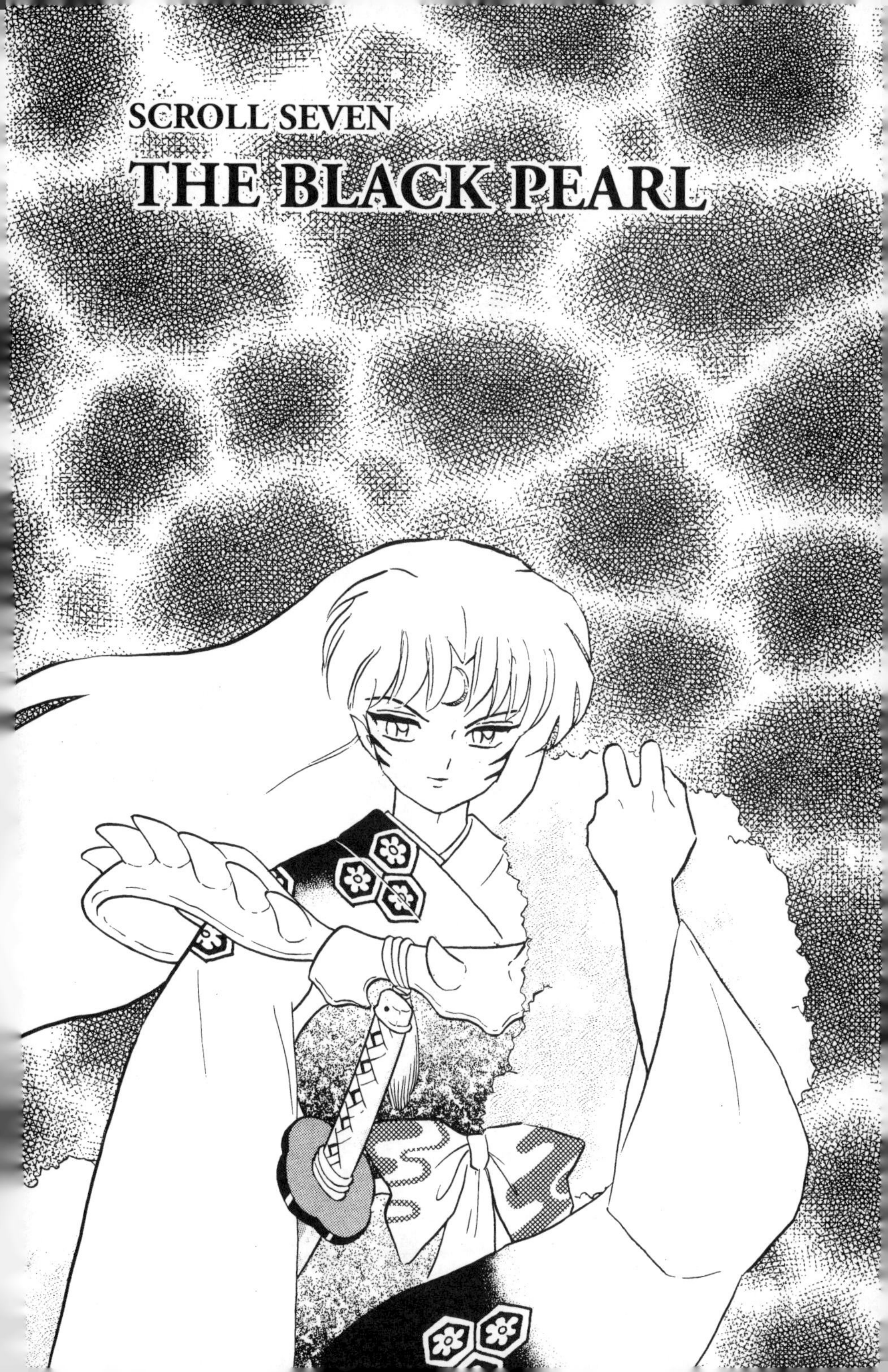
SCROLL SEVEN
THE BLACK PEARL

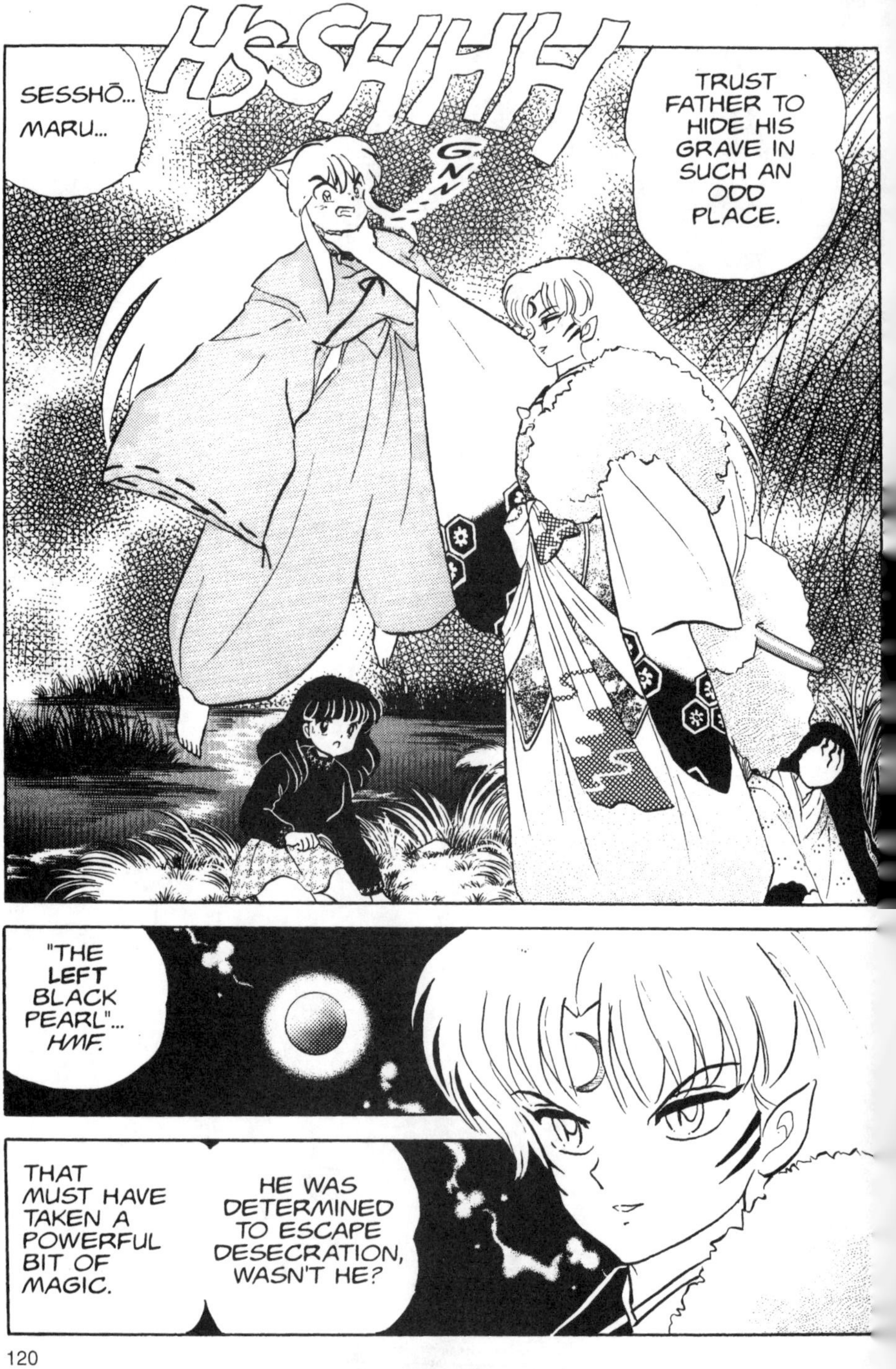
HSSHHH
SESSHŌ... MARU...
GNN
TRUST FATHER TO HIDE HIS GRAVE IN SUCH AN ODD PLACE.
"THE LEFT BLACK PEARL"... HMF.
THAT MUST HAVE TAKEN A POWERFUL BIT OF MAGIC.
HE WAS DETERMINED TO ESCAPE DESECRATION, WASN'T HE?

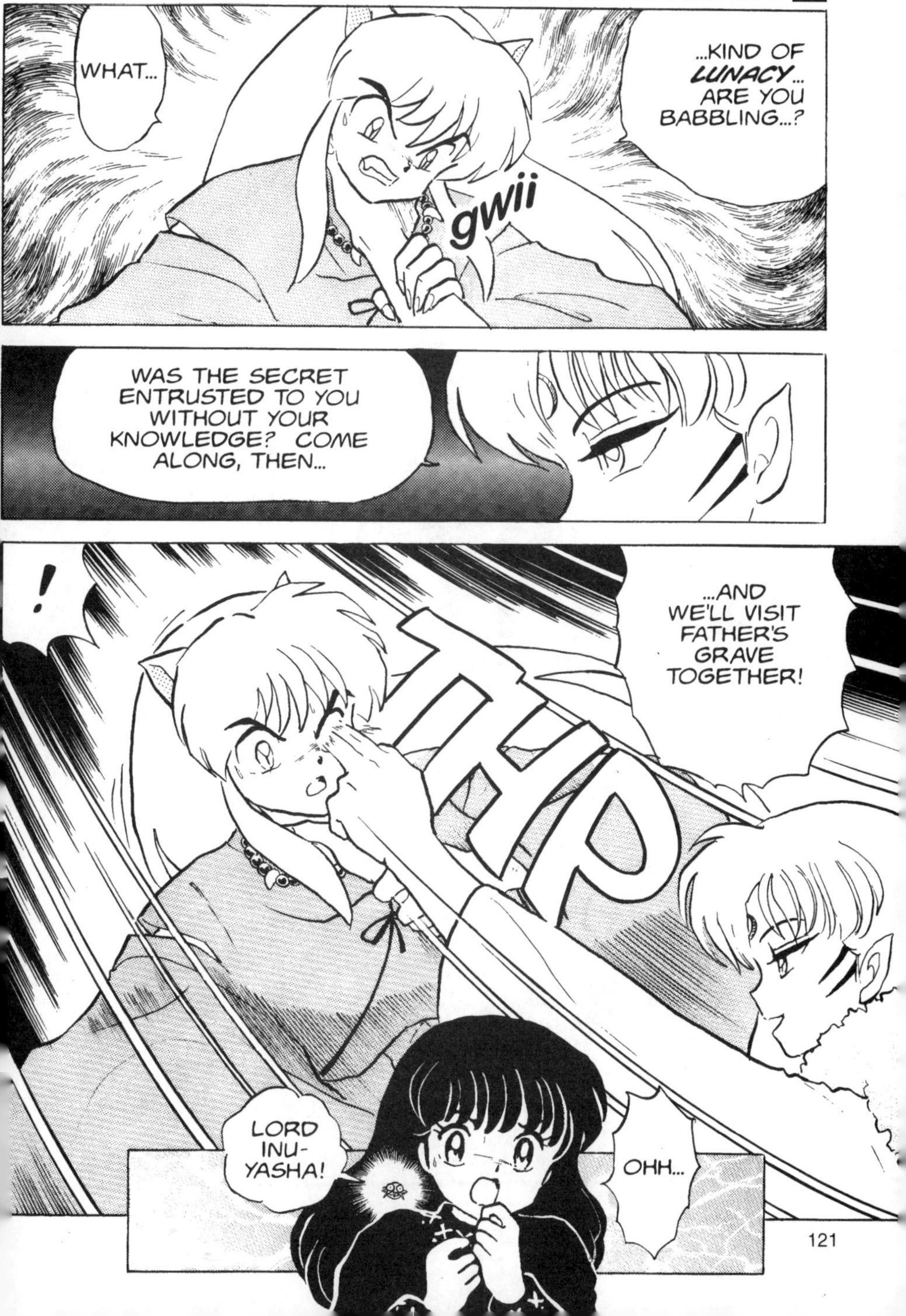
WHAT...
...KIND OF LUNACY... ARE YOU BABBLING...?
gwii
WAS THE SECRET ENTRUSTED TO YOU WITHOUT YOUR KNOWLEDGE? COME ALONG, THEN...
!
THP
...AND WE'LL VISIT FATHER'S GRAVE TOGETHER!
LORD INU-YASHA!
OHH...

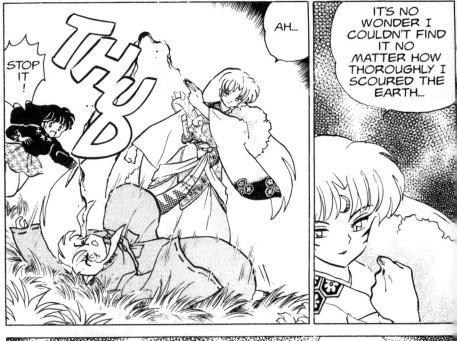

AH...

STOP IT!

IT'S NO WONDER I COULDN'T FIND IT NO MATTER HOW THOROUGHLY I SCOURED THE EARTH...

I HAD ONLY ONE CLUE TO THE GRAVE'S WHERE-ABOUTS...

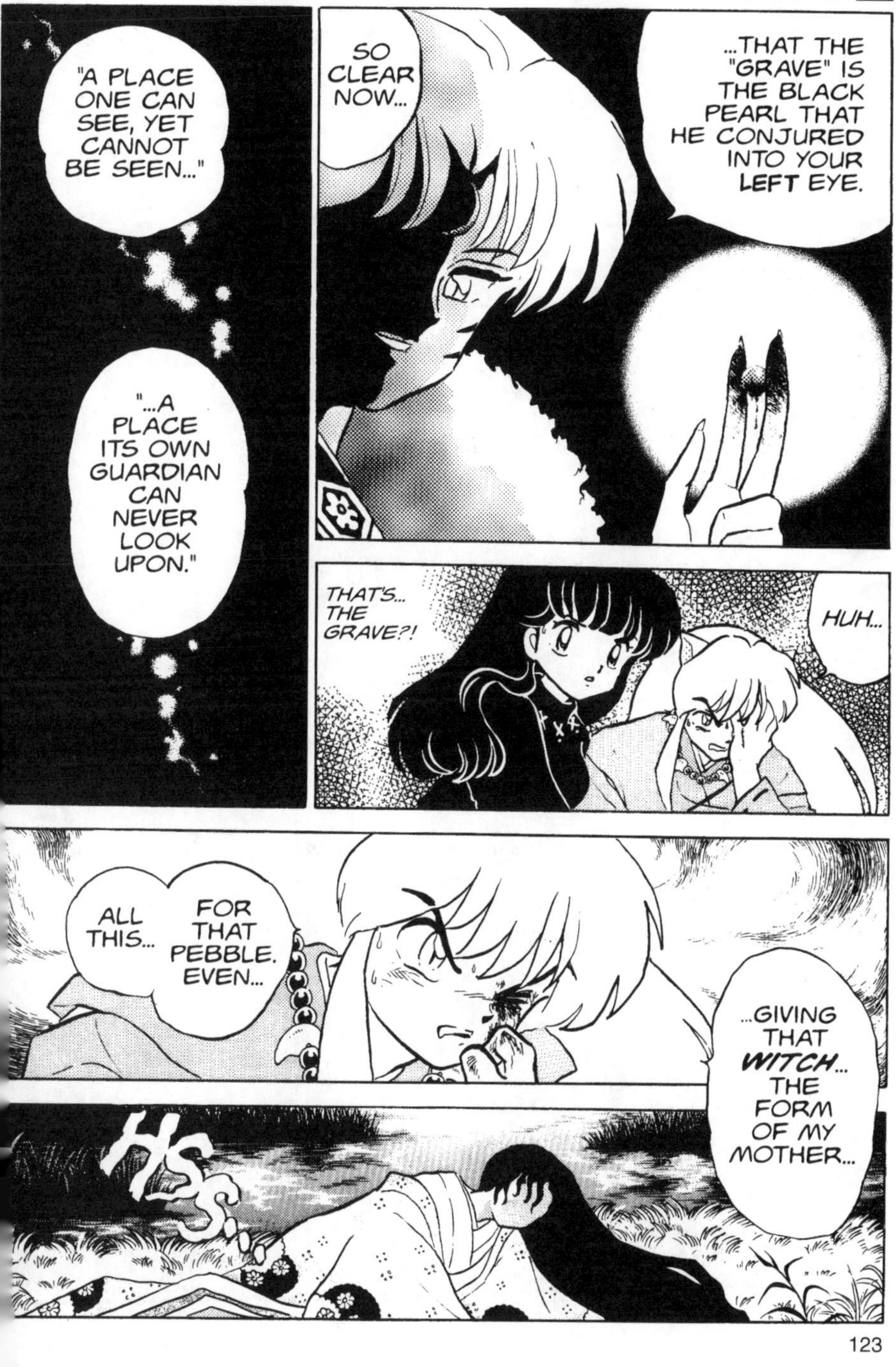
"A PLACE ONE CAN SEE, YET CANNOT BE SEEN..."
"...A PLACE ITS OWN GUARDIAN CAN NEVER LOOK UPON."
SO CLEAR NOW...
...THAT THE "GRAVE" IS THE BLACK PEARL THAT HE CONJURED INTO YOUR **LEFT** EYE.
THAT'S... THE GRAVE?!
HUH...
ALL THIS...
FOR THAT PEBBLE. EVEN...
...GIVING THAT ***WITCH***... THE FORM OF MY MOTHER...
HSS

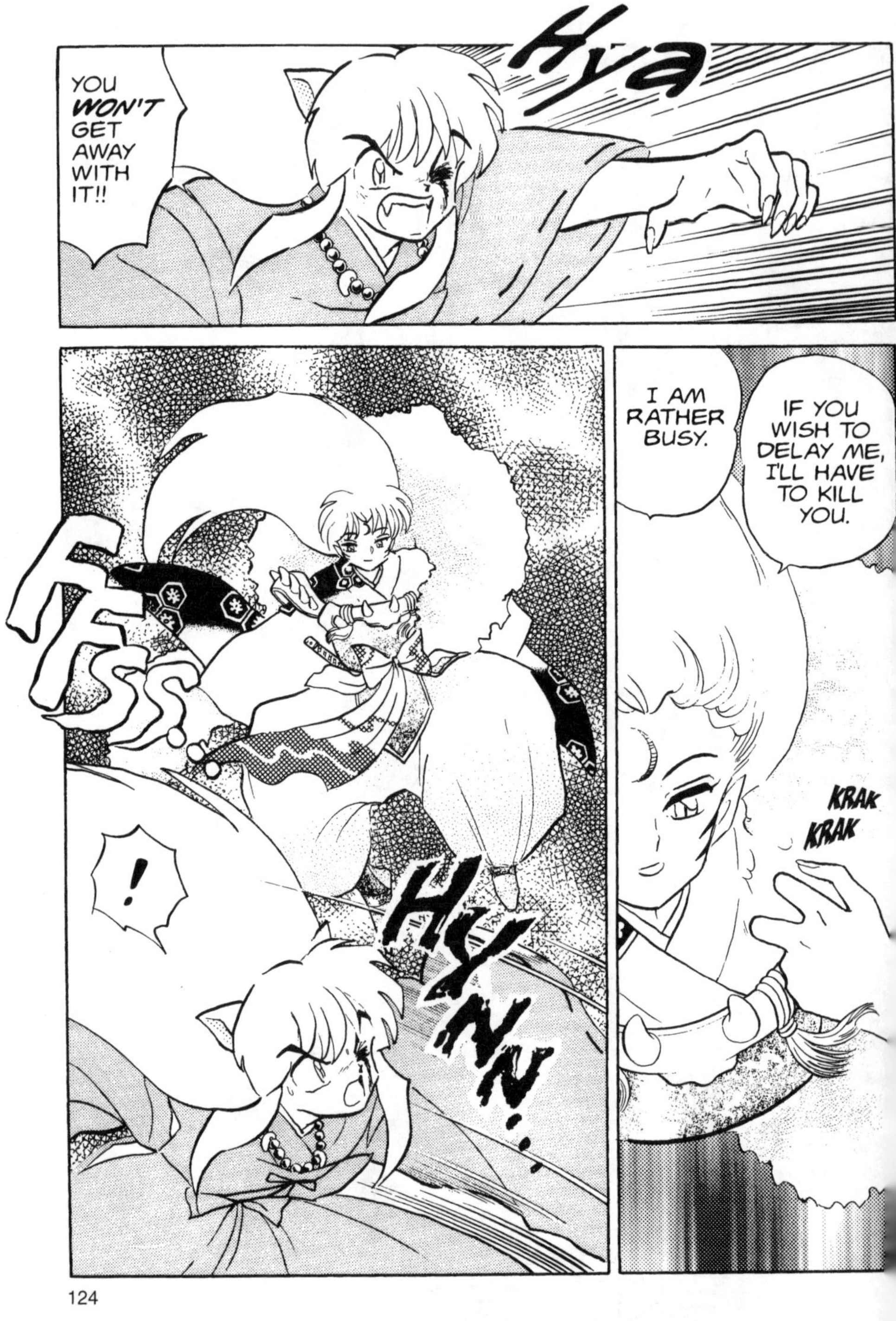
Kya
YOU WON'T GET AWAY WITH IT!!
FSS
!
HYNN..
I AM RATHER BUSY.
IF YOU WISH TO DELAY ME, I'LL HAVE TO KILL YOU.
KRAK KRAK

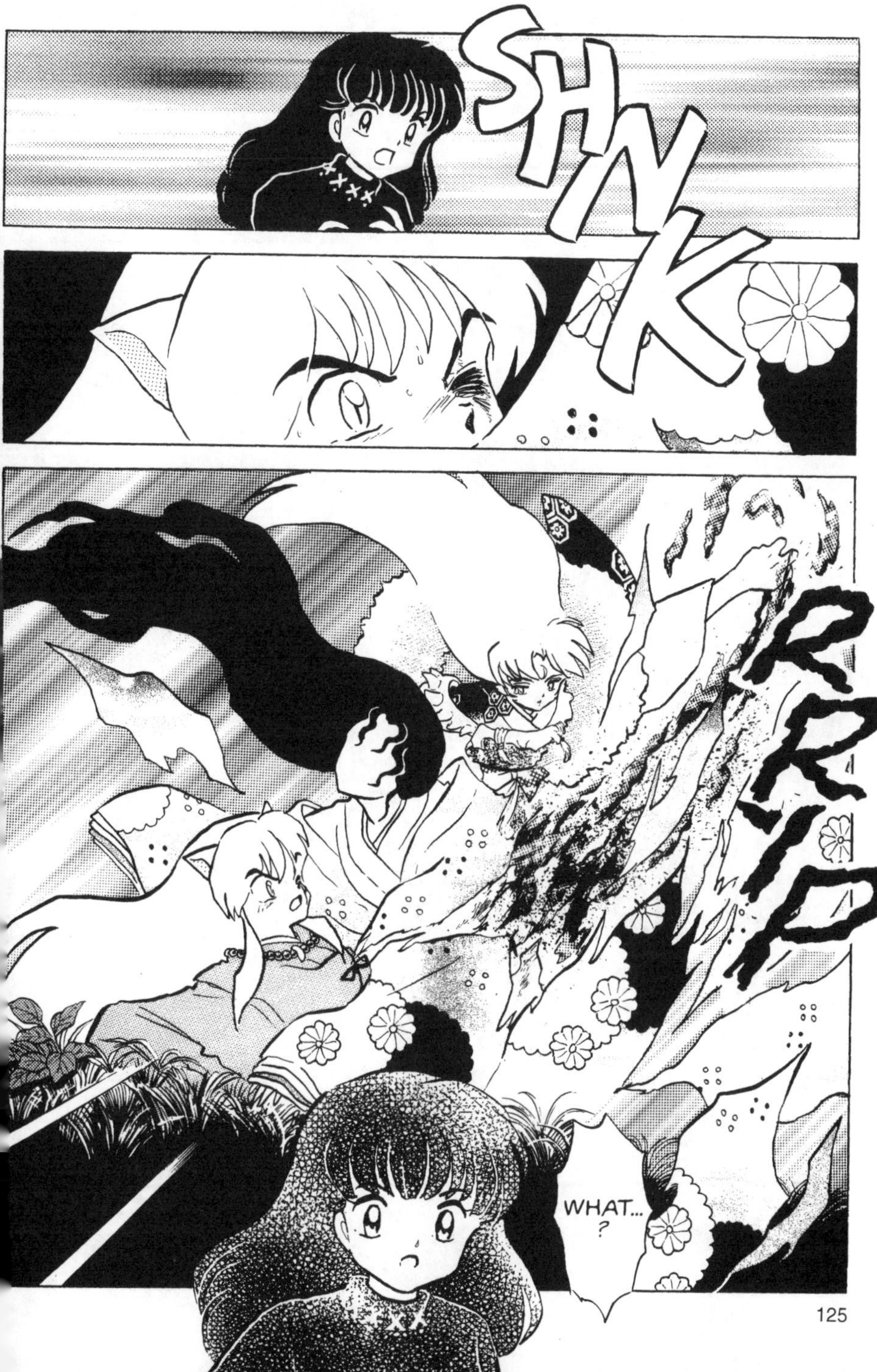
SHNK
RRIP
WHAT...?

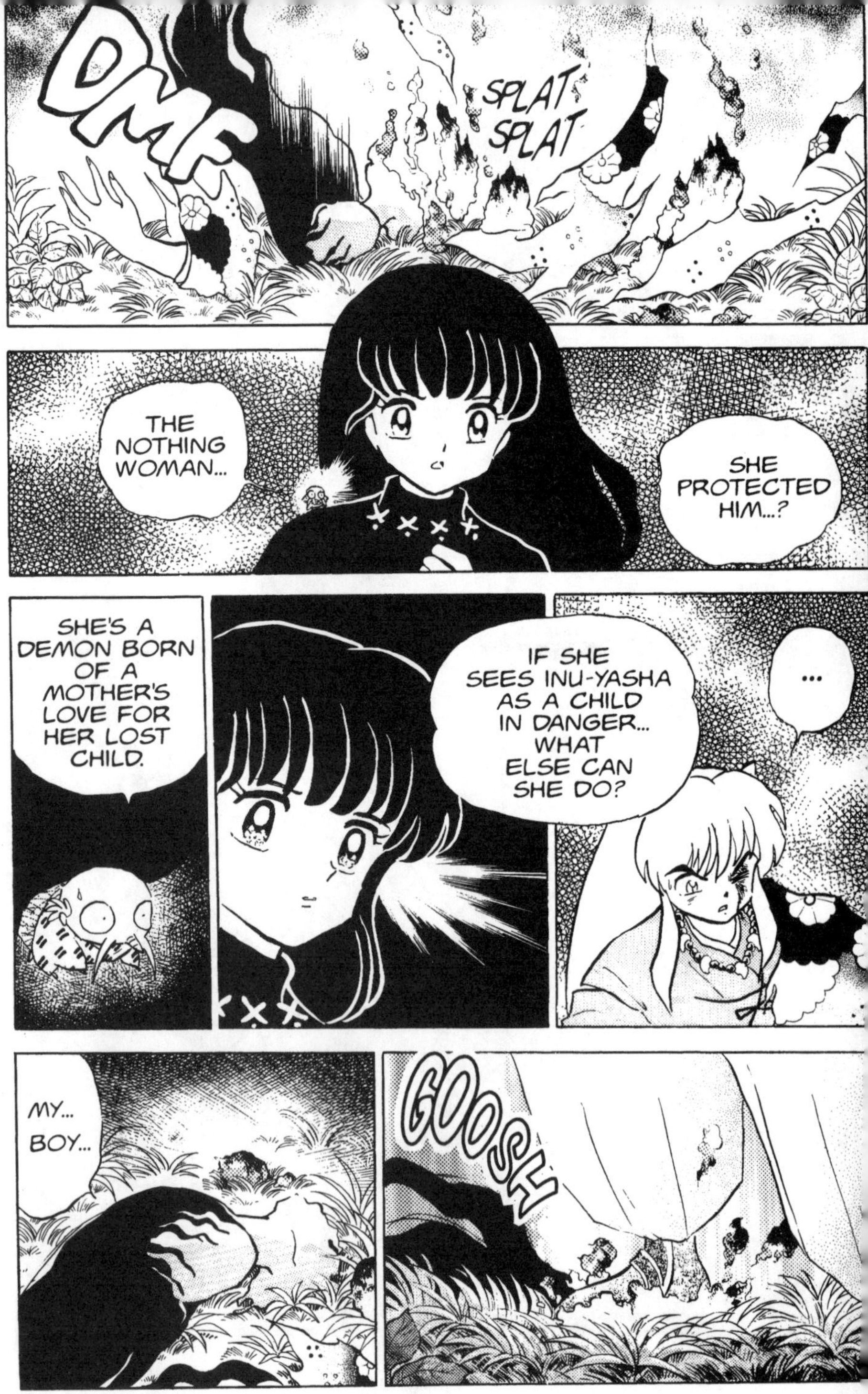
DMF
SPLAT SPLAT
THE NOTHING WOMAN...
SHE PROTECTED HIM...?
SHE'S A DEMON BORN OF A MOTHER'S LOVE FOR HER LOST CHILD.
IF SHE SEES INU-YASHA AS A CHILD IN DANGER... WHAT ELSE CAN SHE DO?
...
MY... BOY...
GOOSH

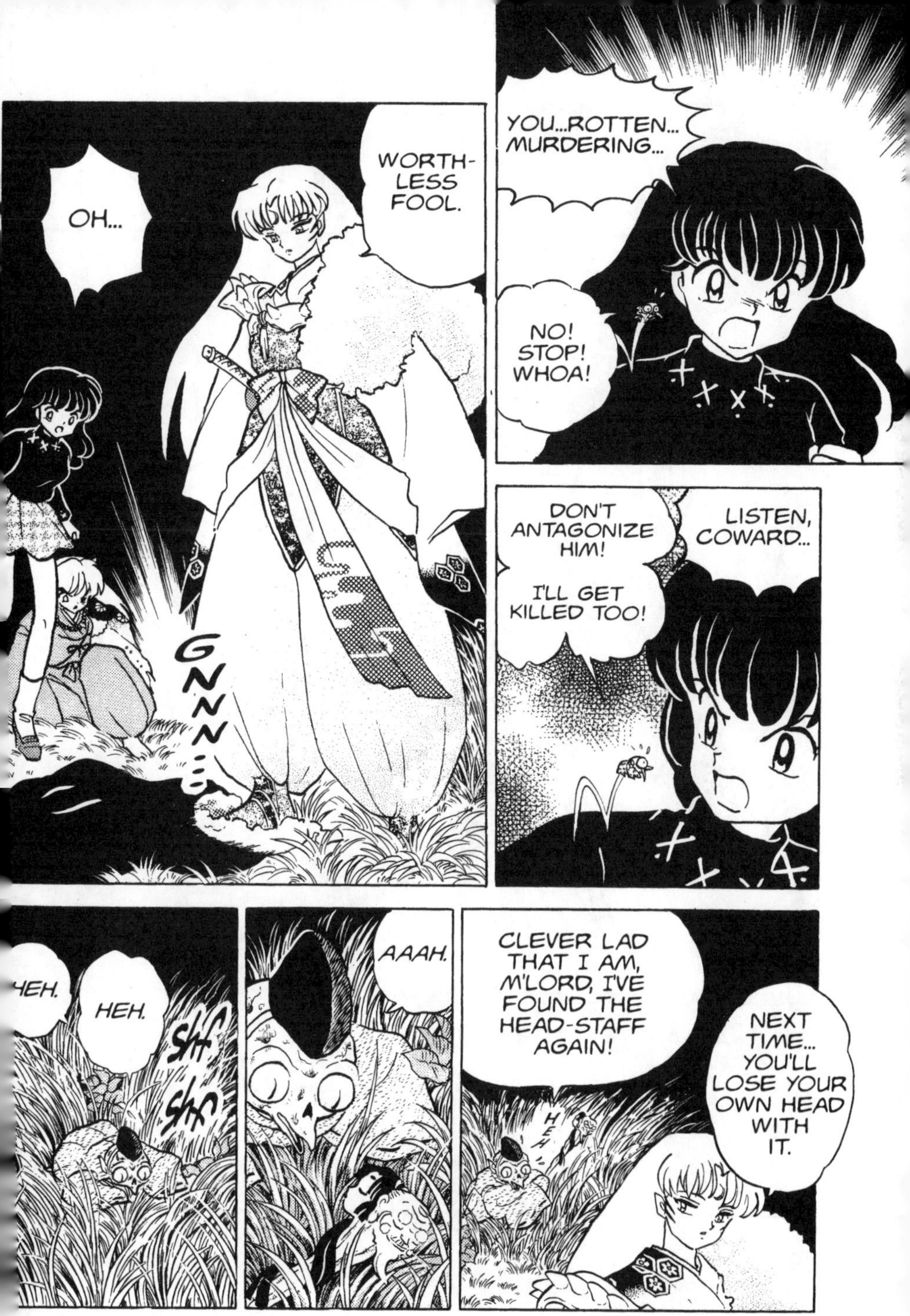
OH...
WORTH-LESS FOOL.
GNNN...
YOU...ROTTEN... MURDERING...
NO! STOP! WHOA!
DON'T ANTAGONIZE HIM!
LISTEN, COWARD...
I'LL GET KILLED TOO!
HEH.
HEH.
SHF SHF
AAAH.
CLEVER LAD THAT I AM, M'LORD, I'VE FOUND THE HEAD-STAFF AGAIN!
HEH
NEXT TIME... YOU'LL LOSE YOUR OWN HEAD WITH IT.

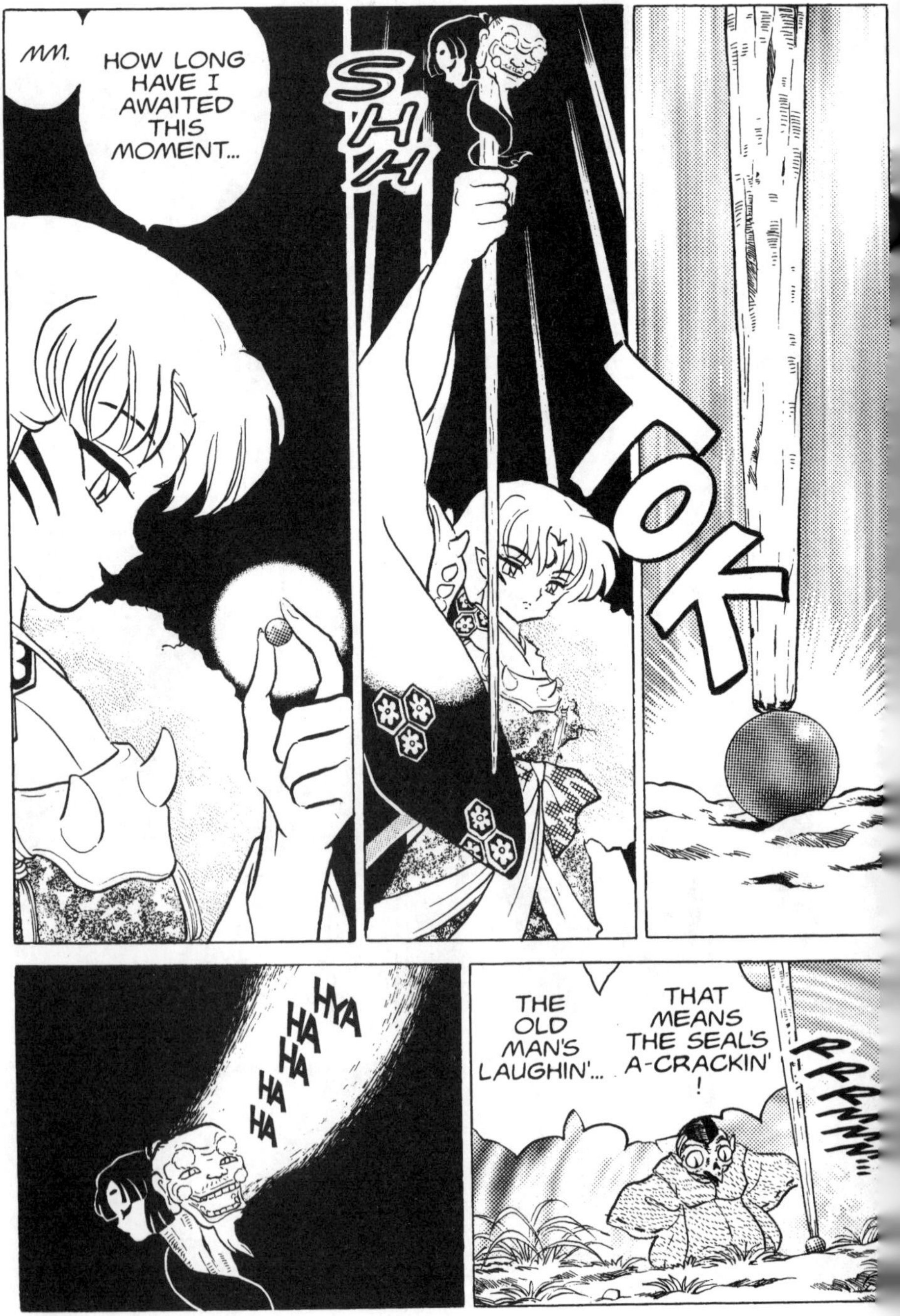
MM.
HOW LONG HAVE I AWAITED THIS MOMENT...
SHH
TOK
HYA HA HA HA HA
THE OLD MAN'S LAUGHIN'...
THAT MEANS THE SEAL'S A-CRACKIN' !
RRRNNN...

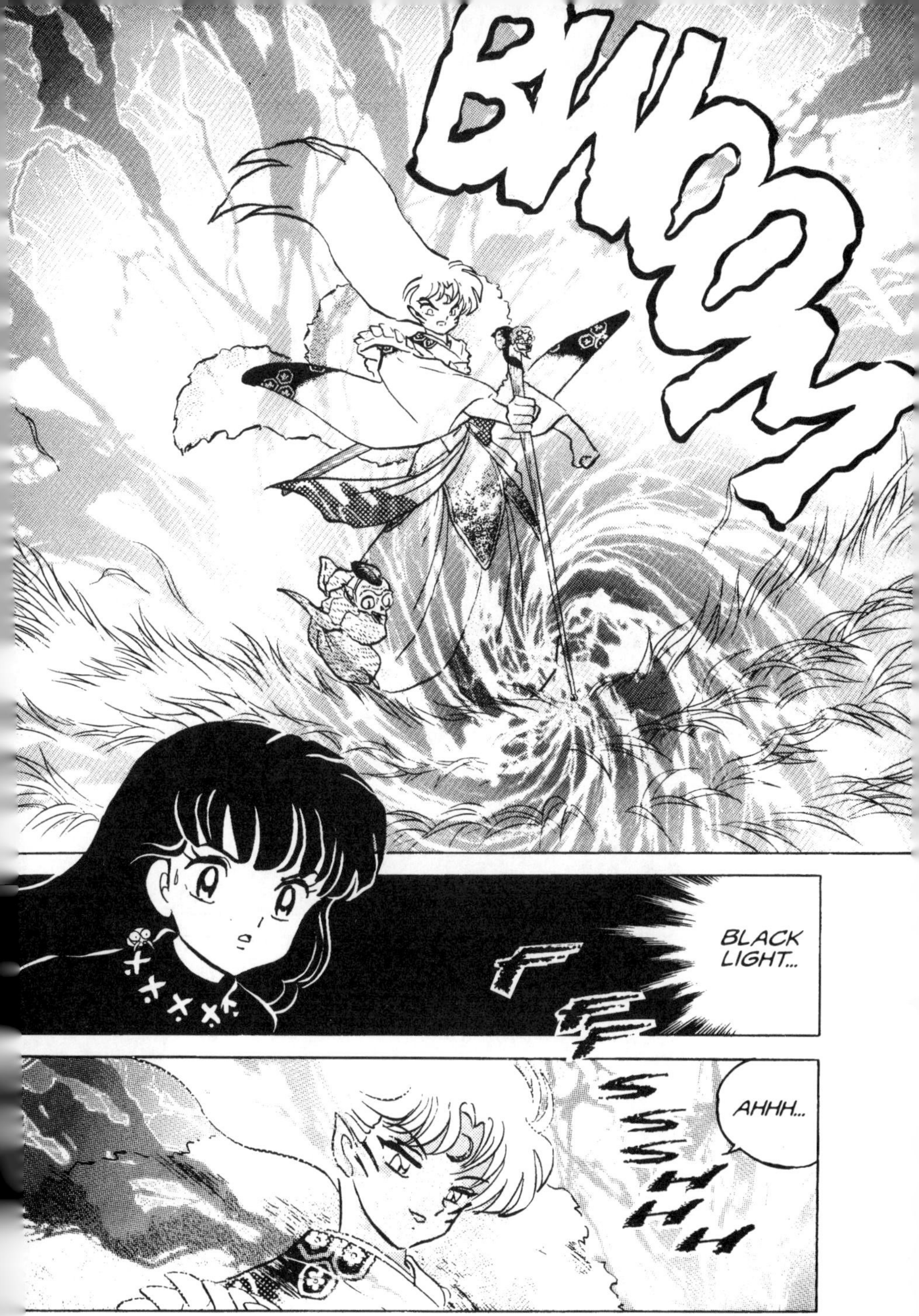
BLOOM
BLACK LIGHT...
FFFSSSHHHH
AHHH...

SHOOMP

WHERE...?

LORD INU-YASHA!

BOUND AFTER 'EM BEFORE THE GATEWAY SHUTS!

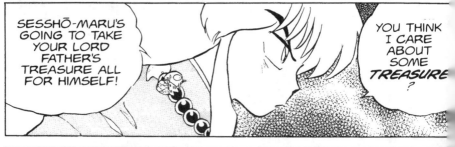

SESSHŌ-MARU'S GOING TO TAKE YOUR LORD FATHER'S TREASURE ALL FOR HIMSELF!

YOU THINK I CARE ABOUT SOME *TREASURE*?

B-BUT, LORD...

SUCH A WASTE...!

SHUT UP!

DID I SAY I WASN'T GOING AFTER THEM?!

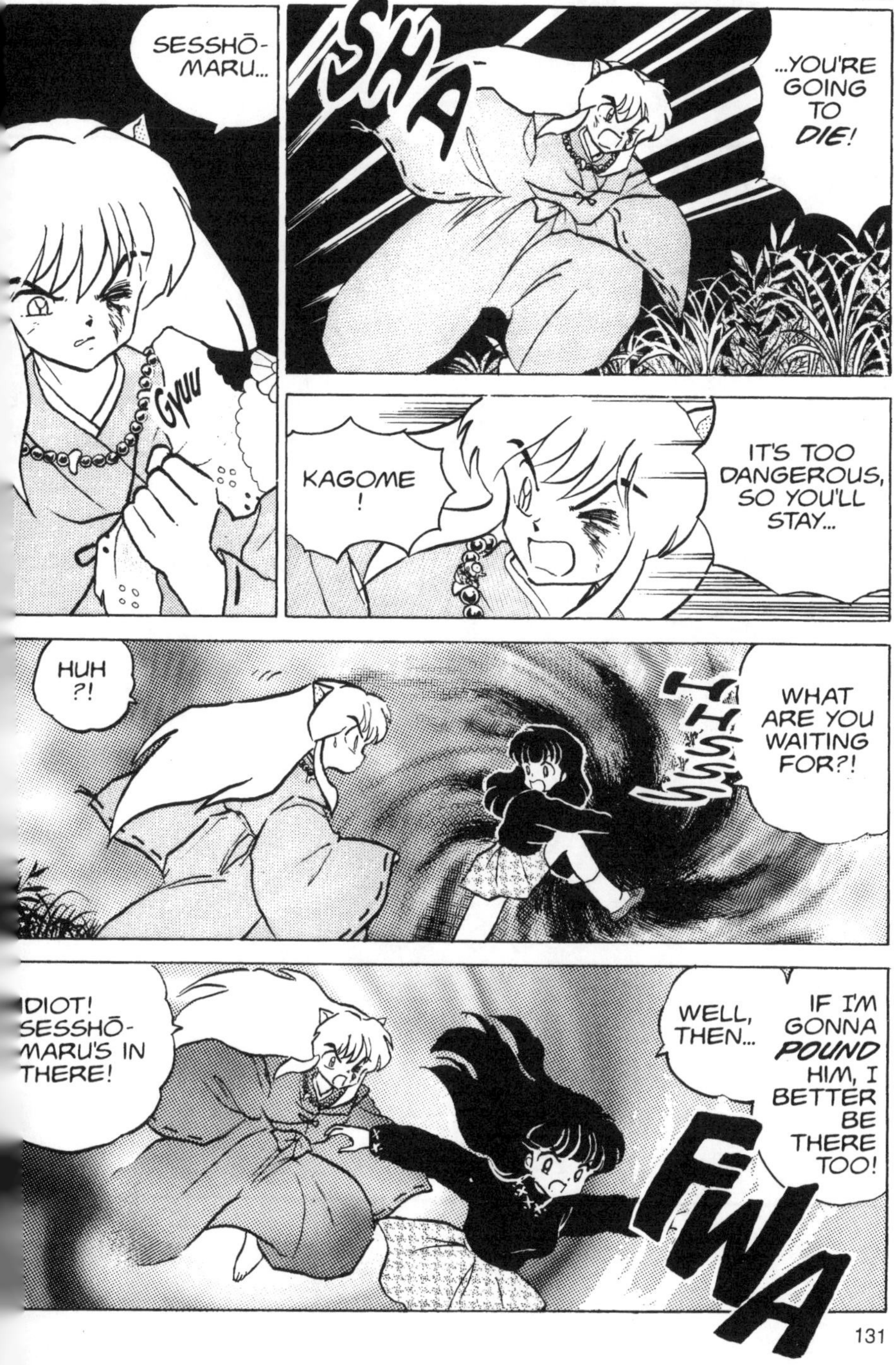
SESSHŌ-MARU...
Gyuu
SHA
...YOU'RE GOING TO DIE!
KAGOME!
IT'S TOO DANGEROUS, SO YOU'LL STAY...
HUH?!
HISSS
WHAT ARE YOU WAITING FOR?!
IDIOT! SESSHŌ-MARU'S IN THERE!
WELL, THEN...
IF I'M GONNA POUND HIM, I BETTER BE THERE TOO!
FWA

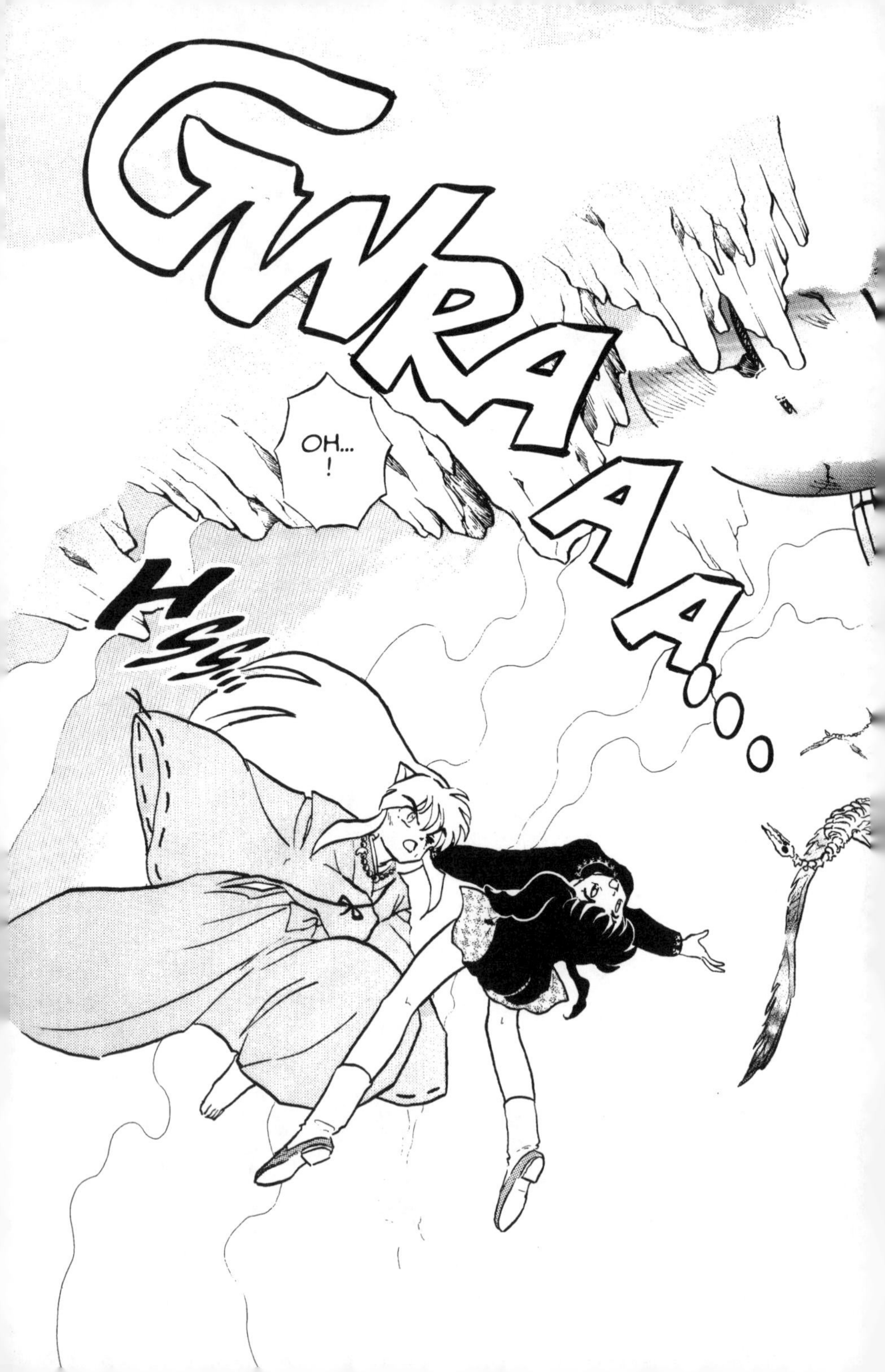
GWRAAAA...
OH... !
HSSS!!

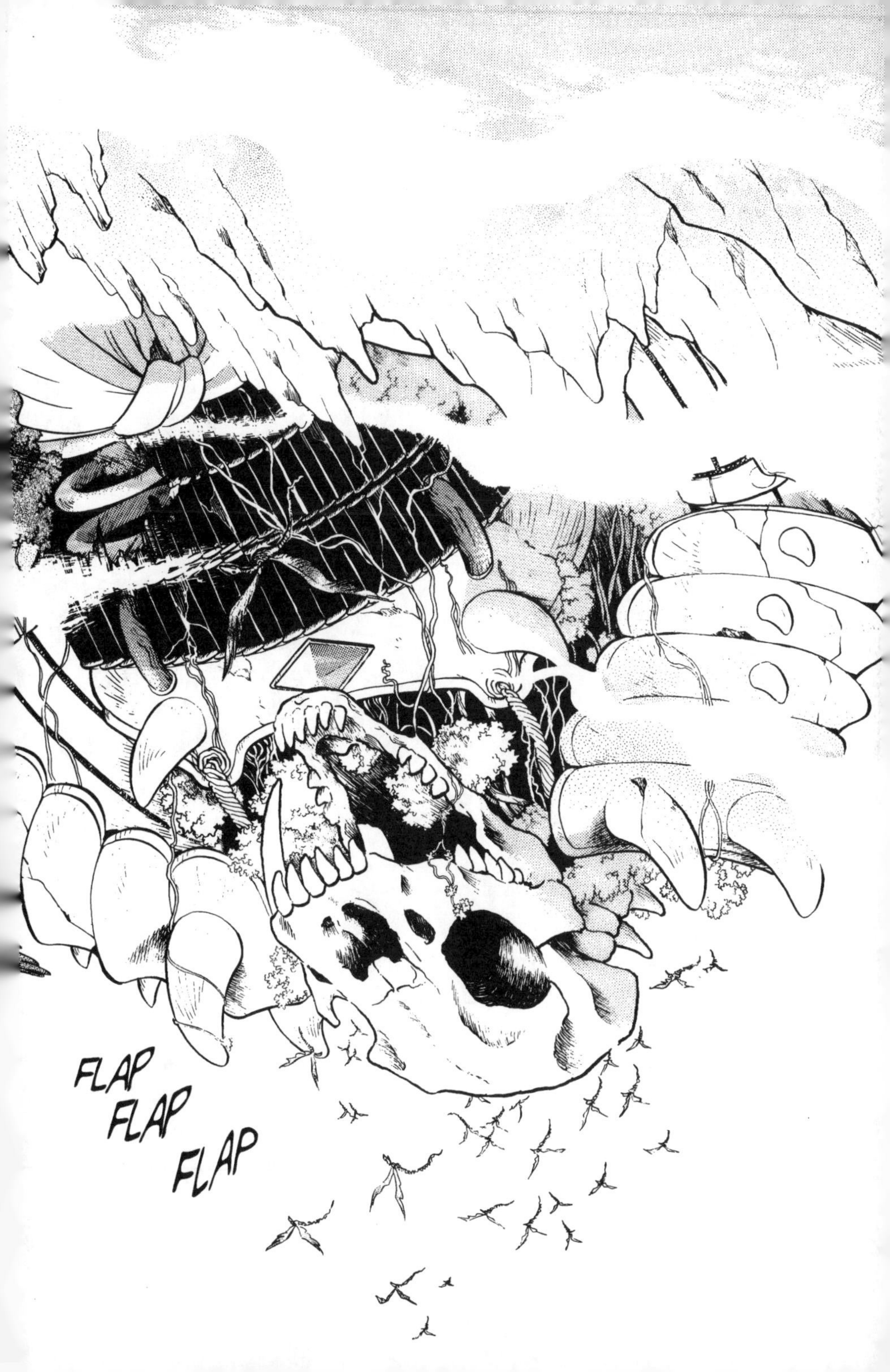
FLAP
FLAP
FLAP

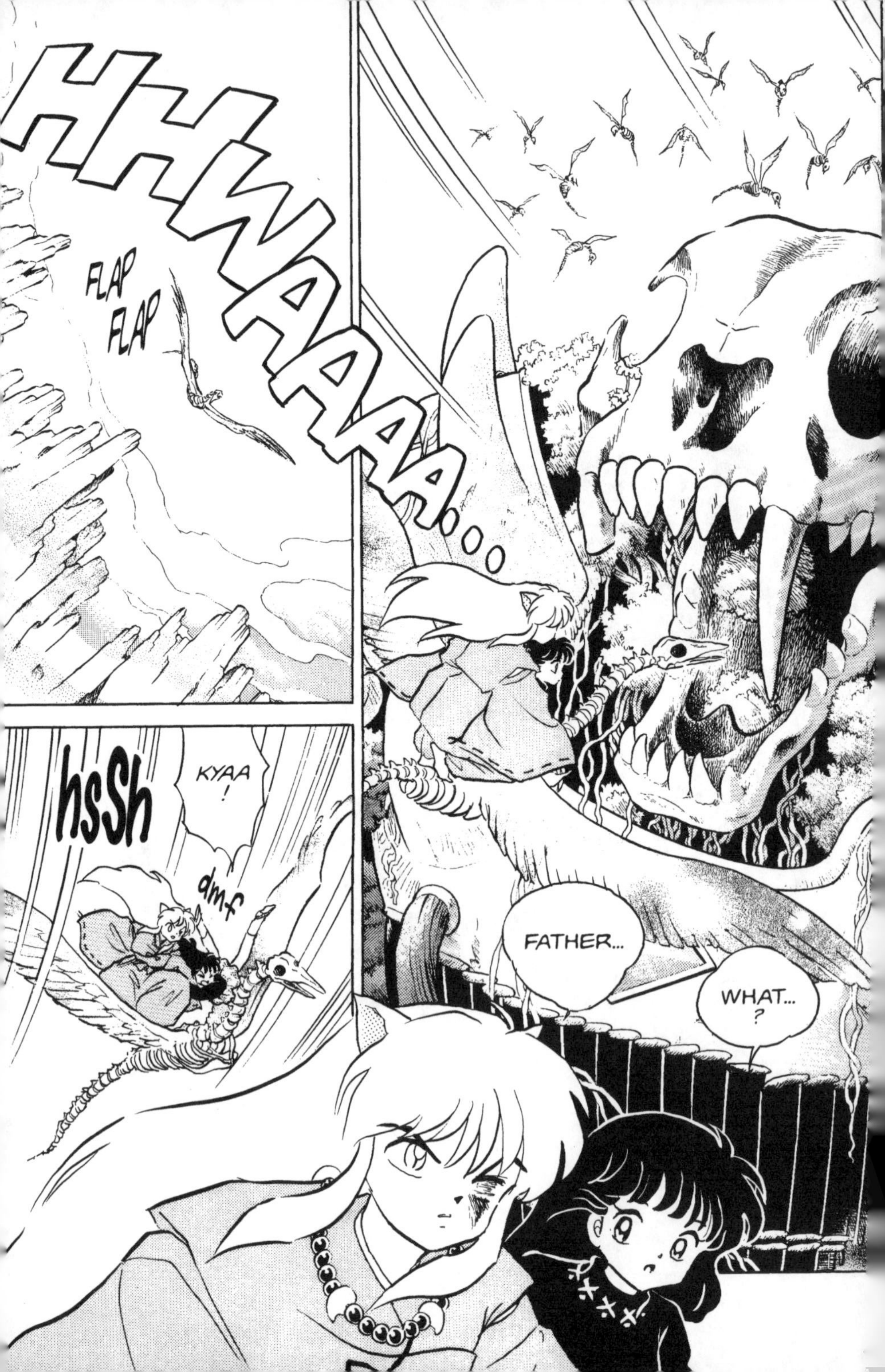
HHWAAAAA...
FLAP
FLAP
hsSh
KYAA!
dmf
FATHER...
WHAT...?

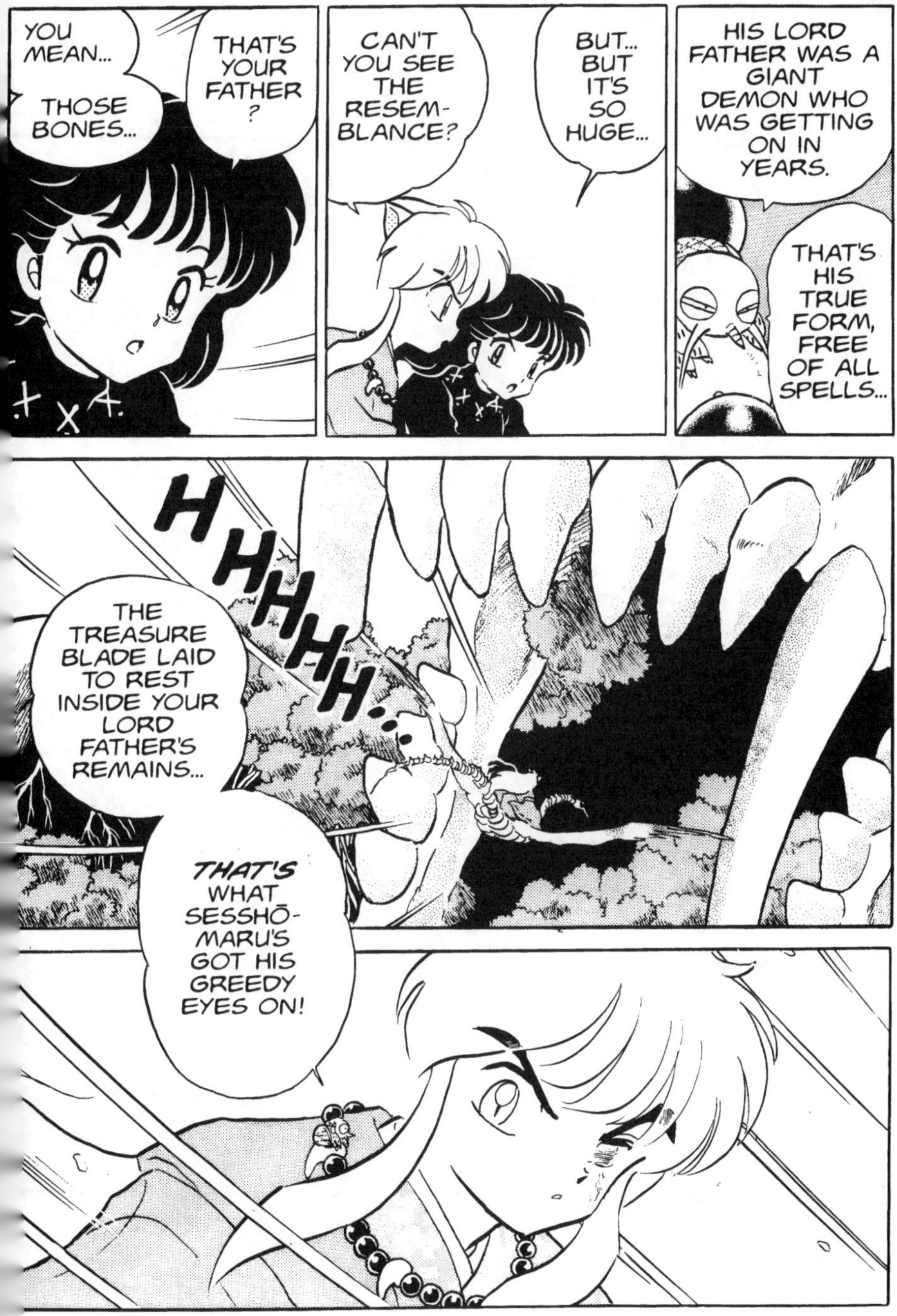
YOU MEAN...
THOSE BONES...
THAT'S YOUR FATHER?
CAN'T YOU SEE THE RESEMBLANCE?
BUT... BUT IT'S SO HUGE...
HIS LORD FATHER WAS A GIANT DEMON WHO WAS GETTING ON IN YEARS.
THAT'S HIS TRUE FORM, FREE OF ALL SPELLS...
HHHHHHH...
THE TREASURE BLADE LAID TO REST INSIDE YOUR LORD FATHER'S REMAINS...
THAT'S WHAT SESSHŌMARU'S GOT HIS GREEDY EYES ON!

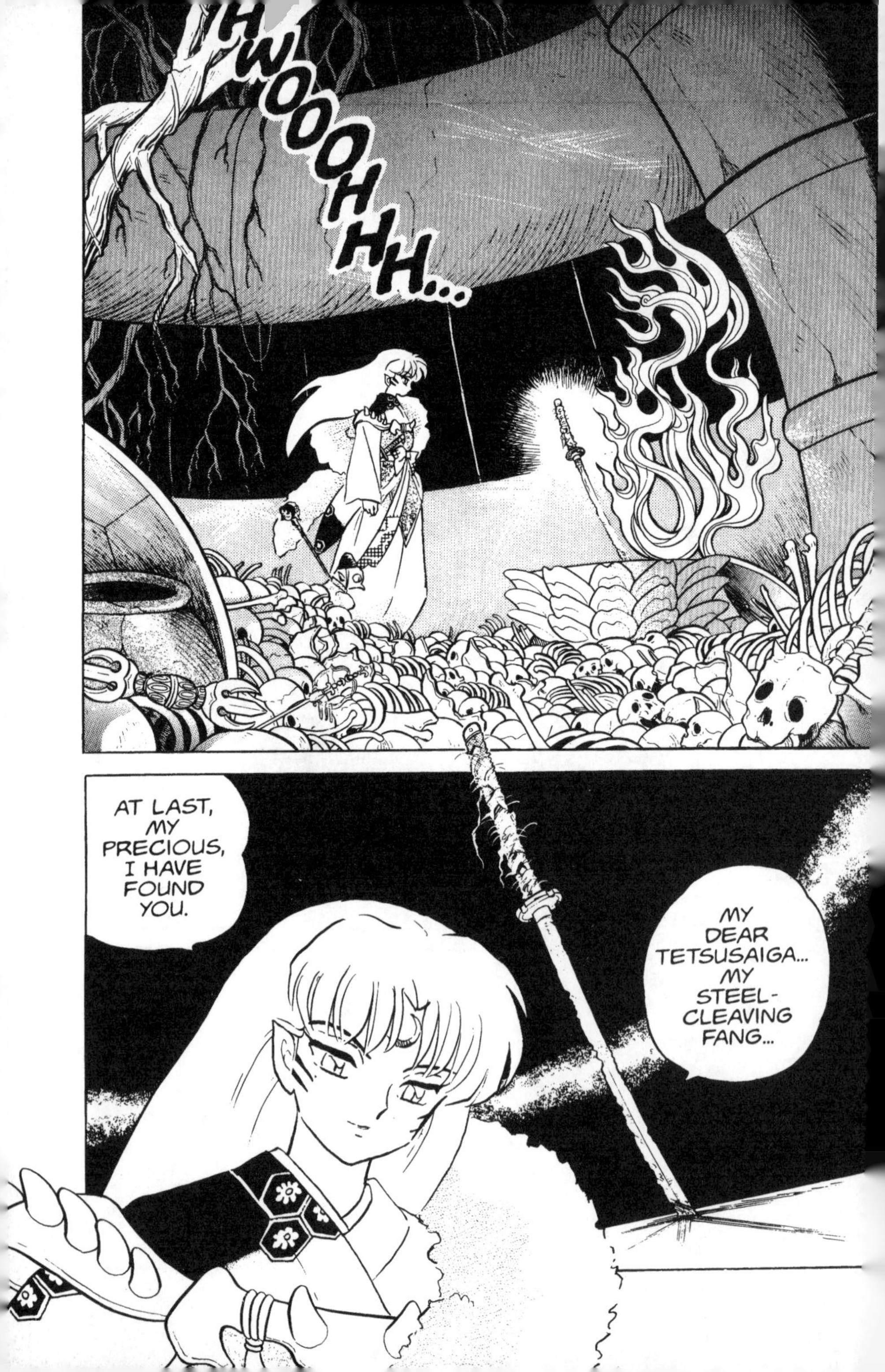
HWOOOHHH...
AT LAST, MY PRECIOUS, I HAVE FOUND YOU.
MY DEAR TETSUSAIGA... MY STEEL-CLEAVING FANG...

SCROLL EIGHT

THE FANG OF STEEL

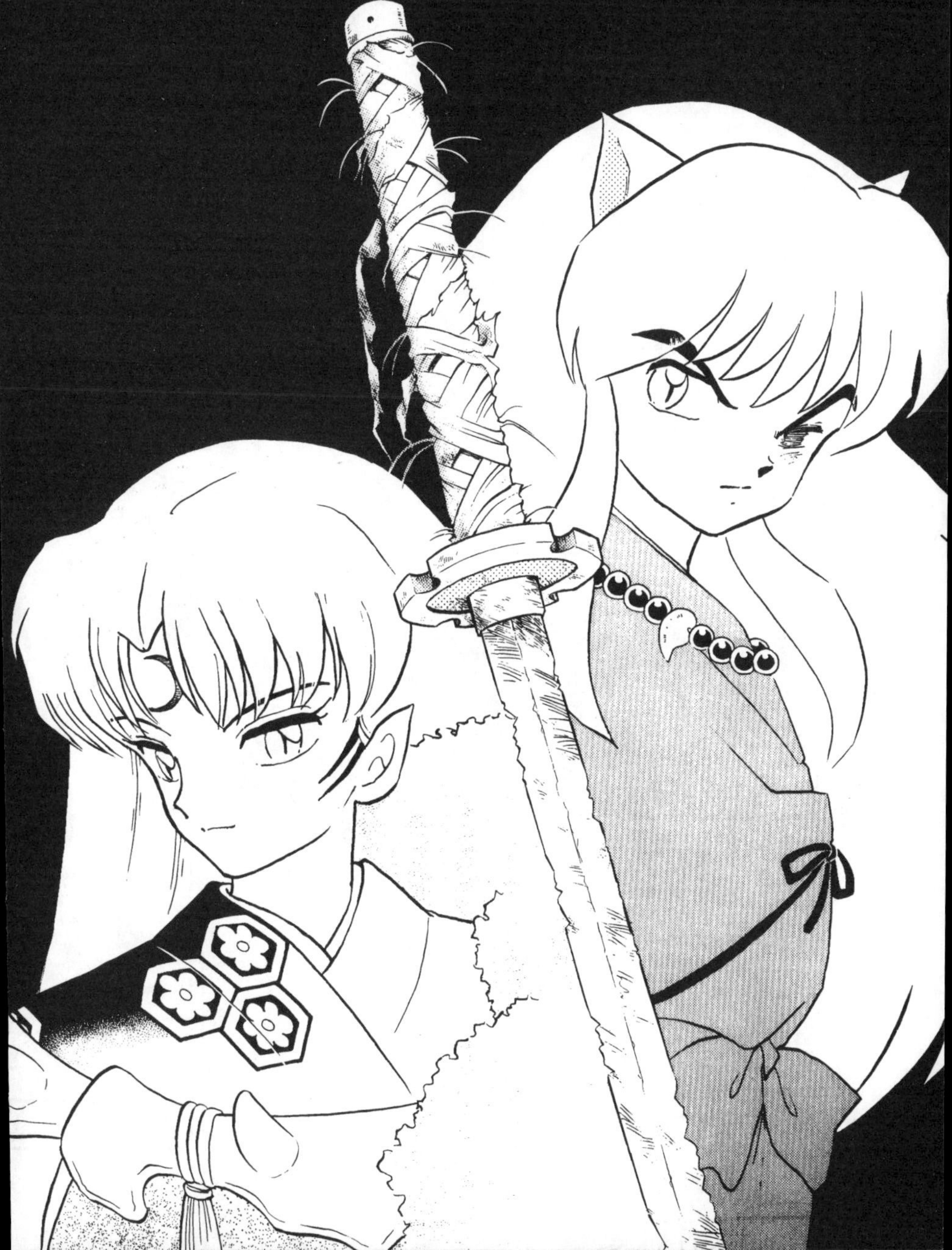

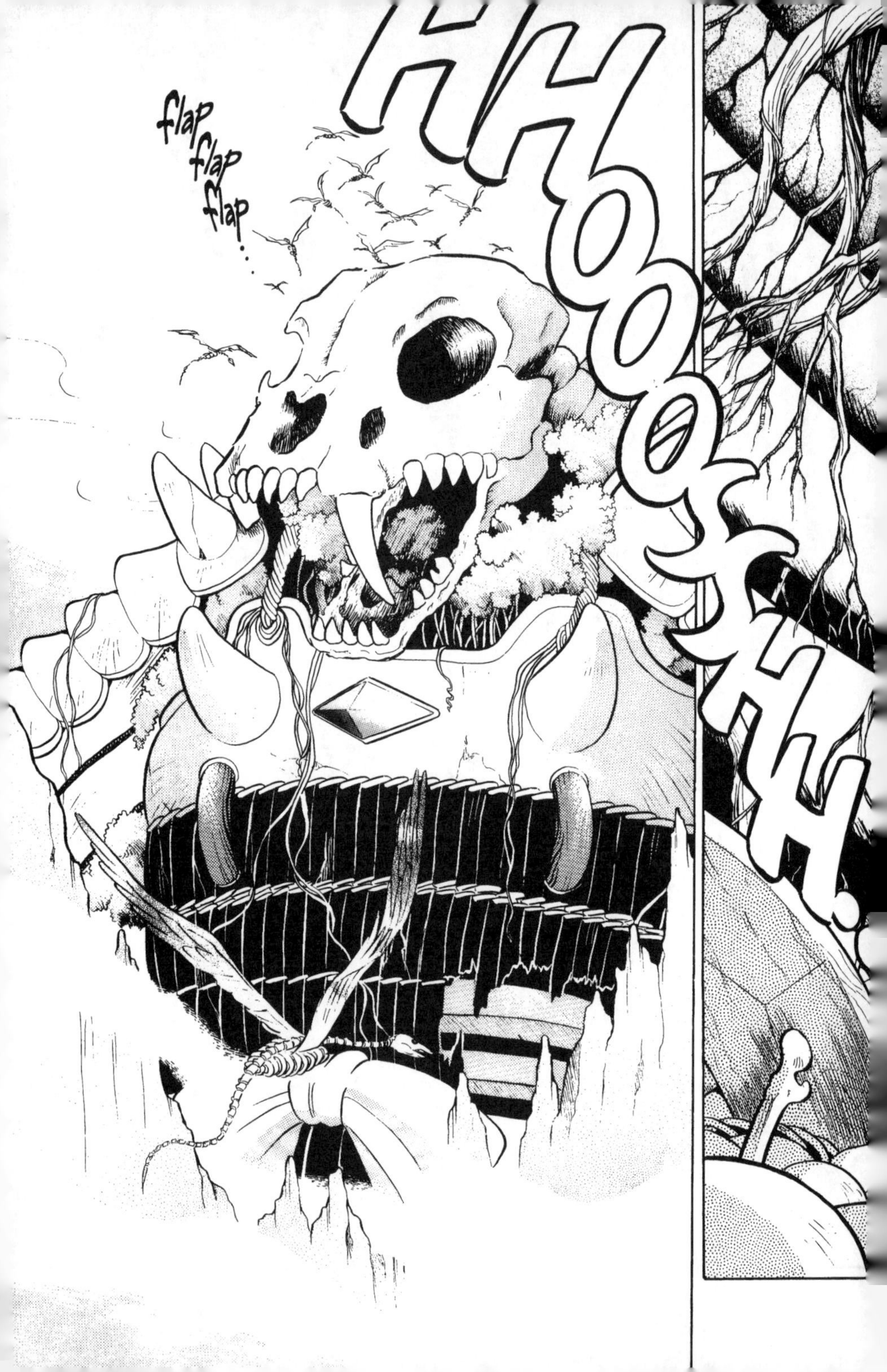
flap flap flap...
FHOOOOSHH...

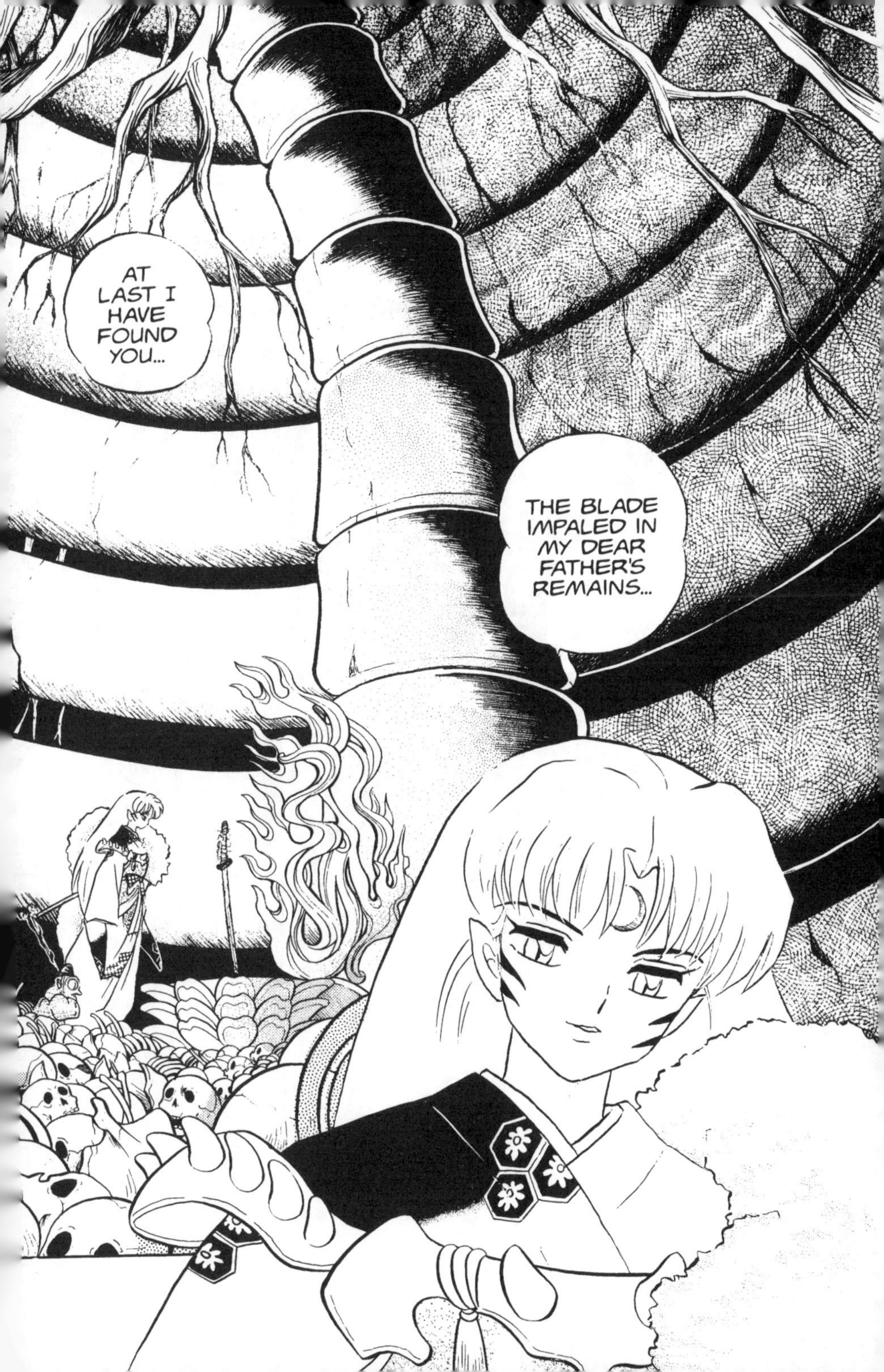
AT LAST I HAVE FOUND YOU...
THE BLADE IMPALED IN MY DEAR FATHER'S REMAINS...

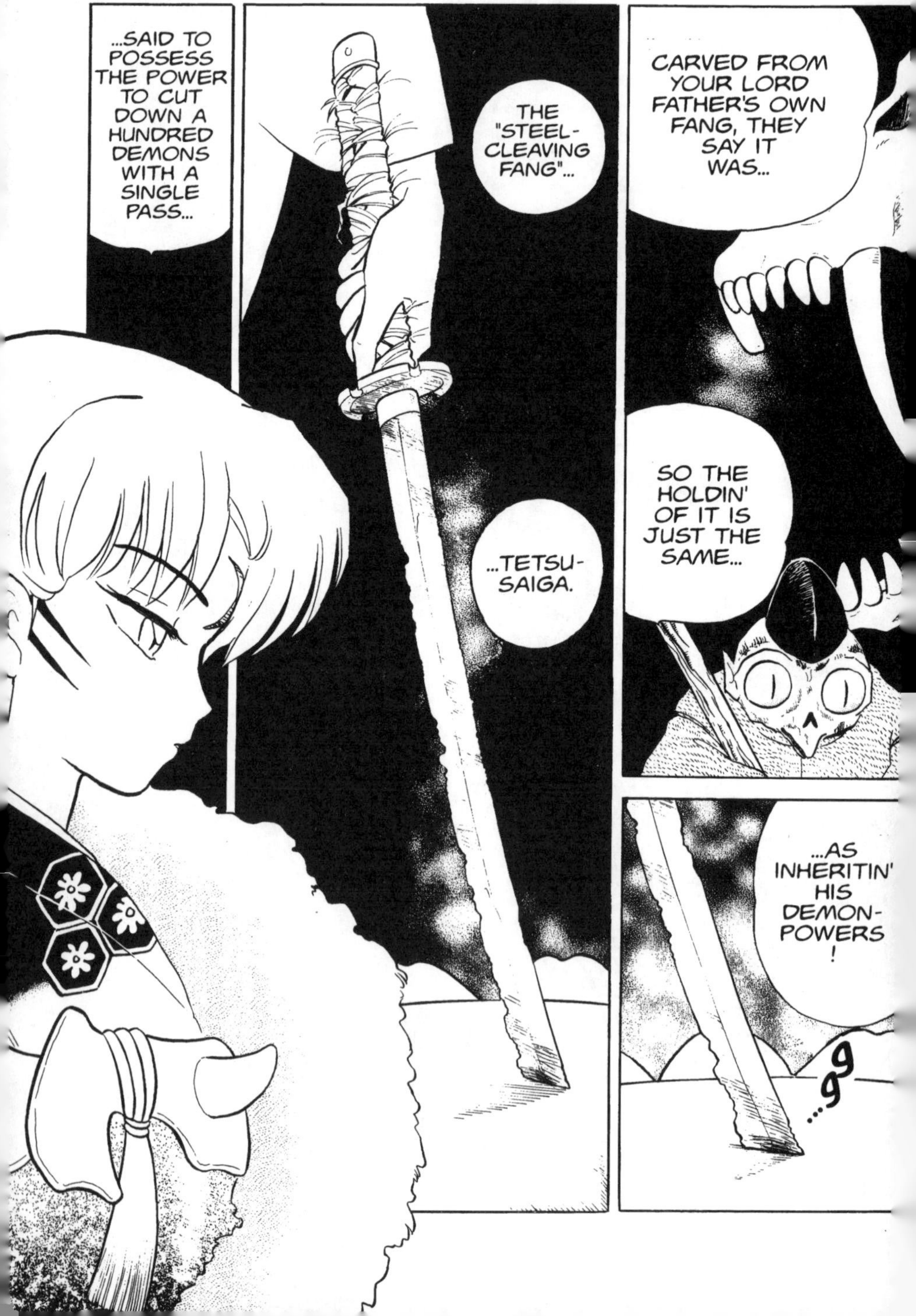
...SAID TO POSSESS THE POWER TO CUT DOWN A HUNDRED DEMONS WITH A SINGLE PASS...
THE "STEEL-CLEAVING FANG"...
...TETSU-SAIGA.
CARVED FROM YOUR LORD FATHER'S OWN FANG, THEY SAY IT WAS...
SO THE HOLDIN' OF IT IS JUST THE SAME...
...AS INHERITIN' HIS DEMON-POWERS!

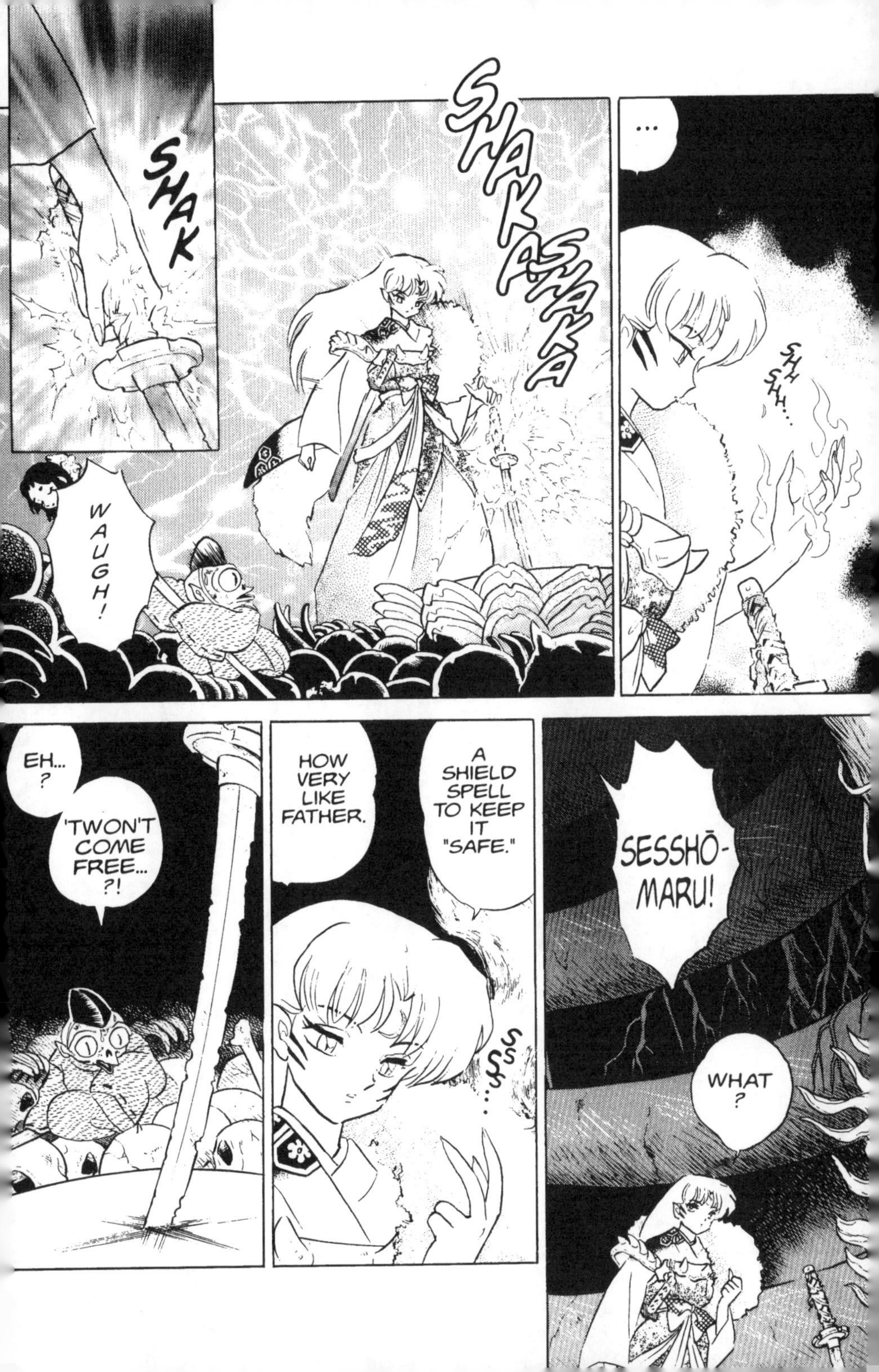
SHAK
SHAKASHAKA
WAUGH!
...
SHH SHH...
EH... ?
'TWON'T COME FREE... ?!
HOW VERY LIKE FATHER.
A SHIELD SPELL TO KEEP IT "SAFE."
SSS...
SESSHŌ-MARU!
WHAT ?

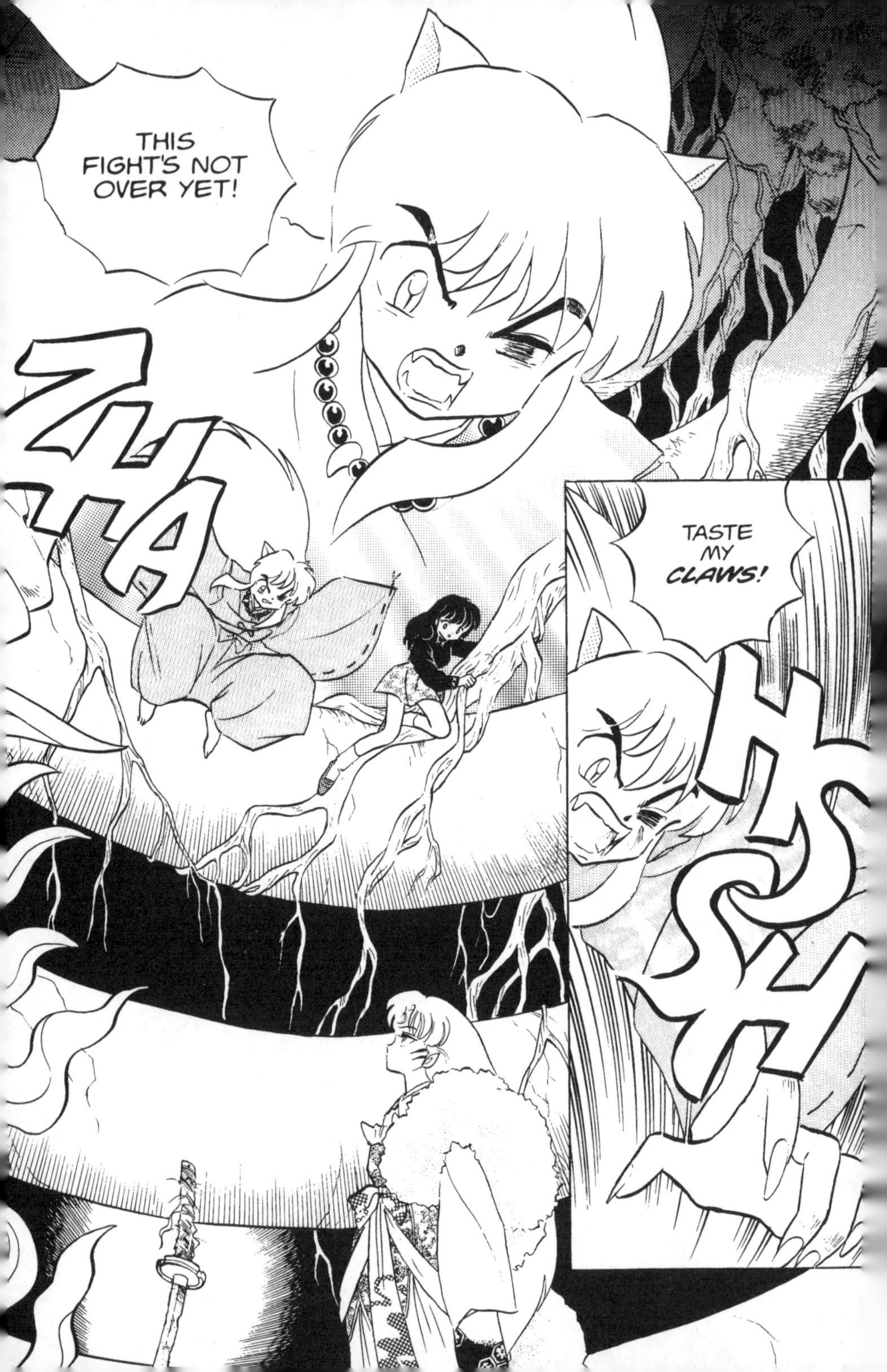
THIS FIGHT'S NOT OVER YET!
ZHA
TASTE MY CLAWS!
HSSH

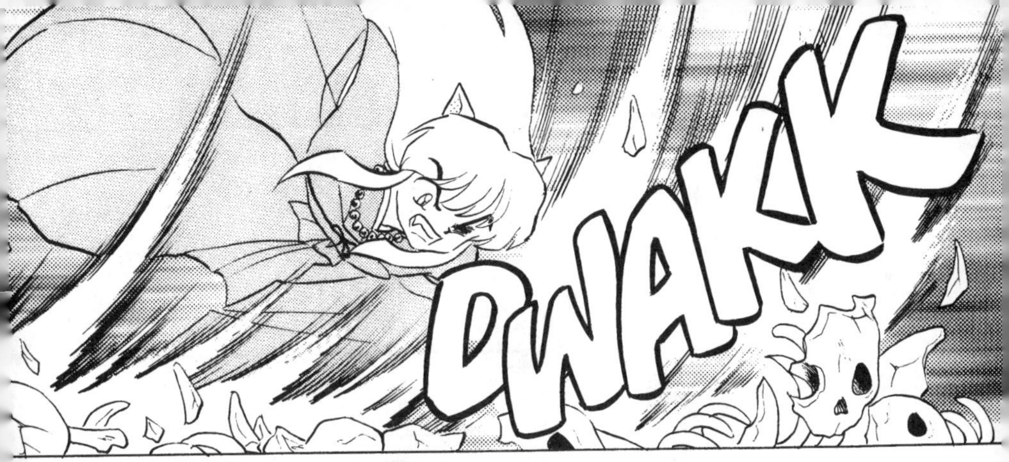
DWAKK

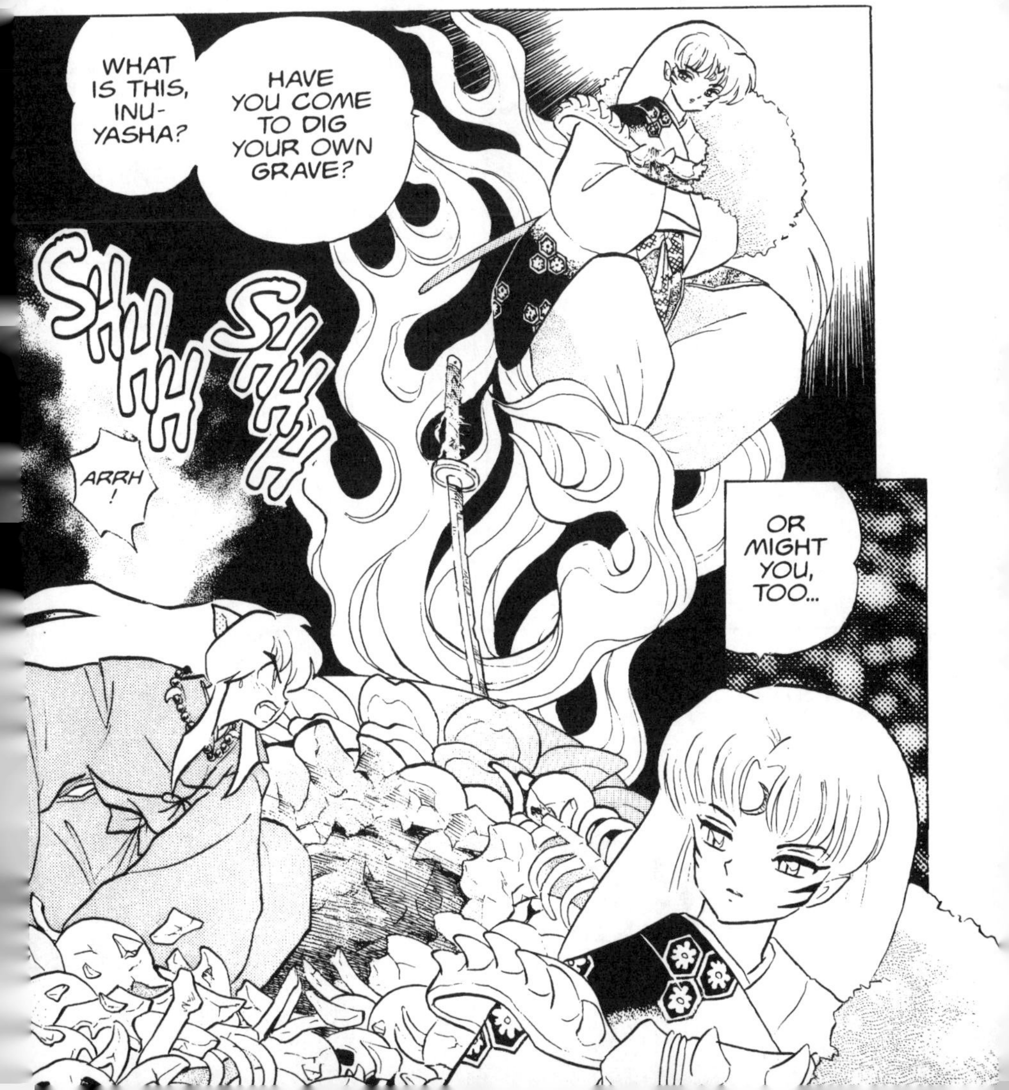
WHAT IS THIS, INU-YASHA?
HAVE YOU COME TO DIG YOUR OWN GRAVE?
SHHH
SHHHH
ARRH!
OR MIGHT YOU, TOO...

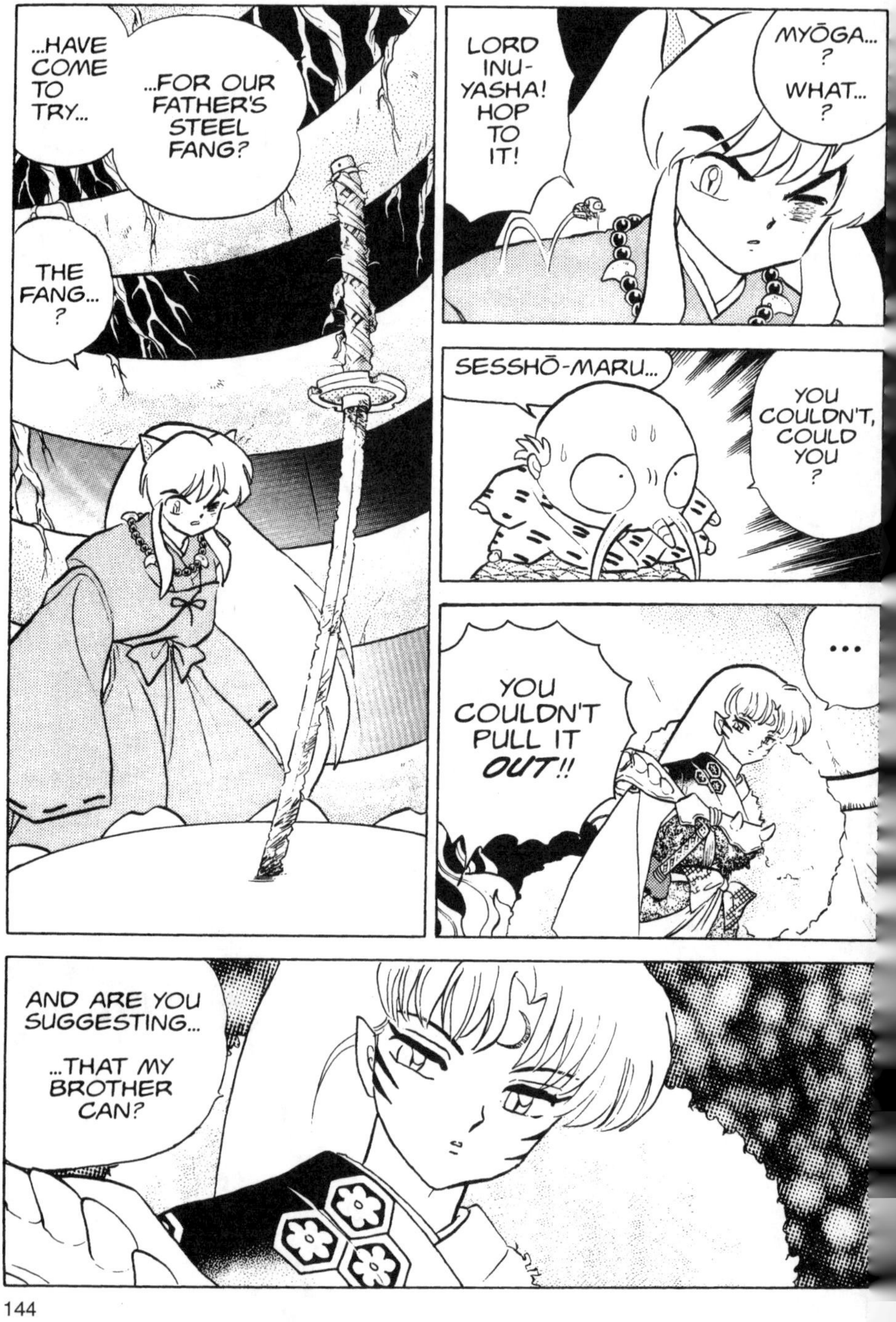
...HAVE COME TO TRY...
...FOR OUR FATHER'S STEEL FANG?
THE FANG...?
LORD INU-YASHA! HOP TO IT!
MYŌGA...? WHAT...?
SESSHŌ-MARU...
YOU COULDN'T, COULD YOU?
YOU COULDN'T PULL IT OUT!!
...
AND ARE YOU SUGGESTING...
...THAT MY BROTHER CAN?

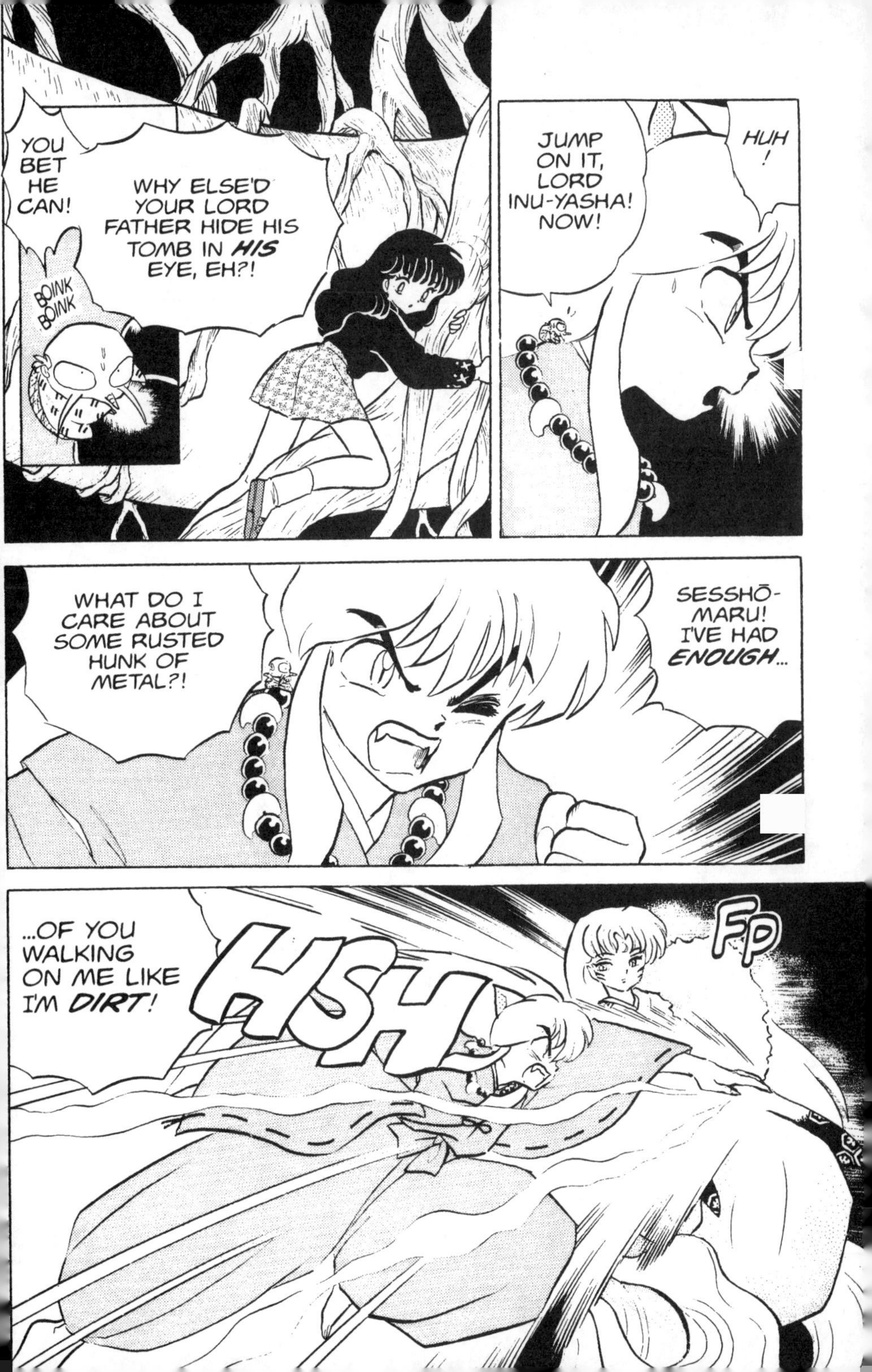
YOU BET HE CAN!
WHY ELSE'D YOUR LORD FATHER HIDE HIS TOMB IN *HIS* EYE, EH?!
BOINK BOINK
JUMP ON IT, LORD INU-YASHA! NOW!
HUH!
WHAT DO I CARE ABOUT SOME RUSTED HUNK OF METAL?!
SESSHŌ-MARU! I'VE HAD *ENOUGH*...
...OF YOU WALKING ON ME LIKE I'M *DIRT*!
HSH
FP

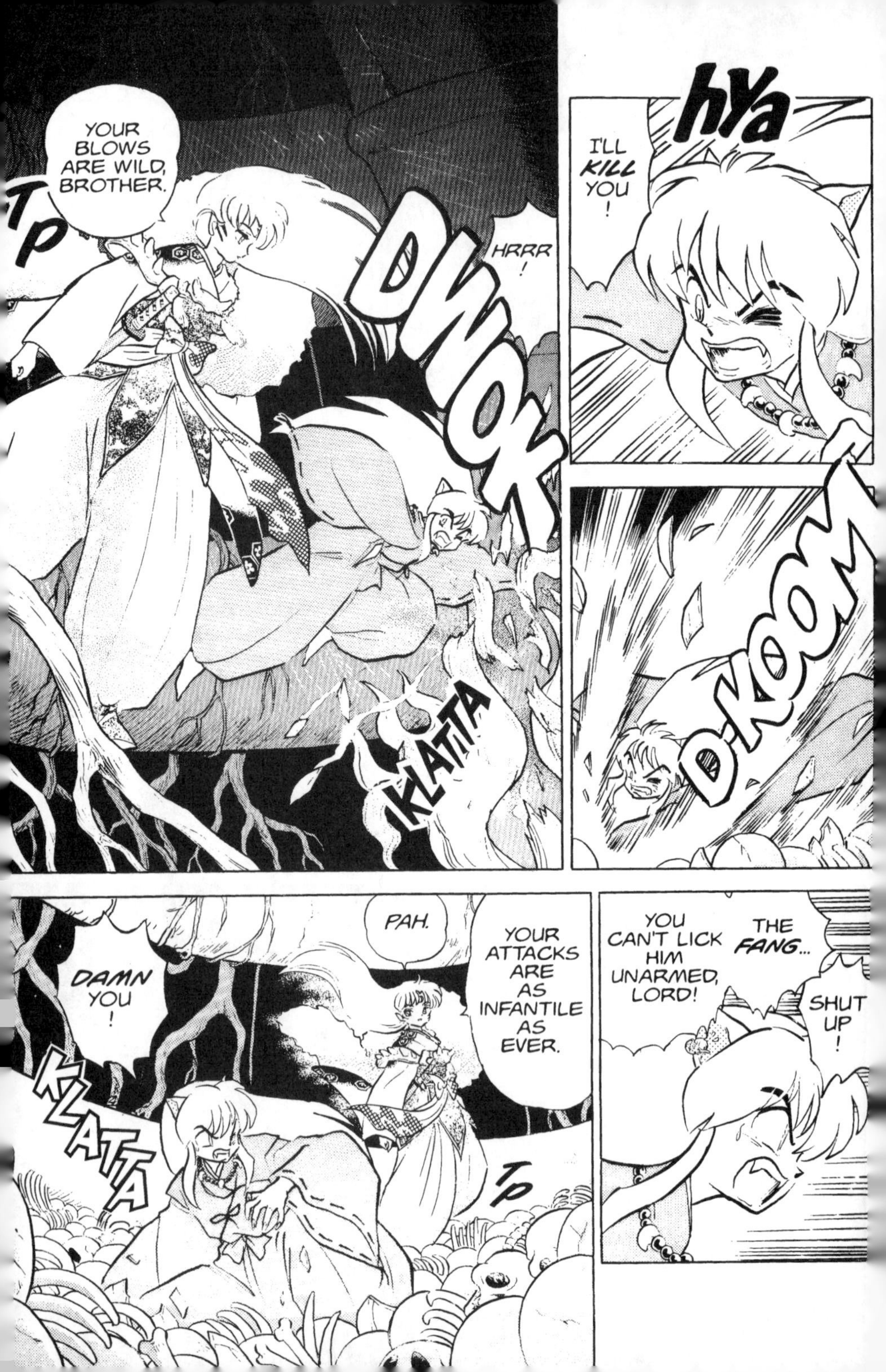

Tp
YOUR BLOWS ARE WILD, BROTHER.
DWOK
HRRR!
KLATTA
I'LL KILL YOU!
hYa
D-KOOM
DAMN YOU!
PAH.
YOUR ATTACKS ARE AS INFANTILE AS EVER.
KLATTA
Tp
YOU CAN'T LICK HIM UNARMED, LORD!
THE FANG...
SHUT UP!

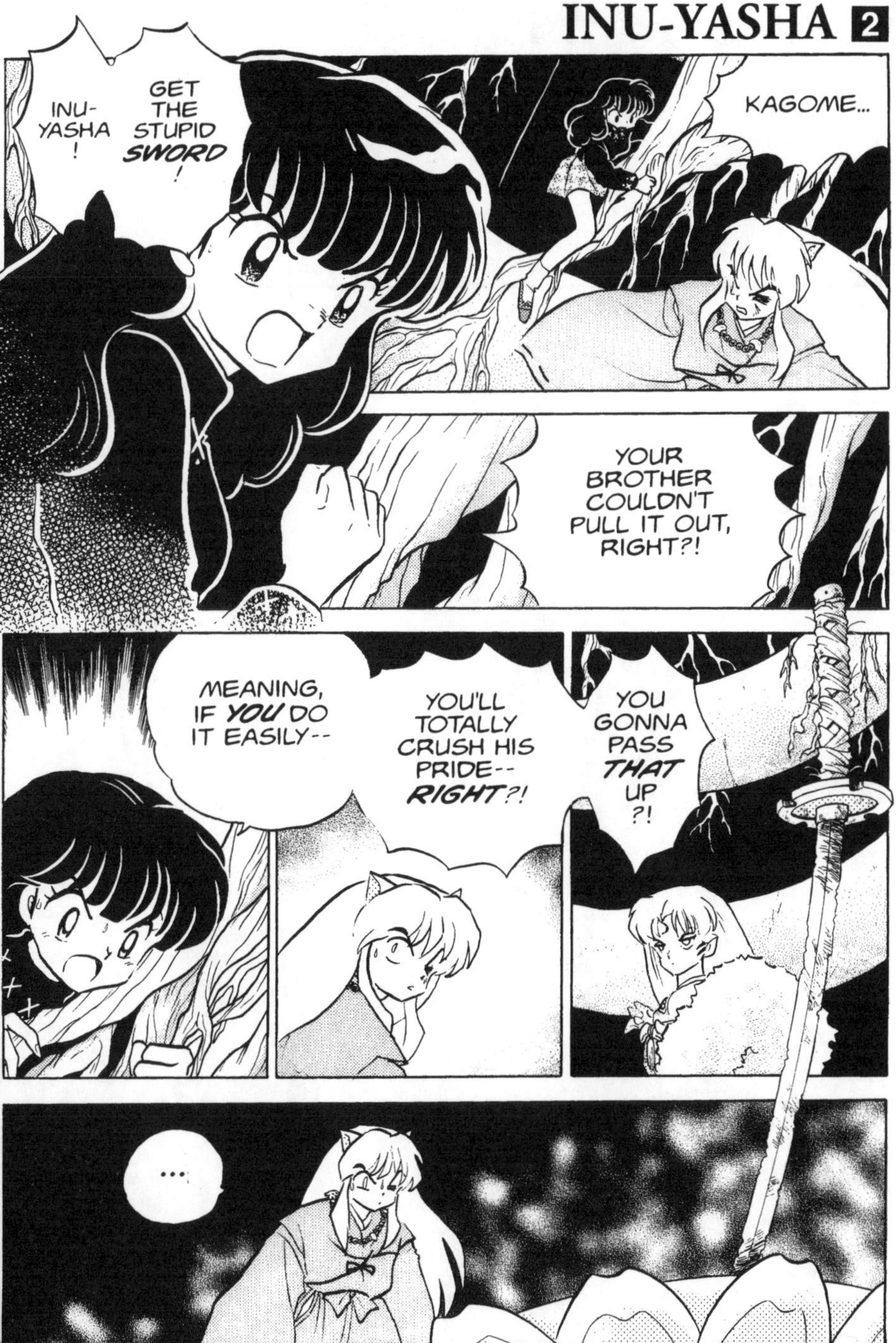
INU-YASHA!
GET THE STUPID SWORD!
KAGOME...
YOUR BROTHER COULDN'T PULL IT OUT, RIGHT?!
MEANING, IF YOU DO IT EASILY--
YOU'LL TOTALLY CRUSH HIS PRIDE--RIGHT?!
YOU GONNA PASS THAT UP?!
...

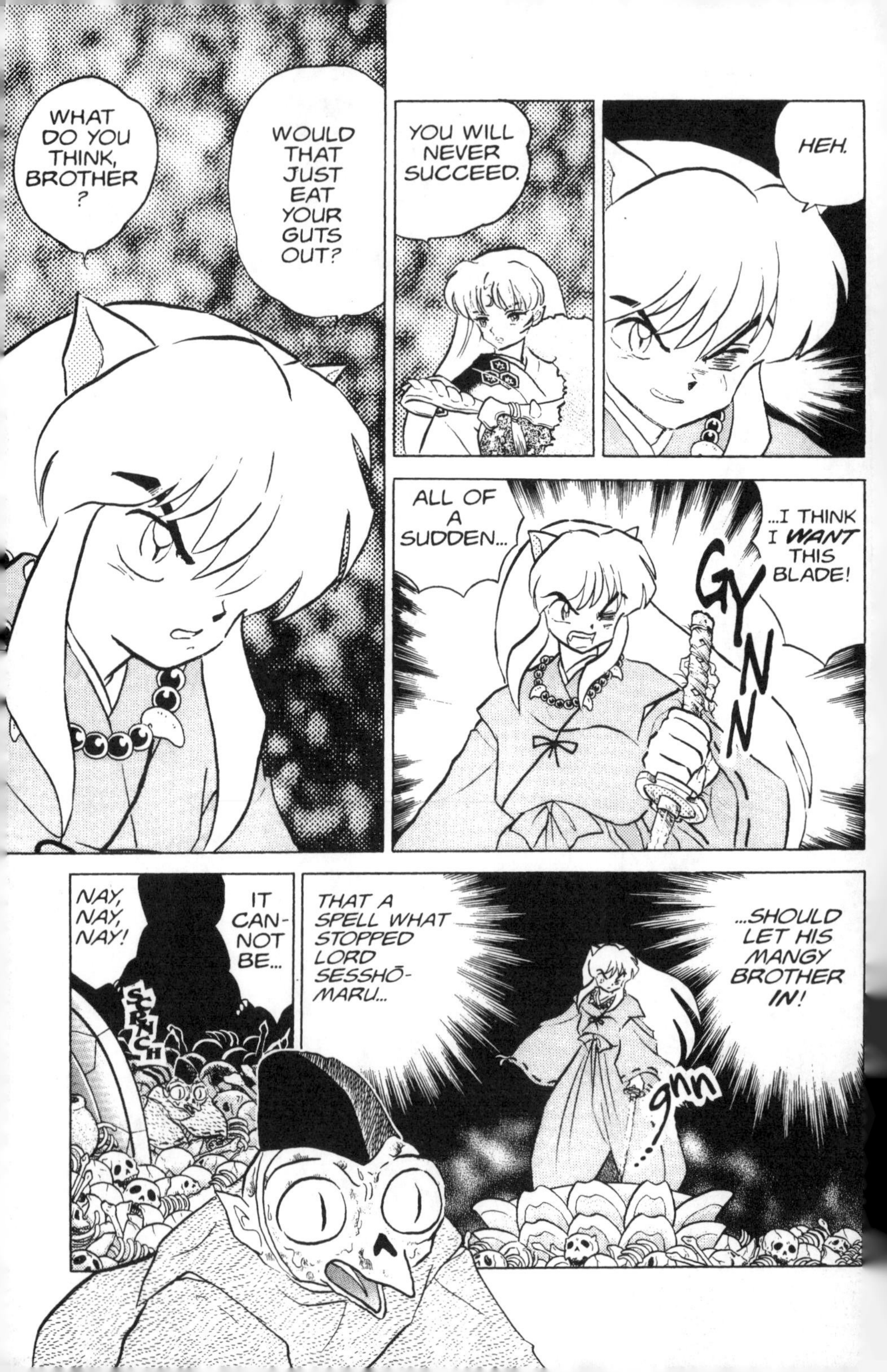
WHAT DO YOU THINK, BROTHER ?
WOULD THAT JUST EAT YOUR GUTS OUT?
YOU WILL NEVER SUCCEED.
HEH.
ALL OF A SUDDEN...
...I THINK I *WANT* THIS BLADE!
GYNNN
NAY, NAY, NAY!
IT CAN-NOT BE...
SCRNCH
THAT A SPELL WHAT STOPPED LORD SESSHŌ-MARU...
...SHOULD LET HIS MANGY BROTHER *IN*!
...gnn

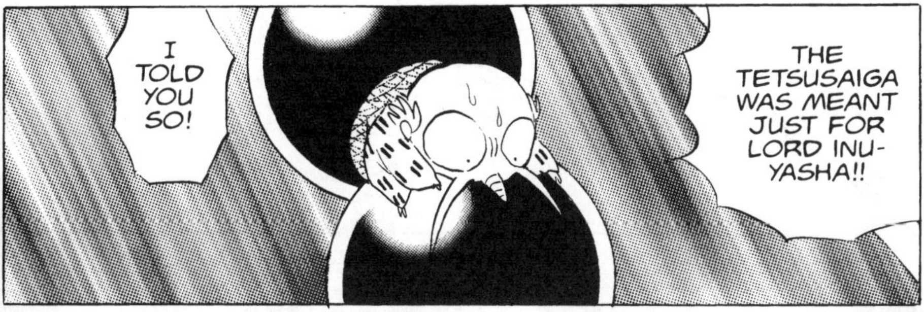
I TOLD YOU SO!
THE TETSUSAIGA WAS MEANT JUST FOR LORD INU-YASHA!!

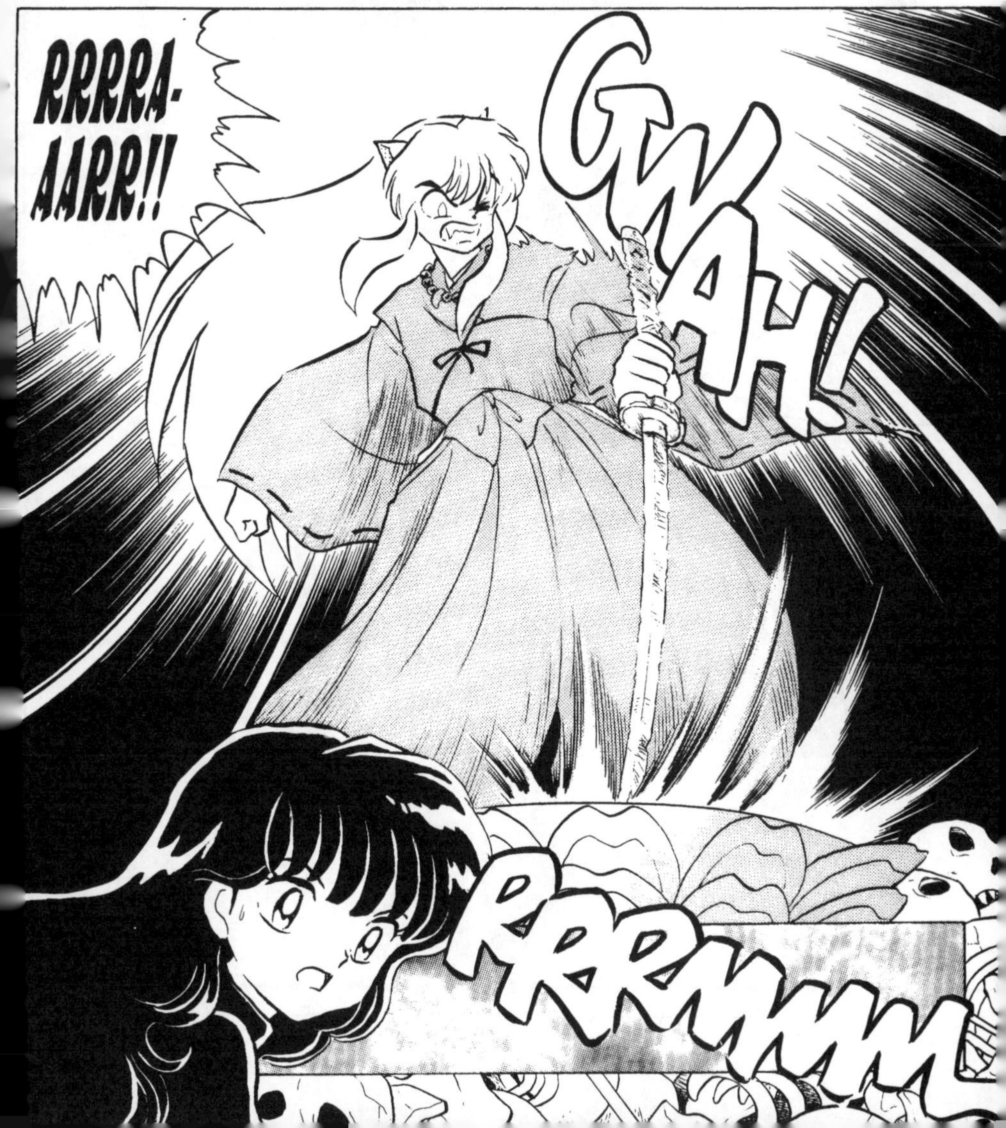
RRRRA-AARR!!
GWAH!
RRRMMMM

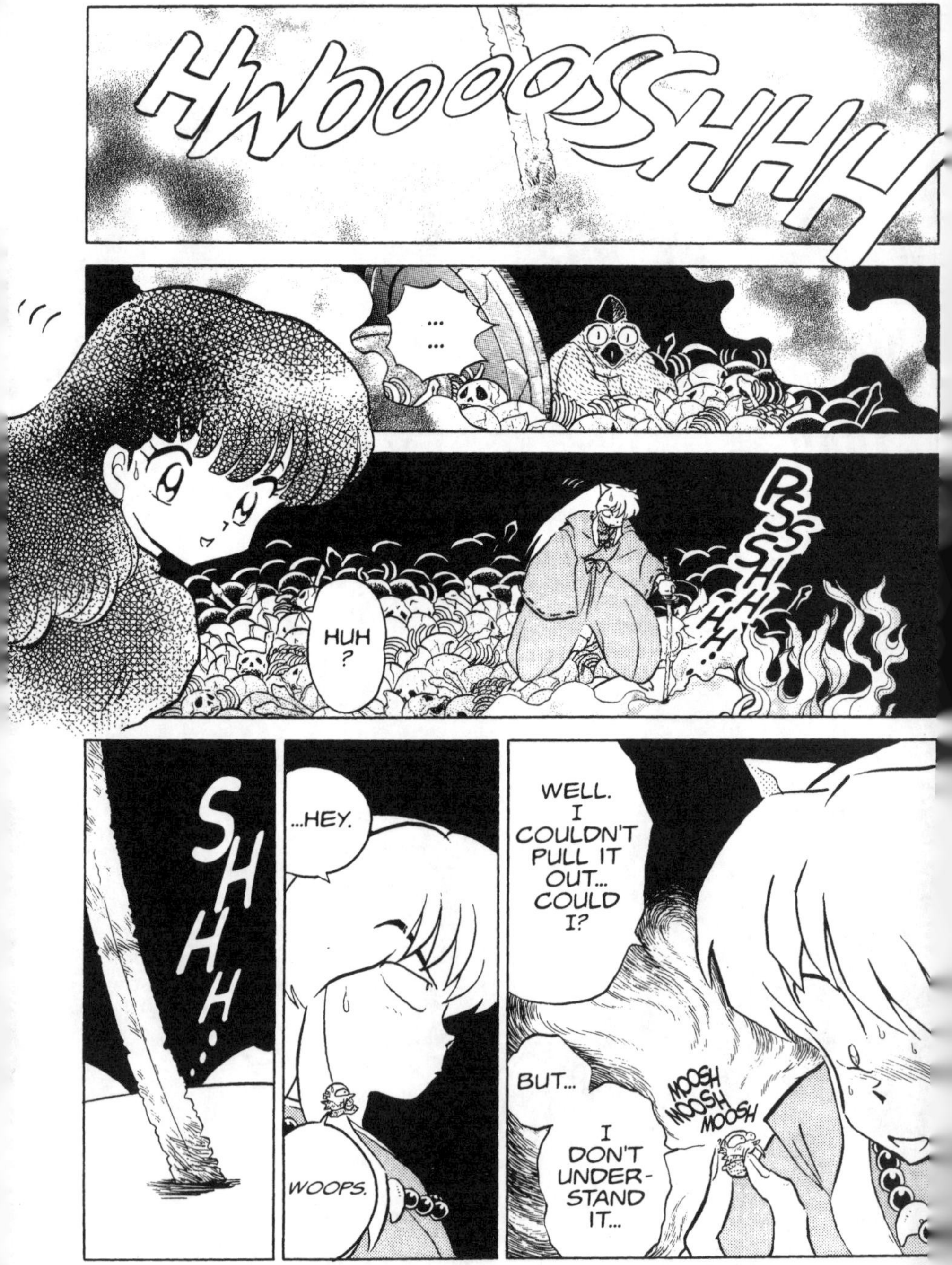
HWOOOSHHH
…
…
HUH?
PSSSHHHH…
SHHH…
…HEY.
WOOPS.
WELL. I COULDN'T PULL IT OUT… COULD I?
BUT…
MOOSH MOOSH MOOSH
I DON'T UNDERSTAND IT…

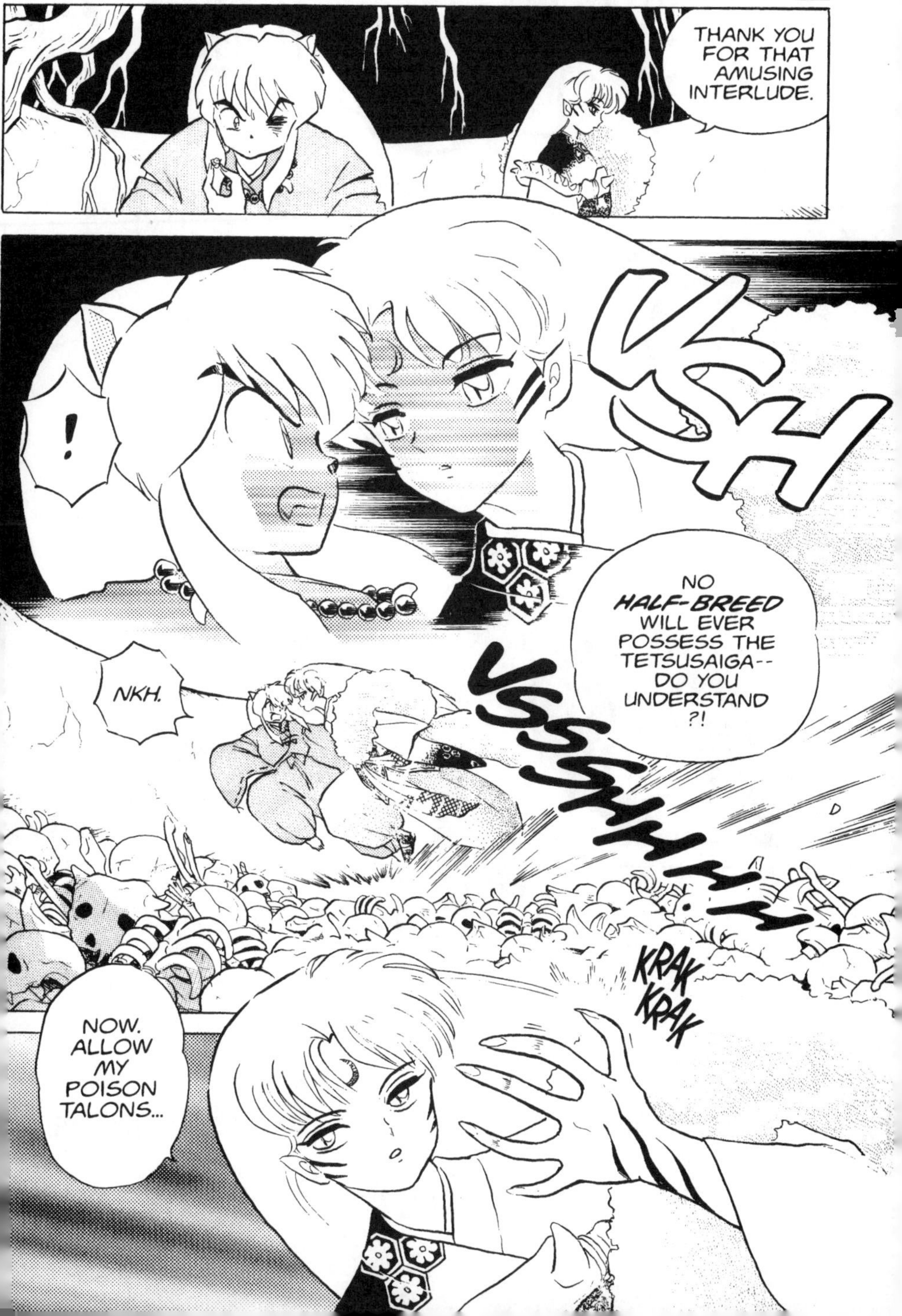
THANK YOU FOR THAT AMUSING INTERLUDE.
!
VSH
NO *HALF-BREED* WILL EVER POSSESS THE TETSUSAIGA-- DO YOU UNDERSTAND ?!
NKH.
VSSSHHHH
KRAK KRAK
NOW. ALLOW MY POISON TALONS...

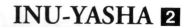

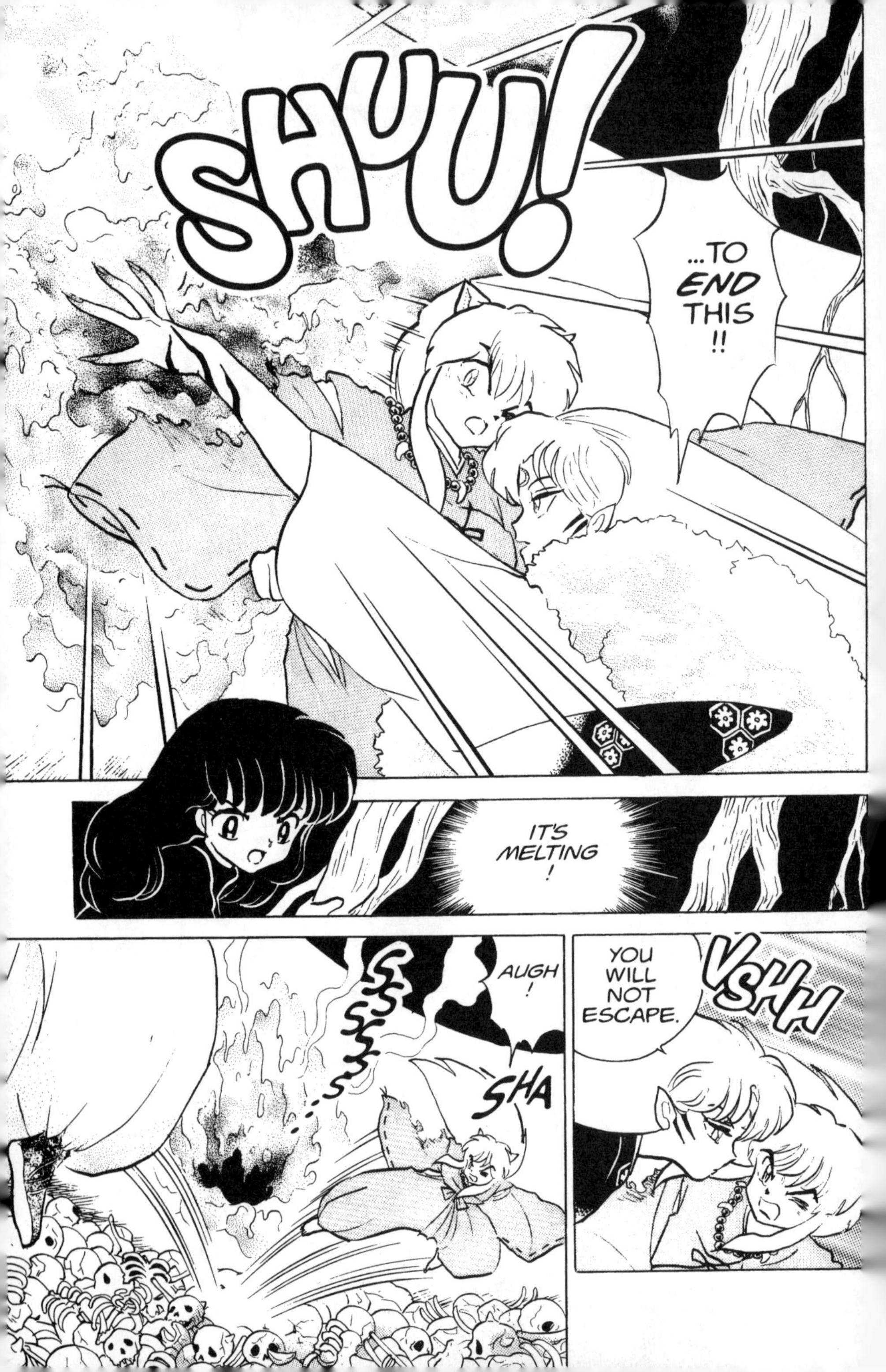
SHUU!
...TO END THIS !!
IT'S MELTING !
SSSSSS
AUGH !
SHA
YOU WILL NOT ESCAPE.
VSHH

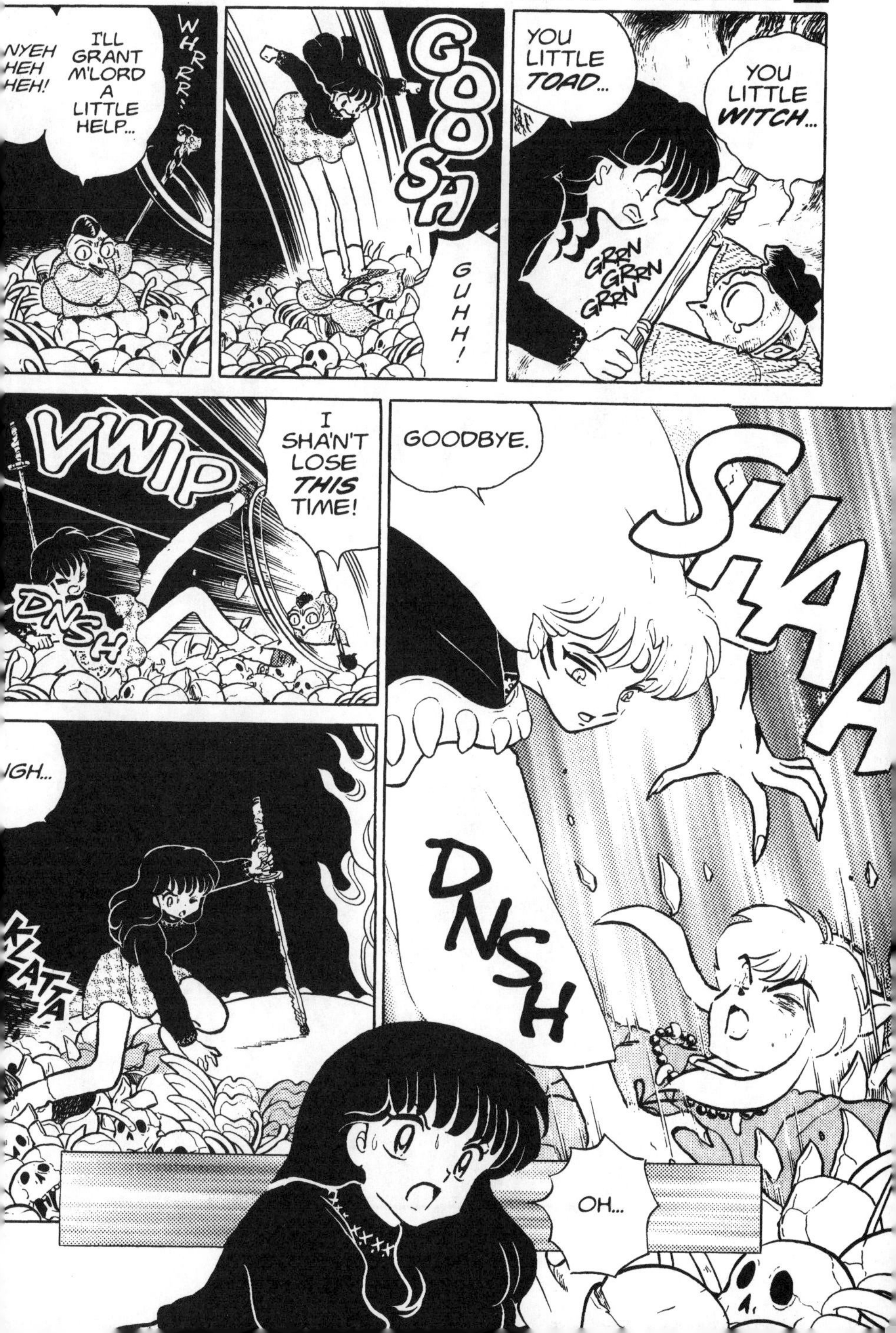
NYEH HEH HEH!
I'LL GRANT M'LORD A LITTLE HELP...
WHRRR...
GOOSH
GUHH!
YOU LITTLE *TOAD*...
YOU LITTLE *WITCH*...
GRRN GRRN GRRN
VWIP
I SHA'N'T LOSE *THIS* TIME!
DNSH
GOODBYE.
SHAA
IGH...
KLATTA
DNSH
OH...

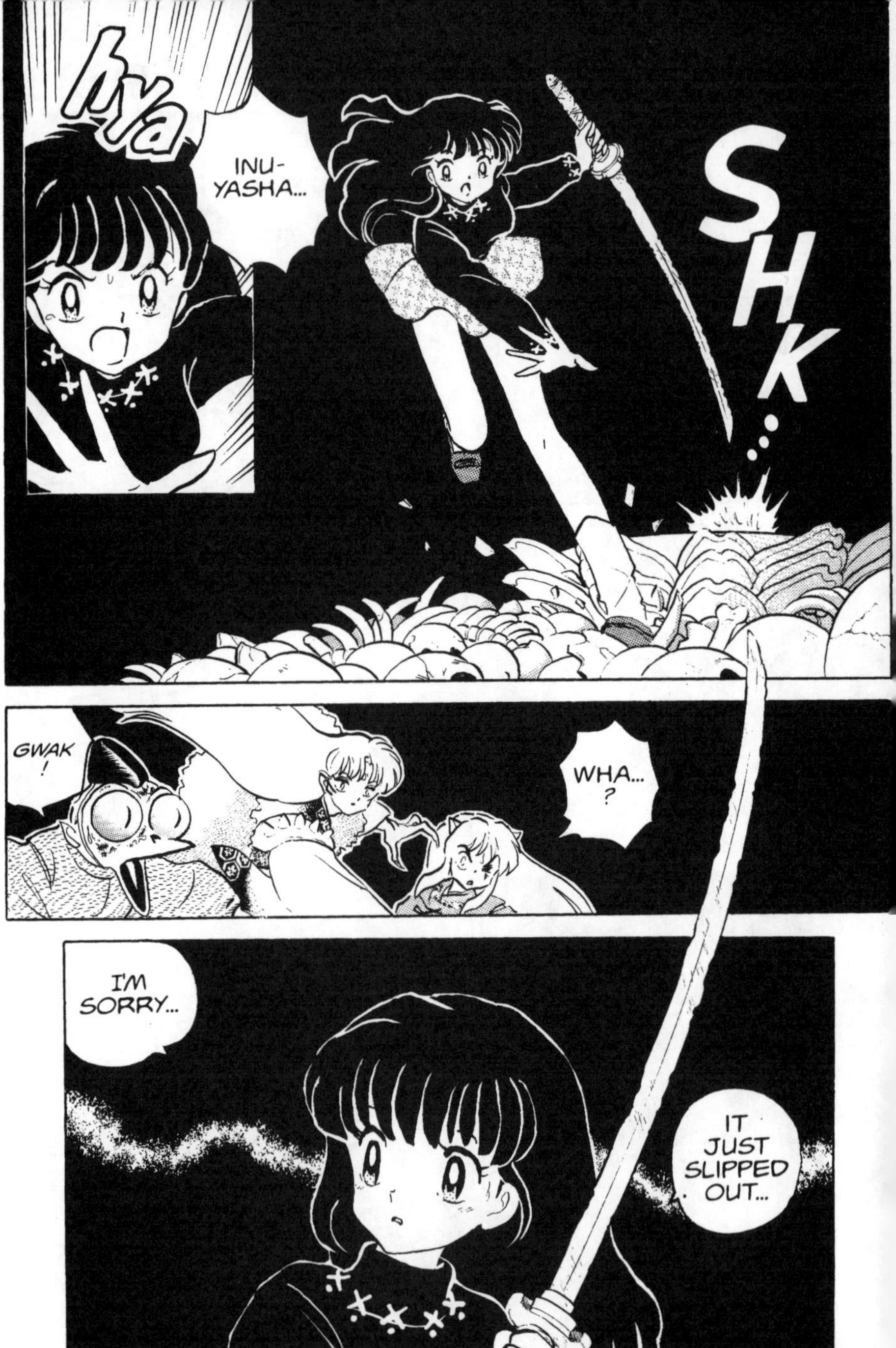
hya
INU-
YASHA...
SHK...
GWAK!
WHA...?
I'M
SORRY...
IT
JUST
SLIPPED
OUT...

SCROLL NINE
THE TRANSFORMATION

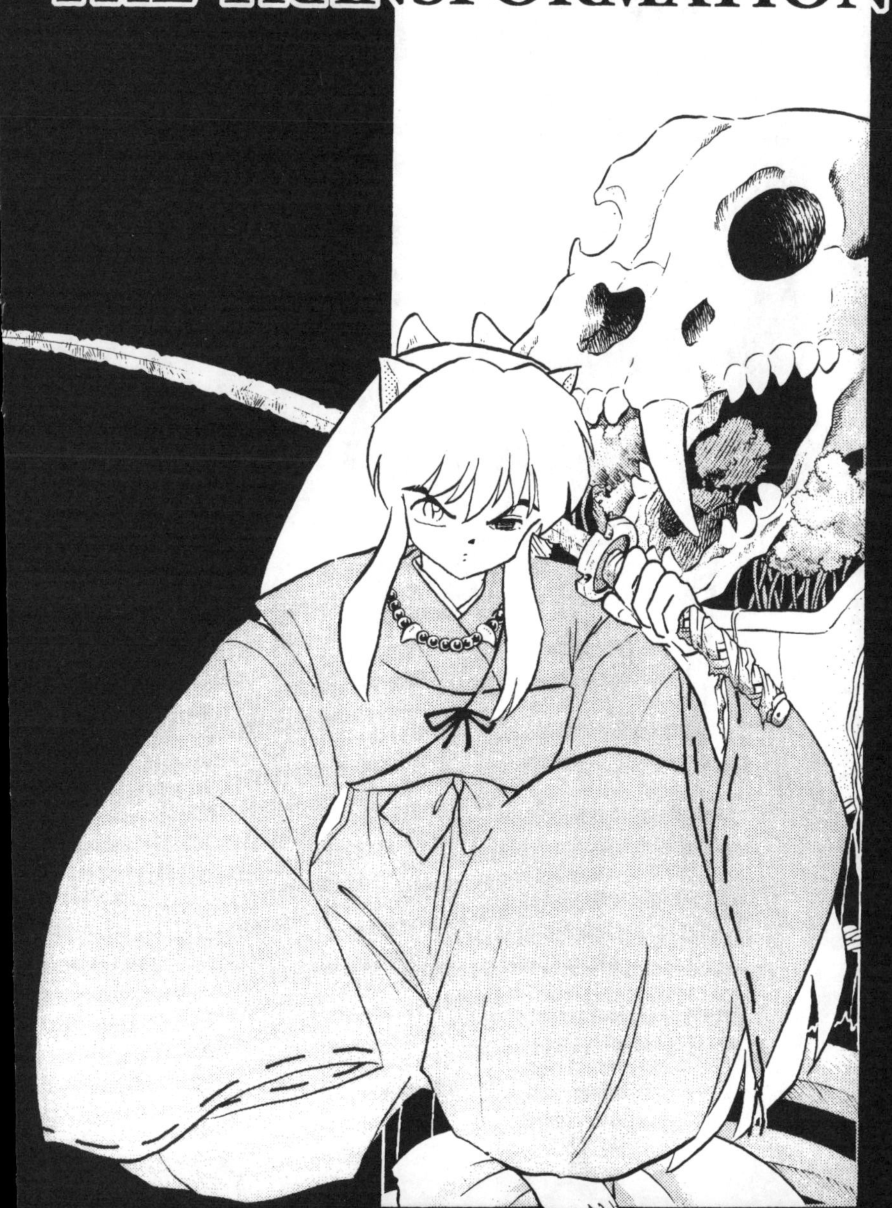

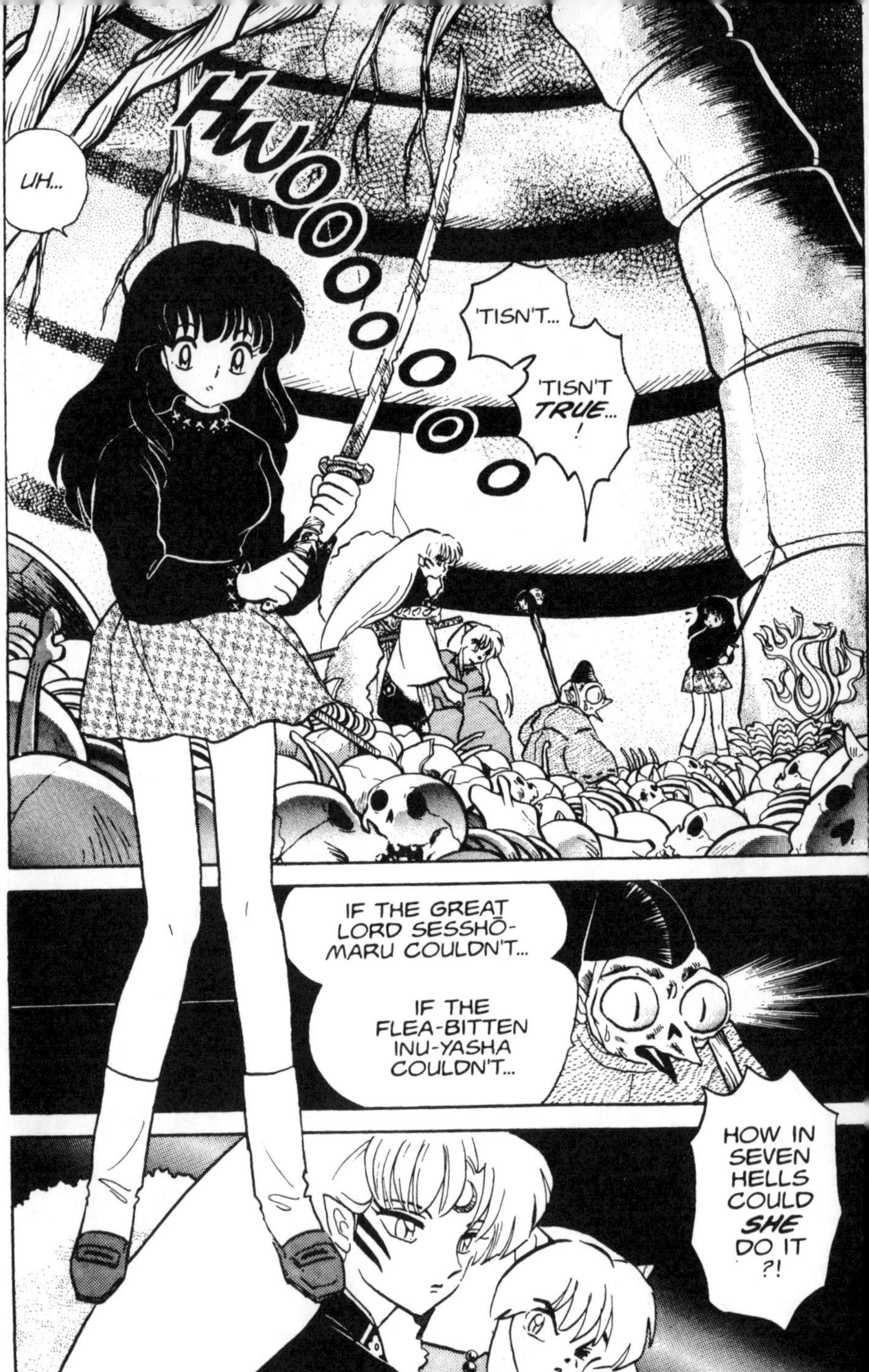
UH...
HWOOOOOOOOOO
'TISN'T...
'TISN'T *TRUE*...!
IF THE GREAT LORD SESSHŌ-MARU COULDN'T...
IF THE FLEA-BITTEN INU-YASHA COULDN'T...
HOW IN SEVEN HELLS COULD *SHE* DO IT?!

NEVER TAKE YOUR EYES OFF *ME!*

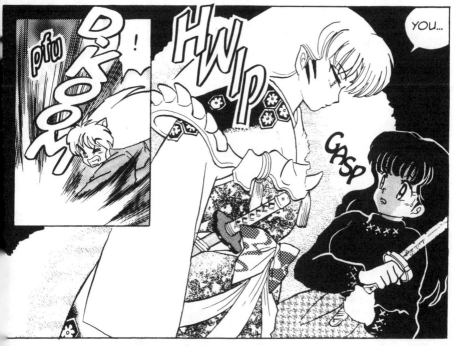

YOU...

GASP

GUH...

LOOKS LIKE YOUR LORD BROTHER'S LOST INTEREST IN YOU...

LUCKY FOR YOU!

SHUT UP, BUG!

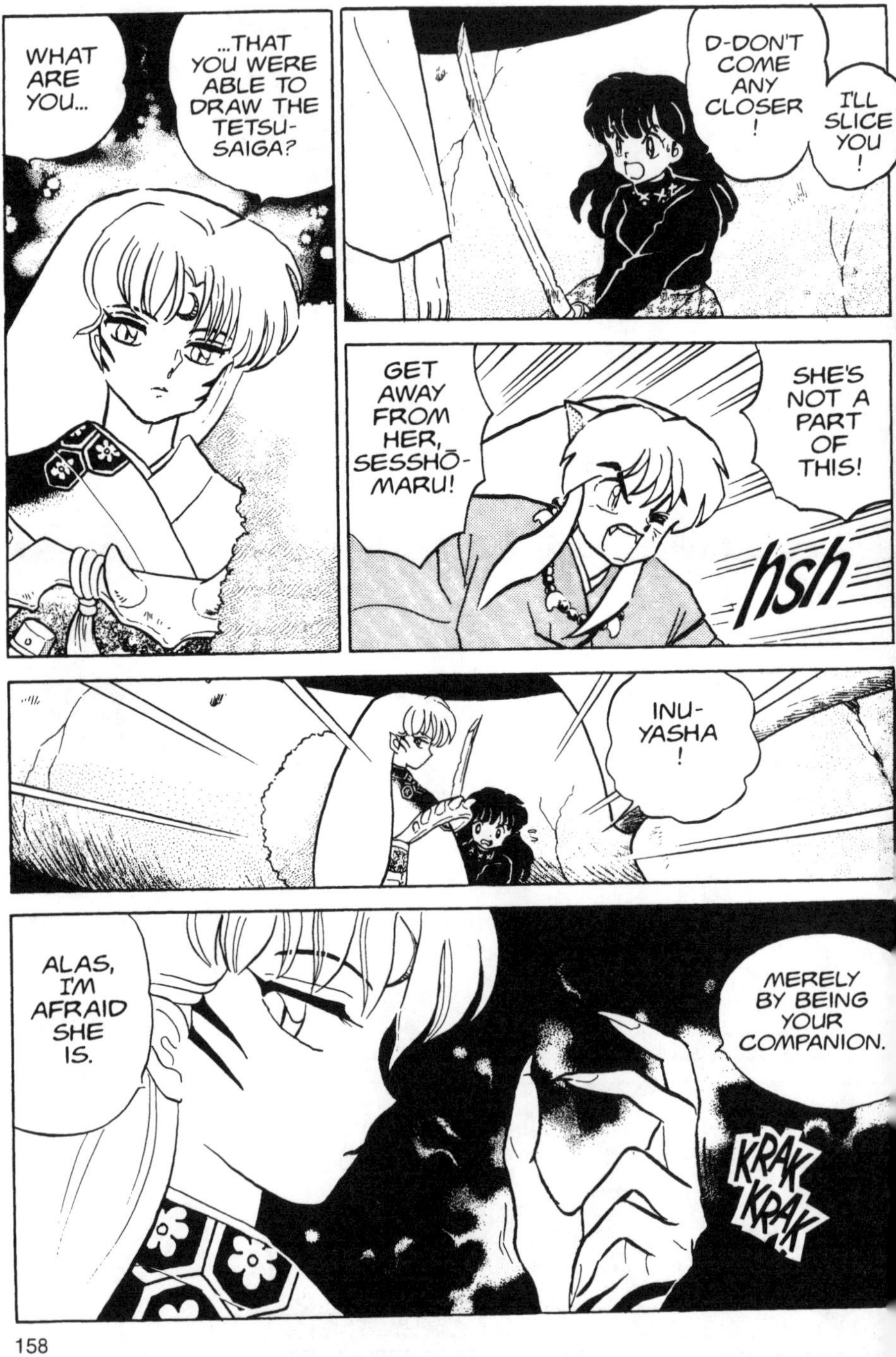
WHAT ARE YOU...
...THAT YOU WERE ABLE TO DRAW THE TETSU-SAIGA?
D-DON'T COME ANY CLOSER!
I'LL SLICE YOU!
GET AWAY FROM HER, SESSHŌMARU!
SHE'S NOT A PART OF THIS!
hsh
INU-YASHA!
ALAS, I'M AFRAID SHE IS.
MERELY BY BEING YOUR COMPANION.
KRAK KRAK

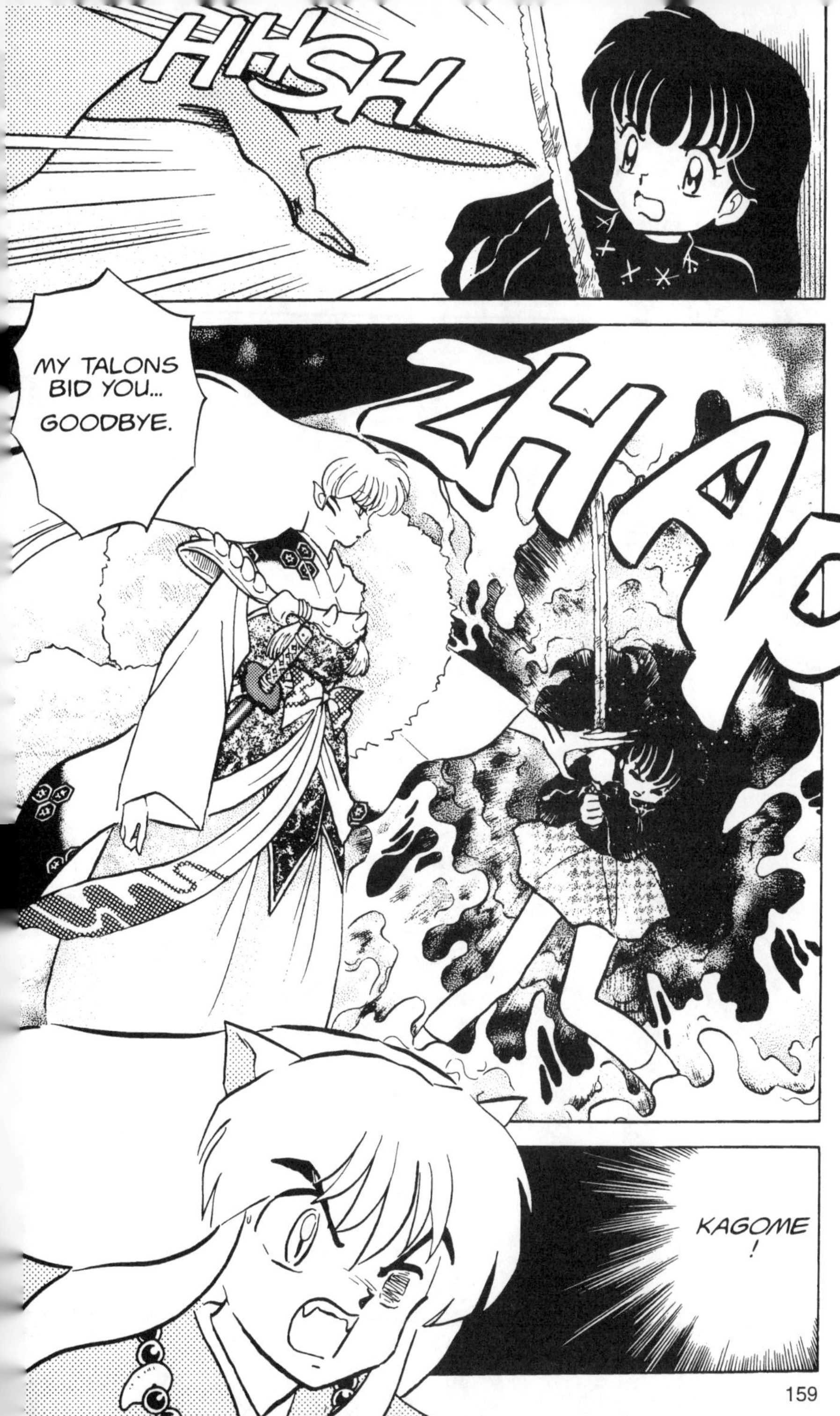
HHSH
MY TALONS BID YOU... GOODBYE.
ZHAP
KAGOME!

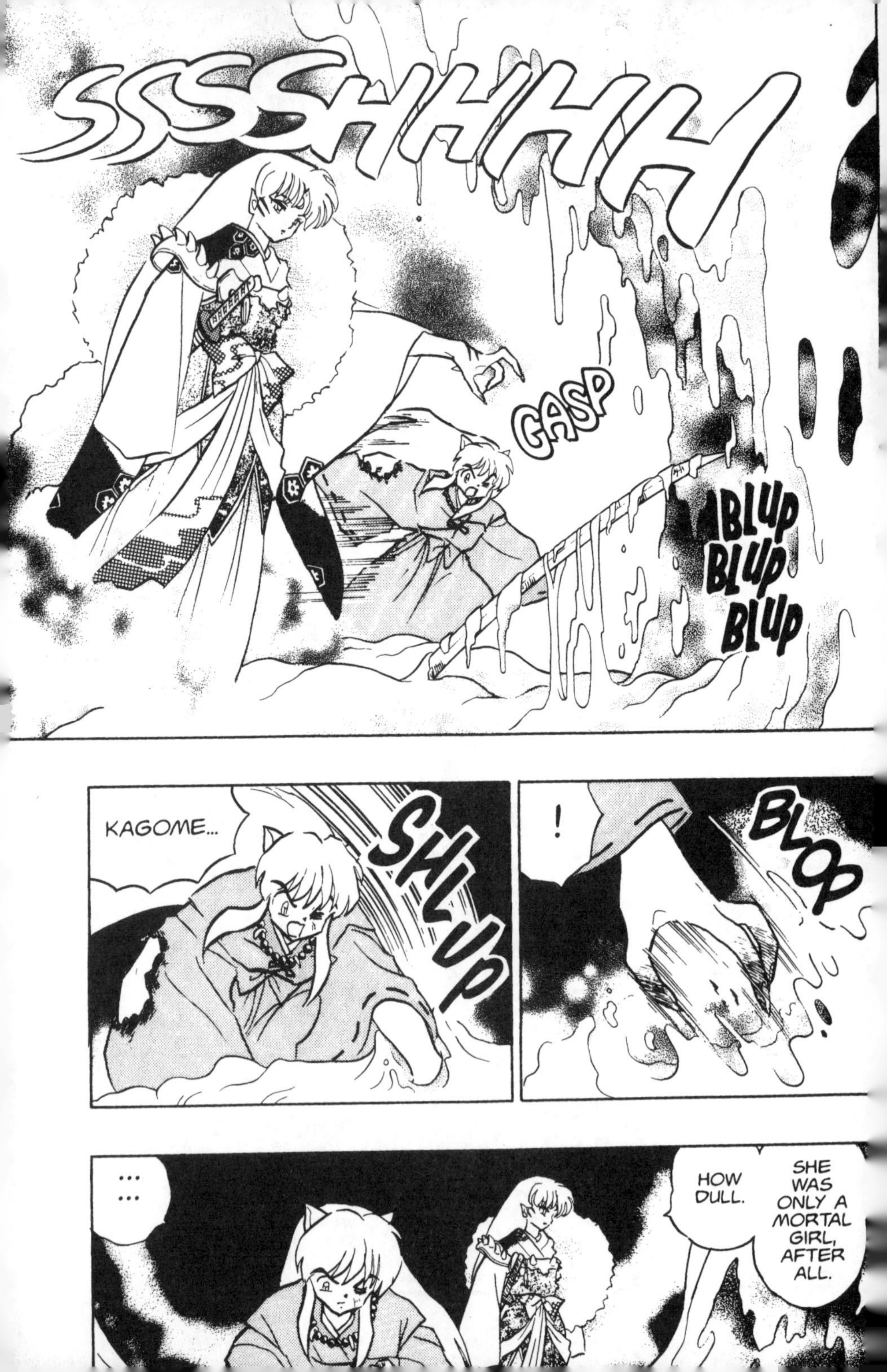
SSSHHHH
GASP
BLUP BLUP BLUP
KAGOME...
SHLUP
!
BLOOP
...
...
HOW DULL.
SHE WAS ONLY A MORTAL GIRL, AFTER ALL.

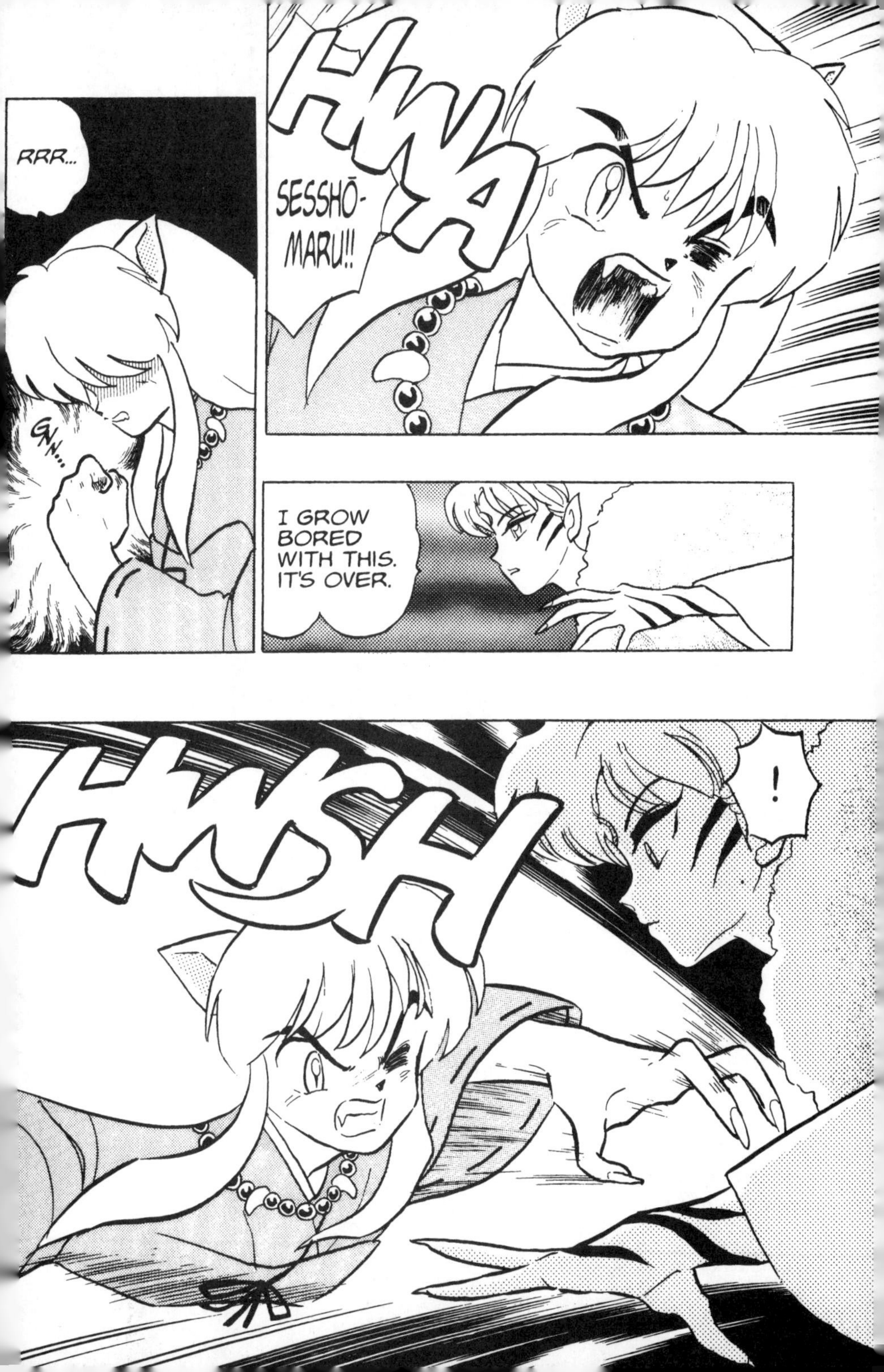
RRR...
GNN...
HWA
SESSHŌ-MARU!!
I GROW BORED WITH THIS. IT'S OVER.
HWSH
!

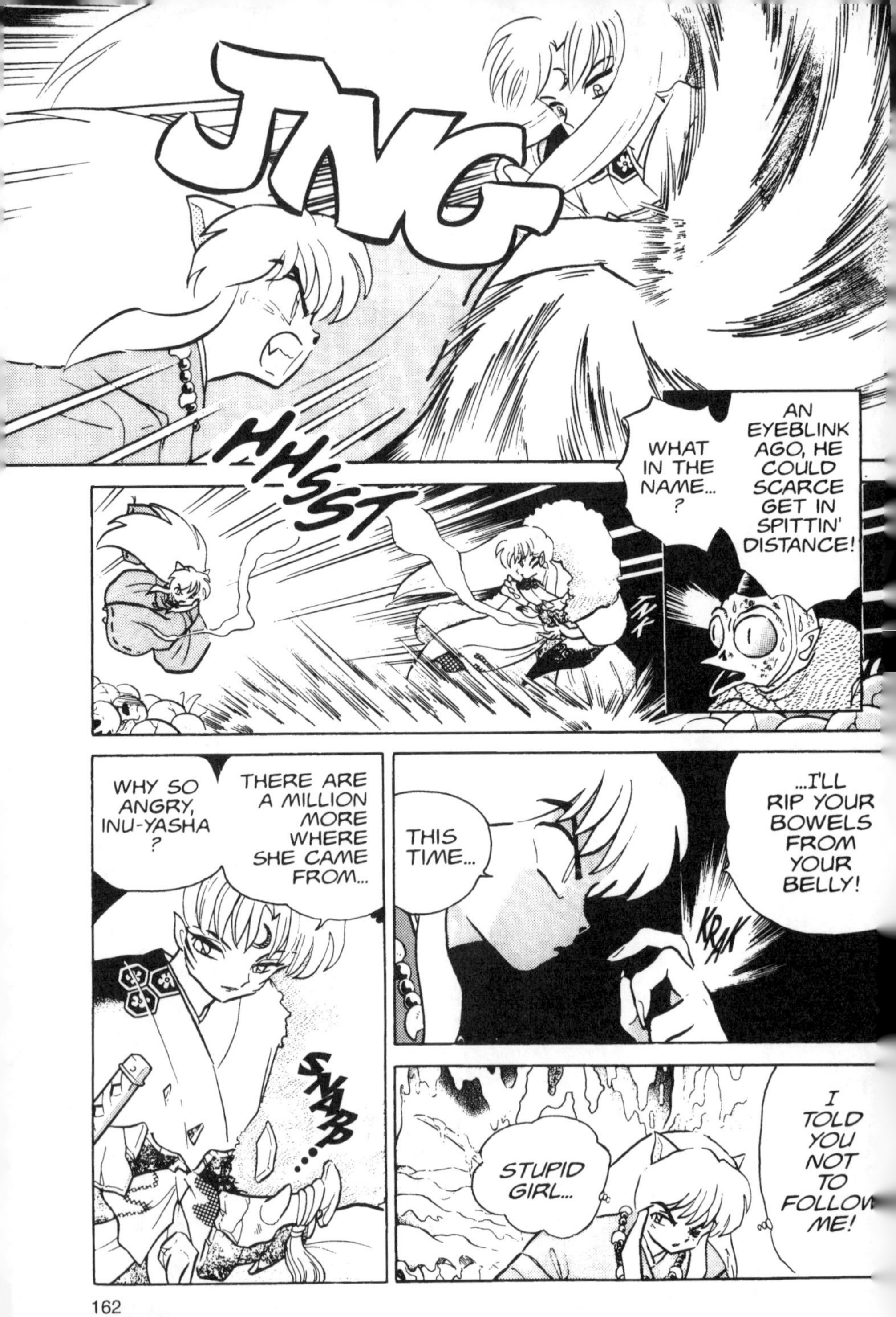

JING
HHSST
WHAT IN THE NAME...?
AN EYEBLINK AGO, HE COULD SCARCE GET IN SPITTIN' DISTANCE!
WHY SO ANGRY, INU-YASHA?
THERE ARE A MILLION MORE WHERE SHE CAME FROM...
SNAP...
THIS TIME...
...I'LL RIP YOUR BOWELS FROM YOUR BELLY!
KRAK
STUPID GIRL...
I TOLD YOU NOT TO FOLLOW ME!

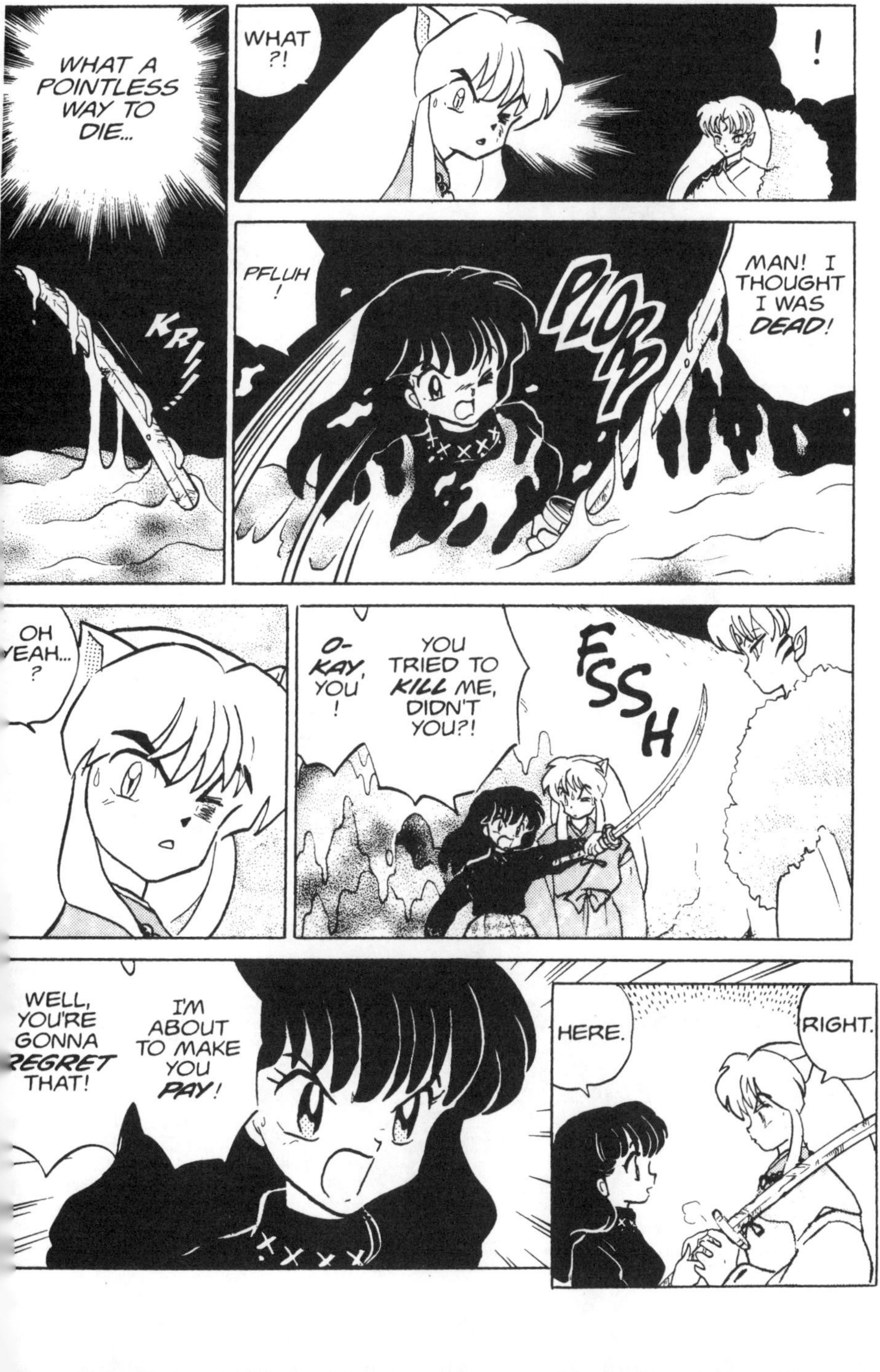
WHAT A POINTLESS WAY TO DIE...
KRI!!...
WHAT ?!
!
PFLUH !
PLOP
MAN! I THOUGHT I WAS DEAD!
OH YEAH... ?
O-KAY, YOU !
YOU TRIED TO KILL ME, DIDN'T YOU?!
FSSH
WELL, YOU'RE GONNA REGRET THAT!
I'M ABOUT TO MAKE YOU PAY!
HERE.
RIGHT.

THIS SWORD LOOKS REALLY *AWESOME*!

GO *TO* IT!

TELL ME...

WHY ARE YOU SUDDENLY SO... BOUNCY?

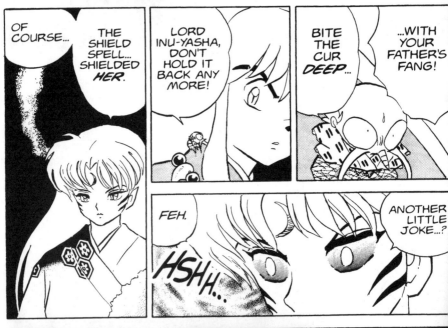

OF COURSE...

THE SHIELD SPELL... SHIELDED *HER*.

LORD INU-YASHA, DON'T HOLD IT BACK ANY MORE!

BITE THE CUR *DEEP*...

...WITH YOUR FATHER'S FANG!

FEH.

HSHH...

ANOTHER LITTLE JOKE...?

LET US SEE WHAT A HALF-BREED LIKE YOU CAN DO WITH THE PURITY OF THE TETSUSAIGA...

ZAWA ZAWA

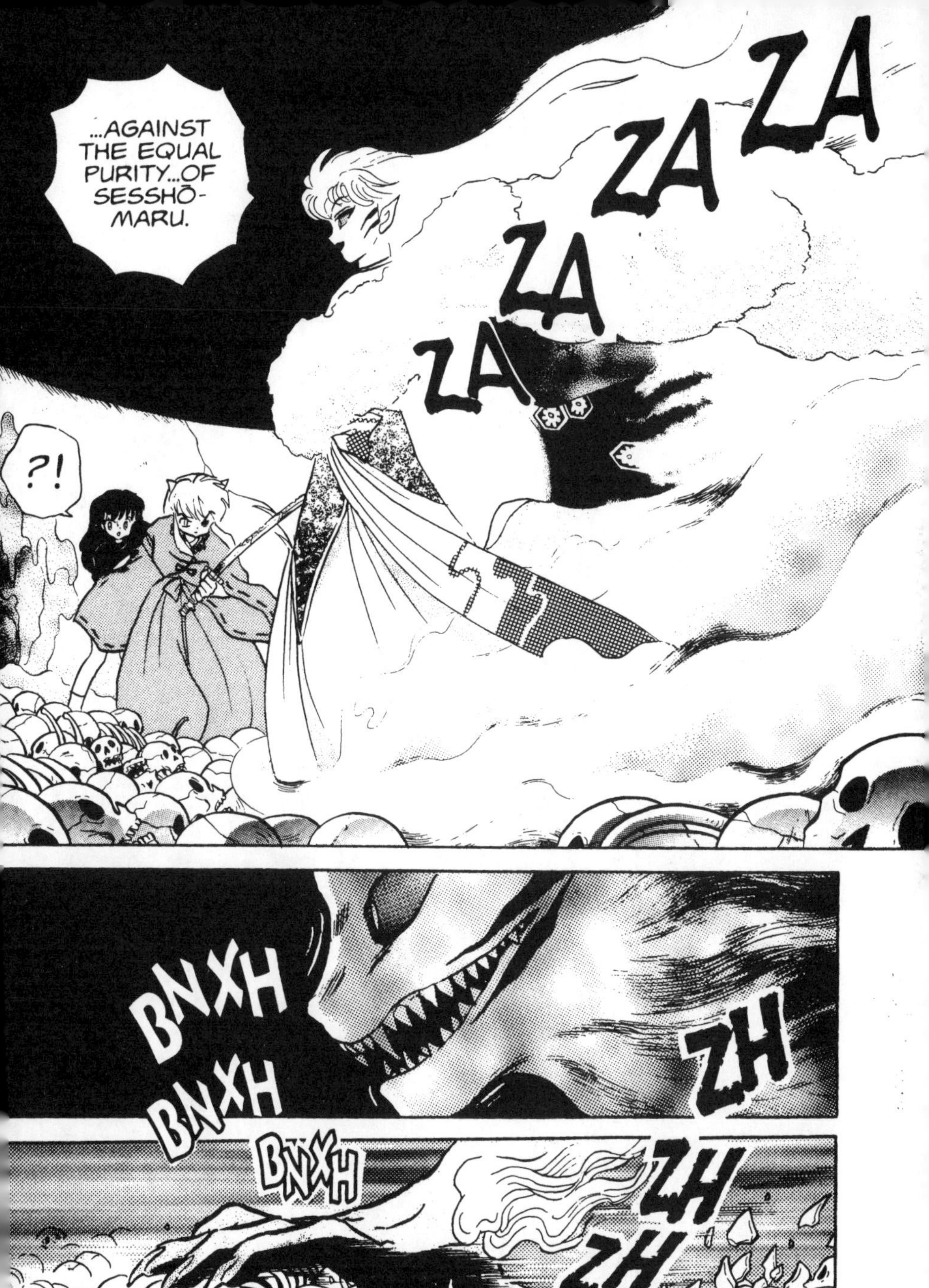
...AGAINST THE EQUAL PURITY...OF SESSHŌ-MARU.
ZA ZA ZA ZA ZA
?!
BNXH BNXH
ZH
BNXH
ZH ZH

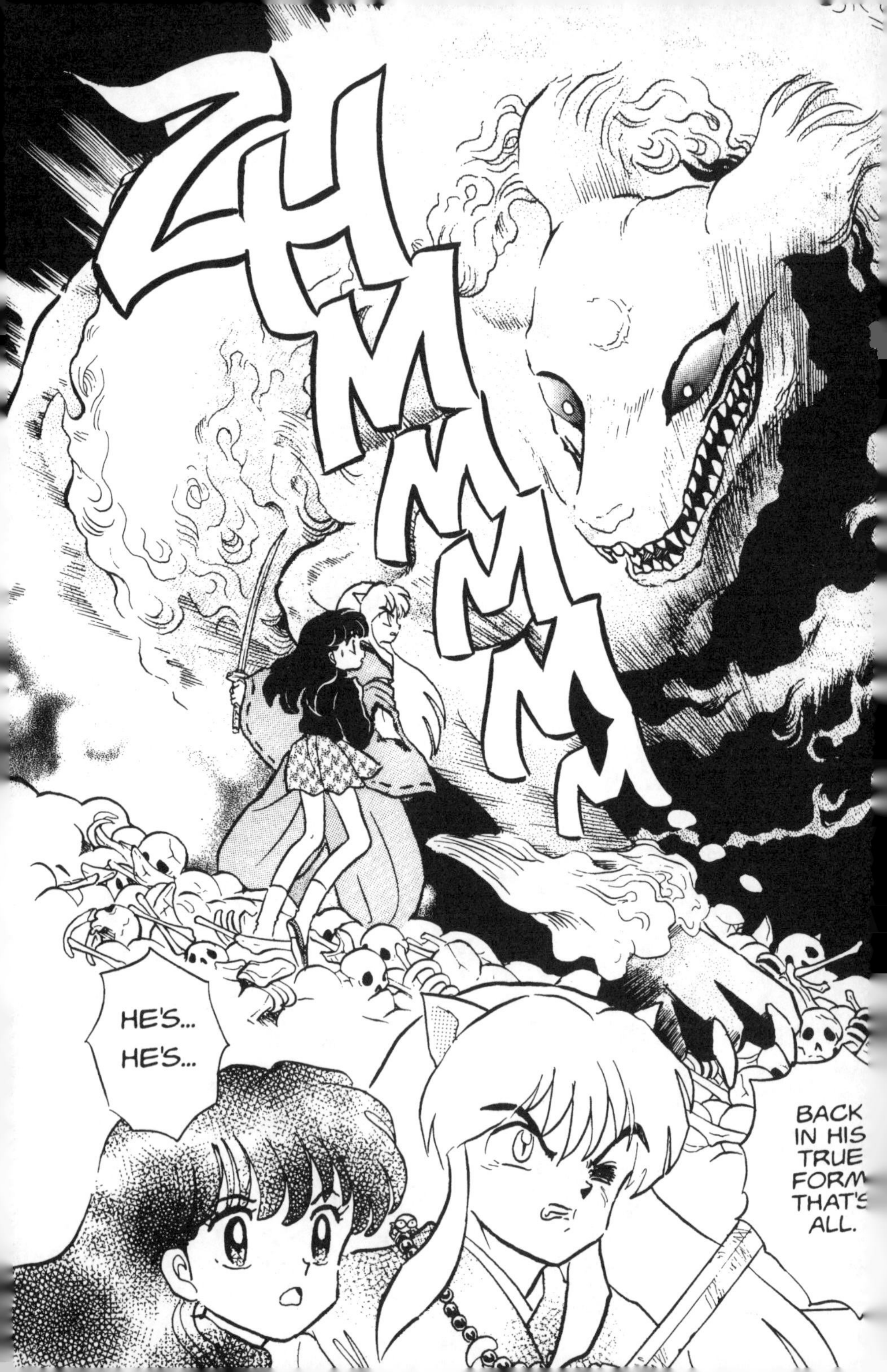
ZHMMMMM
HE'S... HE'S...
BACK IN HIS TRUE FORM THAT'S ALL.

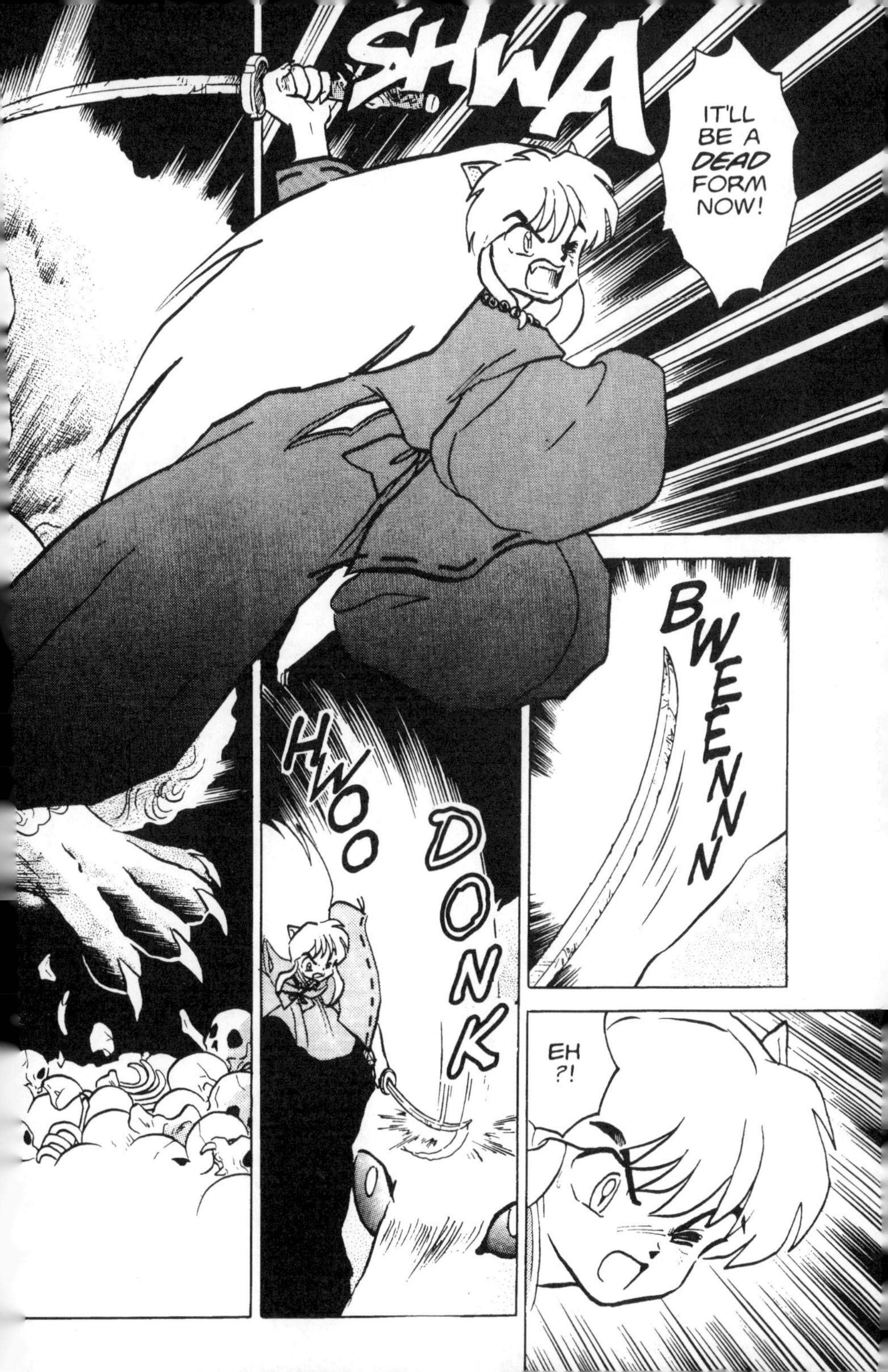
SHWA
IT'LL BE A DEAD FORM NOW!
HWOO
DONK
BWEENNN
EH ?!

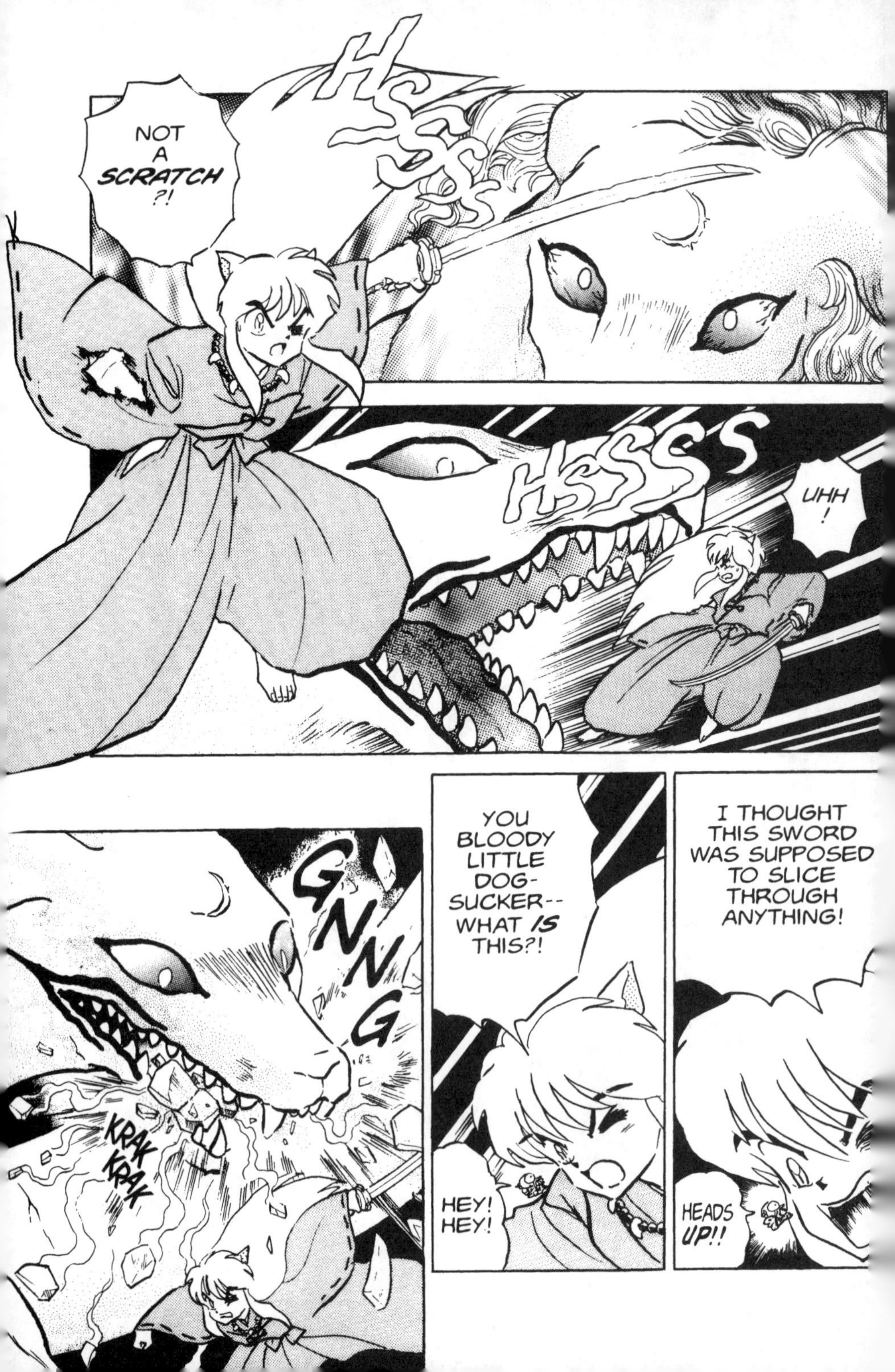
NOT A SCRATCH ?!
HSSS
HSSSS
UHH !
GNNG
KRAK KRAK
YOU BLOODY LITTLE DOG-SUCKER-- WHAT IS THIS?!
HEY! HEY!
I THOUGHT THIS SWORD WAS SUPPOSED TO SLICE THROUGH ANYTHING!
HEADS UP!!

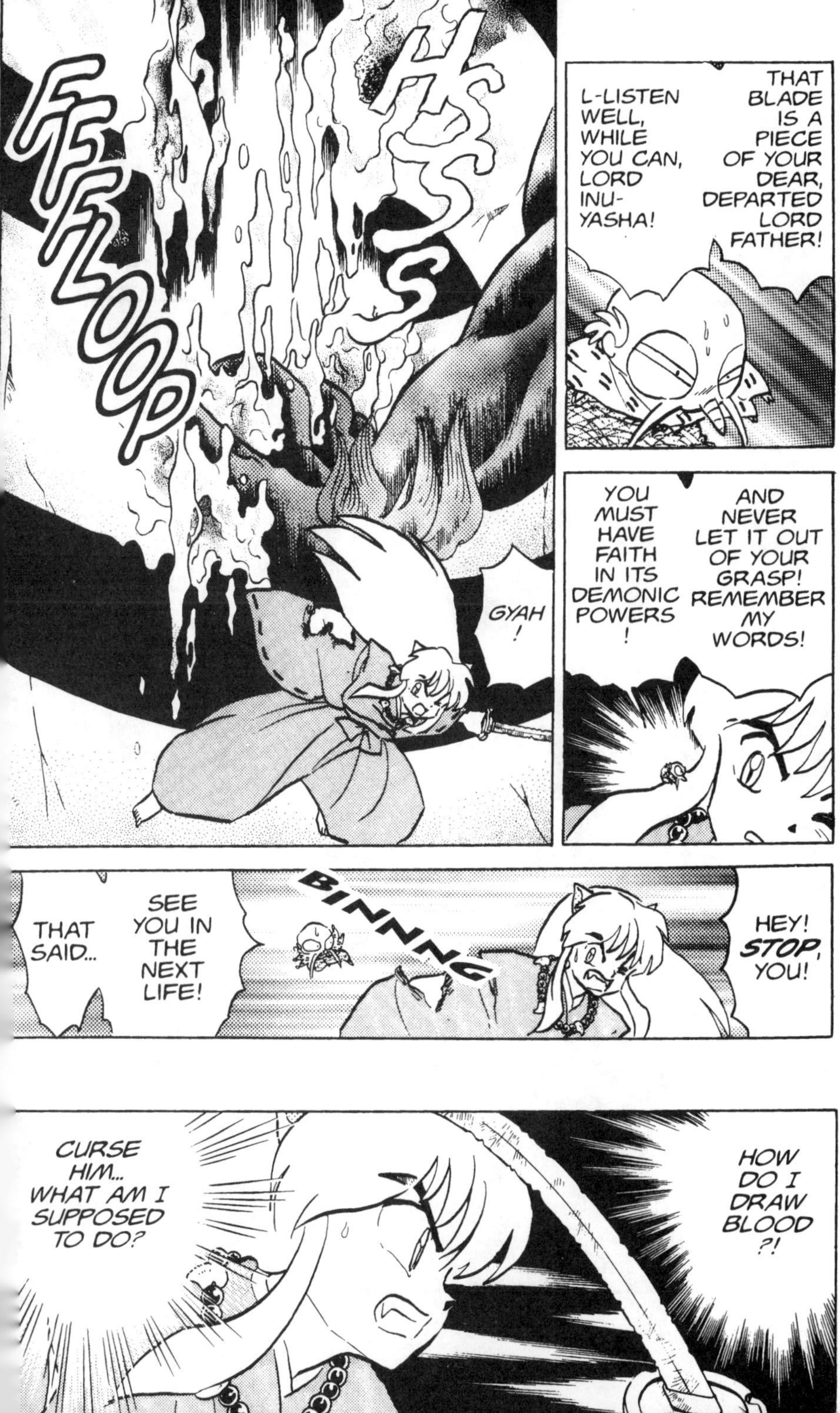
FFFLOOP
HSS
GYAH!
L-LISTEN WELL, WHILE YOU CAN, LORD INU-YASHA!
THAT BLADE IS A PIECE OF YOUR DEAR, DEPARTED LORD FATHER!
YOU MUST HAVE FAITH IN ITS DEMONIC POWERS!
AND NEVER LET IT OUT OF YOUR GRASP! REMEMBER MY WORDS!
THAT SAID...
SEE YOU IN THE NEXT LIFE!
BINNNG
HEY! **STOP**, YOU!
CURSE HIM... WHAT AM I SUPPOSED TO DO?
HOW DO I DRAW BLOOD?!

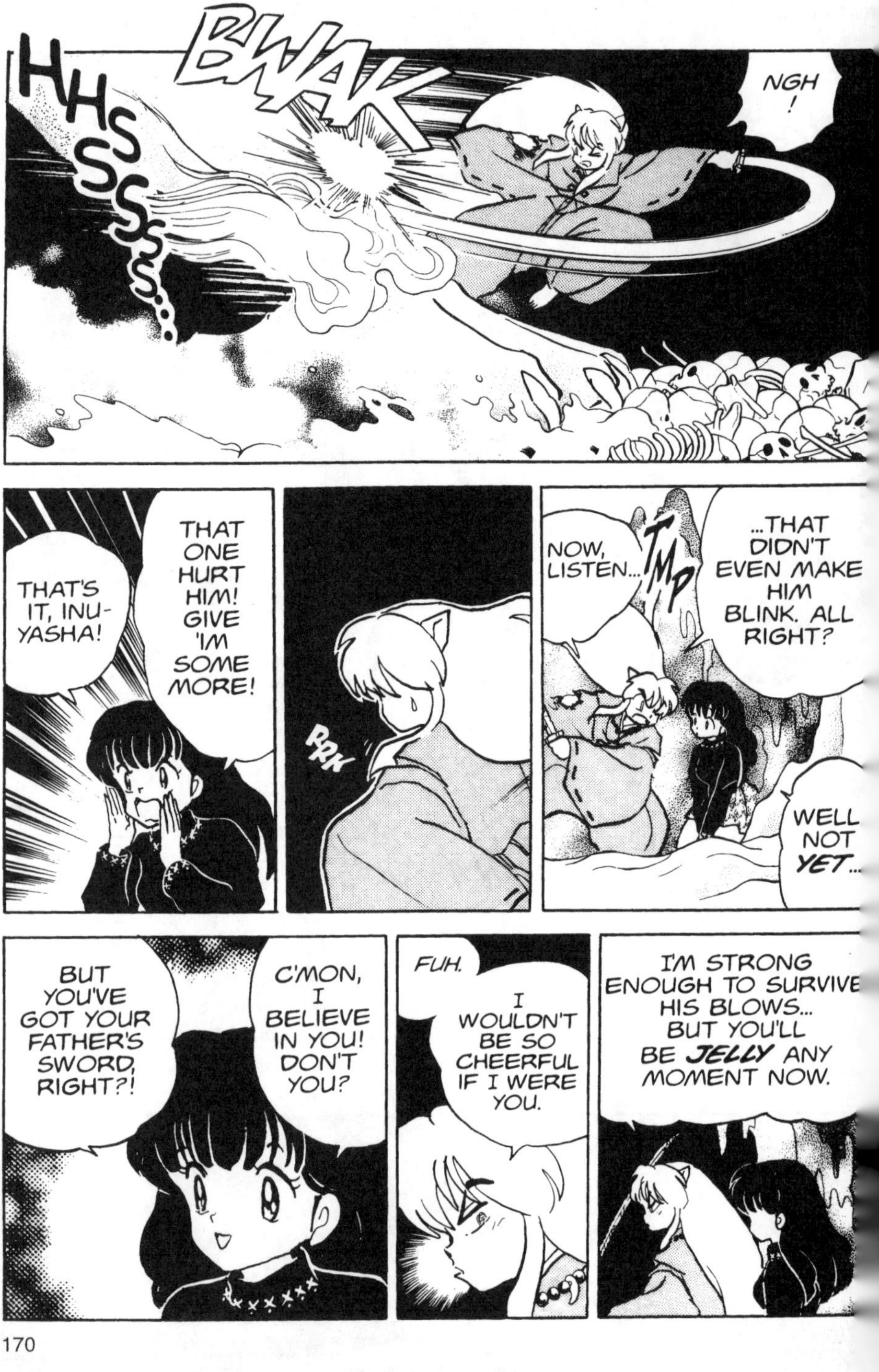
HHSSSSSS...
BWAK
NGH!
THAT'S IT, INU-YASHA!
THAT ONE HURT HIM! GIVE 'IM SOME MORE!
RRK
NOW, LISTEN...
TMP
...THAT DIDN'T EVEN MAKE HIM BLINK. ALL RIGHT?
WELL NOT YET...
BUT YOU'VE GOT YOUR FATHER'S SWORD, RIGHT?!
C'MON, I BELIEVE IN YOU! DON'T YOU?
FUH.
I WOULDN'T BE SO CHEERFUL IF I WERE YOU.
I'M STRONG ENOUGH TO SURVIVE HIS BLOWS... BUT YOU'LL BE JELLY ANY MOMENT NOW.

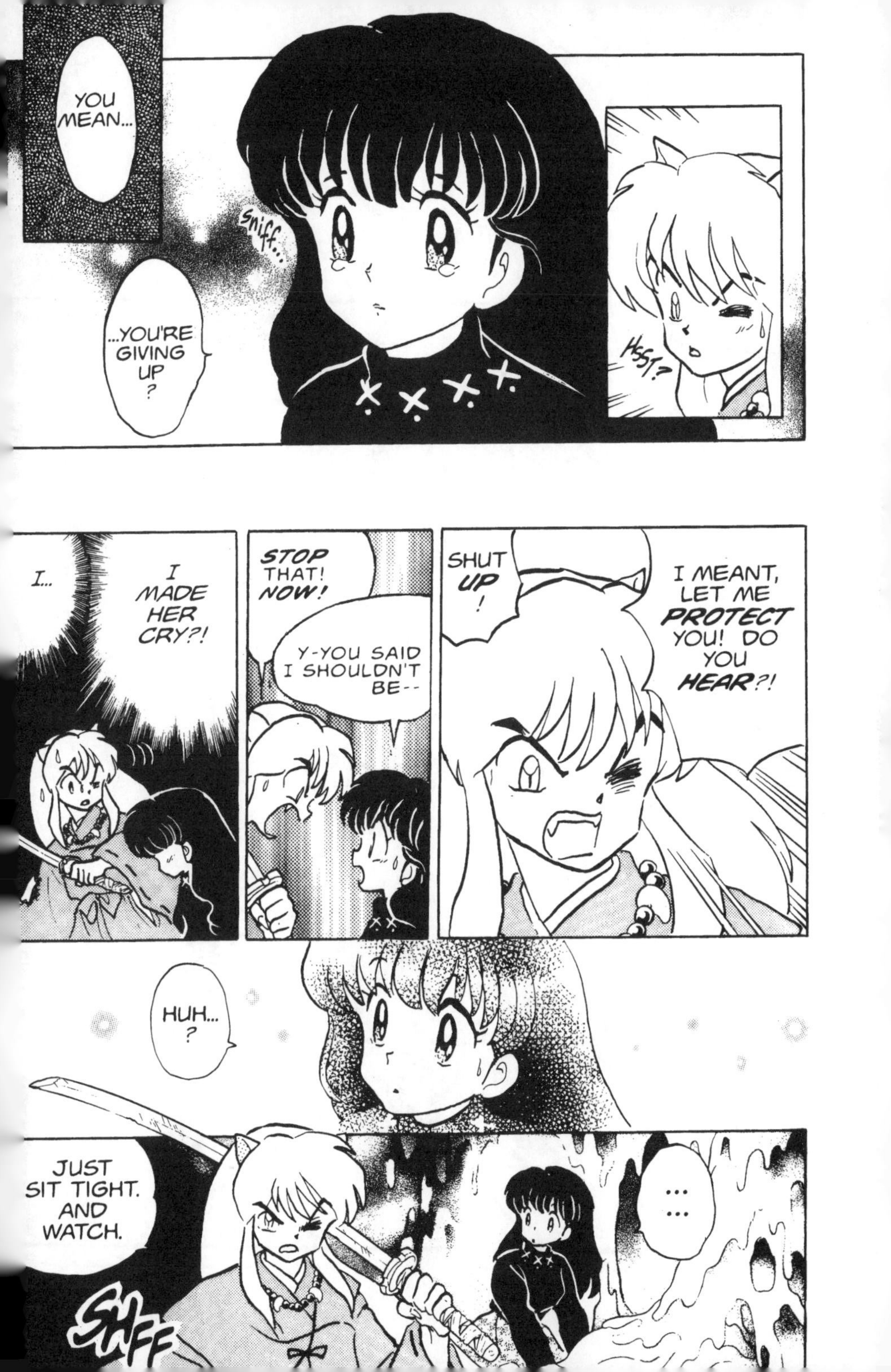
YOU MEAN...
sniff...
...YOU'RE GIVING UP ?
HSST?
I...
I MADE HER CRY?!
STOP THAT! NOW!
Y-YOU SAID I SHOULDN'T BE--
SHUT UP !
I MEANT, LET ME PROTECT YOU! DO YOU HEAR?!
HUH... ?
JUST SIT TIGHT. AND WATCH.
SHFF
... ...

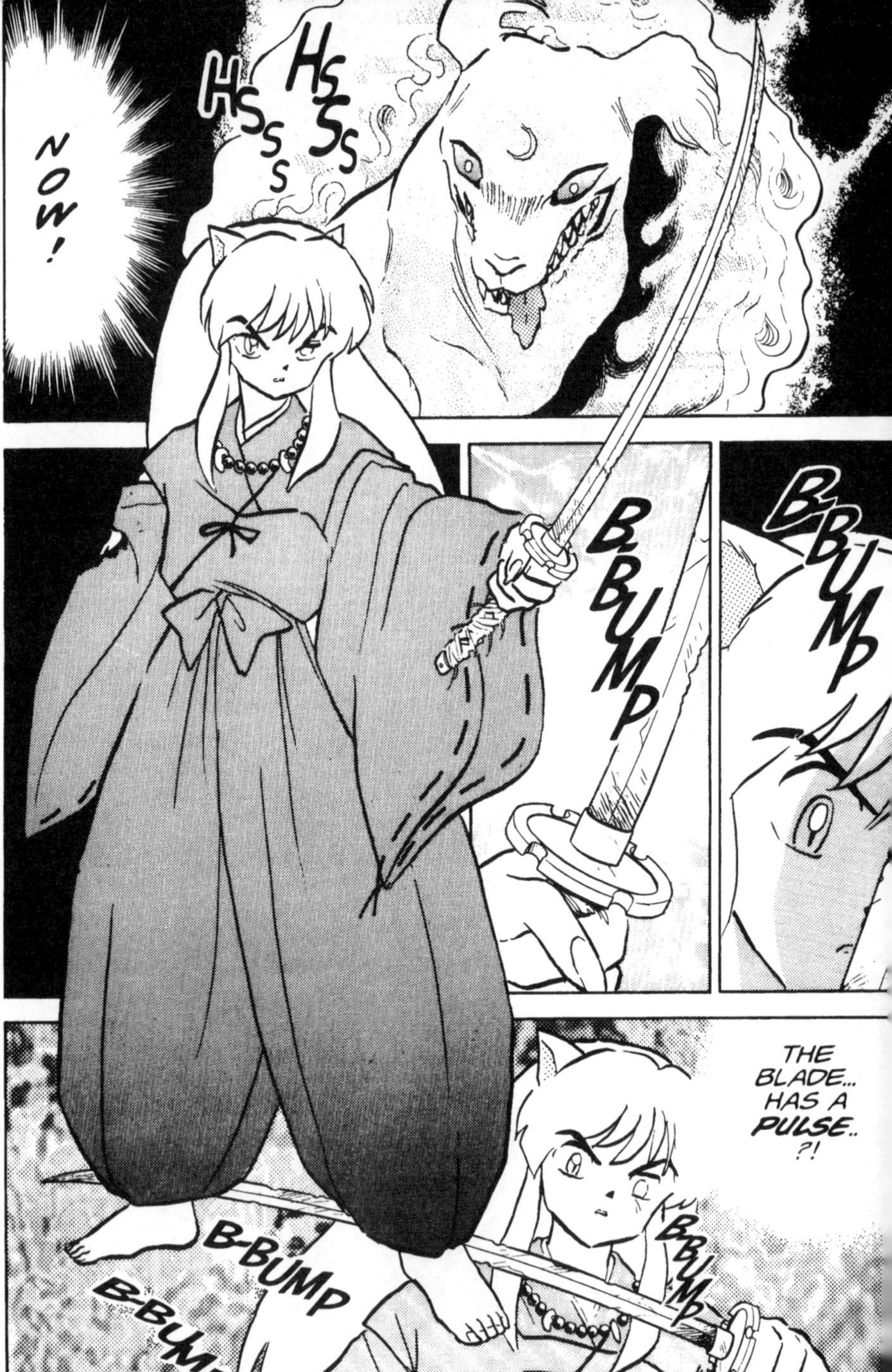
NOW!
HSSSS
HSSSS
BBUMP
BBUMP
THE BLADE... HAS A PULSE.. ?!
B-BUMP
B-BUMP
BBUMP

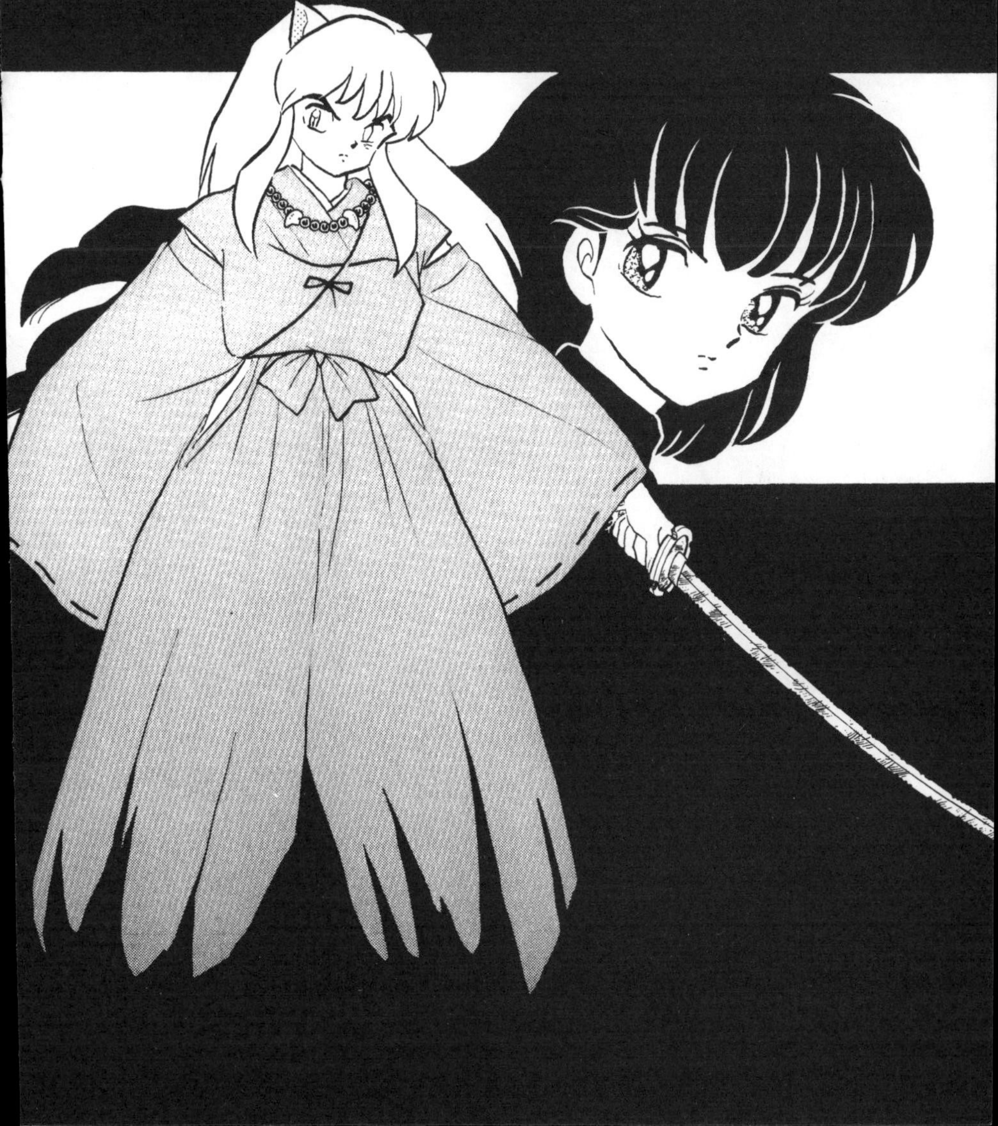

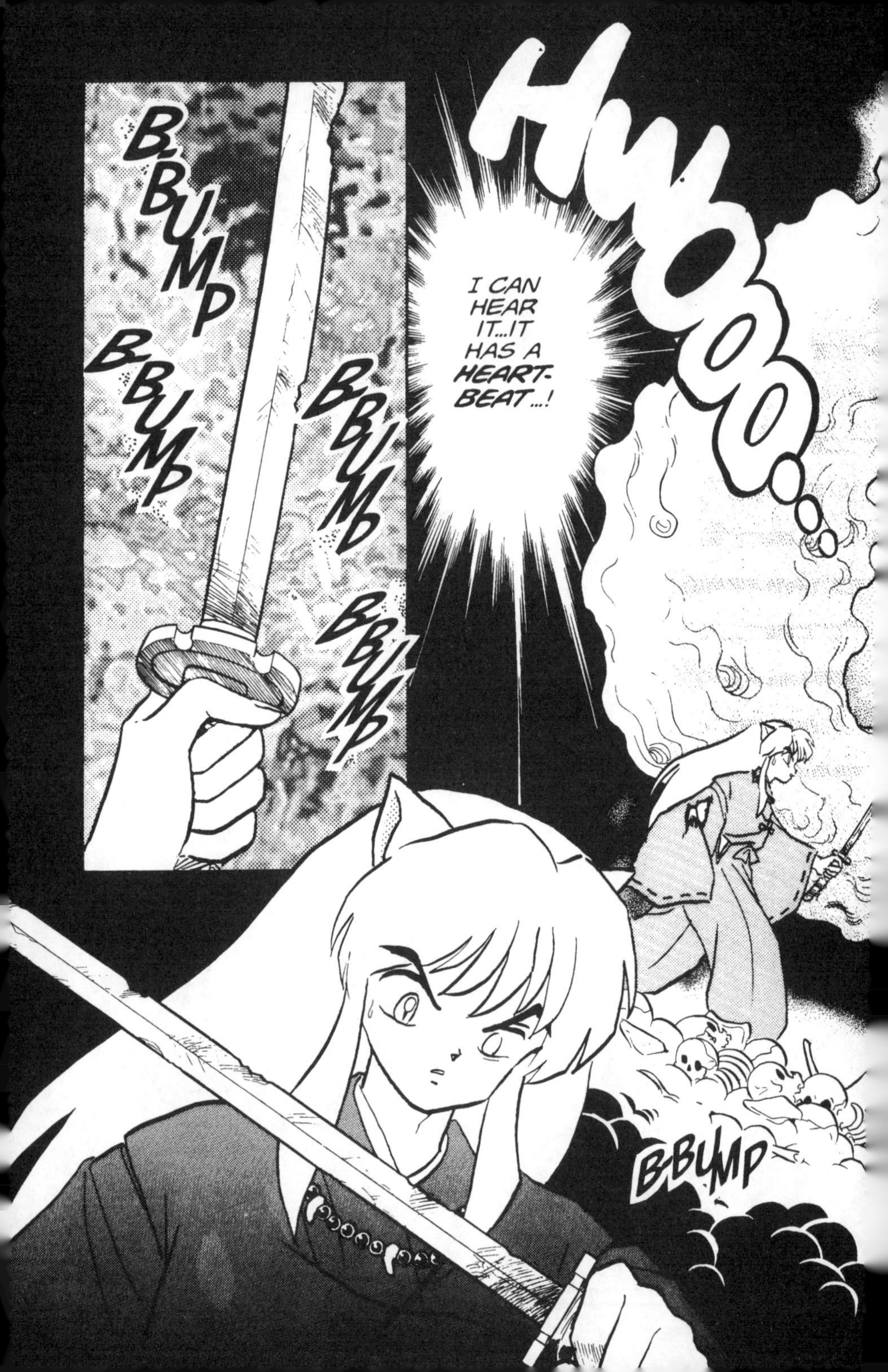
BBUMP
BBUMP
BBUMP
BBUMP
HUOOO....
I CAN HEAR IT...IT HAS A HEARTBEAT...!
B-BUMP

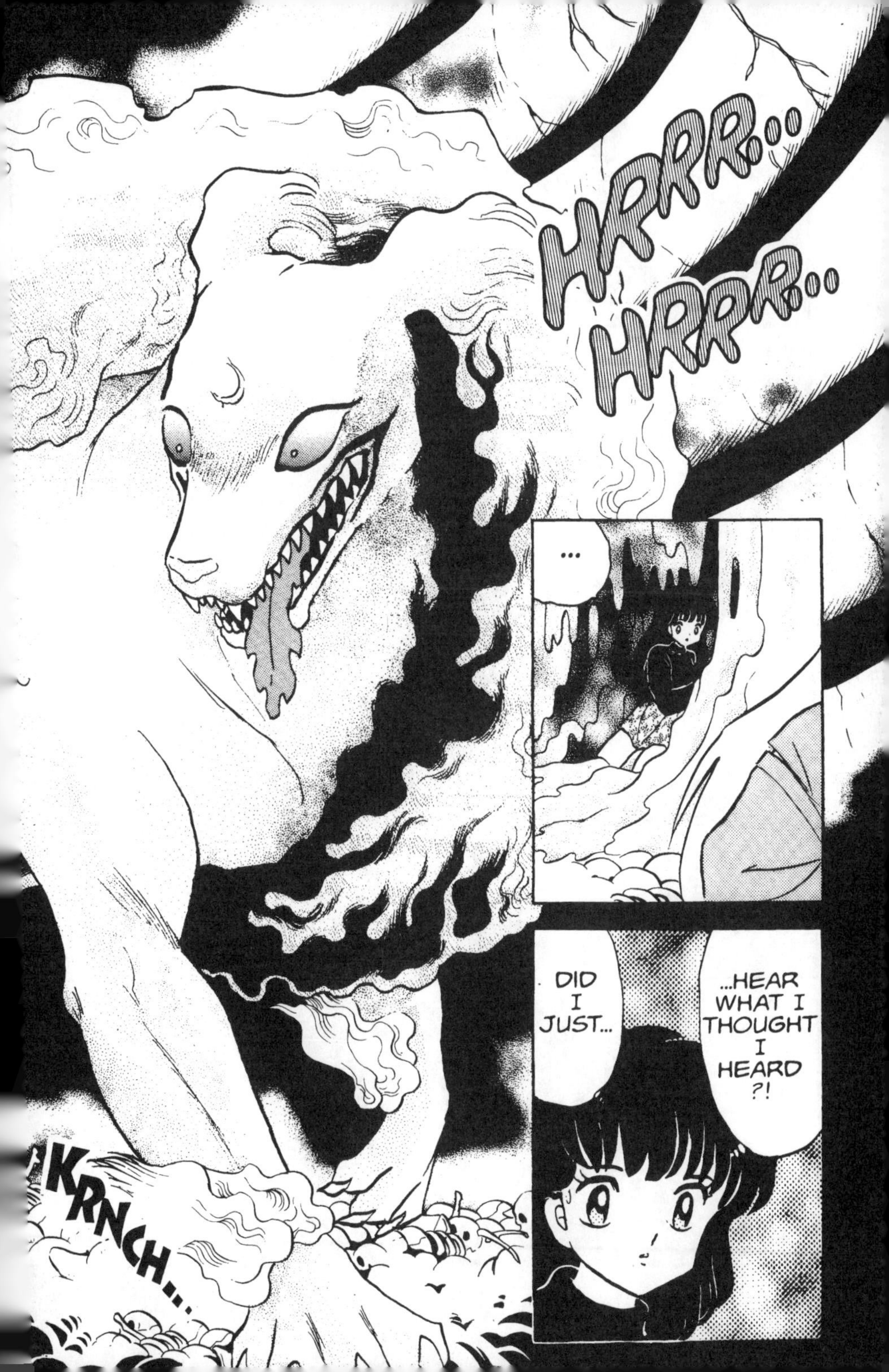
HRRR...
HRRR...
KRNCH...
...
DID I JUST...
...HEAR WHAT I THOUGHT I HEARD ?!

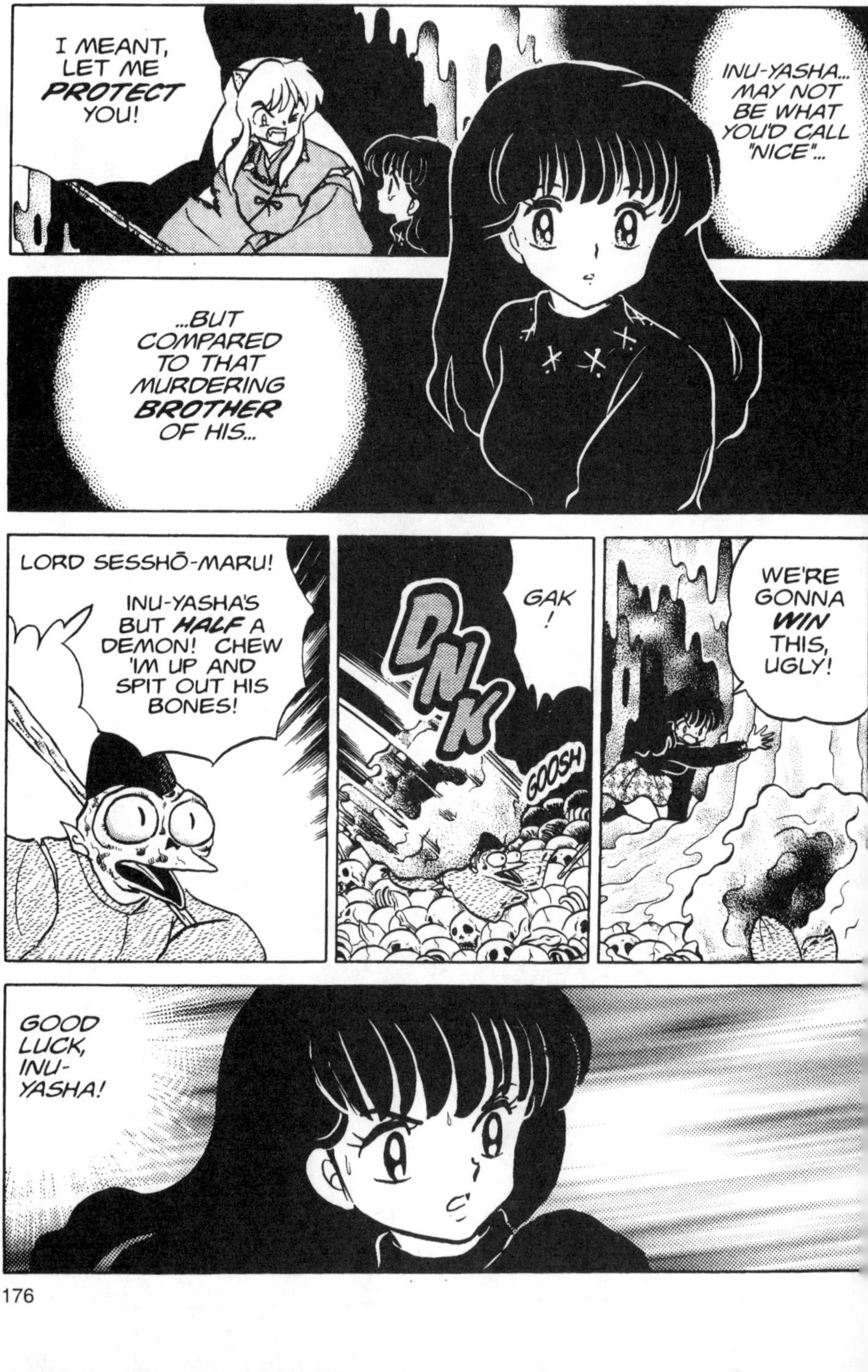
I MEANT, LET ME PROTECT YOU!
INU-YASHA... MAY NOT BE WHAT YOU'D CALL "NICE"...
...BUT COMPARED TO THAT MURDERING BROTHER OF HIS...
LORD SESSHŌ-MARU!
INU-YASHA'S BUT HALF A DEMON! CHEW 'IM UP AND SPIT OUT HIS BONES!
GAK!
DNK
GOOSH
WE'RE GONNA WIN THIS, UGLY!
GOOD LUCK, INU-YASHA!

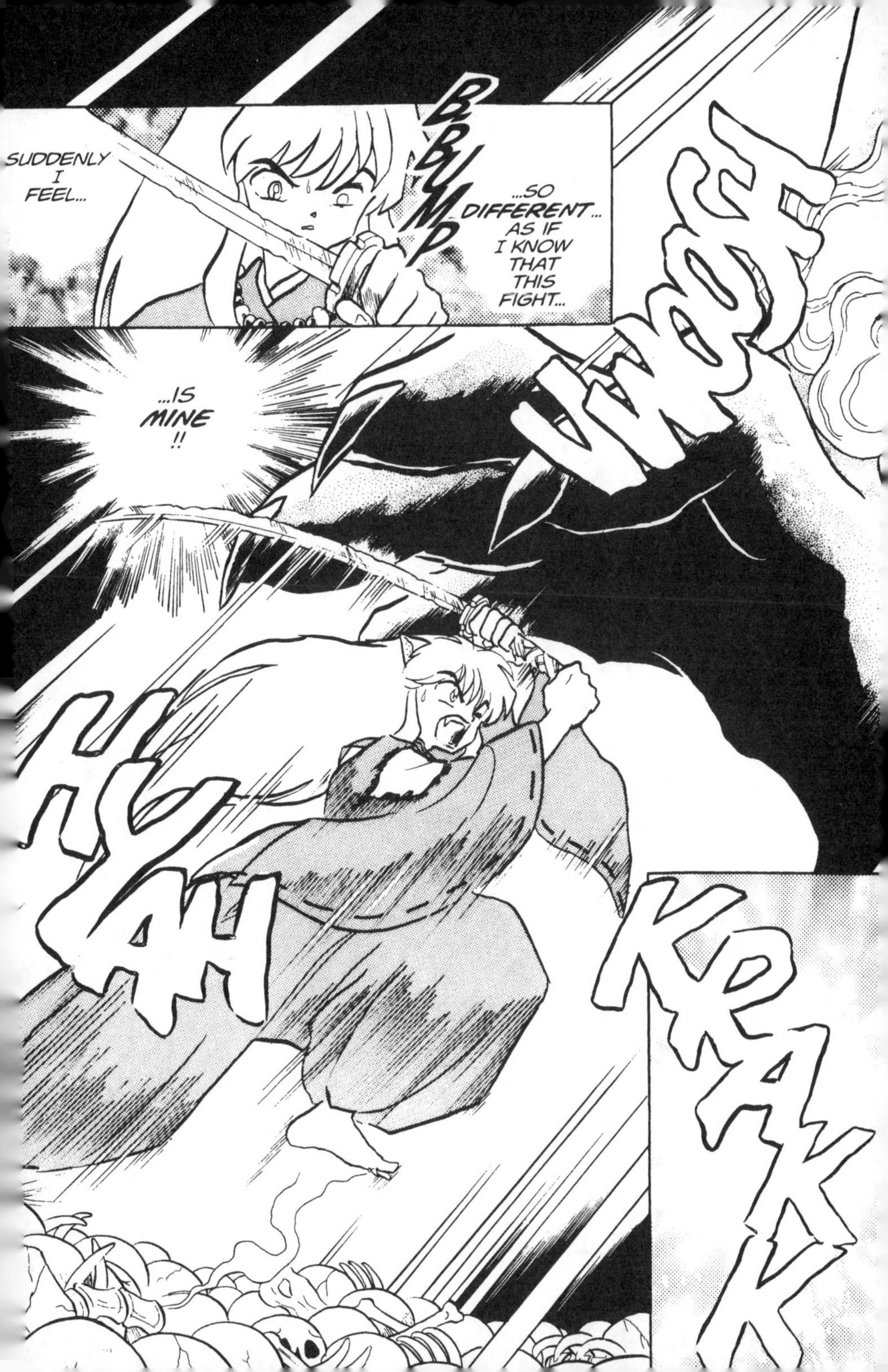
SUDDENLY I FEEL...
BBUMP
...SO DIFFERENT... AS IF I KNOW THAT THIS FIGHT...
VWOOSH
...IS MINE !!
HYAH
KRAKK

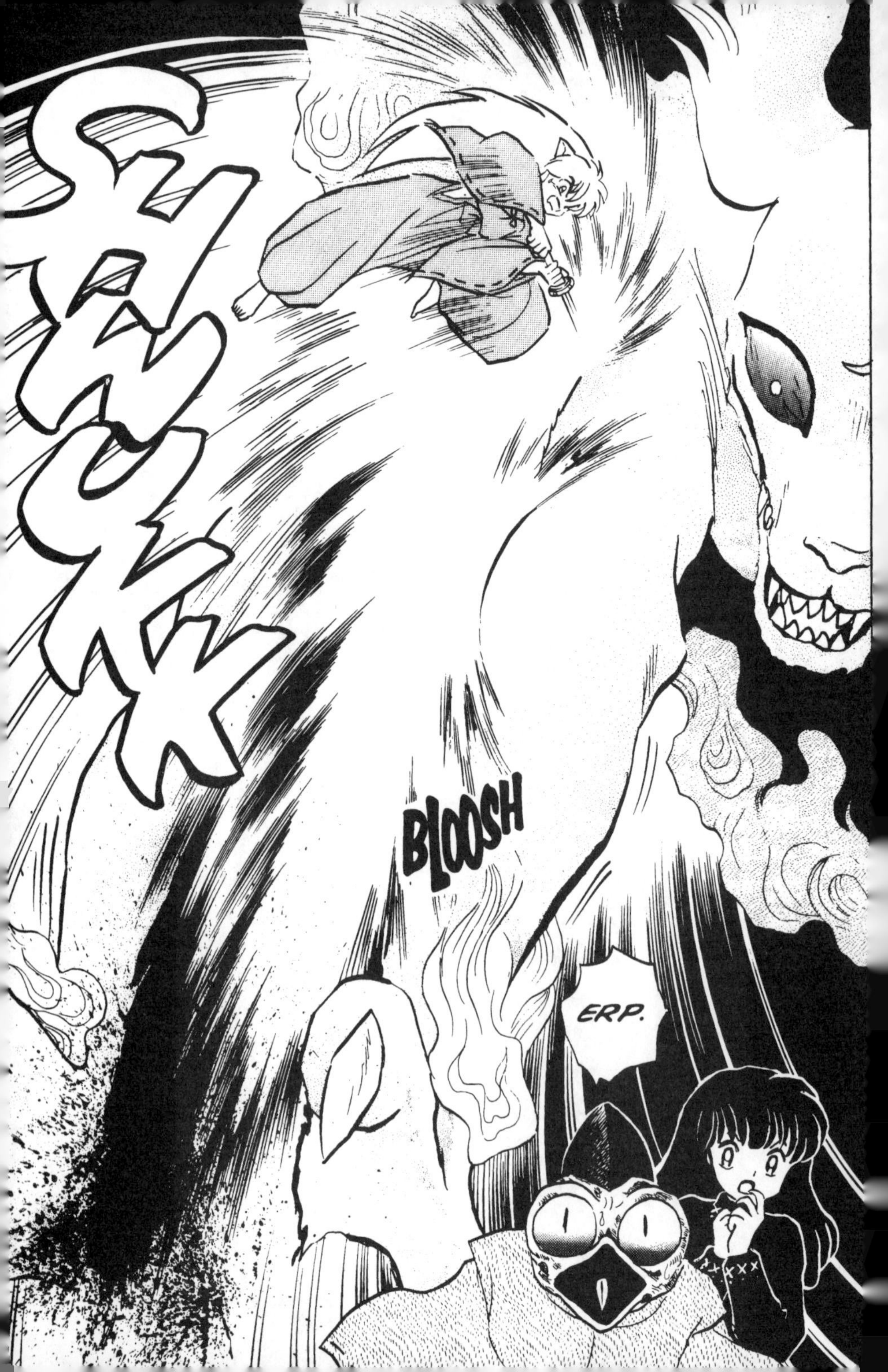
SHUNK
BLOOSH
ERP.

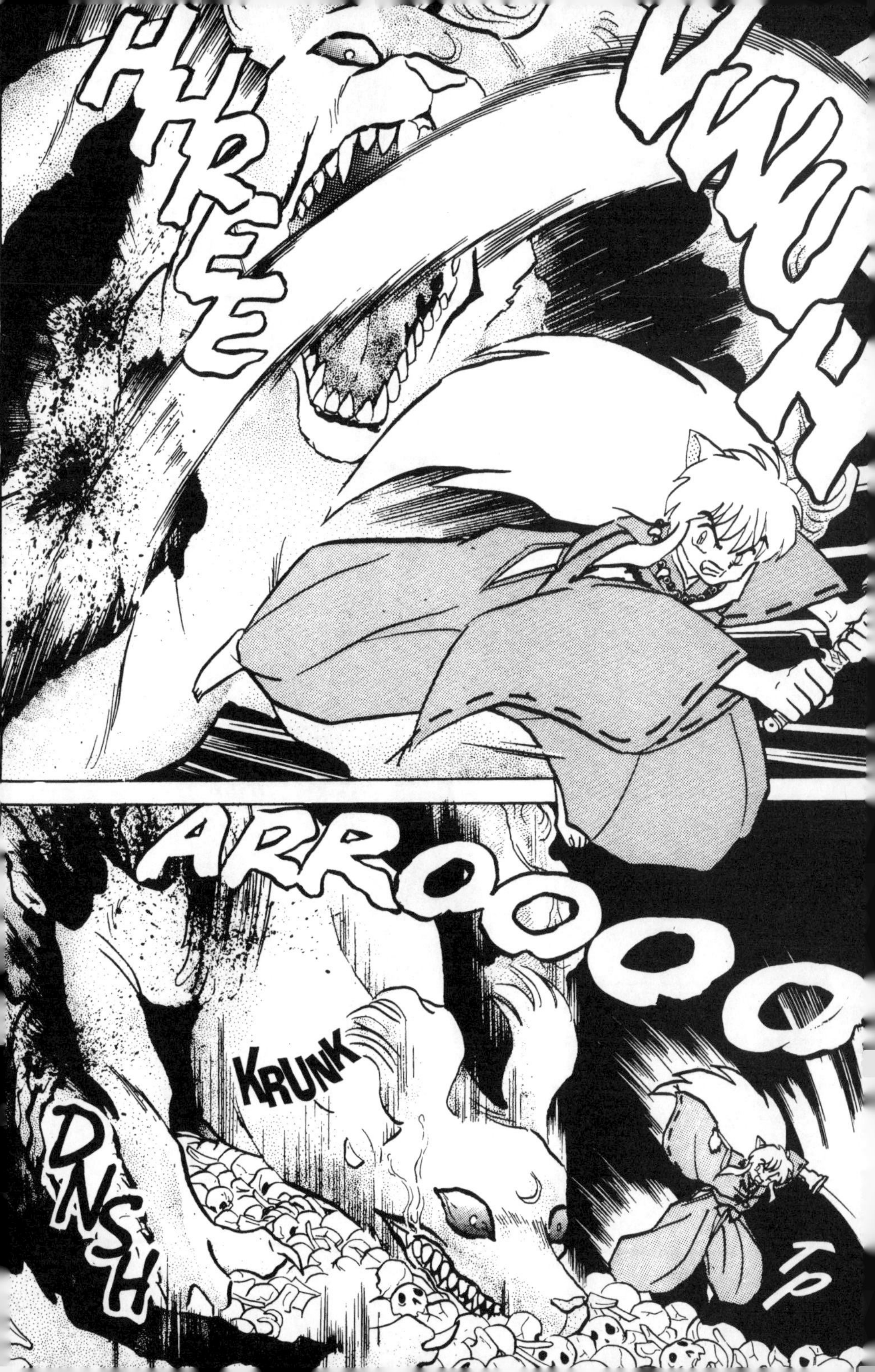
HIREE
VWUH
ARROOOO
KRUNK
DNSH
Tp

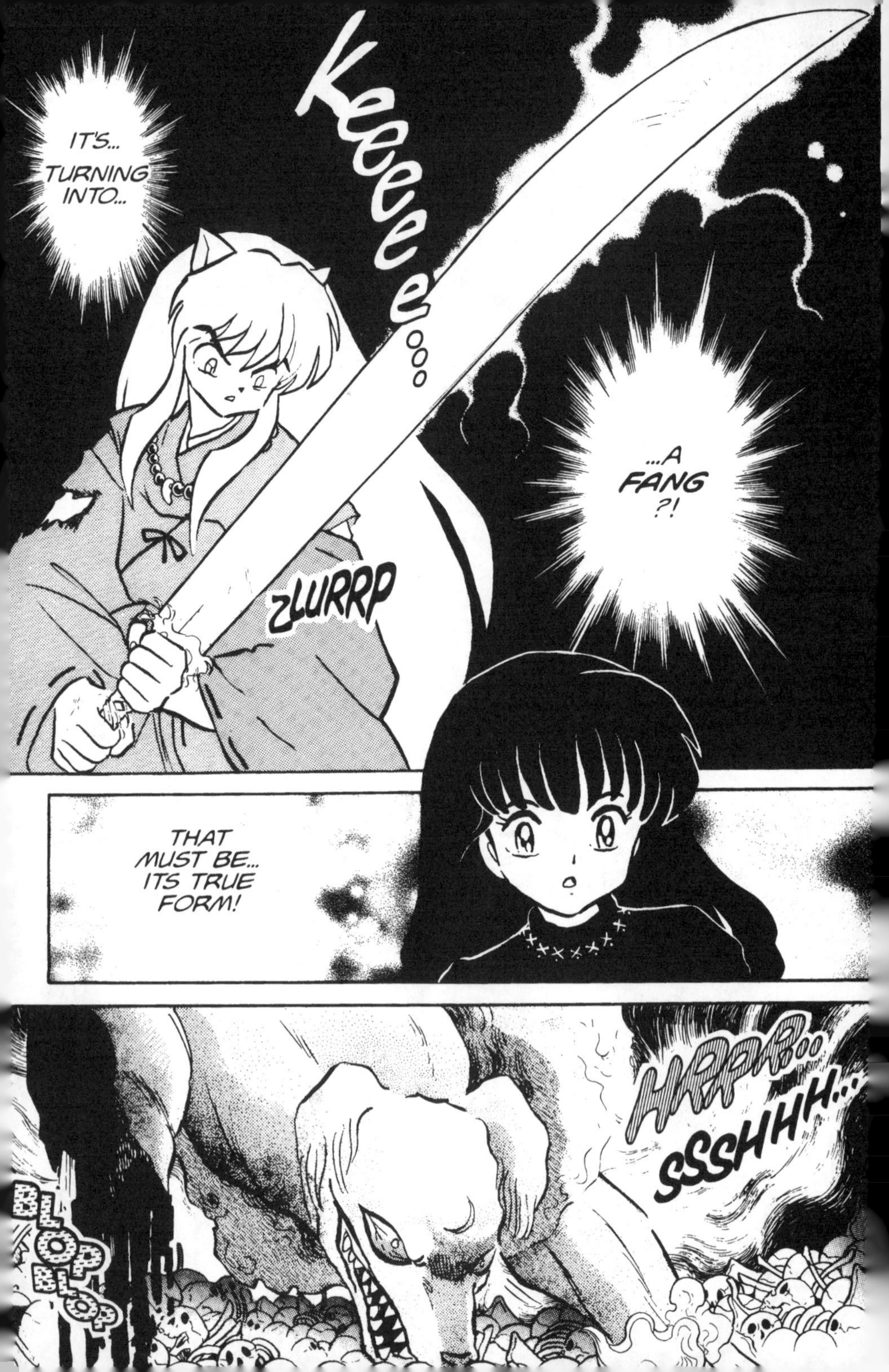

IT'S... TURNING INTO...
KEEEEEEooo
...A FANG ?!
ZLURRP
THAT MUST BE... ITS TRUE FORM!
BLOP BLOP
HRRRR...
SSSHHH...

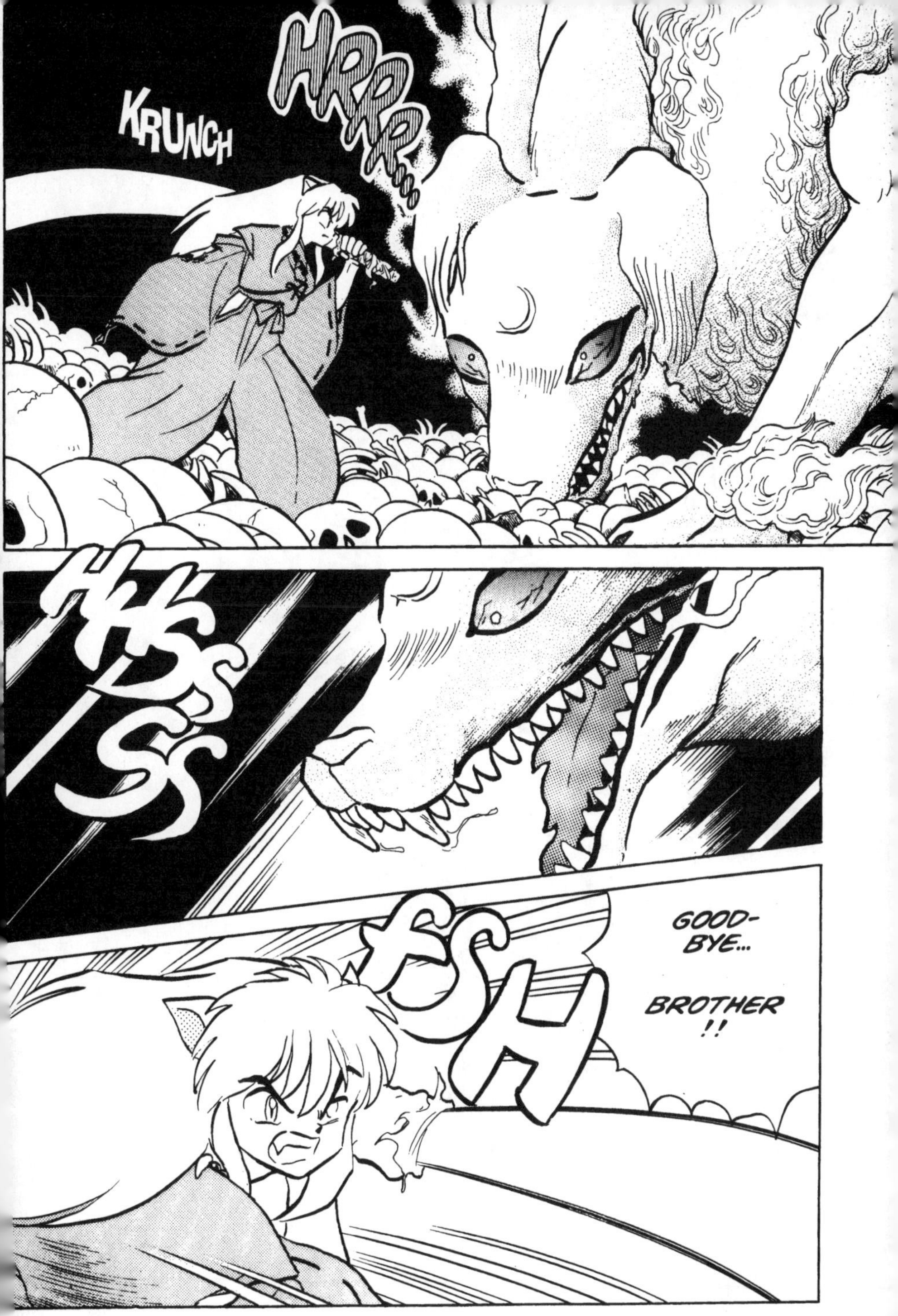
KRUNCH
HRRR...
HISSSS
FSH
GOOD-BYE...
BROTHER!!

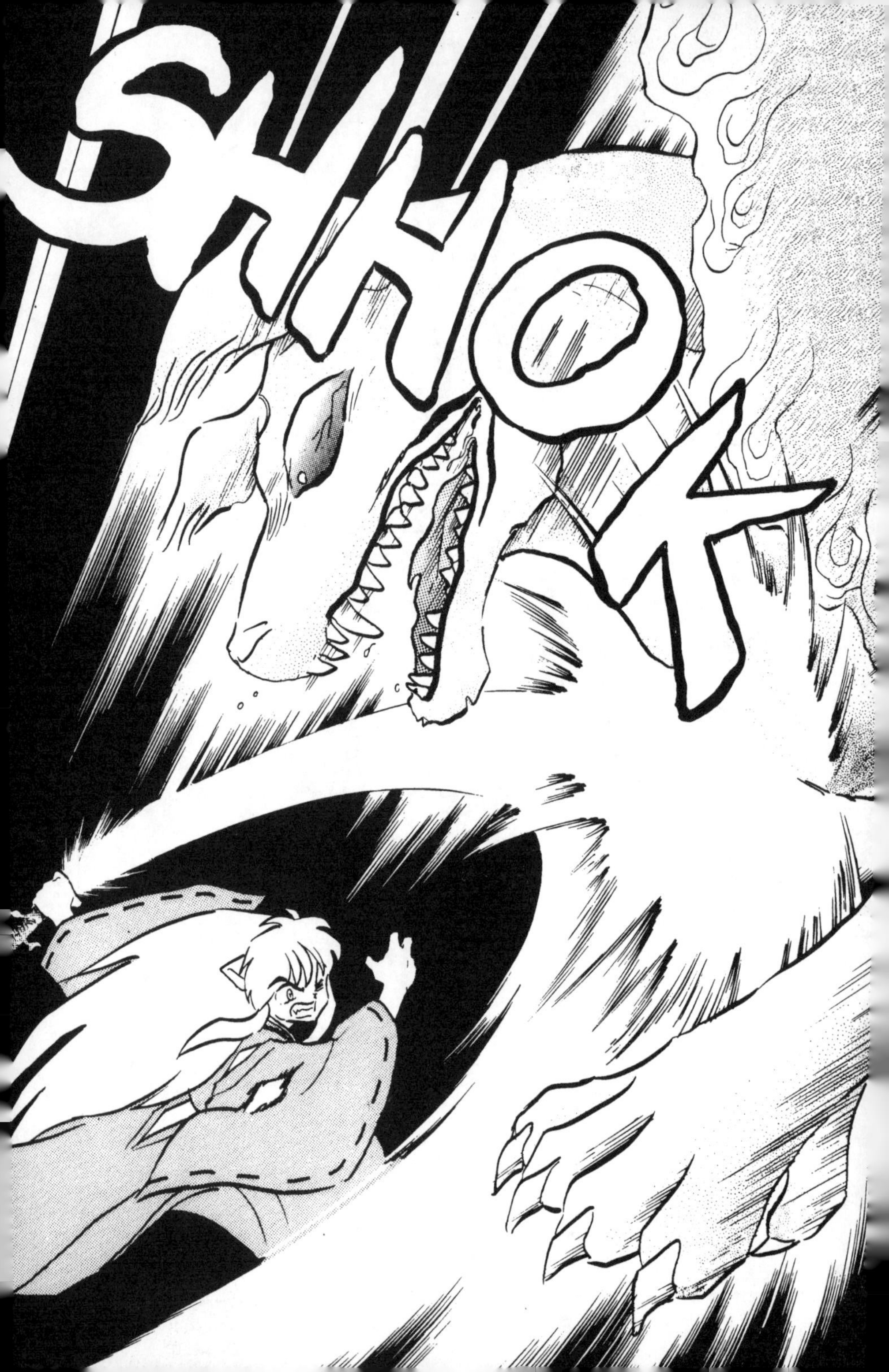
SHHOK

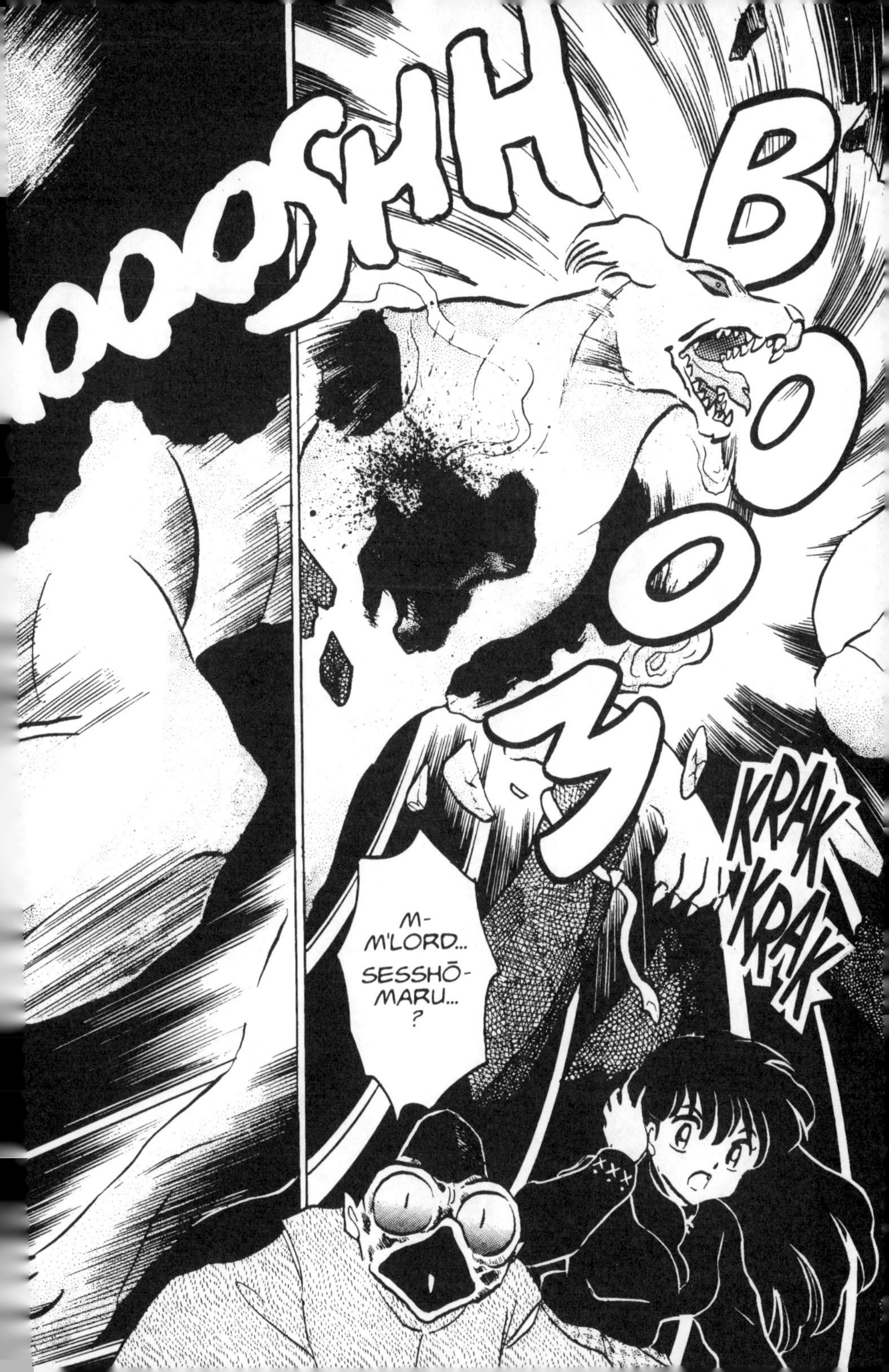
OOOSHH
BOOM
KRAK KRAK KRAK
M- M'LORD... SESSHŌ-MARU... ?

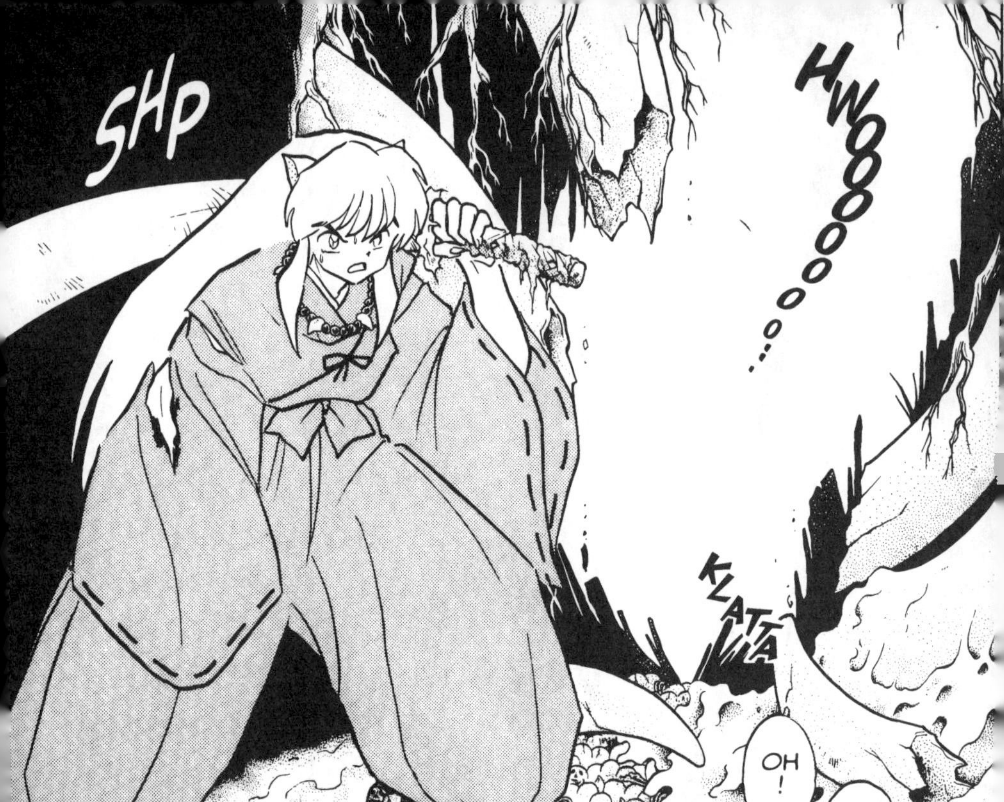
SHP
HWOOOOOOOOO...
KLATTA
OH!
OH!

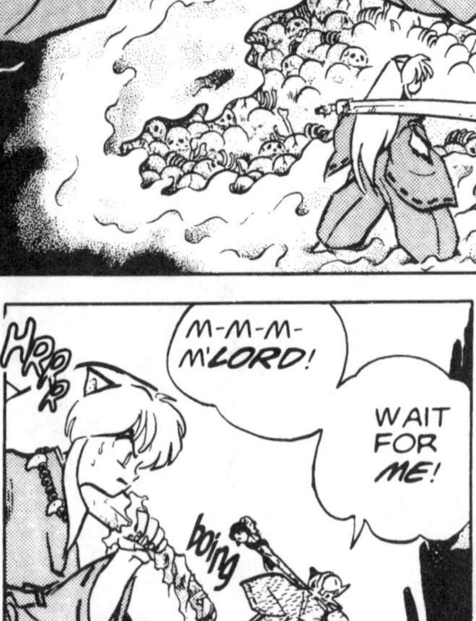
HRRR
M-M-M-M'LORD!
WAIT FOR ME!
boing

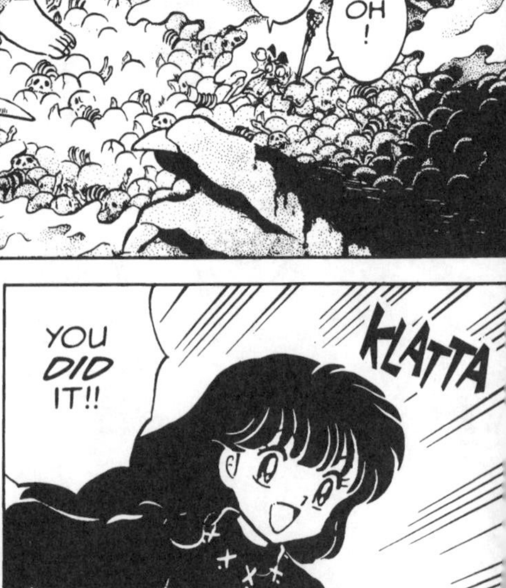
YOU DID IT!!
KLATTA

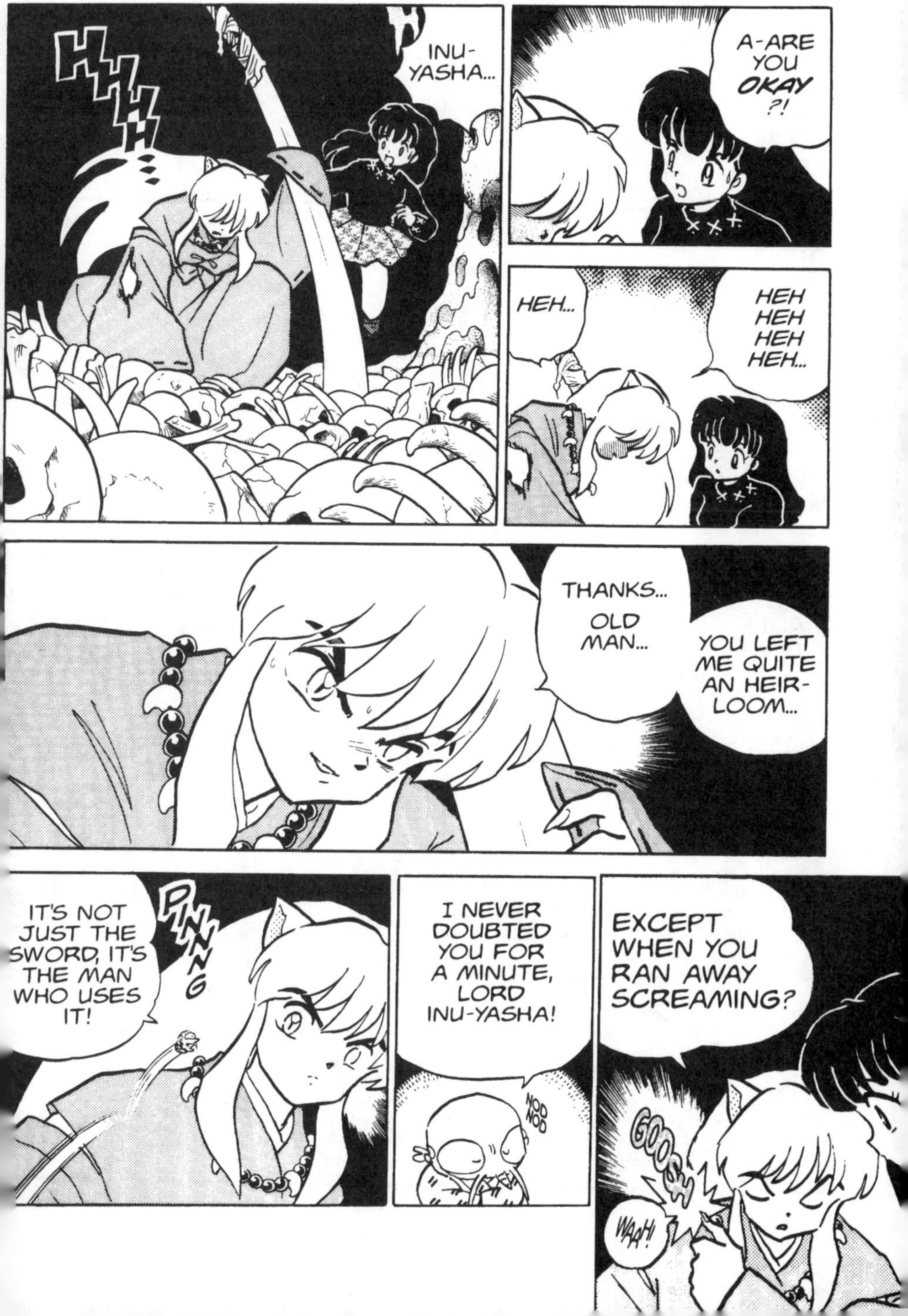
HHHH
INU-YASHA...
A-ARE YOU OKAY ?!
HEH...
HEH HEH HEH HEH...
THANKS... OLD MAN...
YOU LEFT ME QUITE AN HEIR-LOOM...
IT'S NOT JUST THE SWORD, IT'S THE MAN WHO USES IT!
PINNNG
I NEVER DOUBTED YOU FOR A MINUTE, LORD INU-YASHA!
NOD NOD
EXCEPT WHEN YOU RAN AWAY SCREAMING?
GOOSH
WAAH!

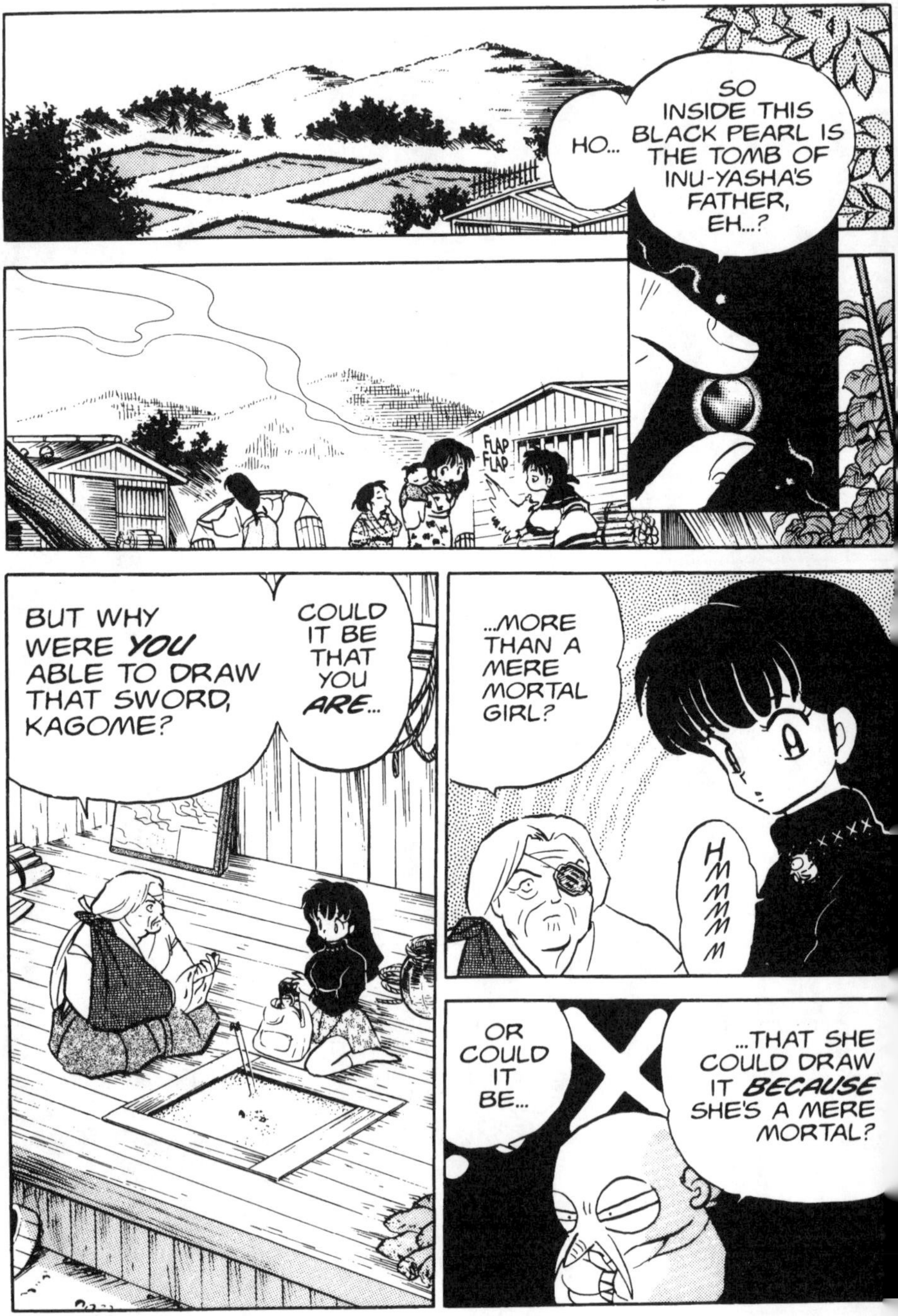
HO...
SO INSIDE THIS BLACK PEARL IS THE TOMB OF INU-YASHA'S FATHER, EH...?
FLAP FLAP
BUT WHY WERE YOU ABLE TO DRAW THAT SWORD, KAGOME?
COULD IT BE THAT YOU ARE...
...MORE THAN A MERE MORTAL GIRL?
HMMMMMM
OR COULD IT BE...
...THAT SHE COULD DRAW IT BECAUSE SHE'S A MERE MORTAL?

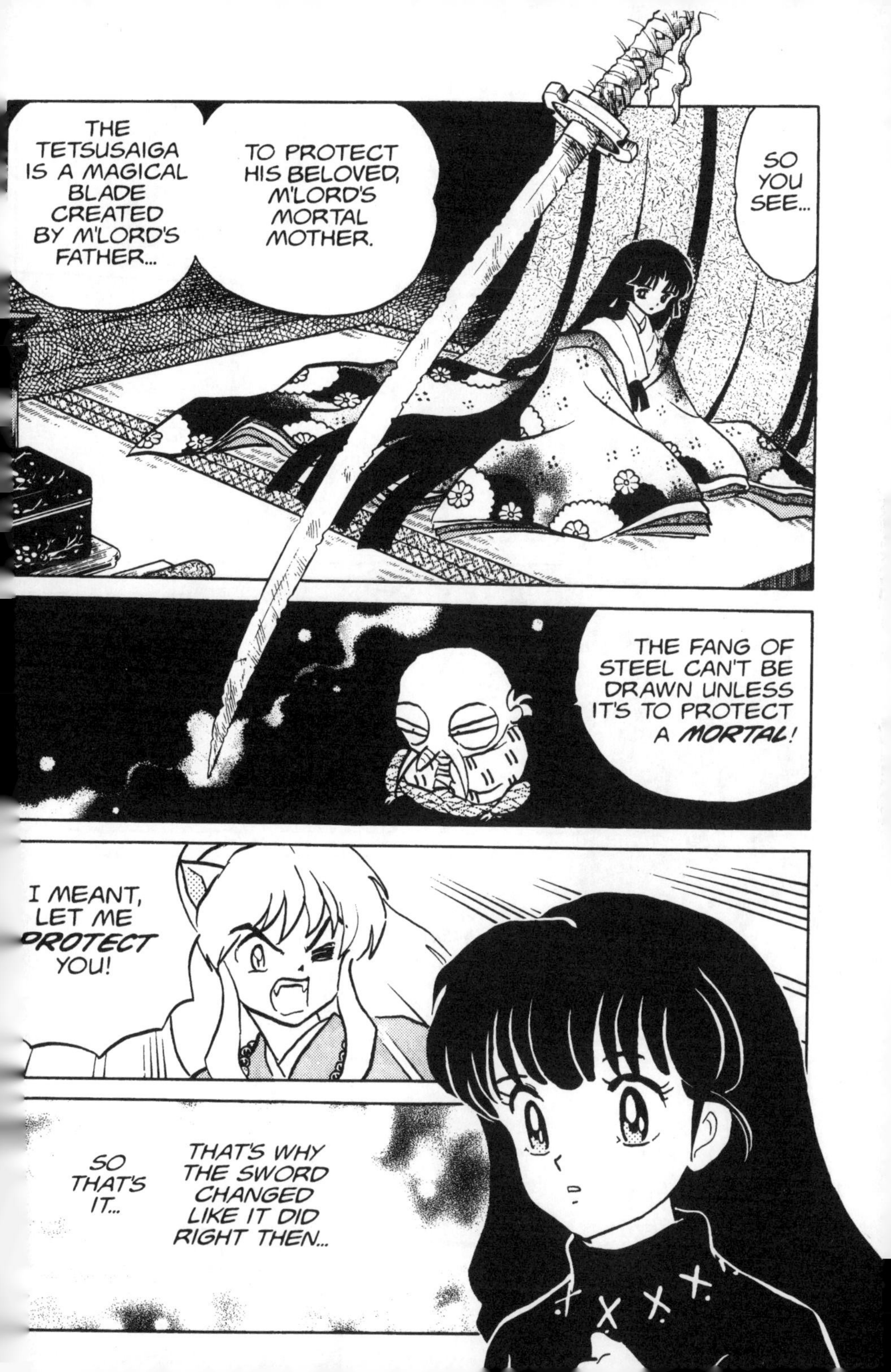
THE TETSUSAIGA IS A MAGICAL BLADE CREATED BY M'LORD'S FATHER...
TO PROTECT HIS BELOVED, M'LORD'S MORTAL MOTHER.
SO YOU SEE...
THE FANG OF STEEL CAN'T BE DRAWN UNLESS IT'S TO PROTECT A MORTAL!
I MEANT, LET ME PROTECT YOU!
SO THAT'S IT...
THAT'S WHY THE SWORD CHANGED LIKE IT DID RIGHT THEN...

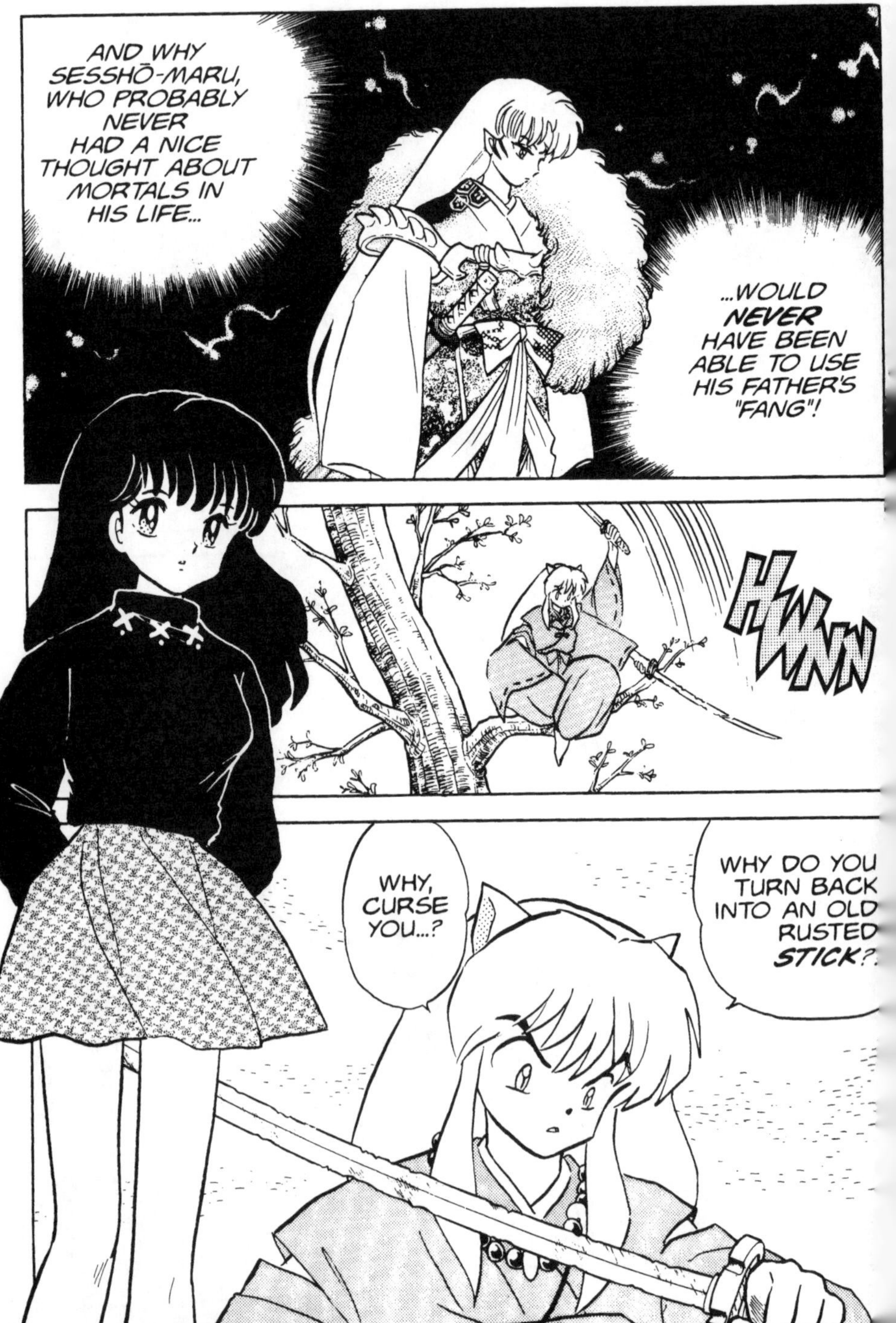
AND WHY SESSHŌ-MARU, WHO PROBABLY NEVER HAD A NICE THOUGHT ABOUT MORTALS IN HIS LIFE...
...WOULD NEVER HAVE BEEN ABLE TO USE HIS FATHER'S "FANG"!
HWNN
WHY, CURSE YOU...?
WHY DO YOU TURN BACK INTO AN OLD RUSTED STICK?

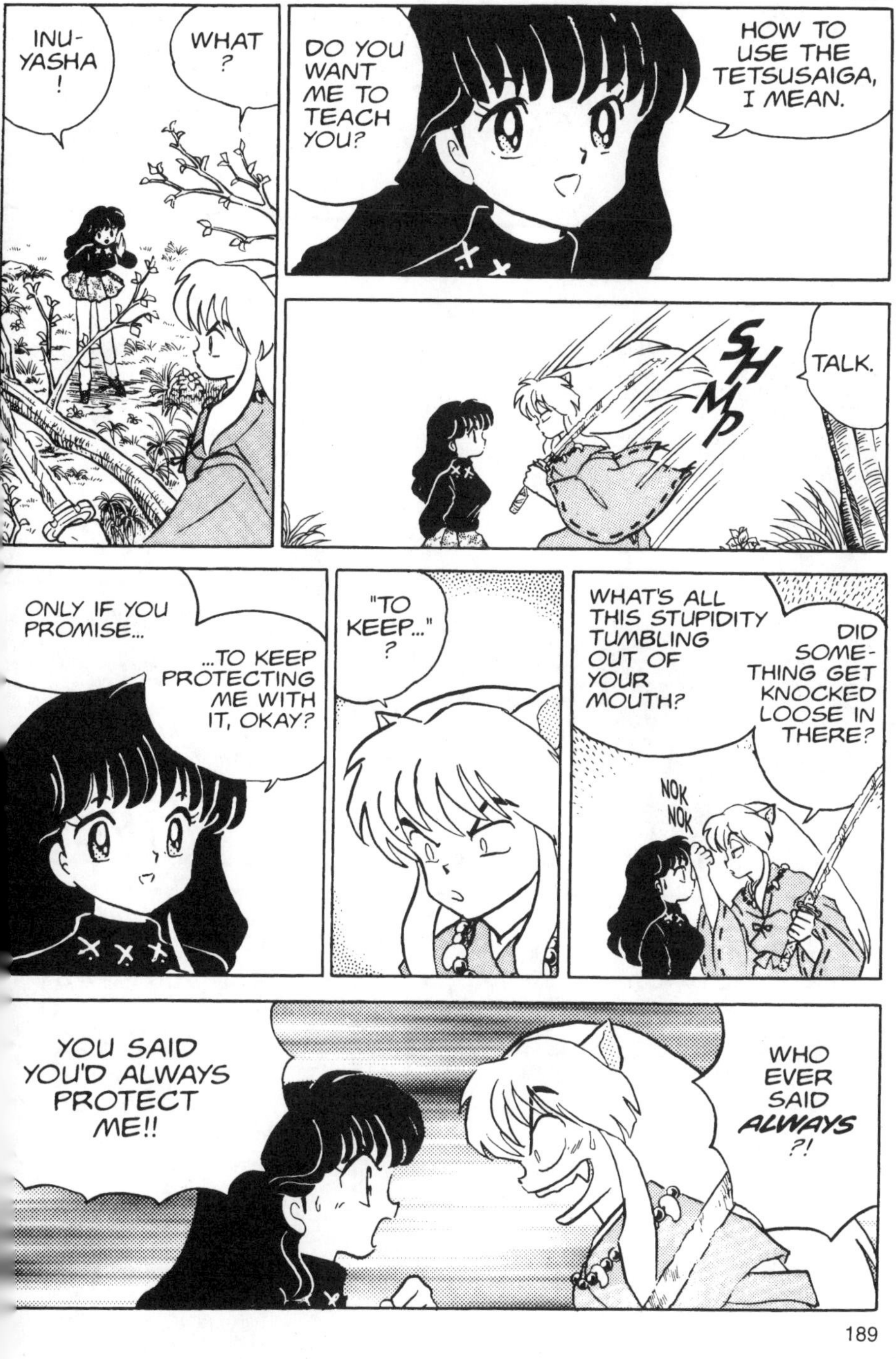
INU-YASHA!
WHAT?
DO YOU WANT ME TO TEACH YOU?
HOW TO USE THE TETSUSAIGA, I MEAN.
SHMP
TALK.
ONLY IF YOU PROMISE...
...TO KEEP PROTECTING ME WITH IT, OKAY?
"TO KEEP..."?
WHAT'S ALL THIS STUPIDITY TUMBLING OUT OF YOUR MOUTH?
DID SOMETHING GET KNOCKED LOOSE IN THERE?
NOK NOK
YOU SAID YOU'D ALWAYS PROTECT ME!!
WHO EVER SAID ALWAYS?!

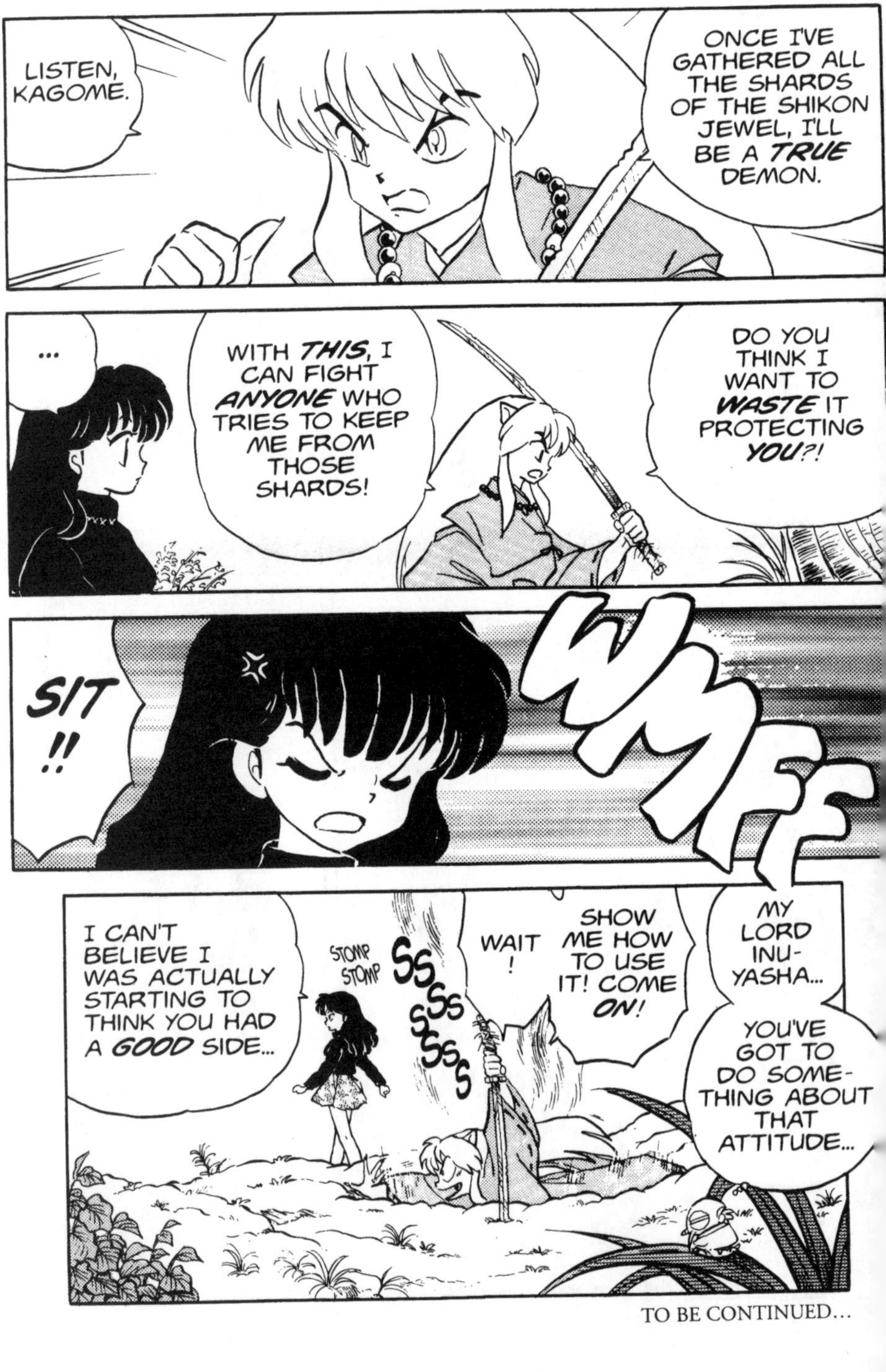
LISTEN, KAGOME.
ONCE I'VE GATHERED ALL THE SHARDS OF THE SHIKON JEWEL, I'LL BE A ***TRUE*** DEMON.
...
WITH ***THIS***, I CAN FIGHT ***ANYONE*** WHO TRIES TO KEEP ME FROM THOSE SHARDS!
DO YOU THINK I WANT TO ***WASTE*** IT PROTECTING ***YOU***?!
SIT!!
WMFF
I CAN'T BELIEVE I WAS ACTUALLY STARTING TO THINK YOU HAD A ***GOOD*** SIDE...
STOMP STOMP
SSSSSSSSS
WAIT!
SHOW ME HOW TO USE IT! COME ***ON***!
MY LORD INU-YASHA...
YOU'VE GOT TO DO SOME-THING ABOUT THAT ATTITUDE...

TO BE CONTINUED...

Rumiko Takahashi

Rumiko Takahashi was born in 1957 in Niigata, Japan. She attended women's college in Tokyo, where she began studying comics with Kazuo Koike, author of *Crying Freeman*. In 1978, she won a prize in Shogakukan's annual "New Comic Artist Contest," and in that same year her boy-meets-alien comedy series *Lum*Urusei Yatsura* began appearing in the weekly manga magazine *Shônen Sunday*. This phenomenally successful series ran for nine years and sold over 22 million copies. Takahashi's later *Ranma 1/2* series enjoyed even greater popularity.

Takahashi is considered by many to be one of the world's most popular manga artists. With the publication of Volume 34 of her *Ranma 1/2* series in Japan, Takahashi's total sales passed one hundred million copies of her compiled works.

Takahashi's serial titles include *Lum*Urusei Yatsura*, *Ranma 1/2*, *One-Pound Gospel*, *Maison Ikkoku* and *Inu-Yasha*. Additionally, Takahashi has drawn many short stories which have been published in America under the title "Rumic Theater," and several installments of a saga known as her "Mermaid" series. Most of Takahashi's major stories have also been animated, and are widely available in translation worldwide. *Inu-Yasha* is her most recent serial story, first published in *Shônen Sunday* in 1996.